FALL-OUT

Also by Kenneth Royce

THE XYY MAN
THE CONCRETE BOOT
THE MINIATURE FRAME
SPIDER UNDERGROUND
TRAP SPIDER
THE WOODCUTTER OPERATION
BUSTILLO
THE SATAN TOUCH
THE THIRD ARM
10,000 DAYS
CHANNEL ASSAULT
THE STALIN ACCOUNT
THE CRYPTO MAN
THE MOSLEY RECEIPT
NO WAY BACK
THE PRESIDENT IS DEAD

Kenneth Royce
FALL-OUT

Hodder & Stoughton
LONDON SYDNEY AUCKLAND TORONTO

British Library Cataloguing in Publication Data
Royce, Kenneth, *1920–*
    Fall-out
    Rn: Kenneth Royce Gandley   I. Title
    823'.914[F]

    ISBN 0 340 49603 7

Copyright © Kenneth Royce 1989

First published in Great Britain 1989

All rights reserved. No part of this publication may be
reproduced or transmitted in any form or by any means,
electronic or mechanical, including photocopying,
recording, or any information storage and retrieval system,
without either the prior permission in writing from the
publisher or a licence, permitting restricted copying.
In the United Kingdom such licences are issued
by the Copyright Licensing Agency, 33–34 Alfred Place,
London WC1E 7DP.

Published by Hodder and Stoughton,
a division of Hodder and Stoughton Ltd,
Mill Road, Dunton Green, Sevenoaks, Kent TN13 2YE
Editorial Office: 47 Bedford Square, London WC1B 3DP

Photoset by Chippendale Type
Otley, West Yorkshire

Printed in Great Britain by St Edmundsbury Press Ltd,
Bury St Edmunds, Suffolk

FOR STELLA

1

The death cloud moved above him, silent and unseen. Zotov was dazed, not quite certain what had happened but vaguely aware that he had escaped. He was alone, and around him was nothing but a terrifying silence which he expected to be broken at any time by those who would hunt him.

He was afraid and the fear grew as he wandered on into the darkness. He could not remember the last time he had been completely alone, yet somehow he knew that there had been such a time and he was filled with dread, praying he would not recollect. Like a little boy, he suddenly wanted the comfort of a mother. He no longer knew the name of his mother or what she had looked liked, and as his mind wandered he tried to cope with the belief that somehow he had had two mothers and that both had given birth to him.

He staggered on, hands clamped to his head, trying to shake off such thoughts. Suddenly he tripped and fell. The jolt and the pain overrode the horrors building up in him. He pushed himself to a sitting position, panting from the effort and slowly rubbing a grazed elbow. The fall disorientated him even further and he was no longer aware of direction. He groped around to feel a hard, rough surface but could see nothing in any direction, and the silence, that dreadful, painful silence, formed pressure pads over his ears. There was not even the sound of a breeze or of any form of life, no matter how minute. Had he gone deaf?

He must be on a road of some sort; it was too evenly surfaced to be anything else. Rising shakily, he straightened himself and continued on but for all he knew he was returning to his starting point. He bumped into something hard and groped around it. A small truck was facing his way.

Zotov could not remember if he had ever driven a truck or car; there was a block in his mind but it failed to cut out a rising terror that produced a whimper. He tried to get a grip on himself. His hands trembled as, blindly, he explored the truck. He managed to open one of the doors. Could he drive? He was not certain. There were no keys and it occurred to him that the truck might have broken down and been abandoned. He tried every switch he could find but nothing happened, not even the lights flickered on; the battery must be dead. But at least the truck was some indication of life, something to cling to.

Just where was he and why was there nobody around? Why was it so utterly quiet? So empty? It might be better to find the edge of the road and stay there until dawn. There might be a ditch he could rest and hide in. He needed some more pills, an injection to calm him down, yet paradoxically the need and the thought made him tremble with fear. He was uncertain of everything now.

He found a drainage ditch by crawling on all fours and he slipped down into it. It was chill but he did not really feel cold and the ditch provided some form of comfort. Briefly he considered finding the truck again and resting in its cab. But that meant close confinement and another form of prison.

Zotov curled up. He gazed out into the blackness and was now able to convince himself that he had not gone blind. To his left there was a strange red glow in the sky. Raising himself he could see that, in fact, there were two separate glows joined by a faint pink streak. He followed a line down beneath them to just above earth level and now he could see deeper glows and realised that those in the sky were reflections. It was impossible to judge just how far away they were but there was a threatening weirdness about them.

For a while he stared, then lay back with closed eyes. He must have dozed for when he opened his eyes again he was facing the other way and there was no immediate sign of the strange glows in the sky, just the total darkness and the uncanny silence. The stirrings of panic began to creep through him. The surrounding dark space brought back a kind of terror he had experienced before but could not recall when and where. He changed position so that the ditch was touching him on all sides and only then, as it brought back a kind of reality, did he begin to calm down. But he prayed for daylight and for some sense into his present situation.

The guard pushed his way down the narrow corridor of the coach, his heavy greatcoat hampering his movements. It was true that another guard was at the rear and the driver was also armed, but that gave him little comfort. In his view the passengers should have been chained or handcuffed; a concerted attack by them could succeed but fortunately there was no co-ordination and they had had no time to plan. Also, in the middle of the night, minds did not operate too well. Even so, most of the stares Smolin received as he forced his way down the aisle were baleful.

It had all been so rushed. Madness. Evacuate. Just like that, no explanation. But the command was unmistakable, and even the doctors had not argued. Coaches, and ambulances for the really sick, together with extra guards, had been sent up from Kiev and boarding them had been a shambles. Some of the patients, or prisoners as Smolin always thought of them, had shown a childish glee in the belief that it was all a night-time play period; some thought they were being herded to their deaths; others, more thoughtful, were suspicious in a different way.

Except for those on duty at the time, they all wore night clothes, even some of the doctors, but the coaches were warm and few people were cold. There had been some attempt at orderliness on reporting in the exercise yard, and after a hasty roll-call patients had been divided into coachloads. The buildings had been cleared and checked but it was all done in an atmosphere of panic. Something terrible had happened.

Smolin reached the end of the coach and gazed along the rear bench seat, ignoring the resentful gazes. The interior lights were poor, some were not working, but all the seats seemed to be occupied. The coach lurched. Smolin put out a hand to steady himself, turned to make his way back to the front of the coach again, and then stopped. He swung round towards the rear seat. The patients were too spread out. He realised there was room for one more prisoner. He now took more interest in the faces about him. Was someone missing? By the time he reached the front of the coach again he knew with a sinking feeling that they were one short. He knew too who it was. Zotov.

"All right?" Smolin's colleague was standing beside the driver's seat but facing up the coach.

Smolin's first urge was to cover-up, say nothing. Then he realised he was damned whatever he did. For once he wished he was not the senior guard.

"I think Zotov is missing," he said heavily. He swung his machine pistol from his shoulder.

"Missing? Do you want me to check? You might have missed him."

"Go ahead. Count as you go. We're one short."

When Smolin's squat, solid, colleague returned he was clearly uneasy. "How could it happen? We checked them all before boarding. Perhaps he's on another coach?"

Smolin shook his head, his heavy features distraught. "It was dark. Everyone was panicking, some were half asleep. It would be easy to slip away. Nobody knew what was happening but everyone wanted to get out quick."

There had been no official explanation but rumours were rife and they had all seen the strange glow in the sky.

"What are you going to do?"

Smolin noted how neatly the responsibility had been planted on him. He could not argue but it was clear that he was now on his own. He did not reply because he did not know the answer.

"Let them find out the other end," his colleague went on. "It's their fault, they should have left it till daylight. Anyway Zotov is no great loss. A nobody."

Smolin thought he knew why the evacuation could not be left until daylight but he was more inclined to agree about Zotov being a nobody. None of the staff knew why he was there except, perhaps, one or two of the doctors. It would be madness to turn back, and orders were orders – reach Kiev soonest. But he would have to report the escape; there was no safe alternative.

* * *

By the time dawn broke Zotov was shivering. The grey misty light pervaded the damp air which reached his bones and forced him to rise. It was only a matter of minutes before he could see the spectral outline of the truck further down the road. As the light strengthened he gazed up and down the road and across the flat plains both sides of it. The whole world had emptied; there was no sign of life anywhere.

He walked back to the truck and was now able to give it a more thorough examination, now realising that at some time in his past he must have been familiar with engines. The ignition key was on the floor of the cab and he tried it as though he was holding some new form of scientific instrument. He turned the key; the battery was dead. He walked away from the direction the truck was facing.

He continued on into a gradually lifting mist. He was well built but rather slight. Average height, grey hair still thick despite middle age. He had once been a very fit man and had maintained that fitness as far as various institutions had allowed.

As the light became increasingly strong, most of Zotov's night-time terrors faded. He strode out, but did not know where he was going, nor did it matter to him. What did matter was the strong need to get back to some sort of life he could recognise and to get as far away as possible from the dreadful place he had left.

His escape had been almost casual. He had been among the first in the queue for the coach, one of the first to answer his name, and then he had gradually edged to the rear and faded into the darkness. There had been so much noise, so much shouting, so many guards herding the patients and shouting orders, so many engines revving and diesel fumes in the air, so much general panic, that he had no difficulty in drifting to the outer perimeter of activity and then beyond it. After that he simply walked away. It had been easy to take advantage of guards besieged by their own fears.

He had no plan. He expected to be found and picked up now that he was in full view in open country, but he was experiencing a wonderful kind of freedom. Cold as he was, it was good just to stride out and to breathe in the damp air with nobody watching him or telling him where to go. As he continued he realised how hungry he was and wondered if he would ever eat again. He looked up at the sky; the glow had gone, robbed of strength by the increasing daylight, but he knew it was still there. Not that it mattered. Not much did any more.

The grey ghostly outlines were eerie. Because of the remnants of ground mist the walls rose as if floating. But the indistinct concrete buildings were no fairy castles. Even at a distance Zotov could see the stark buildings were those of a large town. On the upper floors a weak sun reflected on the windows of tall apartment blocks. What was uncanny was the total lack of traffic on the road. Something, surely, should be moving.

The town could only be Pripyat. Even incarcerated one learned these things, and when he first arrived at the institution the route had taken him through the outskirts of the town. It was a place of little character with a population of over forty thousand.

His first instinct was to get off the road and find some form of cover but he was drawn forward by the complete unreality of the scene. The place seemed dead, a ghost town. Nothing moved. There was no sound. Empty streets faced him. If anyone was here at all then they were behind locked doors. But increasingly he believed that everyone had fled.

Now Zotov understood what had been puzzling him. Either there had been some plague of highly virulent disease, or the reactors had blown at nearby Chernobyl.

2

As he strode along one of the main streets Zotov felt hemmed in by the box-like, prefabricated nine-to-twelve-storey buildings which had sprung up all over Russia. Yet he also felt like the last man on earth, and his tremendous sense of loneliness returned. He was fascinated by the utter barrenness of what he saw.

The whole town must have been evacuated. There were no vehicles that he could see. Here and there garments had been dropped in the rush to get out. A hat was rolling along in the face of a piercing breeze. The vastness of the town, the complete deadness, the utter soundlessness made Zotov suddenly feel puny and totally unrelated to what he was seeing. Nor was there anything to hear. It was all so unnatural and overpowering that he fell to his knees, trembling as a kind of agoraphobia engulfed him.

He bunched up, head covered by his arms, and shook uncontrollably for some minutes. Space. So much of it. Gradually his terror eased but for some time longer he remained crouched. When he finally lifted his head his face was almost grey with strain, his eyes haunted. He rubbed his face, ashamed at the fit and wondering why it had happened. Just what had provoked his fears? Emptiness. He understood that, but why?

Climbing unsteadily to his feet Zotov stood swaying in the middle of the street, a solitary figure in a deserted town. It was uncanny after the confines of so many institutions. He stood breathing deeply and this helped him. He had gone from one extreme to another far too quickly. But his underlying desire to stay free gathered strength.

He was looking for another truck or a car but he could see none down the wide street, nor, as he explored the intersections, was any other form of transport in sight.

Suddenly something clattered ahead of him and in the deadly silence it was like a bomb-blast. He jumped, then saw two scavenging dogs running from a doorway, each with something in their jaws.

His calls to them hung in the air, then he let out a full-blooded yell. The sound travelled, bounced off the empty buildings and spread down the side streets, coming back to him in a variety of volumes and timings. The weirdness of the erratic echoes made him laugh but it was a laughter of disquiet. He realised he was walking between two rows of shops. Outside one of them was an avos'ka lying in the gutter. He picked up the string bag.

Something sparked in his memory. It was not the empty shops that bewildered him so much but the lack of the constantly jostling queues he associated with them, almost always comprised of timelessly patient women. There should be queues for ordering the goods, another for paying for them, and yet a third for collecting the goods now paid for. Three queues for the same goods and at the end of each one, more often than not, an unhelpful and rude assistant. It was an irrelevant thought, yet it seemed terribly important, prodding him into a belief that once he had known a life other than the one he had just left.

He wandered over to a clothes store. Looking into the window he saw the bearded reflection of himself and staggered back in shock. It was not *his* face he was looking at. He turned away to steady himself but was so shaken that he had to crouch again. Eventually he went over to the wall supporting the glass and clung on to it. If it was not his face then whose was it? *How could he have somebody else's face?* Sweat was running off him.

Staring again at the window, he smashed his booted foot into it and the sudden crash of sheet glass made him jump back as pieces shattered crashing all around him, the sound again out of all proportion because it was the only noise in a dead city. When the last splinter had tinkled on to the pavement Zotov belatedly realised that he had a whole range of clothes to choose from without the need of coupons or the aid of the black market.

He stepped through the window treading on glass and

glad of the crunching noise it made; anything was better than the silence. He found the men's department and took his time choosing clothes and shoes.

To strip off his blue uniform, which he had hastily put on over rough issue pyjamas, was a magic moment. When he was dressed he forced himself to face a mirror. If there were clothes here, somewhere, there had to be food.

On the streets again he kept to the middle of the road as if, for escape, that gave him an option of direction. It cost an effort because it created space again when he could have crawled along the walls, but it also gave him more vision.

Taking a side street he suddenly heard a series of strange sounds, animal noises, whimpering and howling. He hurried on, took another turning and gazed at the pitiful sight of a *ptichiirynok*. The stalls of the pet market were still standing, the various cages still on them, the animals inside desperate to escape, their eyes pleading.

Zotov felt sick. He knew only too well the terrible feeling of imprisonment. He realised that the circumstances were unnatural but he could not bear to see the animals suffer like that. He went along the stalls and unlatched every cage and basket until dogs, rabbits, cats, birds and the rest were free. When he found a food store he smashed down the door and distributed anything there was. They would have to find water for themselves but the Pripyat river was nearby.

He gazed with immense satisfaction at the feeding animals and then went in search of food for himself, to eat now and to carry on his journey.

The complication of housing over forty thousand people from Pripyat was bad enough with virtually no notice. The colonel rightly convinced himself that finding secure accommodation for the patients from the psychiatric hospital near Pripyat was not really his domain. He understood why the military had been called in to assist civilian authority; apart from anything else their experience of logistics was considerable, but everyone was being rushed off their feet. So he delegated the problem of the hospital refugees to Major Dubas who made contact with the main hospitals in and around Kiev.

The problems of organisation were enormous at such short notice but crisis often brings out the best in people and Major Dubas was no exception. Overriding everything else, however, was the shadow of Moscow. The Ukrainians had to show that they were more than up to dealing with the crisis, one they considered had been brought on by the incompetent planners in the first city. Ukrainians never forget that Kiev was the 'mother of cities', dating back to the sixth century, and was the country's capital when Moscow was still 'a wheel track in the forest'.

But this was a life-or-death situation; all the stops had to be pulled out. Rumours were rife that many were already dead. So when Smolin presented him with the news that the prisoner Zotov had escaped Dubas was not all that impressed. What the hell did it matter? But he listened and he made a note of it.

The small office Dubas had been allocated off the teachers' rest room in one of the schools had been hastily furnished with a telephone extension. The classrooms were being adapted as dormitories for as many refugees as could be crowded in. Together with their guards the hospital patients had been crammed into three of the larger rooms pending reallocation to other hospitals with security facilities. The whole place was milling with people and everybody seemed to be speaking at once. Throughout the city, wherever there was space to put a bed-roll, it was the same. Kiev was bursting at the seams.

The little office with the small desk was filled with people seeking direction from Dubas who felt he was doing the colonel's job. Amongst those in the overcrowded office were reporters from *Pravda, Izvestia*, and a stringer from the satirical magazine *Krokodil*, but there would be no lampooning about this crisis. A patient had escaped on the way down from Pripyat. It was unimportant as news went. Who? Yuri Zotov. Probably a dissenter. So what! There were hundreds dying out there and probably thousands of sick, if not now then there would be later.

The news that Zotov had escaped occupied just a few

lines in *Izvestia* the following day. Very few saw it and those who did raised no eyebrows; the nation had a massive crisis on its hands and the world was watching to see how it was handled. But Yelena Belenko in her small Moscow apartment saw it. The paper shook in her hands. She lowered the newspaper unaware that she was crumpling it into a ball. Her fear-filled eyes stared into space. Chernobyl was a dreadful national disaster. With Zotov loose the ultimate disaster could be far worse than that; the Soviet Union itself could lose all credibility in the eyes of the world.

Her personal danger suddenly struck her. After all these years. Where could she go? Her emotions were high and she was torn, old memories tumbling back to scramble her mind. Tears trickled down her face as recollections grew stronger. She felt a tremendously strong urge to help Zotov. But how? And equally she realised that, if he were quickly captured, life could go on undisturbed as before.

In her early forties Yelena Belenko was still a beautiful woman. With the high cheek-bones of the Slav, she had not plumped out as do so many Russian women. She had been a ballet dancer of note and now taught the art. Still slim, she had the carriage of a dancer and not a little hauteur. But there was no hauteur about her now. If Zotov remained free her comparatively high position would not save her. Nothing could.

She stood in the middle of the well-furnished room, a slight, almost regal figure, the newspaper still crumpled in her hands. There might be others at risk. She would have to move quickly and there would be no time to wait for her pianist husband to return from rehearsal. For a dreadful moment she wished that Yuri Zotov had died all those years ago. And then she accepted that most of her tears had been caused by her desperate need for him, even after all the time that had passed.

3

When he had fed, and drunk some bottled water, Zotov felt better. He had stolen shaving gear and found a public lavatory where he braced himself to remove the beard he had had for as long as he could remember. He was aware that there were massive gaps in his memory. He could recall nothing at all about his childhood or his teenage years and even later. He had been good at his job before he had entered his first institution because the doctors had told him so, yet he could remember nothing about working.

He could not remember as far back as the first institution he had been in. He could vaguely recall the Yartsevo mental hospital near Moscow and Stolbovaya some time later. He must have been in Christopol prison because he thought he had been there when Anatole Marchenko died inside. He did not think he had any connection with Marchenko, it was simply one of those useless recollections. That was his problem; what little memory he had was disjointed as though large tracts of it had been extracted from his mind, and there were times, when he had brief flashes of reasoning, he believed that was precisely what had happened.

He had been filled with drugs and bombarded with psychoanalysis and the treatment had gone on for years. He was convinced that the doctors – and they had varied as each took on a new stage of his development – had never been content with the result. He had not improved as they had hoped, or so it seemed to him, and often, during the rare moments when he felt less fettered, he wondered why they had taken so much trouble for apparently so little result.

They had called the years of incarceration, hospitalisation, but it had never felt like that. He could recall one visitor and he had not seen him for many years. An elderly man had called every two months and in secrecy because, unlike the others, Zotov had been allocated a private room for these visits. He had always known when the visits were pending by the increase of drugs until he was barely aware of himself when confronted by the visitor.

The man had always shown a strange kind of concern. Zotov had at times felt it to be a love yet they never so much as shook hands let alone embraced and the man had always looked so sad and had never introduced himself at any time. The encounters had been most odd, yet somehow Zotov had needed them. And then they had stopped. Nobody explained why. Perhaps the visitor had died but no one would answer his questions on the subject.

Once he thought he had been visited by a woman but it was so long ago and the recollection so feeble that he guessed he had imagined it. Yet, in his mind, he could still savour her perfume. As he thought and dozed he was sitting in an armchair in one of the major stores. There were beds too, if he felt tired, and for a few days, he would have all the comfort and food he would need. The thought that it might be contaminated often crossed his mind but he was beyond caring. He now knew that he would rather kill himself than go back.

His contentment was increasingly tempered by the need of the drugs he had been given for so long, both orally and injected. He began to shake and doubled forward hoping the attack would pass. What helped him during this time was a cross German Shepherd dog who had attached himself after being released. Once fed it had followed Zotov everywhere and now licked his face as Zotov groaned in pain. Eyes screwed tight, Zotov put out a hand to the probing head and clung to the comfort it brought.

When the attack passed he was left sweating again and wondering whether he could cope without the drugs. The dog put a large paw on his leg and Zotov saw that he now had someone to talk to and would perhaps understand him far better than the doctors had done. He searched around the dog's neck; there was no collar. "I'll call you Pripy," he told him, scratching the dog's ears. "After the town where you were deserted and adopted."

There was something strange about his voice and he realised these were the first words he had uttered since escaping. It was good to have the dog with him; but he would have to move on. The town was deserted now, full of eerie emptiness, but it would not last for ever. Some time, days, weeks or even months, scientists would be back to test for radioactivity and to decontaminate. During that time he could put a lot of distance between himself and this place.

Meanwhile he did not think they would search for him here. In the first place they would not risk contamination; in the second he could not see that he was worth it.

Smolin felt relieved that he had reported Zotov's escape and that Major Dubas had dealt with it from then on. What Smolin had not done, however, was to report the matter to the doctor who had been treating Zotov. The escape was a security matter not a medical one, so, as yet, nobody of real importance had been advised. Even had he considered it, Smolin would have rightly assumed that he had no direct responsibility to the doctors, but only to his own head of security. Nobody was to blame for what followed and the knowledge was slow to filter up to those who really needed to know.

Zotov's psychiatrist only discovered he was missing a day later. He had brought the medical files with him in order to supervise the patients' medication. With patients distributed around various institutions it took time to discover that Zotov had actually escaped.

Doctor Nagornoy had been treating Zotov for the last four years. He had read through all the earlier reports and the various treatments which had changed as drugs themselves had changed together with some psychiatric techniques. Right from the start he had been warned that the case was special. An appendix to the report suggested that when Zotov had been admitted he had not known who he was or where he was.

There was nothing new about amnesia. What had at first shaken him was the fact that, as far as he could judge, no actual attempt had been made to restore the memory; rather it had been built up from the time of admittance on the known facts of Zotov's background. He had been given another memory based on what was known about him. Zotov had been made to learn about his life all over again without him ever actually recalling his earlier memories.

Nagornoy had quickly recognised the importance of all this and he strongly suspected what might have happened during the earlier days of treatment. The original doctor had died some twelve years ago and it must have been he who had reconstructed Zotov's background, presumably with the help of researchers, people, parents, relatives, whoever had known Zotov at the time. But why had no attempt been made to cure the amnesia itself? It had made him wonder if there ever had been a loss of memory and that admittance had another, more perfidious reason.

Zotov's medical history was bound to provoke such thoughts in any doctor, but those who worked in certain of the psychiatric hospitals knew better than to investigate too far. The other unusualness about this case was its length. It was clear that Zotov was never to leave an institution unless he could accept the past life that had been built into him. It had been obvious for many years that that would not happen. Perhaps, in the beginning the treatment had been too harsh, results wanted too quickly. In twenty-odd years treatments had become more sophisticated and it seemed to Nagornoy that an early crash course was not the way to get the right results. But perhaps there had been a strong reason for haste.

Nagornoy had never been happy about the Zotov case because he suspected that the doctors who had treated him over the years had never received the full story. There was more missing than Zotov's memory and he often wondered if attempts had been made to remove the memory and to restore only what was prudent. Or rather to implant a background that had never been there in the first place.

There was one more issue which he had always found disquieting. There was a footnote to the file in heavy red printed letters so that nobody could possibly miss it. If anything happened to Zotov in any way, illness, death, or escape, an Aleksei Chernov had to be informed immediately.

The Moscow telephone number was printed in the same heavy ink.

Nagornoy had little idea of Chernov's position at the time Zotov had been admitted, the note was the original but had been inked over as the first ink had faded with time, but he well knew of his power now. And yet there had been a strong rumour that Chernov had retired. It made no difference, the instructions had not been changed.

He rang the number and a precise, impatient voice answered. "Yes?"

"This is Doctor Nagornoy. I am a resident psychiatrist at the Guliyev Hospital in Pripyat. We've been evacuated and I'm calling from Kiev."

"What is your problem, Doctor?"

"Zotov escaped during the evacuation."

"Zotov? Is that supposed to mean something to me?"

"There is a priority instruction on his medical records that should something like this happen to him, Comrade Aleksei Chernov was to be called on this number."

"I see. Well I'm not Comrade Chernov. I'll pass on the momentous news, Doctor. I wish you all well down there in your time of crisis. Just one thing; is this a fairly recent instruction?"

"It's over twenty years old."

There was a pause. "Perhaps it's not quite so urgent now."

Aleksei Chernov was fat, bald, and cold-eyed. In his sixties he was enjoying a rest at his dacha at the Black Sea resort of Sochi. Late April was not the warmest time but one of the quietest. By the end of summer some two million visitors would have passed through. He was lounging on a day-bed looking out across the water and felt more relaxed than for many years. He had given unstinting service to his country; it was time to ease out, let someone younger carry the burden.

His peace of mind was flawed by the terrible tragedy of Chernobyl but death was not new to him and his concern was for the effect on the country as a whole. It made Russia appear incompetent and this angered him. Even so he had the capacity to push aside such crisis; time would take care of memory.

There was a breeze crossing the veranda and he had a light blanket over the lower part of his body, the hump of his belly only partially covered. Behind him, in one of the bedrooms, he could hear his wife shaking out sheets. He gazed at the sky; there was no risk of fall-out down here.

The telephone rang and his body jerked. Constantly ringing telephones were almost in the past. But not quite; he still had an extension on a stool within reach. He grunted and picked up the receiver in a huge hand. He listened without expression then cut in brusquely, "Ring me back on the scrambler."

He rolled off the bed and waddled through the lounge and into a small study locking the door behind him. He unlocked a desk drawer and took out a red telephone, then lowered his bulk into a sturdy captain's chair. He lifted the receiver at the first ring and at once growled, "You should have used this in the first place."

"About an escaped patient?"

"It should have been enough that there was an instruction to contact me." Chernov did not approve of his successor designate. He had fought hard to promote his own man and the in-fighting had been vicious. The new Secretary-General, Gorbachev, was far too soft in Chernov's eyes and he had fought all the way to keep State Security in hands that really understood the problem and the dangers to the State. There were powerful forces against the comparative liberalism of Gorbachev and Chernov was amongst them. "Tell me about it."

In Moscow Joseph Zhadin was seething. He and Chernov were of equal rank although Chernov had far more service and carried the old guard with him, which was the bulk of the hierarchy of the KGB. Most of his colleagues saw Zhadin as a new broom and that sent ripples through the whole organisation. Opposition or not he had no intention of being talked to by Chernov or anybody else as if he was a new recruit, his loyalties suspect.

"I know no more than I've already told you. If you want more information contact Doctor Nagornoy. He's a resident at the Guliyev Hospital in Pripyat, at present evacuated to Kiev. Clearly this should be between the two of you." Zhadin rang off.

Chernov was not as angry as he might have been. It was best that Zhadin was left out of it. And the less experienced Zhadin had played right into Chernov's hands with his bullish reaction. It was a nuisance to track down the doctor but there were minions to do that and Chernov set the wheels in motion. Within half an hour he had not only located Nargonoy but was speaking to him on an open line, thus contradicting his rebuff to Zhadin. It had seldom been a problem to Chernov to extract what he wanted from people and that included reactions.

Nagornoy had little more to offer even under Chernov's experienced technique. Nobody knew where Zotov had gone or even what direction he had taken. Chernov went back to his day-bed and watched the breeze form minute white-caps on the dark water. His peace had been dramatically shattered and he lay gazing out watching coloured sails billow from masts. He knew what to do; it was a question of how to do it.

It would mean using the vast organisation of which technically he was still head, but realistically from which he had really retired. He knew better than anyone that his term of office finished when his present leave finished. That was the arrangement. Zhadin officially took up his new responsibilities on the day following the last day of Chernov's leave. He had two weeks to go.

Chernov was only too aware that he should advise Zhadin of any action he might take, put his successor in the picture, and give him the whole background which clearly he did not know. Very few people did. And some of those had died. But he had goaded Zhadin into handing over the problem. It was a flimsy ploy, but it was all he had and he believed it was enough. He did not want Zhadin in on this. The increasing openness of Gorbachev would prove disastrous and he was unwilling to take any chances with Zotov.

My God, he thought. Twenty-five years had passed yet Chernov had had no problem in recalling the whole business in detail. It was more than likely that even Gorbachev did not know. Who had heard of him twenty-five years ago? Not a man to rush decisions, Chernov lay tight-faced and still for some time before he decided what to do. He was in a very delicate position and would have to move carefully. There must be some form of compromise.

He rose from the bed, went into the bedroom where his wife was still folding sheets and said, "I must return to Moscow".

His wife, built on similar lines to Chernov, did not turn from her task. With her back to him as she opened a cupboard to pack away the sheets, she replied, "Telephone when you are returning, I will have a meal ready."

"It won't be for some days. Anyway, our time is our own in two weeks. We can stay on here longer."

He had been recalled so many times from so many holidays that his departure meant little to her. She preferred to be as distanced from his job as possible. Her only friends were wives of his colleagues. Outside that circle women were reluctant to confide in her, knowing the position her husband held. There was no need to pack a bag for him; he always had one ready. And there was no need for him to reserve a flight back to Moscow. He would be on it whoever else might be kicked off. She did not know how she would be able to tolerate him once he had fully retired.

Yelena Belenko knew that she must leave but was not sure how best to do it. If she left a note for her husband she might compromise him. If she simply walked out he would be worried and eventually warn the police. That would at least indicate his innocence, something the KGB, when they arrived and that was inevitable, would have to accept.

As she gazed round the apartment her affection was for it rather than for her absent husband. All her things were here, her bits and pieces. None was from Western Europe, for she had always been denied an exit visa. When the ballet company had gone on its periodic world tours, Yelena had always been described as not up to standard at that time or some other excuse had been offered. She knew the real reason. As the years passed she was allowed to visit most of the Eastern Block countries but the moment she ceased publicly to perform, she was back to internment.

Yelena had learned to live with it and she had never been short of privileges within the country. In fact she believed that she benefited far more than her colleagues as if to make up for her restrictions on travel. She had not been persecuted in any way except that on her trips to the satellite countries she was well aware that she was watched all the time. It was a standing order with the KGB.

To walk out would not torture her husband too much. He would quickly recover. Music had drawn them together and had become their only bond. In almost every other respect the marriage had been a failure. And she was well aware of her husband's infidelities; she had indulged in one or two affairs herself.

Right now she had other problems. If she took a suitcase it would be discovered that she had packed and therefore had deliberately fled. If she took nothing but simply walked out her absence would leave an air of mystery about her disappearance. A compromise was the packing of a few things in two old carrier bags; her husband would not know what clothes if any were missing. She put the few empty hangers in a wardrobe drawer, took one last tearful look round the apartment, and left.

Yelena had friends in the Bolshoi but they could not be trusted in this situation and she had many friends in the Kirov ballet in Leningrad. She had to go somewhere and Leningrad seemed to be the immediate answer. Flying was impossible; passenger lists and ticket counterfoils were too easy to check. It would have to be by train.

As Yelena took the elevator to the ground floor she marvelled at her own cold-blooded reasoning. It made her realise that the threat to her had never really receded and that the planning, haphazard as it was in some respects, must have been mulling in her subconcious for all those years, ever since she was in her late teens. She fought back the tears and strode out into the Moscow streets, straight-backed and with long elegant strides. She could still turn heads, but the last thing she wanted just then was to be recognised.

4

Zotov strode round the streets hearing nothing but his own progress. The new shoes he had taken from one of the stores were pinching slightly but he now wore thick socks. He was already getting used to the bizarre emptiness, the blank windows, the glass reflecting nothing but the image of himself which he had such difficulty in accepting, and that of Pripy who trotted beside him dragging a birch broom in his strong jaws. The broom, which had been lying in a gutter, had obviously been dropped by a bubushka, one of the cleaning women who were also used to fill in holes in the road. An old memory returned but it surfaced painfully. A Soviet joke; the bubushkas, usually women of good middle-age, were said to be, 'not only the equal of men but of tractors and bulldozers, too'. The recollection surprised him; from which stage of his life had it stirred? Meanwhile, whenever he suffered the agony of withdrawal pains he could rely on Pripy staying with him and trying to stave off his distress.

Although it could be nerve-racking at times he had by now provided himself with another distraction, a luxury in the form of a transistor radio. He heard the news which confirmed what he had expected about Chernobyl. The number of deaths distressed him and he suspected that they were higher than announced. There was not one mention of his escape in any of the bulletins but he did not see himself as anyone of importance. That he was so important that news items dare not be broadcast about him would never have entered his head.

Apart from the periodic pangs which at times nearly tore him apart, Zotov was happier than he had been for as long as he could remember. There were drugs for the taking in a pharmacy but he had no idea what drugs he had been fed over the years, only that their withdrawal could at times make him crave for them. It was of no use taking drugs at random, and anyway, he must break away from them. It was the only hope of finding out about himself. It was something he felt he must do above all else. Somehow he must unscramble his mind, but he knew that it would take time. Meanwhile he must bear the mental dullness and the constant blockages of his thinking. He had learned long ago not to try to force his mind into grasping something that was beyond it.

He would not go in the direction of Kiev, the whole world would be there. And obviously he could not go to Chernobyl. It was already too near. He must try to get out of the country but that would still keep him in the Eastern Block; unless, by some freak, he could get beyond that. It would also mean following the route of the radioactive cloud if the news was accurate. What could it matter now?

As the evening approached so his nervousness increased. Daylight kept the buildings in view. Unattractive though the prefabricated slabbed apartment buildings were, and in spite of their eternal sameness, they provided a reality which night-time removed. Darkness was space and the cold unknown. A world of nothing, no tangibles, no substance. The store in which he had set up his home was large but at night it became infinite. These were his worst moments and he would cuddle up to Pripy so grateful that the animal understood without probing and pushing and piercing him with yet another needle filled with a strange concoction to see how he might react. Pripy accepted him unreservedly, something he could not recall ever having happened, and he was not ashamed, when the shaking and the depressions grew worse, that he buried his face in the thick fur and silently cried for an understanding of all that was happening to him.

Why? What terrible thing had he done?

On arrival in Moscow Chernov went straight to his apartment. By Russian standards the place was luxurious, adorned with paintings and objets d'art from many countries. He was not a connoisseur and understood little of what was in the rooms, but he did understand the prestige such articles conveyed in an essentially spartan society. Visitors were impressed; what they saw was only a faint reflection of the power Chernov possessed, and that he could display them so blatantly endorsed their awe of him.

Twenty-five years ago Chernov was already one of the chosen within the organisation. His loyalties were still clear and had not changed; it was others who had changed and who wanted change and he would oppose them whatever their exalted position.

He poured a stiff Polish vodka; it was better than the Russian but he would never admit it publicly. His ears were still buzzing from the flight and he sat down to enjoy his drink in solitude. Chernov never tired of his own company, it gave him time to think unhindered. He sipped the first half of the drink slowly, his cold eyes almost lost in the slits of the folded lids. He emanated presence, a man who could not be missed even if stationary at the back of a crowded room. He was also frightening in a way that was difficult to define. Friendship was something he had not been able to accept. Loyalty was another matter and it was this that he was thinking about. Whom could he still trust for what he wanted?

The second part of his drink went down at a gulp and he rose from the chair without the aid of strong hands, suggesting that beneath the fat were layers of muscle. He put the glass down once he was on his feet.

Chernov removed a gilded Florentine mirror from the wall. No effort had been made to conceal the safe behind it. In fact the safe was very old but nobody but a madman would try to break into this apartment let alone attempt to open the safe. The biggest security weapon the home possessed was the fact that everyone knew to whom it belonged.

The only thing that had been changed on the safe was the locking system. About fifteen years ago a combination lock had been fitted but the old double tumbler still remained on the door. It would have been cheaper to have bought a new safe but one of Chernov's strengths was to return loyalty; the safe had been a good friend and was about to prove its real value.

He unlocked the tumbler, then the combination and swung back the heavy door. The interior was small, no more than twenty-five centimetres in depth and height. He removed a cash box and some documents with elastic bands round them and laid them on a side table. He fumbled at the back of the interior with spatulate fingers. Then suddenly the base sprang up to reveal a further cavity. He took from it a folded file. He put everything else back and locked the safe but left the mirror off the wall.

Pouring another drink he sat down in his favourite armchair to study the file. As he read he became more disturbed. The amateurish typing had faded, he had typed it himself one-fingered and some of the errors had not been rectified. The room was silent except for occasional rustling as he turned a page. His flabby features hardened the more he read. Afterwards he went through the doctors' reports which had been attached to the file. The reports on the progress of the first two years following Zotov's admittance had been monthly, and then for the next five years, half-yearly, and from that time to the present, annually.

There was no doubt that medical progress had been made but not as effectively as hoped. The memory had virtually been obliterated but the building up of a new personality had produced big flaws. There was no way that Zotov could ever be released unless some new drug came up to help convince him to accept a life he had never lived. He had taken to his new name without trouble. That was a plus. And Chernov himself always thought of him by that name. It was infinitely safer to do so. There could be no lapses. Like learning a foreign language one had to think in it to be really at home with it.

But this was no language. Chernov groped for his drink and drained it. He yearned for the return of Nikita Khrushchev. In those days Chernov had not been in the position of power he now enjoyed; there had been something of a turnover in KGB chiefs about then. Knowing that, Khrushchev had looked for a man of permanency to entrust with the greatest secret of all. The two men had known each other for some years and Chernov had been helpful in taking care of some of the General Secretary's enemies without obviously linking himself. The two men had enjoyed much in common in spite of the difference in rank.

Khrushchev had been shrewd with an eye on the future. And where Chernov was concerned he had been proved right. The only real disappointment Chernov suffered over his idol was when he backed down over the Cuban affair; but Chernov understood that on such a matter he would have been stepping too far out of rank to pass any comment. But for a while it had shattered his faith.

What should he do now? Khrushchev had kept the matter close to his chest but obviously there were others of the Politburo who were still alive and knew the facts. Few, very few, had known the facts and the following detail. Few wanted to know. There was a problem and it was revealing just how many were willing to leave it to others to solve. From then on matters had been so deliberately confused, discipline and threats so harshly applied that everyone wanted to forget as soon as they could. Except for those left to clear up the mess . . . That largely had always been in Chernov's trusted hands and there was no better man at keeping it there.

Even those who had known the problem had been led to believe that, within a few months of it arriving, it had been dramatically and permanently closed. It was dead.

It had never been dead. With hindsight Chernov realised what should have been done at the time. Nobody would have agreed with it, not even Khrushchev. But it had to be done now. And at once. Radioactive cloud or not, searchers had to go out and find Zotov. Chernov well knew what he was up against and that the two weeks left of his official service were exceedingly feeble grounds for doing what he had to do.

Nobody could predict how Zotov would react as the effect of the drugs wore off. He might collapse mentally and become insane. Or he might, just might, recover some of his memory. Zotov had to be found and killed and buried deep where he could never be resurrected. Chernov prepared a plan to circumvent Joseph Zhadin.

* * *

Zhadin rose and came round his deck to shake hands with Chernov. They were like two boxers about to start a fight and trying to psych each other. Chernov had the edge on experience but he was far from unfriendly. And Zhadin, as a matter of policy, managed a smile. He was taller than Chernov, younger, of course, and fitter. A typical Ukrainian, he had dark thick hair with heavy brows and deep, impenetrable eyes.

"It must be strange for you to come in here as a visitor," Zhadin deliberately went back behind the desk.

Chernov smiled quietly, at his most dangerous. "A visitor? I haven't retired yet, Joseph." A Ukrainian should never be sitting in his chair, but his face remained placid. "But I don't intend to embarrass you. I hope you find the seat comfortable, not sagging too much after so many years of my weight."

"I'm sure the chair has hardly noticed it," Zhadin quipped, aware of Chernov's double-meaning. "You've called about this Zotov fellow?"

"I thought I'd better clear it up while I still have the time. And I certainly don't want to clutter you up with anything so trivial."

"You flew back from Sochi for something trivial? How times have changed."

Chernov gave a full-throated laugh that filled the large office. "Just so, it is trivial. But it goes back such a long way that everyone has forgotten about it. Zotov is really of no further importance but the matter does need tidying up. Can you spare me a small office and a red telephone? Anywhere will do?" Chernov was craftily placing himself in Zhadin's hands.

"Shouldn't I need to know about it? Surprisingly I can find no files. After I rang you I had a search made as you had clearly shown it to be a scrambler matter. The computers hold nothing and the old files down at Dzerzhinsky Square are equally unobliging. Was nothing ever filed on this man?"

"It's so long ago. They may have been shredded and burned. There was a time during Brezhnev's reign when some of the old records were thinned out. Even micros take space. In spite of my flying back the matter is trivial. I only came because time is running out. In two weeks you'll be rid of me. I'm probably the only person around who remembers anything about Zotov." Chernov appeared mischievous. "The scrambler bit was to goad you. I was resting at the time."

Zhadin nodded. "Tell me what you know."

"You mean what I remember. Zotov was crazy. He was making a lot of noise about people in high places that could have been damaging. It would have been a joke but for the fact that he had picked up one or two factual items about high rankers which was not so funny. Where he got those little bits of news from nobody ever found out.

"He became so voluble, especially to the Western press, that he had to be brought in. Treatment failed to provide the answers about his source. He was an engineer of sorts and a malcontent. My guess is that someone fed him with bits and pieces and used him as the instrument to voice them. It was embarrassing at the time. Now, most of those he defiled are dead. But not all. On the loose it's just possible that he might start again. That's why there was a note on his file to advise me if he did, at any time, escape."

"Or die."

"That too. Obviously if that had happened the case would be closed. I didn't mislead you when I said it was trivial. That's exactly what it is. But I'd like him found and I'd like to know what, if anything, he remembers. It would be a nuisance if he started his old games."

"What were the sort of things he was saying, and about whom?"

"Come on, Joseph. You know better. What on earth is the need to know? If his file has been destroyed I am the only person who can probably recall any of the things he said at the time. I've forgotten most of them. If he's remembered it should jog my memory and I'll then know what best to do. Siberia, I suppose, where nobody gives a damn about anything anyone says. It shouldn't take me long to clear it up."

"I'll attend to it for you, Aleksei. With pleasure. Go back to Sochi."

"Joseph, I've never handed over one of my cases in my life and I don't intend to do so just before retirement, especially when I can clear it up."

"But you yourself say it is trivial. How come the Chairman was handling such a piffling issue?"

"I wasn't Chairman at the time. Far from it. It's true I had long forgotten it but the case still remains mine. I just want to finish it. Is it worth a slanging match? Do I have to pull rank at so late a stage? Be reasonable. I'm bored stiff at Sochi. I'm not a family man. Give me this to occupy my time. If you don't then the little I do know remains in my head unless you want to arrest me for lack of co-operation and start a scandal before you've fully taken over. Come on, Joseph. Let me arrange a search to find him."

"Supposing he's in a contaminated area?"

"Then the problem is solved. He'll die sooner or later. Anyway nobody but a fool would go into the radioactive zone to search for him. He's probably between Pripyat and Kiev."

Zhadin took out a packet of papirosas. He offered them to Chernov.

"No thanks. I've never been able to get on with those cardboard holders. I'm a cigar man." He waited for Zhadin to light up and then said, "What about it? Give me something to do."

Zhadin would not be rushed. He was not entirely fooled by Chernov but was it worth fighting over? If Zotov was of any real importance there must surely be something on him somewhere. He threw up his hands in apparent surrender. "You can have Colonel Sokolov's office. He's on sick leave. When do you want to start?"

"Now. Zotov's out there somewhere roaming loose. For his own sake, apart from anything else, he should be brought in."

Zhadin pressed a desk switch. He was thinking that he should get Sokolov's office bugged before Chernov moved in but it was a risky thing to do; Chernov had associates throughout this massive building which was tucked away off the circumferential highway outside Moscow. And those that were not Chernov's disciples were in fear of him.

Zhadin had yet to build up his own acolytes; Chernov would get to know of any bugging in no time.

The ball was poorly struck and rolled well wide of the putting hole. "I'm too old for this, Gerald. The damp has got into my bones." Sir Brian Carter straightened his lanky frame and grimaced. "More to the point I was never any bloody good at it. Stupid game."

"Are you asking me to let you win? Satisfy your ego?"

"The only thing that will satisfy my ego is a damned big Scotch at the nineteenth. Look, it's going to rain, why don't you come to the point? Nobody in their right mind would ask me for a game of golf unless they want something from me." Carter rubbed his back and cocked an eye at the sky. He crossed over to the stationary ball and kicked it towards the hole. It went down cleanly. "I was always better at soccer." He turned to the younger Gerald Woods and laughed. "I don't know what you're going to make of that on your score card."

Woods was smiling broadly. He rammed his putter into his bag and grabbed the trolley handle. "Okay. If you're not in the mood, let's have a drink."

They wheeled round and walked slowly towards the club house.

"Zotov," said Woods.

"Who's he?"

"There's a file on him. From your day."

"Really?" The rain began to spatter but neither man hurried. "What does it say?"

"Just that. Zotov. Question mark. Not a large file."

"At that rate it wouldn't be, would it? We knew how to keep the paper work down in those days."

"So you remember?"

"Did I say that? Good Lord."

"Are you going to tell me?"

The grass was already wet under their feet but neither man opened the umbrellas in their bags. "About what?"

Woods looked exasperated. Carter was now in his seventies but there was little sign of it. His near-senility act did not convince; he had used it in his fifties; a defenceless amiability that often lulled people into believing him to be something of a bumbling, absent-minded idiot. He was still imitated in the department.

"There was a snippet in *Izvestia* which our people picked up. Naturally it was vastly overshadowed by the Chernobyl disaster but we won't be the only ones to have noticed. Apparently he escaped from a psychiatric hospital near Pripyat during the evacuation of that town. We did a routine check and there was his name; literally that was all there was. Clearly the name sparked somebody all those years ago." Woods adjusted his cap as the rain became heavier. Not as tall as Carter, and some twenty-five years younger, he appeared a little pale and unhealthy beside the ex-MI6 chief.

Carter halted and gazed pensively at the fine turf. "Well, well. After so long."

"Is it something we need to know?"

Carter took a golf ball from his pocket, tossed it and caught it. "Who'd have thought it?" He suddenly gazed at Woods. "I need to talk to Moggy about this, Gerald. No reflection on yourself but he needs to know and it had better be from me."

'Moggy' was Sir James Morgan, the present head of MI6. There had been one other head before him since Carter.

"You want to contact him yourself or shall I ask him to give you a call?"

"I'll deal with it. Did Moggy tell you to contact me?"

"Yes. But as a routine check, nothing more. Clearly there is more."

Neither man had taken a further step towards the club house, well aware that it was not a topic for conversation at the bar. The shower eased off and the cloud split to show signs of a struggling sun.

"All there is," replied Carter, "is speculation. That's why the file is so empty. There was nothing to add at the time and perhaps not even now. But it was extremely fascinating then. I'd love to be in on this but I don't suppose Moggy will let me. Have we anyone in that part of Russia?"

"Kiev, perhaps. We try to keep an ear in the Ukraine. But

I doubt that there's much going for us in Belorussia where he could possibly be."

Carter laid a hand on Woods' damp shoulder. "I'm glad you've caught the drift. What about Poland? How are we placed there?"

"That's a different matter. We're well represented there but it's a long way from Pripyat."

"If Zotov's mind is still functioning he'll know that. Better than Czechoslovakia. Friendlier for what he might need."

They started to walk again. "If you're thinking about getting him out there must be more than speculation involved. And, anyway, in that part of the country it will be virtually impossible to find him, let alone find him first."

Carter's eyes smouldered with recollection. "You're right. If we want him their need will be a million times stronger. But if they really go flat out to retrieve him it will at least endorse some of our speculation."

"Your speculation, Sir Brian. Nobody else seems to have any and it does not seem that you intend to tell me. Let's have that drink."

Carter chuckled. "It won't loosen my tongue, young Gerald, but I'm sure that you didn't have that in mind."

Colonel Borya Kanavsky entered the office unsure whether he had heard correctly. When he stood in the doorway, at first he could not believe his eyes.

"It's me, Borya. No ghost. Your eyes do not deceive you. Come in and close that door."

Kanavsky stared round the comparatively small office and then back to the large figure of Chernov sitting behind a desk too small for him. After all these years he simply could not equate the two.

"Comrade General, I thought someone was playing a joke. I understood you had retired."

"Not quite, Borya. I'm still on the payroll for a week or two more. I want General Zhadin to get used to the feel of my old office; it wouldn't be fair to hold him up. Sit down, for God's sake, there's work to do."

Kanavsky sat, still bewildered. He was trying to get used to a new boss and now the old one was back.

Chernov drew on an enormous Cuban cigar and filled the office with its rich aroma. He was amused by Kanavsky's embarrassment. "At ease, Borya. You're sitting there like a *zven'ia* waiting to feed the pigs. General Zhadin has let me have this office while I'm still here, so don't worry about mixed loyalties. He knows what I am doing." He paused, easing out a long plume of smoke while he studied the close cropped, clean cut image of Kanavsky across the desk. "I would like to think, however, that for the brief time I'm here your loyalty to me will be as strong as ever it was. It was something about you I always admired."

"I can only say I'm so pleased to see you back, Comrade General. Others will be pleased too."

"I hoped you would say that. I am about to rely on you entirely." Chernov waved his cigar, forming a spiral of smoke. "Did I tell you that before I went on leave I recommended you for promotion? I shall be gone before I see the result of that, and of course, the decision will be out of my hands. But I still have clout, Borya. I expect it to happen."

"Thank you, sir. You can rely on me to do what you want. As always."

"Then let's get down to it. A man called Zotov, someone of little distinction, escaped from a medical institution while being evacuated from Pripyat. He's still loose and I want him found. He's part of an old case of mine and I want it tidied up before I finally go."

"To find him in normal times would not take too long, but the whole area is buzzing down there, every bit of transport commandeered. In fact the authorities in Kiev are crying out for anything that moves."

"Borya! Have you gone so far back in the short time I've been away? Of course transport is short but all we need are a couple of helicopters and experienced observers. Just tell the Kiev office to do it and that you'll accept no excuses. I want Zotov in. Quickly."

"With respect, sir, would the directive not be better coming from you? They dare not argue with you?"

"You're right, Borya. But everyone thinks I'm fully retired. Look at your own reaction. There isn't time for cross-checks and references to be made. Simply tell them that it's Code Four and to get on with it. There's a Doctor Nagornoy down there who will help with Zotov's description."

"Code Four? So important?"

"I haven't the time to explain to you and you haven't the time to listen. Just do as I say."

"Where should we search?"

"You obviously start from the hospital area. One helicopter north and one south. And cover Pripyat itself. A deserted town would be attractive to someone on the run."

"North would take them into the contaminated zone."

Chernov struck the desk. "What's happened to you? That's not our problem. There are men at this moment flying over the blown reactor at low level to drop sand on it. Again and again and again. Brave men. Some have already given their lives to save thousands of others and you're worried about contamination? See that they get some of that protective clothing, whatever it's called. Get the helicopters down from Moscow, Leningrad, anywhere. But you'll probably find a surplus of machines down there by this time."

"Yes, Comrade General."

Kanavsky started to rise. He didn't know why he should be so surprised at the order. Perhaps he had already got used to the idea of another Chairman, or perhaps it simply did not seem so important that a man had escaped.

"Sit down," Chernov instructed. "There's one more thing." He passed over a slip of paper with an address on it. "As soon as you've dealt with the search I want Victor and Yelena Belenko picked up and taken to Lubyanka. I want them in separate cells and let me know when you have them."

Even though the Belenkos were well known, this was better understood; a matter of routine. Just the same Kanavsky considered Chernov had gone a little strange in the short time he had been away. He waited for the dismissal and then set about his tasks.

Chernov knew that he could not have put the matter in better hands; Kanavsky was a first-class administrator and, in his way and away from the direct influence of his master, just as ruthless. Chernov had always been strong on the art of delegation.

Zhadin was aware that Chernov was using Borya Kanavsky. He would not have expected anything else; Kanavsky had always been at Chernov's side. Zhadin also recognised that Chernov's influence would be around for some time, even after he finally left. He himself could come the heavy hand and make demands on Kanvasky but that would drive Chernov into another tunnel. It would take time for him to make his own mark and he wanted to do it his way and not Chernov's. But at no time did he consider the matter of Zotov as trivial. Never in Chernov's life had he wasted time on trivialities.

What Zhadin had to keep his eye on more than anything else was that Chernov did not set up his own network within the main network. He had to find out what was happening without causing too many ripples within the service. It was also important that he and Chernov did not appear as enemies. That would confuse loyalties which must be made to shift his way.

In an organisation so vast and world-wide and for which he had become responsible, the issue of Zotov appeared minute. Yet Zhadin's instinct told him that the first dangers to his new position were already under his feet and emanating from the small office which temporarily housed Chernov. Chernov would not work against the State, he was too much a patriot and too hard in his views. But it was a matter of definition as to how the State's interests were best served and whether he was capable of change in its real interests.

5

Zotov heard the thud of blades about the same time as he spotted a car. The sound sent tremors through him, but when he searched the sky he could see nothing in any direction. Yet there was a helicopter about somewhere and he had only to look at Pripy whose ears had pricked up, turning this way and that like elliptical discs.

It dawned on him slowly that the sound was magnified because it was so deadly silent everywhere. As though he was slowly turning up the volume of his transistor the thudding grew stronger and that could only mean it was approaching. Pripy suddenly barked and Zotov almost jumped out of his skin.

They had to get off the streets and at once Zotov was sorry that he had not made a makeshift lead for the dog. It was too late now. He ran along a side street making for one of the stores he had broken into. Pripy loped along beside him. The sound of the helicopter grew noticeably louder and he tried to run faster, disgusted at his condition. The monotonous thudding was so close now that the empty streets and buildings were beginning to act like an echo chamber, the roar rumbling down every avenue. Yet still he could see nothing.

As they turned into one of the main streets, Zotov slowed down, his breath rasping. Seeing the pile of broken glass he ran through the window of a store. Pripy had learned the route round the broken glass and followed just after, at last realising that this was no new game. It was the store where they slept and as Zotov tore further into its bowels he saw that he had not remade the bed. He frantically tore blankets, sheets and pillows off and crammed them under the bed as Pripy ran round behind as if to protect him.

The roar of rotary blades was now deafening as though the whole sky was filled with helicopters. Zotov crept nearer to the front of the shop to get a better view of what was happening. He crouched behind some furniture. The machine sounded as if it was actually in the shop and the sound swelled until he thought his eardrums would burst. The effect on Pripy was worse; his sensitive ears were being hammered and he was barking at the unseen devil who was torturing him.

At last Zotov saw a faint shadow cast by a weak sun and it was coming down the street at snail's pace. Then he saw the skids of the machine itself about twenty feet above the ground. The down-draught blew into the shop like a gale, and anything loose started to flap or rattle. The helicopter hovered outside and then began to descend.

Zotov guessed that the crew had seen the smashed window. Were they looking for him? Pripy was going berserk and there was nothing Zotov could do to restrain him. The engine thumped at a slower rate and he guessed they were shutting down and that could only mean they would climb out to investigate. He scurried back into the rear of the shop to hide behind some long rolls of carpeting. For once Pripy did not join him and Zotov feared the dog would give them both away.

There was no point in calling out. There was still too much noise but at least it covered Pripy's incessant barking although that would only be effective until the engine was switched off. Then it was, and the following silence was almost as painful as the ugly noise had been. There was still the slow swish of the blades and then that stopped too. Pripy stopped barking and began to snarl.

Nothing happened for some time and Zotov raised his head above the carpet roll. Pripy was growling and then started to bark again as two figures dressed like space men appeared through the broken window. Zotov gazed at the hazy forms, felt his stomach give an enormous kick and vomited just before he passed out.

The two men approached with visors raised. "Vandals," remarked one of the men. "Thieves. There's always someone to take advantage of tragedy."

The second man joined him. "It's understandable though. My wife's been waiting months for a broom head to go with the stick she bought. They never reach the shops together. We might as well help ourselves while we're here."

The pilot shook his head. "You're a fool, Leonid. Would you take contaminated goods home?"

"Someone has. This isn't the only shop with smashed windows. It must have been done during the evacuation; if it was after then there might still be people here."

They stood just inside the store gazing around and not happy with the job they had been given. "I'll shoot that dog if he doesn't stop barking." The second man removed a glove and drew an automatic pistol.

Pripy backed away but his barking got louder and the man fired. Pripy howled as the bullet grazed his head and then cowered. The airman took more careful aim. Pripy lurched sideways just before the gun roared and came round fast in a frightening leap to bite viciously into the gun hand. The man screamed and the pilot reluctantly drew his own gun, cursing his comrade for being so stupid.

It was the gun roar that roused Zotov from his faint, as well as the fact that his head was down and the blood better able to get back to his brain. But the shots had sounded like cannon in the store and he came round to the screams of one of the men. He peered slowly over the carpet roll, saw what was happening and realised that he was about to lose the only friend he'd had for as long as he could remember.

Pripy wasn't making himself an easy target as he pulled the airman round with him. Blood was gushing from the man's hand, and his face in its protective hood was white with pain. The pilot was trying to get round for a shot when Zotov, having crept forward quickly, hurled a wooden bed knob at the right-hand section of window which still had glass in it. Desperation gave him accuracy.

The heavy wooden knob hit the glass, shattered it and a whole long strip crashed down. Pripy lost his grip, then hared back into the store to the waiting arms of Zotov who had thrown himself behind a settee. Zotov clung desperately to Pripy who was shaking in anger and still growling loudly. He could see where a tuft of hair had been ripped from the dog's head near one of its ears and blood was trickling into the fur. There was no way of hiding his position now but Zotov clung on and kept out of sight.

The two airmen had spun round, assuming at once that the glass had merely dislodged itself, perhaps aided by the reverberation of the shots. "You fool," shouted the pilot at his colleague who was holding his bloodied hand. "You should have left the dog alone, there are probably dozens of them around." As if to confirm it, some of the abandoned dogs which had been freed by Zotov appeared outside the store attracted by Pripy's barking.

"We'd better get a dressing on that. Let's get back."

"I could be contaminated. My God."

"You asked for it. There's nothing here but animals. Even if Zotov is here we'd never find him. It could take weeks and we'd need an army to make sure he didn't double back all the time. We'll do one more circuit, then get back."

The blades started to rotate and the deafening roar returned as the helicopter lifted off.

Zotov did not move. He was trembling more than Pripy who had calmed down in his arms. The thunder of the helicopter could still be heard slowly traversing the streets so that the crew could at least put in a reasonable report. It would go sooner or later but what now disturbed Zotov was the knowledge that they were definitely looking for him. What was it about him they saw as important enough to send men into a contaminated zone? And what had made him pass out like that?

When the last faint sound of the helicopter had gone he warily came out from behind the settee with Pripy close beside him. The silence had returned; the other dogs had wandered off, and Zotov seemed to have the town to himself again. As they stepped out on to the street the dog gave a last chorus of barking to show his cockiness now that the enemy had gone; then he trotted back into the store and returned with something in his strong jaws which he dropped at Zotov's feet.

It was the gun the airman had dropped. Zotov bent to pick it up with a strange feeling of familiarity. As he held it in the flat of his hand he knew that, at some time or other, he had held a similar object. He watched, fascinated, as his hands, apparently working without instruction from his mind, released the catch to pull out the magazine, counted the number of rounds and pulled back the breech to eject the round in the chamber. He picked the round up and pressed it down into the magazine making sure that the rim did not overlap the one below it to cause a jam. The pistol was an eight-shot, 9 mm Marakov.

He stared at the gun again and applied the safety-catch. He had done all this before. When? It must have been years and years ago. But he had done it and although he could not recall the time it was clear that his instruction had been thorough for him instinctively to do the right things now. It both pleased and worried him. He slipped the gun into his hip pocket and even that small action had a vague familiarity about it.

They had to get out of town in case the men came back. He said to Pripy, "Let's find that car again. It was only a few streets from here."

In the helicopter the pilot watched out of the corner of an eye as his comrade put a dressing round his hand. The dog had bitten deeply and very painfully; the wound was ugly and still bleeding and the flesh around it was turning blue. When he had finished the airman said, "I'll get this treated as soon as we arrive in Kiev. At least it shows we got out to search." Suddenly he froze and felt frantically around his waist. "I've left my pistol there."

The pilot looked across. "You must have dropped it when the dog bit you."

"We must go back."

"We will when you've been treated."

"I can't report without a pistol; I'll be crucified."

"You need that bite sterilized and you need a booster tetanus jab. We'll go back later."

"No. The jab can wait. A few minutes will make no

difference. Please. I'm in enough trouble letting a dog disarm me. I'll never live it down. Let's go and get it."

The pilot shrugged, looked at his fuel gauge, then said, "Okay. At least we know where you dropped it. Radio back a report as we go. That'll show we're keen. Mention the dog but obviously not the pistol." He swung the helicopter round, almost on a pivot, and sped back towards Pripyat.

Jan Mirek was in Warsaw when Ian Pascoe sought him out. They met in a spartan, two-roomed apartment which was considered a safe house.

"You're a raving lunatic," Mirek said heatedly. "You could have contacted me some other way."

"I was careful and I was helped by friends of yours. Anyway, it's urgent, I had to come."

Mirek was still fuming. He had been in and out of Poland many times, assisting with political agitation, anything that might help his father's people rid themselves of slavery and the Russian yoke. He had even been to prison for a short spell and his cover had held up well. He had done odd jobs on false papers and was funded by London. This meant that he had to move fairly frequently so as not to cause too much curiosity.

In late 1939 Mirek's father had fled to Britain to become a bomber pilot in the RAF. He was still alive in London, speaking English with an atrocious accent which had changed little despite the forty-seven years he had lived in Britain. Jan Mirek, on the other hand, spoke English with an accent which verged on the over-refined as if to make up for his father's lack of linguistic ability. He spoke Polish, his father's native tongue, with equal aplomb and could slip from one language to the other with complete ease. He also spoke very passable Russian and reasonable French.

At thirty-eight, and about five feet ten, Mirek was quite powerfully built with dark, crinkly hair, and a fresh English complexion. He was physically fit and had always been mentally alive. His deep eyes were seldom far from smiling. Mirek could see the funny side of life and swore that it was only that which kept him sane. He was irreverent about most things and had never been deeply religious like his father. But he had developed his father's deep hatred of the Russians who had occupied his country and directed its affairs through a quasi-government.

At the moment, however, Mirek was far from humorous. For a British Embassy official to call on him in this fringe-of-town apartment he saw as absolute stupidity. Even though Pascoe was no fool he had done a very foolish thing.

Reading his mind Pascoe said, "Calm down, Jan. You're showing your genes. I know I'm followed; but I'm not cracked. A diversion was arranged by some of your friends. Nobody but you knows I'm this side of town. Am I invited to sit?"

Mirek gestured helplessly to a rough wooden kitchen chair. "You brought some coffee?"

Pascoe smiled, feeling an edge of thaw. "Of course." He lowered himself carefully on to the chair, a tall, thin, fair-haired figure, normally well dressed, but dressed down, not too harshly, for this visit. He produced a packet of coffee beans from inside his top coat. "You'll enjoy these. Good coffee."

"Where's your car?"

"Other side of town. As it will be watched awaiting my return, I've arranged for it to be picked up by a friend. That should irritate them. I came by a combination of taxis and public transport. Now, have you cooled down enough to listen?"

Mirek pulled a chair up to a small table covered with magazines and newspapers. "Go ahead," he said wearily.

"There was a little item in *Izvestia* a few days ago. Chap called Zotov escaped from a mental hospital, prison really, near Pripyat. Our people attach a great deal of importance to this. He's apparently wandering free."

"So?"

"They'd like you to nip over the border and pull him out. They'd very much like him in London."

Mirek stared. His lips twitched and then he laughed. "You're off your chump. This isn't a needle in a haystack, more like a grain of sand in a desert. Those silly sods in London really are the limit."

"It's not as bad as that. The number of routes between here and there are extremely limited."

"Sure. And they're all under a cloud of radioactive dust."

"The cloud will have moved on by now. The damage is done, but it's dissipating all the time. It was the people on the spot who suffered."

"I'm still young enough to be around in another twenty years. And so are you. Do we have to add to the existing risks? I'd never find him. It's hopeless."

"Bullshit. It's an instruction."

"Christ, he could be anywhere. He might be dead. If he's heading towards Kiev he'll be caught sooner or later, anyway. If he heads north he'll run straight into the Pripyat marshes. Have you any idea how massive and deserted that bog-land is?"

"Oh yes. The biggest peat bog in Europe. The unlovely landscape of Belorussia. But put yourself in his place. What are his options? If he really wants to escape he can't head haphazardly into the marshes. He's got to have some idea of direction."

"He could go for the Czech border."

"Would you? In his position? The Soviets have things pretty well tied down there at the moment, unlike Poland. Which would you take?"

It was an almost endless speculation. Czechoslovakia was nearer to Western Europe but probably carried greater dangers. Mirek waved his hands in exasperation. "It doesn't matter, does it? You're throwing me to the wolves on a tinpot idea. Nobody can be that important. Known dissidents don't rate that sort of risk, and I've never heard of this one."

"Nor have I. He apparently goes back to Brian Carter's days."

"Then let him bloody well find him. That was in the dark ages when I was still at school." Mirek reached across the table to clutch the packet of coffee beans as if he half expected Pascoe to take them back. "Besides, it's not my scene, not what I'm best at. I'm no Pimpernel."

"Who knows?" Pascoe shrugged. "You've done plenty of disappearing acts here."

"No." Mirek was at once deadly serious. He shook his head slowly. "I'd need to know far more if I'm to put my head on the block. Who's idea is this?"

"Moggie's. The directive is from him personally."

Both men were silent, Pascoe because he wanted Mirek to have time to think it over without pressure, and Mirek because he realised that it was a serious matter and nobody was going to tell him why. For a while Mirek still sat with an elbow on the table his head lowered bull-like. In that position his gaze suddenly came up to meet Pascoe's. "I refuse to go in blind like this. Haven't we anyone nearer?"

Pascoe hesitated and it was clear to Mirek that he had been given strict instructions on how much to concede. "We've been in touch with our cousins to see if they can help as they're heavier on the ground in Russia. They have a bone marrow transplant specialist who has offered the services of his techniques and is being flown from California to Moscow. It seemed a God-sent opportunity to have someone with his ear to the ground; someone who would be in a strong position to ask questions in high places. He is highly thought of in the medical world. He would have to be for the Russians to let him in on this sort of issue."

"And?"

"The Americans won't touch it. There's a powerful chance of goodwill arising from the visit and they're not willing to endanger it for something so indefinite. Either that or they've asked him and he's refused. It's a pity because he could have expressed a genuine interest in someone roaming wild in an evacuated area. But there it is."

Mirek nodded slowly. It was plain why Pascoe had told him this. He was showing that the matter had to be of the utmost importance for Britain to have gone to such lengths in an attempt to compromise a well-known American surgeon. "I suppose Moggy told them as much as you've told me? Damn all. What could be the result of Zotov finishing up in London?"

"It could bring the so-called morality of Russia to its knees. They would lose all credibility. And in so doing almost world-wide support. It could make a great chunk of their supporters sick at heart. Only the maniacs would be unaffected. And you would have achieved what you've always wanted." Pascoe paused knowing that he at last had Mirek interested. "It could," he continued calmly not wanting to inject too much drama into his tone, "expose the greatest fraud in history."

Mirek sat back. "Could or would?"

"I've told you all I know, so don't push me. However, I don't believe that Moggy, or anyone else of authority in the service, would send you out on a death run without the highest possible motive. In spite of rumours to the contrary, intelligence agencies have the welfare of their agents very much in mind. The system could not work otherwise; they'd never find recruits. Think how the Russians look after theirs."

"I didn't suggest I was being set up. What about Annya?"

"Why don't you take her with you? A couple would look better than a bloke on his own."

Mirek rose and placed the coffee beans in a small, battered refrigerator. "How do you think she'd get time off? Anyway, I wouldn't want to drag her into anything as dodgy as this."

"Speak to her. She might be able to fix it, and she's used to taking risks. Before she turned to teaching she was a nurse, wasn't she? That could be useful."

Mirek sat down again. "I'm really beginning to dislike you, Ian. You've been digging too deeply into my affairs."

"I've been covering your back. You're in deep with Annya; it's my job to know."

Mirek wished he had a photograph of her but it was highly inadvisable to have one either on him or in the apartment, or anything that could be traced back to her should something happen to him. In her absence he had to create his own vision of her but it was not difficult. In her early thirties she was as dark haired as he was, but she cropped it into a thick bob which encased the high cheek-boned lines of her face. Beneath the fringe were defensive blue eyes that had, at times, shown a fair amount of suffering. Her husband had been killed a few years ago in one of the early riots. Mirek had known her about eight months and their relationship had gradually deepened, although sometimes he wondered if she had really recovered from that loss.

Mirek knew he would ask her because she would do anything to get back at those whom she hated and blamed for her husband's death. "What can I tell her?"

"That you're going to try to find a man called Zotov. The truth."

"As we know it," Mirek added drily. "I'll put it to her when she comes in. I'll need funding and some papers."

"Of course. They're being done now. I'll get them round to you."

Mirek controlled his anger. "You were bloody sure of yourself weren't you?"

"Not at all. I was sure of you, though. I knew that you wouldn't be able to resist. If we can pick up anything from Kiev I'll let you know."

When Victor Belenko came home he found the apartment empty. This was not something new but usually there would be a note and a meal in the oven. At the moment he had no concerts on, but was involved in constant rehearsal. Most of his life seemed to be spent either at his dummy keyboard, which was propped up against the Cuban mahogany sideboard, or at orchestral rehearsals or studio recordings. Music was his life and almost anything else an intrusion.

A tall, slightly stooped man, his greying hair was brushed straight back with two thick wings of it curling over his ears. He had fine, aristocratic features which displayed a certain degree of arrogance in the grey, sometimes indifferent eyes. Belenko knew he was a fine pianist and believed, against other expert and sometimes jealous opinion, that he was the best. He certainly filled the concert halls and was internationally known; but it always aggravated him that he was not allowed to perform abroad in spite of many invitations. He often suspected that it was because of some earlier misdemeanour of Yelena's.

Yet his wife added to his stature for she was at least as well known and as a couple they were highly envied. The marriage worked well on the ground on which it was founded but that had nothing to do with love. Both of them loved their work and that was enough.

He was searching for something to eat when the bell rang. He opened the door grudgingly to see two blank-faced thugs outside who looked like thieves. It was a fact that crime was on the increase, and he started to close the door quickly, but it was thrown back against him and Belenko went reeling against the hall wall. Breathless, the indignity of it overcame his natural fear.

"Do you realise who I am? I shall call the police unless you leave immediately."

"We are the police, Comrade Belenko." Warrant cards were flashed in the same way the world over.

"Then how dare you come barging in like this?"

"You are under arrest. Where's your wife?"

Belenko could not grasp what was happening; he was not a political animal but perhaps these weren't political police? But they were plain-clothed. "May I see your identities again? There is clearly a dreadful mistake."

His request was ignored. Instead the senior officer asked, "You are Victor Belenko? The pianist?"

Belenko drew himself up. Recognition was almost as satisfying as his music. "Of course . . . "

Before he could say more he was grabbed, turned, thrown face against the wall, hands grasped viciously and his wrists handcuffed behind his back. He was in a state of shock as the front door was slammed and he was left in the small hall while the two men rushed into the apartment. He heard them running wild with little respect for the furniture and after a while they returned.

"Where is she?"

Belenko had managed to turn round and supported himself against the hall wall. He was now pale and full of fear. "She wasn't here when I got back. What's happening?

What have I done? There will be trouble over this; you two louts will pay."

They looked at each other and then one of them laughed. "Is she normally here at this time of day? What is the usual thing?"

The questioning went on for the next half hour during which they sometimes prodded and pushed him, never actually striking him, but enough to bewilder and bruise him. The whole unsavoury episode was so foreign to him, so unaccountable, and so sickening that he gave confusing and conflicting answers as he was gradually stripped of all dignity. He simply could not grasp that any of this could be happening to him. At one point he was on the verge of tears.

By the time they bundled him into the ominous black car waiting below, Belenko's smug life had become a screaming nightmare. When they arrived at Lubyanka he almost passed out from shock.

6

Zotov found the car again. It was a small compact Moskvich made by the AZLK plant in Moscow. This recognition did not tax him too much; he had read about them in some of the technical magazines he had been allowed in hospital. It was well clear of the kerb in one of the outer streets away from the city centre and had obviously been abandoned in a hurry. The keys were still in the ignition.

This fact depressed him somewhat for it smacked of a breakdown like the truck he had found before reaching town. He was almost afraid to climb in to try it. He opened the nearside door and told Pripy to jump in and then went round to the driver's seat. It was a pity the car was red; too easily distinguished, especially from the air. He turned the ignition. The car fired at once.

Why had it been left? He could only think that in the panic to leave the carburettor had been flooded and that the owners had left by other means. A couple of garments on the rear seat seemed to confirm this. Zotov sat at the wheel and ran his hands through his hair. He was filled with both excitement and apprehension.

After being confined for as long as he could remember too much was happening to him in too short a time. He had spent only three nights in Pripyat since escaping, four nights of freedom altogether. Already it felt like years and being reborn. Everything was so strange and the world was empty. Not for the first time he appreciated the loving presence of Pripy. Even if the dog couldn't understand he at least paid attention.

Zotov revved the engine up, getting the feel of the pedal and examining the dials. He had driven before, he was sure. The tank was full, enough fuel to take him some considerable distance. Tentatively, he tried the clutch and then attempted to drive away. The car shot forward in a series of back-jarring bumps. After a while he got the knack and drove carefully along the street, taking corners slowly but knowing that there were no other moving vehicles to hit.

He kept to the outskirts, wanting both to try the car out and to examine the perimeter of the town, but he found it none too attractive and turned back towards the city centre. It was important to conserve fuel, but he also had to stock up for the journey north-west. He knew he could not go in the Kiev direction.

He came to the main street where he had broken into the stores near to the one he slept in. No sooner had he turned the corner than he was braking furiously. He had already found the brakes to be less than perfect but this was no time for confirmation. Standing broodily in the middle of the street was a stationary helicopter.

Why hadn't he heard it approach? In his panic he realised he should have skirted the machine and driven straight on, and belatedly he tried to do this, releasing the brakes and veering as he accelerated. He mounted the pavement and the steering wheel became alive in his hands.

Zotov glimpsed the two airmen dash into the street and the pilot had a gun in his hand and stood his ground as Zotov tried to go round him. The car grazed the side of a building and there was a terrible shrieking of metal and then more as the pilot fired and hit the car. Zotov lost control as the car lurched back on to the street and he thought he was about to crash straight into the helicopter. He rammed on the brakes finding too little response, and the effort sent him into a skid which had the car bouncing up the kerb again until it finally came to an unsteady halt.

Zotov was in shock and trembling, his hands frantically gripping the wheel as if it was the only thing he could believe in. His drugged system wasn't attuned to what was happening to it. He was dazed and scared as the pilot and his colleague came racing up to yank open the door.

"Out," ordered the pilot. "And be careful how you do it." He had his gun levelled at Zotov who climbed out only half aware of what he was doing. He was still bemused about not hearing the helicopter.

"Keep still against the door. Just stay there." The pilot realised his luck. In the confines of the car and with the noisy engine running, Zotov simply hadn't heard them, and they had come in low, straight down the main street. "Where's the gun?"

Zotov tried to clear his head. His nerves were screaming and his withdrawal pains almost impossible to bear. But he had to hang on and somehow, like a boxer who had just been hammered, tried to clear his head. "What gun?" He thought he was going to faint and clung to the door frame. Behind him Pripy was trying to get out but Zotov stopped him by blocking the door.

"When we came before my colleague dropped his gun in that store. It's no longer there. Where is it?"

"I've just driven in. You've given me such a shock." Zotov waved aimlessly. "A helicopter in the street; my God, you could have killed me."

"Has the dog just driven in too? He was the one who bit me." The second man, his hand bandaged, stepped forward. "And the car was already plotted. We know where it was. You must have been in the store while we were there. The dog was protecting you. I should slay you for that." He moved towards Zotov but the pilot stopped him.

"Is your name Zotov?"

He had no papers of any kind on him. "No."

"No? Then you'd better tell us what it is and what you are doing here."

They hadn't bothered to ask him for his papers; they knew who he was. "Igor Smolin." The name of one of the guards was all he could think of.

The airmen glanced at each other and smiled. They had entered into a sort of game; a little mental torture to make up for all their trouble. "And where are your papers, Igor?"

"There was no time to get them. We had to evacuate too quickly."

"From Guliyev Hospital?"

"From here. Pripyat. I got left behind. I've been roaming the streets."

"And smashing windows and stealing goods. That won't look good, Igor. They won't like that back in Kiev. Looting carries the maximum sentence. Why did you lie to us? About just coming in to town?"

Zotov realised that they were playing with him; it happened to him on various occasions in hospital when he had exasperated the staff and they goaded him in retaliation. But this was different. This was the end of the line. He tried to get his mind working but his thoughts were clawing through glue, ponderous and ineffective. He simply did not know what to do or say. All he did know was that he could not go back with these people. So he just stood there, frightened but determined.

The airmen glanced at each other once more. The game was over, short and disappointing. The pilot said, "Step away from the car and turn your back towards my colleague. You are coming back with us."

If he turned his back Zotov realised that the gun would be on view. "The dog will jump out if I move away. He'll go for you."

"Never mind the dog, just move away." The pilot had his gun pointing at the spot where Pripy would emerge once Zotov moved.

Zotov knew what was about to happen and that it might also happen to himself once Pripy had been shot. He steadied himself against the open door with one hand and put the other behind him to grasp the door frame. His hand brushed the gun. He knew that he had to act convincingly and equally that he wasn't conditioned for it. He reeled back a little and saw the airman with the bandaged hand come forward to grasp him.

It wasn't easy to grip the gun without being obvious and to ease off the safety-catch. He was aware that there was no round in the breech and that there was no way he could cock the weapon without using both hands. As he moved away from the door he produced the gun and aimed it at the unarmed man who stepped back and froze, gazing at the barrel. He said to the pilot, "You shoot the dog and I'll shoot your friend."

Pripy, sensing the danger, had at first hung back growling but now he hurtled forward across the seats and leaped at the pilot. The pilot hesitated because of the sudden danger to his colleague and jumped away instead of firing but Pripy went after him. The other crewman hurled himself at Zotov whose concern for the dog momentarily distracted him. Belatedly seeing him coming Zotov slashed the gun across the man's face and saw him reel back.

Meanwhile Pripy had the pilot by the leg having failed to reach the gun hand now held high. It gave Zotov time to cock his gun. The pilot, still struggling with the dog, realised that he had been fooled and loosed off a wild shot at Zotov. This made Pripy bite deeper and the pilot screamed. Despite his pain he regained some control and took a steady aim at Zotov who was the greater danger.

Zotov fired. At first he thought he had missed but then he saw the change of expression on the pilot's face as he began to sink to the ground. As the pilot made an effort to raise his gun Zotov fired again and the bullet struck him in the head. Even though he was down Pripy continued to savage him.

The second airman was squatting, hands covering his face and blood streaming between his fingers. He was barely conscious. Zotov had fired at the pilot in self-defence, but now he had to act quickly again before the other airman realised what was happening. He stepped behind the man and shot him through the back of the head.

Zotov gazed down at the two dead figures, then crouched in the gutter between them and started to tremble uncontrollably. Pripy tried to comfort him but there was no consolation to be found. If he could justify the first killing, he could justify the other only by his need to stay free. It was not enough, yet he knew he would do it again and again in similar circumstances. Although he had pulled the trigger it was those who had first sent him to be drugged out of his wits who had obliquely put the gun in his hands and provided the innocent targets.

At that moment even escape no longer seemed important and his desire to live was gone. Only the dog gave him the will to continue; to leave Pripy now would be just another kind of murder. Despite that, the temptation to put the gun to his own head was almost unbearably strong.

Zotov sat for what felt like an hour before he could move. And when he did move he stood up shakily and would have fallen if he had not grabbed the door of the car. He had killed two men, but now there would be more after him. And more. This was not the end of his danger but the beginning. He straightened up and tried to think. He went to pick up the other gun. He knew what he had to do; he only hoped he had the nerve to do it. But was it already too late?

Yelena Belenko took the lift from the marble-pillared Metro station and emerged into the crisp, late April air. She found the taxi rank and asked to be taken to Nevsky Prospekt, Leningrad's main street. There she walked slowly along the wide avenue, gazing at shops but never entering them, aware that people noticed her, and, more disconcertingly, recognised her. There was little she could do about that except stay off the streets entirely and her state of nerves did not permit that. She had craved to get out after staying at a friend's cramped apartment for only two nights.

Yelena had more friends in Leningrad than in Moscow for much of her ballet had been done here at the Kirov. Her natural reaction had been to flee to the country's second city where she had always felt at home. Once there she did not know what to do next; running away was a new experience.

Although being noticed worried her it also reassured her; would the authorities be mad enough to do anything rash to one so well-known? Even without being recognised she would be virtually impossible to ignore for she walked with the elegance and assurance of a queen. She knew she looked good and it was difficult not to be vain. But she knew too she was in grave danger. It was no more difficult to find her in Leningrad than in Moscow.

Fortunately all the talk had been about the horror of the Chernobyl disaster and Yelena's state of mind had been misinterpreted among friends who had fussed over her. They had no knowledge of the deadly secret she carried. And yet, in spite of her dire position, when she really considered it, she was glad that she knew. At least Zotov was still alive, although there must have been many times when he would have wished not to be.

Her strength of feeling for him after all those years did

not really surprise her. They had had something special going for them and to this day thought of him warmed her through. It had taken an event as tragic as this to make her realise once and for all that she still loved him. The memory was growing stronger and she feared for him, for without doubt they would be out looking for him. And this time they would kill him.

After a morning of window-shopping and walking many miles she caught a cab to the Summer Palace. It was one of her favourite places, the fifty fountains in the superb gardens a balm to eye and ear. Built by Peter the Great, the architects had been French yet she had always felt part of this scene and she cherished the serenity and splendour.

Fedorovitch Gromov was where he said he would be. Yelena did not hurry although she was late and Gromov came hastening towards her against the background of the cascading fountains. His arms were held wide, his smile of pleasure huge, as he raced up to embrace her. He threw his arms round her and swung her round kissing her on the cheeks as he did so.

"Yelena! Yelena! It's been far too long." Gromov held her at arm's length and she could not help smiling at his genuine pleasure. Only a shade taller than she, he made up for lack of stature by growing a goatee beard and by his ebullient nature. In his fifties, Gromov was a frustrated musician who played the oboe quite well but never well enough. Instead of landing in an orchestra, or better still, conducting one, which remained his real ambition, he had finished up behind a desk in a government ministry. To compensate for his failure he had become an opera and ballet buff, clinging to the fringes of those he would have liked to usurp.

When he calmed down, not really noticing how Yelena had responded to his greeting, he said with conviction, "You are as beautiful as ever and younger than before. How do you do it?"

It was difficult to resist. Yelena smiled happily. "Time has been kind to you, too, Fedor. It was good of you to come. I know how busy you are. At the moment, too, it must be awful with so much tragedy going on."

He slipped an arm through hers and grasped her hand as they walked along slowly. "There is nothing I would not do for you, you know that. I am so happy to see you here in Leningrad; this is where the arts belong. Did Victor come with you?"

She knew the question was not idle. Gromov had made clear his feelings for her many years ago when she had still been dancing. As he had done also to friends of hers. It was as though Gromov believed that every young ballerina he could lay endorsed him as an integral part of their world; it was the only way he could really feel himself to be accepted. His lack of success had added to his frustrations quite simply because most women found him rather odious. But he hid his feelings well and kept trying. "No," she replied, "I'm here quite alone."

"Then where would you like to eat? You will have dinner with me?"

"I'd love to, Fedor. Somewhere very quiet."

Gromov then knew for certain that Yelena wanted something from him. Her phone call had been a surprise, but that she would eat with him was an unexpected pleasure. It would mean he could show her off. "The quieter places are not so good, let's go to somewhere well known where the food is reliable."

She understood what was in his mind. "Would it not be better without distractions? Just the two of us. As you say, Fedor, it's been a long time."

"As you wish. Is there something else I can do for you? You have only to ask."

"I want to go to Poland. Can you arrange a quick visa for me while I'm here? I have my passport with me."

"That shouldn't be difficult. Is there any particular reason?"

Yelena smiled furtively. "I was hoping you would not ask. Would it be sufficient to say that I'd prefer Victor not to know?"

"Yelena. My dear. You surprise me. But then perhaps not. Away from the piano, Victor has always struck me as rather dull." He squeezed her arm. "Why shouldn't you enjoy yourself?"

They walked on in silence but Gromov was clearly buoyant. He did not believe that Yelena would go all the way to Poland to meet a lover. He would arrange her visa just the same. "Let's make a night of it," he said suddenly. "A good meal followed by a few drinks; there's a small hotel I know." He squeezed her hand. "We could have a nice meal and then some drinks. And you wouldn't have to rush away; we could perhaps stay on for a few hours. Then I can attend to your visa first thing in the morning. What do you say?"

She tried not to cringe openly although she knew her hand had stiffened. "That sounds fine," she replied. Already necessity had driven her to this. She fought to hide her revulsion.

Gromov gave a smile of glee. He felt he had achieved a lifetime ambition. He turned to view her beautiful profile.

Belenko shuddered at contact with anything in the cell. It smelled and it was damp and dark and it disgusted him to a point of nausea. How could this happen to him? There had to be some horrific mistake. Someone would pay for it; he had influence in high places, and had once shaken hands with Gorbachev himself.

There were no windows in the cell and the toilet facilities at one end were crude in the extreme. The place stank and he found himself unwittingly dissecting the ghastly odours of urine, unwashed human bodies and, if suffering had a smell, then that too was there. He puked before he reached the bucket and was dragged into utter despair. He was being degraded in the coarsest possible way and the protected life he had led had been no preparation for the obscenity around him.

The narrow bed with the single dark blanket was uninviting but there was no chair and he felt weak and compelled to sit down. When he did sit the bed emitted yet another obnoxious smell and he knew that he could not sleep on it. He could not accept anything that had happened to him.

Belenko shivered, much as Zotov had done, but for

entirely different reasons. Zotov had learned to live with suffering, degradation and incarceration, but Belenko would never learn; he would crack without any assistance from drugs or persecution. All that was needed was to keep him where he was without information and to feed him with the revolting swill that was now pushed through his door.

Aleksei Chernov knew this only too well. He had been to many of Belenko's concerts and had enjoyed them immensely, but the day the pianist married Yelena was when he began to take more interest in him. But the only file opened on Belenko remained in Chernov's head. He had grown to know his man which was why he left the pianist in one of the old cells for the night before visiting him the next morning.

Belenko already looked a wreck, red-eyed and pasty-faced, so that Chernov did not have to ask what sort of a night he had had. The pianist rose from the bed slowly, having been forced in the end to use it. He recognised Chernov at once. "Thank God you are here. There has been a dreadful mistake, Comrade Chernov." But in the back of his mind was the disturbing thought that this man had retired, so what was he doing her at Lubyanka?

Chernov smiled pleasantly. "If there has been a mistake, Victor, we will readily put it right. I'm sorry the cell is so disgraceful. We rarely use it now but at the moment we are so overcrowded. If we find it necessary to keep you here some time we'll do our best to improve the quarters."

Belenko lurched and steadied himself against the wall, hating to touch it or anything else. "Necessary to keep me here for some time? Do you know what that will do to my fingers?" He held them out, long and manicured. "They would seize up in this damp. I would not be able to play again."

"I hope it doesn't come to that, Victor. We would all miss your playing, particularly myself. I've seen you perform many times."

"But what have I done for this to happen to me? It doesn't make sense."

"Not what you've done. What you might know." Chernov's manner was exceedingly pleasant. Nor did he intend to rush the interrogation. When dealing with people like Belenko delay was an instrument of torture.

"Know? About what? All I know is music."

"That's what you specialise in. A master. But you would be a very dull person if your entire knowledge stopped there."

Belenko stood well clear of the bed and as far away from the bucket as he could get while his persecutor stood just inside the metal door.

"I can swear that I know nothing that could possibly be of interest to you." Belenko made a pathetic figure trying to be dignified but destroyed the effort by showing stark fear. He wasn't far off pleading, but first he had to know why he was here. Then he appeared wary. "Has Yelena been mixing with the wrong company? Has she let me down?"

Chernov despised the hypocrisy of it. If anyone was capable of mixing with the wrong company then it was Belenko himself. He wasn't too discreet about some of his affairs. "Why don't you sit down, Victor? Would you like me to have a chair sent in?"

Belenko stared at the bed with open distaste and shuddered. While his mind was on the untold discomforts of the bed Chernov said, "What do you know of a man called Zotov?"

"Zotov?" Belenko appeared easier now that he had at last been asked a question. And his mind was clear on the matter. "So far as I'm aware I know nobody by that name."

"I didn't say you knew him but what do you know of him?"

"It's the same answer. The name means nothing to me."

"Really? Are you saying that Yelena has never mentioned him to you?"

"So it is about Yelena. I thought it might be. What has she been doing?"

"Answer my question, Victor. And make sure that you reply correctly. Think very carefully indeed. Think back, right to the day when you first got married. Did she ever mention such a man?"

Belenko saw that his freedom might depend on his reply, so he cast his mind back. He wasn't in the best condition for mental exercise but he tried desperately hard. Finally he shook his head apologetically. "I'm sorry. I can see that this is important to you, but I give my word that the name means nothing to me. I've heard the name but in no particular context. I know nothing about such a man."

Chernov nodded slowly. "Aren't you now curious about him?"

"Why should I be? If he has brought me this kind of trouble I don't want to know anything about him."

"You really mean to tell me that Yelena didn't mention her first lover to you? Well, the first we know about, but in truth I think Zotov was the only man she really cared about. Until you came along." Chernov smiled cynically.

"Her lover." Belenko shrugged in a way that sought pity. "Now you know what I've had to contend with. No, she never mentioned him. But then I wouldn't expect her to tell me about her previous love affairs."

"Where is she now, Victor?"

"Probably at home, although she hadn't arrived by the time I got there, which is unusual. Haven't you tried the apartment?"

"She seems to have disappeared completely although there's no sign that she's moved out. You'll have to go through her things for us, tell us what is missing."

Belenko nodded; he doubted that he would know.

"Where is she likely to go? Where would she run to?"

Belenko couldn't grasp the possibility that his wife would run anywhere. "I don't know. Why should she run away?"

"Think carefully."

"No, I'm sorry. If you explained to me what was happening I might be of more help. I'm totally confused."

"I believe you, Victor. So we'll give you a little more time to think. Yelena must have favourite places to go. Special friends. If you come up with anything interesting knock on the door and tell the guard. I will come round at once."

"You're going to leave me here? Please don't do that. I'd think much better at home."

"You'd have distractions at home, Victor. Just mull over anything interesting that Yelena may have told you over the years." Chernov rapped on the door without turning, his huge frame almost hiding the door completely, his bald head haloed by the closed grid. "Don't take too long over it. Time is important." As the door opened behind him Chernov added, "I'll have your dummy keyboard sent in. It will help keep your fingers supple in this damp." He smiled. "And it will be a constant reminder of what pleasures await you outside. Enjoy yourself."

Belenko sank on to the bed with a loud, plaintive groan.

7

Zotov had seen the petrol station during his tour round the streets of Pripyat. He smashed the pump lock and forced the door of the office. At the rear of the building a store room yielded cans of oil, and empty cans which he filled at the petrol pump. He loaded them into the car. He filled the car's tank and drove off with Pripy sitting upright beside him.

The stranded helicopter came into view like some dark forbidding dream. The scene, in the wide, lifeless street, was bizarre and Zotov hoped it would go away. He pulled up beside the machine, better able to judge his poor brakes by now, and he off-loaded the cans again, despairingly aware of the time it was taking.

Then, one at a time, he dragged the crewmen to the machine. That wasn't so bad but getting them into the cockpit was one long nightmare. He found it easier to shoulder them but had not realised just how much his strength had become depleted over the years. Once on the flight deck he had the extra physical problem of getting them into their seats and then strapping them in. While he did this he wondered how he was so certain that he knew who sat where, yet he had not hesitated.

Once the two dead men were strapped in Zotov was faced with a crucial dilemma. The gun had proved to be valuable. He had taken some rounds from the pilot's gun to top up his own magazine and had then put the pilot's gun back in its holster. The fact that they had been armed at all indicated that the search for him did not fit the usual pattern.

He found the helicopter's fuel cock and opened it. He had already prepared a rough fuse by cutting off a long piece of material obtained from one of the shops. He rammed this into the fuel tank. Finally, one at a time, he emptied the petrol cans over the bodies and the interior of the machine.

He jumped down and crammed the re-capped empty cans into the car. Pripy had been left locked in the Moskvich and was now howling at the strong smell of fumes. Zotov drove straight down the street to a safe distance, pulled up and then ran back to the helicopter. He lit a match and ignited the end of the rough fuse. He ran towards the corner of the nearest building as fast as he could. He was blown off his feet while he was still running, feeling the enormous pressure on his spine as the helicopter exploded, and the searing heat.

He tried to rise but his legs seemed to be paralysed. He was face down as he turned his head to look back. The helicopter was a mass of fire, parts of it flying through the air and screaming like shrapnel. He dragged himself on his elbows until he was round the corner, and protected from the unbearable heat.

Suddenly he realised that his legs were scorching and the agony made him sit up. His trousers were on fire. He beat out the flames and rolled his body so that the smouldering patches were smothered. The smell of burning cloth was lost to him in the greater smell from the raging helicopter. As he changed position and managed to peer round the corner he saw the machine writhing inside the massive fire ball eating through the ugly, swirling pall of black, stinking smoke that was choking him. Behind the flame and smoke the machine was shrinking as it lost shape and heeled over.

Zotov closed his eyes. He was covered in sweat and descending smut. Shreds of molten metal hurled around him, forcing him to roll away again to escape their scorching heat. The smell of burning flesh and rubber was terrible. The whole gruesome image was still contracting and when he stared at the flight deck he could see two incinerating figures, distorted and charred and staring straight at him with burned-out eyes.

As he stared back in horror, they grew smaller and blacker and more shapeless as the flames bit deeper. There was a terrible noise of collapsing metal as what remained of the helicopter compacted further to a stinking flaming scrap heap, with now more smoke than flame. His face felt scorched but gradually there was less heat and he realised that the machine must have been carrying more fuel than he had bargained for.

Above the general racket of screaming metal and fire roar he could now hear Pripy howling with fear. Zotov made a supreme effort to rise. The pain in his legs was excruciating as they took his weight but he managed to stagger towards the car. As far away as he had left it the car was still hot to the touch and he quickly opened all the windows to release the interior heat.

He turned to view the decreasing black stub of the helicopter before climbing in and driving back to the fuel station. He refilled some of the cans and put the remainder back where he had found them. He drove to the store where he had stacked the food and drink, and clothes and equipment he would need for the long journey through the almost uninhabited Pripyat bog-land.

As Zotov took a last look round the soulless windows and the vacant streets, he bade a silent farewell to Pripyat, grateful for the unlimited shelter and sustenance it had exclusively provided. He was sorry to be leaving, for once out on the open road he would be more vulnerable. He had no option, however. He headed for the northern perimeter of the ghost town, now a burial ground for an unknown helicopter crew, and on reaching the fringes took the north-west road towards the marshes.

Annya opened the side window. The battered old Mercedes had a well-tended engine under its dented bonnet. Mechanically it was exceedingly sound. The power-driven windows still worked and the dark-haired girl, sitting beside Jan Mirek, held back her head to let the cooling air blow into her face. "I really don't know why I'm doing this," she said. "I must be crazy." She was using her native tongue although she spoke English with the same fluency as Mirek spoke Polish.

"You're doing it for me," said Mirek without taking his eyes off the road. "I'm irresistible."

She thumped him on the arm, not too hard, for the traffic was still quite thick. The breeze lifted her fringe and better revealed the clear, beautiful eyes beneath the dark brows. "That's the conceit of the English."

"Rubbish. It's the natural self-confidence of the Pole. How did you get the time off?" He pulled up at traffic lights beside an army truck loaded with soldiers; those who could see Annya grinned or wolf-whistled.

She placed an arm along the back of the seats to touch him lightly on the shoulder. "I'm owed a week. It was short notice but I've put in plenty of extra time lately and they know it." She faced him and laughed. "Anyway the head fancies me."

"Who doesn't? Don't get spoiled by it. I don't like the feel of this job at all. It's a stupid mission but if by chance we strike lucky we could be in all sorts of trouble. I did warn you."

"Yes, you did. I've been up against the wall before, Mirek. You know that. And I owe those bloody Russians."

He turned his head quickly and then back to the road. "Don't let hate sway you. It's the wrong motive. It can also colour your judgement. It's our heads on the chopping block. It would be foolish to forget it."

"It's not the first time I've carried false papers."

"That isn't what I mean. Don't take it too lightly, Annya. You mean too much to me."

She lowered her head to his shoulder. "That's nice."

"It's no reason for getting you involved. I'm sorry now I ever mentioned it."

"So you'd have pushed off and left me worrying about what had happened to you. That could have given me even worse trouble."

He didn't argue. He was uncomfortable, not so much that they were flying blind, or that Ian Pascoe had told them nothing more than to set out on a hopeless task to find a man called Zotov, but because he was certain that Pascoe himself knew no more. He had told Annya exactly what Pascoe had told him.

At first she had not relished the idea of searching for any Russian; almost every Pole hated them, but when Mirek told her the possible effects of finding this man and then delivering him to London, her attitude changed as Mirek's had.

"Do you believe Pascoe?" She was reading Mirek's mind.

Mirek swore as he was forced to brake sharply; they were approaching the eastern outskirts of Warsaw. He was not surprised by the question; Annya had dealt with Pascoe almost as much as he. In a volatile political climate occasional direct contact was difficult to avoid no matter how undesirable. "He himself might have been misled, but yes, I believe he's told us what he's been told."

"You don't sound too sure, Mirek." She had called him Mirek from the start. They first met at a clandestine gathering; there had been two other Jan's there and she had cut through the confusion.

He laughed. "It's not Pascoe I'm unsure about. I'm being used out of context. This isn't my normal game. I'm an on-the-spot backroom boy. That's as far as it goes. I'm not a gun-toting swashbuckler."

"Your father was, only he did it at angels one-five. Same thing, though."

"He was a bomber not a fighter pilot. A bus driver, he called it. He got them there and he got them back. He was on the first 1000-bomber raid over Berlin."

"So why are you doing it, Mirek?"

Mirek blew out his cheeks. He replied in English, breaking all the rules. "I don't know. I'm beginning to be sorry for myself."

"Maybe it's because you're trying to find out if you're a Pole or an Englishman."

"No, love. I know what my allegiances are. Maybe it's because I owe it to the way my parents' family disappeared after the Russians entered Poland. Maybe I would like to give Russia a big kick in the arse for the heartbreak that caused." Mirek paused, his hands relaxed on the steering wheel but his eyes were gazing ahead expressionlessly. "And still cause," he added quietly. "The old man has never really got over it. Nor had my mother up to the time she died."

Annya reached out to place a hand lightly over his.

"Anyway," he added, "we're committed to try and help the poor sod."

When it was decided that the helicopter was off the air there was deep concern at base. There were complications, for the two machines involved in the search for Zotov had been commandeered by the KGB for an unspecified time. All communications had been routed back to a temporary KGB field office set up on the northern outskirts of Kiev. A mobile station had been parked on a field giving ample room for helicopter take-offs and landings but there was room for that also at the main base and certain KGB officers were puzzled as to why the base was not used. In addition, a separate mobile radio unit had been parked close to the field station and the normal frequency had been changed.

The two junior KGB officers involved, on the direct orders of Colonel Kanavsky in Moscow, knew all about secrecy and how sometimes it could go against them. Had they been more experienced they would have acted more quickly but in Moscow Chernov had made his orders clear; the only senior officers he wanted to use were those under his direct and visible control, and only where he was sure their loyalty was to him.

So when one of the helicopters went off the air nothing was done at once. The field office presumed there was some sort of technical problem. It was only when about an hour of light was left that the matter was actioned. The senior of the two officers, an acting captain, did not inform the Air Force that one of their helicopters was missing but rang straight through to Kanavsky who gave a ready instruction. Send out the remaining helicopter to search around Pripyat. There was still enough light and Pripyat was near enough to Kiev.

The remaining helicopter crew did not much care for the order. They had been searching the comparatively safe areas of the outer approaches to Kiev. Now they had to go into the contaminated area, and they took the view that whatever had happened to the other chopper was due to radiation. They had no choice. They left with protective clothing.

They made a direct approach to Pripyat, no longer concerned with the missing Zotov, and sighted the burned-out heap quite quickly. The charred wreck was still smouldering but the smoke had abated and they had a clear view of the tragic remains. They knew the KGB would not accept short cuts so they landed and went as near to the burn-out as they could.

The machine was a twisted, shrunken mass, smoke begrudgingly spiralling in odd blackened pockets to tell them that it was still too hot to touch. It was a ghastly sight, yet they had to gather some idea of why it had happened. Neither man considered it to be anything other than a crash.

They looked around. It was difficult to understand why there had been so much fuel left in the tanks. The fire had been horrendous. Neither ventured near enough to touch the crew men; they felt that if they did what was left of the corpses would disintegrate.

They climbed back into their machine. Neither said a word and they were still silent as they took up their positions. They were sickened by what they saw and they could not understand it. They took to the air and did a routine check of the town, then headed for Kiev. Halfway back they radioed the news, then filled in with a description of what they had seen on the streets. It did not amount to much, but they mentioned the solitary truck.

The KGB officer at the field station checked the earlier radio report of the dead pilot and asked what had happened to the red Moskvich. Go back and find it. Later, when it was confirmed to be missing the KGB captain contacted Colonel Kanavsky who in turn informed a shaken Chernov who gave an immediate, most urgent, directive.

8

Zotov had pulled off the main road about three miles back and was now travelling through the bleak mass of unending peat bog, the scene flat and eternally uninteresting. He had the planet to himself and the subconscious analogy produced the familiar trembling of the hands. Loneliness was not what he wanted but it was exactly what he needed. People would have stifled him and with them would have come the very dangers he was trying to avoid. Yet surely he had a friend somewhere, someone he could turn to and trust?

These kind of thoughts had become a mental struggle. There was a blockage like a steel plate separating the two halves of his brain. At times the frustration made him yell in anguish. When he did this Pripy's reaction was to cower and immediately Zotov would try to forget his own problems to comfort his friend.

He was travelling on an uneven earth road but, provided there was no torrential downpour of rain, he would be safe. The main road, although surfaced, was not all that good and, anyway, he wanted to avoid other traffic, sparse as it might be in this wilderness. Making the turn-off had been instinctive. From the air he had no cover whichever road he chose and the forests were too far away. Somewhere, roughly following the same route would be the Pripyat river but he had no idea how far he was from it.

At about the same time as Chernov heard about the burned-out helicopter Zotov decided to stop for the night. The light was getting bad and the last thing he wanted to do was to use headlights. He pulled off the road carefully, making sure that he missed soft spots and that he could get away in a hurry.

Part of the reason for the general emptiness of the main

north road was the disaster at Chernobyl. People were not keen to follow the route of the radioactive dust cloud. Another reason was that most traffic to the Czech and Polish borders came from the direction of Leningrad in the north and from Moscow to his east. This part of the country was virtually uninhabited and had little to offer but bog-peat; the rich grainlands were to the south, in the Ukraine.

Zotov was also aided by desertion caused by justifiable fear. If he was exposed to view he was also protected by calamity. Nobody was going to dally. He let Pripy out to bound away to stretch his legs after being cramped for so long. Zotov poured water for the dog and then heaved out a looted bedroll from the boot of the car.

He ate cold canned food and drank lemonade from a plastic bottle. By the time he had finished the sun had long gone down beneath the flat earth's rim. He was a lone figure in the immense Pripyat marshes.

It was too early to sleep and he tried the transistor. Music came through weakly and then the crackle of news. He would not even have picked up that much had there been intervening hills. But it was useless. He squatted with his back against the car with Pripy contentedly at his feet.

The pain in his stomach was a little easier but he knew he must face up to the day's events. He had killed two men. He made no excuses and delved into no inquest. But arising out of it certain matters about himself had been revealed, points he did not know before today.

In the helicopter he had instinctively known where the pilot and co-pilot sat. He had had little difficulty in finding the fuel cock. At one time he had been familiar with automatic pistols, for when the gun had been in his hand the sensation was not new. He could drive, no matter how shakily. And he loved animals, particularly dogs. So even if his real personality had been subjugated his natural instincts were still there.

What he did not understand was his strong urge to reach Poland. He accepted that he had to get out of Russia. But why was the need to reach Poland so strong? He had been cut off from real news and had little idea of the state of affairs in either Poland or Czechoslovakia. Yet there was no doubt in his mind; it was Poland he must reach. There had to be a reason.

He kept his mind occupied with questions like this for he still dreaded night-time and the darkness it brought. And in such a vast empty area the agony of it was far worse, so he tried to concentrate on other matters. The strongest of these was the nightmare of killing the airmen and burning their machine, yet his increasing feeling of guilt had nothing to do with the airmen. It came from the past, creeping through some shutter in his mind to taunt and to scare him, for he could not pinpoint the source. Eventually, he curled up and trembled against the furry warmth of the only friend he knew.

Captain Penovitch accepted his sudden promotion to Major with some surprise. He was convinced it was a matter of expediency tied up with the search for the mysterious Zotov of whom nobody had ever heard. Had the promotion been granted orally he might have considered it with some suspicion, but the directive had come through over the telex much to the chagrin of some of his Kiev-based superior officers.

He was forced to tell the Commander of the Air Force base from which the lost helicopter had been virtually commandeered. It was necessary to get some crash experts out to Pripyat to judge the cause of the crash, and the resistance to entering an evacuated area kept coming up. His orders cut through the obstruction and his new rank helped. A team was flown out at first light and among them was a pathologist.

Parts of the wreck were still hot to touch but mostly it was now possible to make a close examination. The two crash experts were not at all happy with what they saw. It would be difficult to form a judgement without taking the burned-out hulk back to Kiev. With the right equipment they could perform on the spot but it would take a good deal of time and there was unspoken consent that the sooner they were out of the danger zone the better.

The pathologist agreed. The charred remains of the two corpses needed minute examination. Clearly they had been burned to a cinder but had they been burned to death? It would be difficult to extract the bodies as two separate units; they would fall apart. All these difficulties could be overcome given time but none of them wanted to spend time on the site of the crash. At any other time they would have been fascinated by the challenge.

The pathologist said, "It's obvious that they were burned to death. That's my immediate prognosis."

The senior crash expert openly showed his relief. He glanced at his subordinate expecting no opposition when he said, "Looks like engine failure. She fell straight out of the sky. She's too badly burned out to form any detailed analysis. I can see little point in trying and what can be the urgency? I suggest that when the town is declared a safe zone we come back with lifting gear and get the whole lot back to Kiev. Meanwhile we are satisfied as to the general cause. Are we agreed?"

There was no dissent. None of them had heard of Zotov. The two dead helicopter crew had been part of the original search, and the two still alive had long since been warned of the need for complete secrecy.

When Chernov read the detailed radioed report the morning after the crash he was certain that the crash was no accident. He had no idea of what had happened but he did know that a red car had initially been sighted and that the car was now missing. Somehow Zotov had pulled off a coup. And there were indications that, away from the daily use of drugs, Zotov was beginning to act with some decision. He could imagine the man's torment but he was clearly coping with it. The big worry was just how permanent would be the effect of years of highly specialised treatment.

He was sitting at his desk in his small, borrowed office when Zhadin walked in unannounced. "What do you think?" asked the new Chairman.

"About what?" Chernov replied, uncomfortably aware that he had only caught sight of Zhadin at the last moment and had not heard him enter.

"The crash at Pripyat. What else? It could only have been

as a result of your insistent search for the mysterious Zotov. What do they think in Kiev?"

Chernov knew that Zhadin had access to the report which had come through the usual channels.

"Unfortunate," Chernov growled. "I suppose the helicopters are being overworked due to Chernobyl and are not getting their standard servicing."

Zhadin sat down. "You believe the report then?"

Chernov looked surprised. "What option have I? I'm not down there."

"You think this man Zotov took the car?"

"I can't dismiss the idea. I suppose it could have been anyone but I have to follow what I've got."

"You don't think the crash has anything to do with it?"

"In what way, Joseph? It's connected in the sense that they were out searching for him."

"Perhaps they found him."

Chernov examined the report before him. "It doesn't say so here. But if they did find him the two events are not linked. We're talking of a man who's been in institutions for well over twenty years and had been mentally ill for the whole of that time. What effect could he possibly have had on them? We must continue to search."

"It's still important to you?" Zhadin was watching the wily Chernov closely.

"Nothing's changed. I'll use what time I have left while you're still Chairman designate." He smiled. "After that I'm quite sure you'll kick me out."

"We can't have two bosses, Aleksei. I think I'm being rather tolerant, don't you? Why, you're even promoting some of the Kiev staff without reference. Wouldn't you call that tolerant?"

Chernov showed surprise. "I've promoted nobody. I wouldn't dream of such a thing. What are you talking about?"

Zhadin rose with a smile. "Don't take me for a fool, Aleksei. You'd have told your acolyte Kanavsky what to do. The promotion was unjustified." For the first time Zhadin was showing open antagonism to the great Chernov. "I shall set a limit on the time you have available for this search and it won't extend to the expiry of your leave. I'll let you know in due course what that limit is. So you had better move fast and try not to lose any more men and aircraft. If you want a confrontation then you can have it."

Zhadin returned to his own office and sat down behind his desk. He ignored the incessantly ringing telephones and the constant buzzing of his intercom. Finally he flicked a switch and told his PA to stop all further calls until he countermanded the instruction.

He sat silent and brooding, his dark features impassive. He should kick Chernov out, he knew that. All the time he tolerated him he was weakening his own position and if he allowed that to go too far he could be in danger of losing his control. Not immediately, perhaps, but it could happen before he had time to grasp the real power the job generated.

Everyone knew that Chernov's present leave was part of his retirement present. He had already had his leave. But Chernov's term of office did not officially terminate until midnight on the last day of that leave. It was common practice and in normal times there would be no problem; but it was debatable whether Chernov was within his rights to come back to work out what was left of his contract.

But to challenge him openly on the matter could raise a storm which Zhadin could do without at this stage in his new post. It could appear petty to deny Chernov such a request, particularly as the matter of Zotov was ostensibly so unimportant.

Zhadin was still sitting back when his coffee was brought in. He gave a nod to his secretary and watched the steam rising from the demi-tasse of espresso, a luxury he had quickly installed. The whole hub of Chernov's intrusion was Zotov. Zhadin had done some more research, used every filing device in the organisation and the result had borne out what Chernov had claimed; Zotov was such small fry that there was no file on him and none had ever been raised.

Zhadin shook his head and gazed at the long line of trees which hid the centre from the highway. He reached for the cup, his hand steady and strong. With the loss of a helicopter, accident or not, he was in a position to demand from Chernov what Zotov was all about and if he was so minor then no more helicopters could be wasted on him. It would be easy to do. But Chernov would spin some story knowing it to be uncheckable and use devious methods to get what he wanted done.

There was something about Zotov that made Chernov very uneasy; he was a deeply worried man. Was it possible to discredit Chernov, get rid of him once and for all, and destroy the myth of his impregnability? If he could do that he would scuttle Chernov's hard-core friends within the centre.

At last Zhadin permitted himself a smile, not of satisfaction but of purpose. He raised the main Kiev Station and was put through to the field office. When he spoke to the newly promoted Penovitch and congratulated him on his promotion he knew he had won an ally without pulling rank. He did not want to instil the sort of fear Chernov could generate, but co-operation.

Penovitch was dumb-struck to receive a call from the new Chairman. He was finding it difficult to cope with all the good things now happening to him. But the chief of the KGB was talking and he had better listen.

"Colonel Kanavsky tells me you are doing a good job down there. There is some importance to the matter of Zotov. Do whatever Colonel Kanavsky tells you. This man must be found. Now I want you to listen very carefully to what I have to say. And you are to tell no one. No one at all at any time. Is that understood? Just between you and me, Major."

Penovitch almost fell off his chair while giving reassurances. He listened as he had never listened before.

When Zhadin completed his instructions he added quietly, "Make no mistakes, Major. Enjoy your promotion."

Chernov had managed to keep from Zhadin the fact that the eminent pianist, Victor Belenko, was at present residing at Lubyanka Prison, that part of the old building which, before the Revolution, had belonged to the All-Russian Insurance Company. It was not a difficult thing to achieve; the Chairman was remote from the many arrests unless directly brought to his attention or authorised by him.

Chernov was quietly seething. Nobody had ever dared speak to him before like Zhadin had so if the Zotov affair could be somehow used to depose the new Chairman of the KGB then that would be a bonus and a smack in the eye for the soft-centered Gorbachev. That would be the best retirement present of all. A move back to old standards.

His mood did not influence, however, his second confrontation with Belenko. The pianist had been sick again and he looked wretched. The night had been cold and damp and all the smells had been locked up with him through the long dark hours. He had practically had no sleep at all but at times sheer mental exhaustion had enabled him to doze off against the hard wall. He had been unable to tolerate the stinking bed.

"You didn't sleep well, Victor?"

Belenko could hardly see Chernov against the light and through lids swollen with rubbing due to the dust in the cell. "Please get me out of here. I've done no wrong."

Chernov noticed that the dummy keyboard he'd had sent in was propped just behind the door. He didn't need to be told that Belenko hadn't used it. "Have you thought where your wife might be?"

Belenko made an effort to rise but fell back against the wall. "You mean she has not come home at all?" She had never done that before. To come home in the early hours was one thing but to stay out all night was difficult to understand. He still could not accept that she had fled.

"She's gone, Victor. Face up to it. She's left you. But we must find her."

Until his mind had started to go hazy, sometimes to the point of blacking out, Belenko had thought of nothing else. "She has a lot of friends in Leningrad from her Kirov days. Perhaps she went there."

Chernov grinned. "I knew you'd come up with something, Victor."

"May I leave now?"

"As soon as we've found her. But I'll try to improve your cell. Be brave, Victor, it should not take long."

* * *

The ballet rehearsal was in full swing when the KGB pounced and brought everything to a halt. It was like a wax tableau when the music stops raggedly and the dancers grind to a halt. Two men came in by the stage door and entered the wings of the stage. The third man came down from the rear of the auditorium towards the small group seated in the stalls. As he neared them he called out, "I want Mashenka Lubinov."

Nobody asked who the three men were, nobody needed to. "I am Mashenka Lubinov." The middle-aged ballet mistress rose to her feet angrily. "Do you realise you've interrupted a full-scale rehearsal? What do you want?"

"A word with you, Madam." The tall, thin man bowed apologetically. "I'm sorry for the interruption but this is a matter of some urgency. Is there somewhere we can talk?"

They went to the rear of the auditorium looking ridiculous with Mashenka so small but so graceful beside the lanky, stooped security man. When they were clear of the rest, the man asked, "Is Yelena Belenko staying with you, Comrade Lubinov?"

The question was unexpected and Mashenka had to think quickly. There was no point in denying it. "She was but she's gone."

"When was this?"

"This morning. She didn't come back last night but she telephoned me about two hours ago to say that she'd collected her things and that she was leaving at once."

"Is that all she said?"

"You want to hear the thanks she gave me for having her? The apologies for not returning last night? For goodness sake."

"I want to know where she has gone."

"I don't know where." The diminutive ex-ballerina poured scorn on her interrogator and made no attempt to hide her contempt. "I assumed she went back to Moscow as she had come from there. I didn't ask her and had I done so I don't think she would have told me."

"Why not?"

Mashenka shrugged impatiently. "She was worried about

something. I think she must have had a serious argument with her husband. But I'm guessing. If she had wanted to tell me she would have done. That's all I know." She turned to gaze down the darkened theatre to the oasis of light shining on the restless performers on stage. "I must get back. You now know all I know."

What on earth had Yelena done?

The sun was shining and the coarse grass long and hard as they raced towards the old farm gate with the uneven stone wall stretching to both sides of it. She tripped him as he went past her and he fell face down in the grass to pretend that he was badly injured. He kept the act up long enough to raise her concern but when she bent down to make sure he was all right he pulled her on top of him.

They made love there and then, protected from sight of the farmhouse by the wall. Not too far away was the sound of a tractor and it was this that pulled them to their senses and made them realise that they had not been too careful. Yelena laughed and quickly adjusted her clothes. "We were seen," she teased him.

"Then we'd better pack our bags and go." He laughed, ruffling her hair as she tried to fight him off. "Let them see us again; show them how it's done."

She pushed him off. "Where can we run to when babushka kicks us out?"

He tried to grab her again but she wriggled free. "You know where. Warsaw. That's were we'll go."

They both burst out laughing. It was a standing joke between them. They were always going to run away together to Warsaw. Neither of them had been to Poland, let alone its capital. It might have been Prague or Budapest or East Berlin but it always came out as Warsaw. Their love, like most young love, produced many childish, secret moments and whenever they had felt the need to get away from it all their refuge would come out as Warsaw. They began to build up pictures of it, mostly inaccurate, but the dreams were theirs and their refuge was long established as the Polish capital where everyone would understand their problems and be kind to them and not mind their making love in the open.

They lay there planning their trip knowing that the next day would destroy their dreams for some time. Periodically they would meet at this kulak owned by Yelena's grandmother. It was one of the few small private farms still left after Stalin had killed off millions of the well-to-do peasant farmers allowed to make a profit. It had become a second home to both of them, a place to escape to when not in training.

Yelena slipped off a shoe and wiggled her toes. He could see where they had bled from her ballet classes.

"Are they painful?" he asked.

She was pleased by his concern. "Not when I'm with you." Behind the radiant smile was a trace of sadness. "You have to go back tomorrow?"

"You know I do. And so do you."

She slipped a hand inside his open shirt and cradled up to him. "Whatever it is you're doing it certainly keeps you fit."

He kissed the top of her head. "I have to be fit to keep up with you."

She punched him lightly on the chest. "It is you who wear me out. You are a beast. A savage."

"Let's elope," he said.

"Where to?" And then they both burst out laughing. "To Warsaw," they said in unison and it provided a signal for another, prolonged burst of passion.

Afterwards, near melancholy set in. Neither knew when they would next meet. Yelena was being worked to the limit because of the promise she had shown and already her name was becoming known. And he had to return to his secret training. For once he could give her no prediction as to when he would next be free to come to the haven of the farm.

Yelena did not know where he did his training nor what it was for. Because of the infrequency of the meetings she assumed that he worked miles away from Moscow. He never spoke of his work and she had more sense than to ask about it once he had made it clear that he was forbidden to discuss it. The only hint he had given was on that very day and then only to imply that he might soon be available more often.

They had made the best of this day and they were both sadly aware that it was all too quickly drawing to a close. With the approach of sunset their mood became more sombre and they wanted to keep physical contact if only by the holding of hands. And later, when it was time to part, they embraced so tightly and for so long that they floated on a cloud of love, both sad and ecstatic, which excluded everything around them.

They did not want to part. The feeling between them was so strong that their joke about elopement was close to becoming reality. All they wanted to do was to be with each other, to carry with them the eternal pain of love.

It had to end and it happened that night although neither realised it then. They were to meet only once more and that was to be in entirely different circumstances. Yelena's passion had not waned and the strain on her was enormous. For nights she had cried and for a while, because her health deteriorated so much, she had to give up ballet. She became haggard, her cheeks sunken, her fine body shrivelled.

Friends advised her to get away for a spell. They knew she was suffering from an affair of the heart but they never knew who was involved. For many reasons her affair had been kept secret which was why they always used the refuge of the farm and the warm understanding of her grandmother. She decided to leave the country for a while to convalesce and to go to the place they had always joked about. It was before she saw him in an institution and there was little difficulty in arranging the trip. It was after they had met again and their association was linked that her real problems began and her own life was threatened. She did not know why he had been put away and was too afraid to ask; but for his father making a slip-up she would not have known he was there.

As the engine drone changed note Yelena broke from her dreams and as she gazed at the puffed cloud below her, there were tears in her eyes and she was afraid as she had not been for years. She also felt tainted after the previous night with Gromov. She shuddered at the recollection of his exploring hands and obscene touch.

Her ears hurt as the plane started to lose height and she pinched her nose and blew. The whole nightmare was starting again but worse now, because this time there would be a termination. She thought of Zotov as she had last seen him but in the name she had been compelled to accept until it became a natural reference, and wondered what he looked like now. Perhaps it was best not to think about it. But how could she ignore it? He was out there somewhere needing all the help he could get with greater odds against him than he could probably conceive.

Perhaps that was just as well. There was no hope for him. None. She doubted that there would be any for her either but at least she had moved quickly. Yelena sat back and prayed that she might see him once more, no matter what he now looked like, before they killed him as they had wanted to do so long ago. Only the exalted position of Zotov's father had saved him then, but he had been dead for years and could no longer intervene.

Yelena tried to hold back her tears before anyone noticed. As the plane descended for the landing she had the strong sensation of being carried down into a deep pit.

They stayed at Siedice, an engineering town about fifty-three miles east of Warsaw and roughly halfway to the Russian border. The mileage for the day was poor but they had set out very late and it took them time to get out of Warsaw. Siedice was the last town of any size between here and the border.

Mirek booked them a double-room at a small hotel on the outskirts, near to some factories. It was anything but ideal but suited their needs and they were able to tuck the car away at the back.

They cleaned themselves up and sat down to plan their next move. It was difficult to know what to do but they agreed that it would be better to enter Russia openly and hoped that Pascoe's forgeries were up to standard.

"Where do you intend to cross?" Annya asked as she brushed her hair in front of a mirror.

"Brest-Litovsk. It's the most logical place."

"I've been through it, Mirek. Used to belong to us but the Russians took it. You'll be wildly excited; full of saw mills and cotton mills, and engineering and food processing. Goes back to the eleventh century, though." She gazed at him and saw his broken image in the mirror. "Big. Nearly a quarter of a million people." She half-turned on the shabby stool. "Shouldn't be too difficult to strike south-east from there. But how do we find somebody in the Pripyat marshes? Have you any idea how big they are?"

Mirek sat on the bed, which creaked noisily. "Zotov will have to keep close to the main Kiev road. He'll be pushing his luck if he cuts across the open marshes."

"We don't even know what he looks like. The nearer we get the crazier the whole idea appears." Annya put down the comb and studied her distorted reflection. "I'd better not look too good in this dump."

Mirek was uncomfortable on the bed. "I told Pascoe it was crazy, but there are one or two pointers. We know Zotov's about forty-seven and he's almost certain to be on his own. He's been institutionalised so long that he'll be wary of mixing with strangers. If he tries to get out of Russia, he'll expect more help in Poland than in Czechoslovakia."

Annya swung round. "He won't survive out there, Mirek. We won't be the only ones looking for him and we haven't the same kind of muscle."

Mirek shrugged. "So we go through the motions." He rose and made a gesture of hopelessness. "Okay, they'll find him long before we even get a scent, but we try. I've got to fill the car. You coming?"

There were Solidarity slogans over most of the scarred factory walls as they searched for a pump station. They found the dirty brick walls depressing, the graffiti failing to lift them, and headed towards the town centre. Annya, who was driving, said, "There's little Willie again."

"So you noticed him too?"

Annya glanced in the mirror. "He's been with us all the way from Warsaw."

The car was a Volkswagen which had seen better times. It had an empty roof rack which made it easier to identify, so perhaps it was intended to be seen. But by this time both Mirek and Annya had memorised its number.

"Two men," Annya observed. "What do we do?"

"Ignore them."

Annya spotted a pump station and pulled on to the forecourt. The Volkswagen continued on.

They climbed out while the attendant filled the tank and checked the oil, and walked towards the air pump tucked in one corner. Mirek was thoughtful. "Maybe they're just keeping an eye on us. It happens."

"From Warsaw? Perhaps Pascoe has told more people than you about Zotov."

They turned towards the car. The attendant was topping up the oil. "He wouldn't have done that, but someone else might know just the same."

They walked back slowly to the car with Annya fumbling for the cash in her shoulder bag. "It's a bit too soon."

"I agree. I hoped we had lost them when we reached the hotel."

Annya climbed in behind the wheel. "That explains your erratic driving on the way in. Don't treat me like an idiot, Mirek. I know your intentions are noble, but I'm also in this up to my neck. They'll only put you away for twenty-five years; they'll execute me."

They emerged into a small cobbled square and as they entered the narrow street on the far side the Volkswagen came into view again.

"I won't try to lose them," said Annya. "They're not very good at it but it's best they don't know that we know."

Mirek resisted looking round. He was thinking that the two men in the Volkswagen did not give a damn whether they were seen or not. But at some stage he and Annya would have to try to lose them permanently.

9

The red car stood out like a beacon in the vastness of space. Zotov had considered cutting across the flat bog-land to avoid the possibility of being seen by other motorists, but just stepping off the narrow road, which was little more than a track, was enough to dissuade him. Because of insufficient aeration the vegetation was not completely decomposed and the surface was spongy and badly drained. Mosses and marsh plants were slow to form and gave an acid surface soil. It would be madness to try to cross. But it could be madness to stay on the road.

    The biggest problem was to come to terms with the endless openness about him. The unchanging monotony of the stark scenery made him believe that he was trapped in one of his own frightening dreams, that the journey would never end and that he was caught in a perpetual hell. His only reassurance was the dog, warm and real by his side.

    Zotov was still unable to remember a life before being in a mental hospital. Only facts like his being able to drive indicated that he had ever been outside an institution. It proved that there had been another kind of life but the sweat would stand out as he tried to penetrate the shutter that prevented him from recollecting it.

    He was aware of being in Belorussia and recalled that the Belorussians had become part of the Russian culture, unlike the Ukrainians to the south who considered the Russians inferior in culture and in almost everything else. How he knew this he could not determine but he did not question its validity. He was beginning to accept whatever came to him naturally.

    Now and again he would stop the car for Pripy to exercise and for himself to take stock. Always he switched off the engine. And always he would scan south towards Kiev and try to detect any moving specks in the sky and to listen for the slightest buzz.

He was now travelling due west in the low flat country pancaked between the higher ground of Minsk to the north and Kiev to the south-east. And he had picked up the run of the Pripyat river which brought with it lines of deciduous forest to break the monotony and give an illusion of cover.

During the early afternoon of the day after he left Pripyat he saw an ancient, empty peat harvester. The old tractor, apparently abandoned, stood in the middle of the bog that had mostly been raised, exposing the dark brown earth beneath the turf. The massive trailer was loaded, the near tetragonal shape topped by the rounded hump was strapped down. Behind it were stacks of turf presumably awaiting collection. There was nobody in sight but there had to be someone near by.

Zotov stopped the car and climbed out. Forming a line beyond the immediate bog-land was an uneven run of trees and he guessed that either the main river or a tributary flowed somewhere near. There had to be a dwelling of some sort and it was while he was mulling over this that Pripy picked up the dreaded sound.

At first it was too low for Zotov to hear but Pripy was growling and gazing south; the dog had good reason to hate helicopters and those who flew them. Then Zotov picked up the faint drone himself. When he gazed back into the sky he could see nothing except big cloud patches, but he did not hesitate. He whistled Pripy and jumped into the car.

The ground was too treacherous to try to cross the stripped bog and head towards the trees so he had to take the long way round. The poor road had been churned up by tractors at this point but Zotov had no choice and drove recklessly for the fringe of distant cover.

The car simply wouldn't move fast enough. He was losing his nerve and snatching too often at the steering wheel. He skidded into one of the gulleys and was not sure how he extricated himself but he seemed to do all the right things to correct the skid and get shakily back on to the road. He tried to calm down, but he was being chased by ghosts he barely understood. All he knew was that he must avoid capture.

He tried to concentrate on his driving rather than on his plight. What worried him most was that he could not hear anything beyond the noise of his own engine and the faster he went, the louder it became. The car began to rattle and shake.

He rounded a long bend just managing to keep the car on the road and then up ahead were some trees. He slowed down a little, realising that he would have to leave the road to obtain any cover. Choosing what seemed to be the best place was part instinct, part panic; there was no time to reason. He braked hard, released the brake and then swung off the road to start a hazardous and jarring journey into the trees, trying to avoid hitting them head on.

The stop was bone-shaking. He wanted to go in deeper, but thick bracken and the spongy underlay pulled the car up in a shuddering, violent movement that hurled him forward to crack his head against the windscreen. Somehow, Pripy managed to fare better and was hurled under the dashboard.

Zotov passed out for a few seconds. When he came to he believed he had been unconscious much longer and he struggled out of the car. Something was trickling down his face and he wiped away blood from a small gash in his forehead. He slammed the door to leave Pripy barking inside but he did not want the dog to be seen.

The car looked like a huge deflated balloon amongst the greenery. There was an axe in his stolen supplies and he quickly set about gathering bracken and hacking off small branches to cover the car. The sound of helicopters was now much clearer. He worked frantically and made so much noise that he didn't hear someone approach.

"Are they after you?"

Zotov jumped, and spun round. A narrow, lined face showed through the foliage. The weary grey eyes that assessed him had seen it all, the crusted features were like a visual portrayal of Russian history. Tragedy was there and kindness too wrapped in a backcloth of gentle cynicism. There had been no surprise in the question. Fascinated by what he saw, Zotov was late in noticing the shotgun held waist high and barely visible below a low-hanging branch.

Zotov turned to continue with his work. If the man shot him then his troubles would be over, but he feared the helicopters more.

"Are they after you?" The man hadn't moved but there was now a trace of impatience.

Zotov carried on working. "I think so." What could it matter? There was nothing he could do except draw his gun but the stranger showed no real animosity towards him.

"Then I'll help you." The man stepped forward and placed his gun against a tree. He drew out a long-bladed knife and cut away at the undergrowth with an easy skill. "My name is Georgi Borodin. What have you done to annoy them?"

Zotov was too afraid to pause, the car must be covered, so he just shrugged and shouted, "I don't know what I've done and they won't tell me."

"Bolsheviks." Borodin spat. "You don't have to do anything to upset those bastards."

From what Zotov could see of him as they feverishly worked he supposed that Borodin was in his mid-fifties; he was on the short side but wiry and tough. He hadn't shaved for a few days and the growth was dark and grizzly. He wore old baggy trousers, a check shirt hanging outside and a rough denim jacket on top of that. His hair was matted like the undergrowth and equally undisciplined. His sinewy fingers had knuckles like rope knots but moved deftly and expertly.

The sound of the helicopters was now filling the air, hurting the ears and making Pripy howl inside the car.

"You afraid of the dog being seen? They would recognise it?"

Those who would have done were dead. Zotov had no idea whether or not Pripy had been reported. "I don't know but I can't take chances. The dog has been very good to me."

Borodin nodded sagely. "That ought to do it." He stood back to cast a critical eye over the camouflaged car. "If we move away the dog might stop barking."

They moved further back into the trees until they couldn't see the car at all. In a small clearing Borodin squatted, produced an old clay pipe, thought better of it and put it away again. "Better not let them have a wisp of the smoke. Sit down there. You look pale; you been ill?"

"I suppose so. I've been in an asylum." Zotov smiled faintly. "Don't worry. I'm not insane."

Borodin cocked his head to locate the position of the helicopters. They were so loud that he had to shout back, "It's not the people inside them who are insane, it's the stupid bastards who put them there. My brother was put away. Never saw him again. That was at the end of Stalin's day. He thought everybody was a threat. Killed off more of our people than were killed in the war. I suppose it was cheaper to thin out the nation that way. He was insane."

Zotov struggled. He felt a resistance to what Borodin was saying but could not place its source. He wanted to disagree yet at the same time Borodin seemed to be talking sense. Was he fighting against his own indoctrination? But he could remember nothing except what had been pumped into him.

The thudding of the helicopters pushed everything else from his mind. It sounded as if they were coming down on top of them but Borodin made no move.

"They can't land in the trees," said Borodin drily. "Don't look so scared."

"They'll get out and search. Especially if they've seen the car."

"Of course they will. But we'll keep ahead of them. Leave it to me."

But Zotov was afraid to leave it to anyone and he was getting worried about Pripy. The sound of the machines was bringing back too many fears. Without realising it he drew his gun.

Borodin stared. "That looks like a military issue."

"It is. I won't harm you, you have been very good to me."

Without moving Borodin asked, "You sure you're not insane?" The question came without rancour.

Zotov was irritated, then saw the faint amusement in Borodin's eyes. "I'm satisfied. Only time will make me sure."

"Then put that gun away before it goes off. You're too twitchy. An accidental shot will bring them here quicker than anything else. Listen. They're landing." Borodin climbed to his feet, his head turned to locate the area of descent.

They could feel the down-draught and so realised that the landing must be quite near where the car was hidden. Tree branches were swaying as if in a gale. There seemed to be at least two machines but the noise gradually abated as the rotary wings flapped to a stop. The immediate silence was painful.

Borodin said, "You'll have to trust me. I'll deal with them. Just stay here."

Zotov did not like it. He felt as if he had been lulled into a trap. But if the airmen came into the woods someone had to divert them. "I don't like it," he said bluntly.

"I know you don't. But I could have filled you with buckshot if I'd wanted to. Just stay calm. I've had practice at these things. Stay where you are and I'll be back."

Before Zotov could answer Borodin moved off into the trees. At first Zotov could hear him moving but within seconds there was no sound at all; the trees had stopped waving as the helicopters had shut down. He felt uneasy alone in the clearing and his tension began to build up. He looked at his stolen watch, an ugly, heavy time-keeper. Everything he wore was stolen and he wondered if Borodin had realised this, the newness of everything.

It was concern for Pripy that made Zotov move; the dog would be scared shut in a car that had been covered over and with his master not in sight. He did not head towards the car but to where he thought the tree line would be and from where he might be able to see the road and where the helicopters had landed. He moved carefully.

After a while he became fascinated by his own movements, almost as if survival was something he had been taught. He stopped periodically to listen and during one of these halts he heard voices. He felt for every footstep as he advanced obliquely towards the sound.

The light increased as he neared the fringe of growth and he dropped to a low crouch. He saw two helicopters first. They had both landed on the earth road, not risking the bog, and they were further away than he had expected.

About thirty metres to his right, in clear ground near the tree line, was Borodin and two helicopter crew. Last time there had been two men for each machine so where were the others?

Zotov eased himself down flat so that a casual glance would not pick him out. Borodin was at ease with the airmen and suddenly they all laughed together. He held his shotgun over his shoulder and nobody was concerned by it; he was pointing into the woods in the direction where he had told Zotov to wait and doing most of the talking.

Zotov could not tell why he felt so uneasy. He accepted that Borodin would try to talk his way out of the situation if he was intent on saving Zotov, but they had only just met and Borodin's acceptance was difficult to understand.

Suddenly the three men were laughing again and shaking hands all around. The two airmen walked slowly back to their machines and one of them did a circular movement with his hand over his head. The blades started to rotate and Zotov realised that the two pilots had remained on board. Borodin covered his ears and was obviously going to wait until the helicopters took off. Zotov drifted back into the woods and followed his own rough trail to the small clearing.

The dreadful roar soared above him and he thought the trees would be flattened as the machines scudded over them. Borodin arrived, his approach well covered by the noise of the engines. He waited for the sound to disperse and then clapped Zotov on the shoulder. "Well that got rid of them. It wasn't too difficult."

"What did you tell them?"

"That I know these parts like the back of my hand. That I would have seen a red car and taken note of any stranger. Oh, they were looking for you all right. Come on, I'll take you home for a meal."

"I must let Pripy out first." It was strange how he felt he could trust the dog far more than he was willing to trust Borodin. It was an uncharitable thought but he could not get rid of it. Somehow the helicopter crews had given up just a little too easily.

* * *

Chernov would have liked to go to Kiev and direct the search for Zotov personally. The whole affair was going off at half-cock. But he could not leave Moscow. Zhadin had already shown his suspicion and if Chernov left for Kiev that suspicion would come out into the open. As it was Chernov was reduced to using what help he could muster. He would have liked to flood the whole Pripyat area with aircraft, and cover the bogs with choppers and spotter planes. But the call on aircraft was too great following Chernobyl, so he was restricted to the two helicopters for which Kanavsky had stuck out. It was maddening.

Chernov had considered informing Zhadin of the actual problem and its tremendous importance but he dismissed the idea almost immediately. In the first place he distrusted his successor, because the power of the security services would be diminished under him aided by the craze of *glasnost*. The country could not survive that sort of thinking. Openness was a quick way to ruin. It was the unknown, the hidden fears, that kept the country together and the foreigner out.

The more important reason was deeper and not open to any compromise. Certain people knew what had happened but all of them at the time had solid reasons for closing ranks and for maintaining the secret. It had affected every one who was involved. Political belief played a huge part and without exception all those ensnared held that unswerving belief. Subsequently, to those who still lived, the reasons for silence became more sinister and a simple matter of life or death.

Chernov himself held an unshakeable belief in what he was doing. Nikita S. Khrushchev had been shrewd in his prime. He knew that the Chairmanship of the KGB was at times precarious, particularly during that period. He had chosen a chairman designate, a young man whose loyalty was unquestioned and whose idol was Khrushchev himself. The secret had been sworn, and nothing could make Chernov break that loyalty. Nor could he see any good reason; nothing would be achieved by sharing the secret and much might be placed at risk. *Glasnost*. Chernov shuddered at the very thought.

He paced the small office and felt like breaking down its walls. The cipher room was close by and the constant coming and going was driving him mad. He had been placed in a position to which he was totally unaccustomed and he had to fight down a feeling of recklessness. The hub of his own immense organisation was here in this vast complex, thousands of personnel, and yet he could not safely use them. He had been forced to place his trust in an acolyte, albeit an efficient one, but the restriction stuck in his throat. He had formed a small cell but it was not enough.

Chernov cursed Chernobyl. He cursed it loudly and for anyone to hear. If he had his way he would dispense with those responsible in a way that would warn their successors. But for that disaster Zotov would still be captive and of no danger. At no time were his thoughts on the unfortunates who had died a terrible death or on the brave who had put their own lives at risk, probably, ultimately fatally, in order to save tens of thousands of others. His thinking centered on one man only and his hatred grew.

He lowered his huge frame on to a chair not designed to take his weight. It creaked and he scowled at the intercom, then pressed a switch. He would have to get tougher with Kanavsky. It was ludicrous that Zotov had not yet been found. If it went on like this he would have to go to Kiev and damn the risks that would bring.

10

Borodin had referred to his home as a dacha, but as Zotov stepped inside he realised that was too grand a description. The wooden cottage was an *izbi* and even that was stretching things. It was situated out of sight amongst some saplings, a mile or so from where Zotov's car had been left. There was no indoor plumbing and no electricity. Water was contained in a huge outside tank with a crude inlet into the cottage over a massive stone sink. The place was heated in several ways, butane gas cooker and separate heaters and a solid fuel copper. On a wall of the kitchen hung a long zinc bath.

The house was crude but warm, and with miles of peat bogs around him Borodin would never be short of fuel. It turned out that the old tractor Zotov had seen belonged to Borodin who scratched out a living by lifting the peat to sell at lower than State rates. What he did was illegal but he had been doing it for years and nobody seemed to mind, particularly those who bought from him. He lived alone and preferred it that way. Zotov was reluctant to probe his past as he wanted to avoid the embarrassment of talking about his own.

Borodin was certainly a little odd. The loneliness and the way he chose to live was strange. There was no clue as to how he spent his spare time. A radio was perched on a heap of old papers and looked as if it was never used. And that was all.

Zotov sat down at a rough wooden table, which Borodin had probably made himself, while his host went to the kitchen pantry to bring back a round-shaped loaf with a hole in the middle. When Borodin poured a small quantity of salt into its centre, Zotov's memory stirred. This was not a new experience but he could not recall the last time he had witnessed it. The loaf was a *khlib-i-sil*, Ukrainian symbol of hospitality. Yet here they were in Belorussia.

Borodin saw Zotov's puzzlement. "Yes," he smiled. "I am a Ukrainian. Why do you think I hate the Russians so much? That's why I helped you." Borodin pushed the large plate across. "My meals are simple but wholesome. Help yourself."

They ate cabbage borscht followed by duck swimming in gravy with masses of potatoes drenched in butter. During the meal Borodin provided very powerful home-brewed beer that made Zotov's head swim. He was not used to liquor and had to struggle to keep his senses. In spite of this, when they had finished eating, Borodin insisted that they drink a toast to Zotov's freedom in a vodka distilled from potatoes instead of rye and which was a dirty green in colour.

After the richness of the duck and the drink and the heat from the turf fire, Zotov had to go outside to be sick. When he returned he apologised to Borodin who said he understood and helped him to bed.

The bed was hard and Zotov lay there unable to sleep with the walls misty and moving. He felt ill, but also disturbed. Something wasn't right. He tried to struggle up but the effort made him feel sick again. Eventually he fell asleep vaguely aware that Borodin was moving about in the next room.

He awoke with a headache, and with bright daylight streaming through the only window in the room. He felt dreadful. He climbed out of bed realising that, apart from taking off his shoes, he had not undressed. Pripy had slept at the foot of the bed and Zotov opened the door to let him out. There was a wash basin and a jug of cold water on a small solid table. He splashed his face and raised his head to glance suspiciously into a broken mirror somehow stuck to the wall.

He summoned his courage to gaze at a face that was still not familiar. The image spurred a hazy recollection but of someone else rather than himself. The sensation was both eerie and frightening. He shuddered, but he had to try. He looked at his reflection again. The hair might be grey now but as it was thick he thought he looked better without the beard. He quickly shifted his gaze.

Ostensibly there was nothing to upset him about what he saw; he was very presentable, but he could still not put the face to the man he was supposed to be. It was like looking at an old photograph of someone he had known long ago but had forgotten. But this wasn't a photograph, it was his own face and it scared him that he could not accept it as his own.

He went outside to get some air and found Borodin stacking turf in an old ramshackle shed. Borodin looked up and grinned. "Feeling better?"

"I'm sorry. I haven't had anything to drink for years and yours was so strong." He saw Pripy sniffing around the trees.

"I understand." Borodin came out of the shed wiping his hands. "What do you intend to do?"

Zotov rubbed his face feeling the hard bristle. "I must move on. I'm very grateful for what you have done for me. I can't pay you. I have no money." It was the one thing that he had failed to look for in Pripyat where he had found everything he needed.

Borodin waved a hand. "You are close to insulting me. I've been down to look at your car. It's rutted in but I can get it out with my tractor."

"Is there any damage."

"Not that I can see, but I haven't looked that closely because I didn't want to disturb the camouflage."

Zotov was gazing into the shed where the turf was stacked and where a battered old van was almost hidden. "Does that thing go?"

"The van. Sure. But it creaks and the springs aren't so good." Borodin stretched. "It gets me where I want to go."

"If there's no damage to the car I'll change it for the van."

Borodin screwed his eyes. "Is the car stolen?"

Zotov nodded.

Borodin did not seem too disturbed. "Let's look at it first."

Zotov went back to the house to get his jacket. He stuffed the gun into his pocket and then, on impulse, withdrew it. He released the safety-catch and pulled out the magazine.

It was empty. He pulled back the breech; the chamber round had been removed. He knew then that his doubts had been well founded. Only Borodin could have unloaded the gun. Clearly he was laying some kind of trap for him, having disarmed him first.

A chill filled his veins as Zotov fought off the effects of a hangover. When he emerged from the cottage Borodin had his shotgun with him.

The bar was crowded and cramped and filled with the stink of cheap tobacco. It was not the best place to discuss what to do about the UB, the Polish internal security service; Mirek and Annya were satisfied that the two men could be nothing else. After an indifferent dinner they had gone into the small bar because there was little else to do.

The noise level was high, everybody seemed to be shouting to be heard. There was a good deal of jostling at the bar itself and Mirek had manoeuvred Annya into a corner where they could just raise their glasses without a struggle.

"What shall we do?" said Mirek close to Annya's ear.

It was difficult to engage in this type of talk with so many people around. "We'd better go outside."

"They'll follow. We can't have them following us tomorrow. It would be better if they think we're going back to Warsaw."

Annya shook her head helplessly. "I heard about half that," she yelled. She led the way outside. Even that was a major operation but finally they stood outside the hotel's main entrance on steps just above street level. The bar door opened behind them and she guessed that one of the UB men had followed.

They stood holding their drinks and Annya said quite audibly, "It's impossible in there. Too noisy and too stuffy. I think I'll turn in."

"You don't mind me having another drink in the bar?"

"If you can stand it. Don't be too long." Annya turned and smiled sweetly. She thought she could see one of the men lurking at the back of the hall. She drained her glass then handed it to Mirek. "Take that back with you, darling.

I'll do some packing." She headed for the stairs; the small lift was too often full.

Mirek fought his way back into the bar and managed to order another drink. He felt rather than heard the UB man come in behind him and was relieved when he saw him join his comrade. He hoped Annya knew what she was doing.

Before she came down again Annya slipped on a short dark jacket and she had a scarf over her head. It was chilly outside but she wore no gloves. Once on the street she dived into the first recess and waited. It was something she had done often enough but she was in strange territory and did not quite know whether they had been blown before leaving Warsaw or whether being followed was connected with their other activities. Either way they had to be careful. She realised she looked like a tart standing there in the dim light but there were few people about. It was too soon for the bars to turn out.

Satisfied, she continued on down the street and took the first turning. The old street was dark and dingy and the wrong end of town for a lone woman. She kept close to the walls, and through them, thick though they were, she could hear the noise in the bar. She neared the next corner. At the rear of the hotel was the car park, a rough earth patch which had grimy walls on each side. It was really an overlarge yard, full of grot and covered with discarded bricks and bottles. Annya entered the yard and sparingly used a small flashlight.

The cars were parked haphazardly, mainly because no lines had been painted to form slots. The surface was so uneven that it was difficult to avoid stumbling. She searched for the Volkswagen and found it eventually in a privileged position at the end of a line and pointing towards the exit. The UB men had obviously made their mark with the hotel management. She shone the torch to check the registration number and then set about opening the door to release the hood catch. None of this was new to her.

In the bar Mirek was surprised when one of the security men started to talk to him in quite a friendly way. The exchange served a dual purpose except that the other man did not join in and after a while slipped away from the bar.

Mirek covered his anxiety but realised that he must leave to warn Annya. But by now the man talking to him had introduced himself as Jan Brus and was insisting on buying Mirek another drink. Before Mirek could make an excuse the drinks had been ordered.

Mirek's mind was reeling. If he broke away too obviously he would be sending up a signal, and if he did not he could be leaving Annya in trouble. He finally decided to bluff it out. It might at least allay the suspicions of the man he was with. He raised his drink in a toast and called for more. There was nothing else he could do that would not give the game away.

Annya had the hood raised when she thought she heard a sound. She kept very still but nothing followed. She waited by the car but saw nothing move. It could have been anything. After a while she realised it would be better to get back to her room. Although she could handle weapons she was not really mechanically minded. She produced a pair of pliers, previously used for cutting wire barriers, and simply cut through every lead she could locate by touch around the engine. She had stopped using the torch the moment she heard movement.

She was about to lower the hood when this time she heard something much too close to her. Instinctively she ducked as something swished past her head. Springing from a crouched position she lashed out with the pliers, and hit somebody, for there was a short, agonised cry. A dark figure fell back, slipped badly with arms flailing, and the crack of a head on metal was sickening to hear.

The man slid down the car to crumple quite close to her, groaned and then twisted in a strange way and did not move again. There was the diminishing sound of a bottle rolling away before it was caught up against an obstruction. It was so dark in the parking lot that almost all Annya saw was in hazy silhouette. She looked around quickly. There was nothing but cars and the man at her feet. In desperation she shone her torch at the body.

It was one of the UB men. There was no visible blood but she did not like the way he was twisted nor the fixed grimace on the face. She crouched by the body ready with the pliers should he be feigning but there was something final in the way he lay there that frightened her. She pushed the body quite hard to see if there was any reaction and when there was none she felt for the pulse. No response.

She sat back on her heels scared and near to panic. Something was hurting the palm of her hand and she realised she was gripping the pliers too tightly. She wanted to be sick. How had he died so easily? She forced herself to be practical and explored behind his head. It was tacky with blood but she could feel some give in the bone. She retched and afterwards felt drained.

Annya rose and closed the hood as quietly as she could, aware that her hands were shaking; she clenched them as panic rose up again. She must do something about the body; it could not be left there, nor could it be reported. And she dare not go back to get Mirek.

She leaned back against the Volkswagen and tried to pull herself together. She slipped the pliers into her pocket and then went along the row of cars testing the doors and boots. A few were unlocked.

As she opened the back of one of the cars she realised that she was about to compromise somebody else if she dumped the body in another car. She found she could not do it. She gazed round in despair and eventually saw the shadow of a jutting wall at the back of the hotel.

Annya groped down the line of cars to reach the wall, which she found to be a projection that screened off the back door of the hotel, to hide from view four massive refuse bins. Once behind the wall she felt exposed. The door was large and presumably led to the kitchen and she could see a strip of light beneath it. How many times did staff come out to empty into the bins?

She went back to the Volkswagen and bent to grasp the man under the armpits. To do this she had to turn him and she trod on something hard that turned her ankle painfully. She swore and tried to flick the obstruction away with her foot. She missed in the dark and trod on it again. She reached down and found a gun. Maybe this was what had whizzed past her head? She wiped it and placed it in one of the dead man's pockets.

When she tried to drag him between the cars she found his dead weight difficult to manage but desperation gave her the will to keep going and after several stops she reached the wall. She peered behind it. The door was still closed. The risk had to be taken. She dragged the corpse round to the furthest bin and wondered how she could ever lift it.

Time was passing and she felt weak. She couldn't wait. She managed to prop the body against the bin, knelt down, and pulled the body over her shoulder in a crude fireman's lift. She clung to the bin and dragged herself up by it. She heard someone shout behind the door and fear gave her the extra strength to rise. Once she was upright it wasn't so bad but she was now faced with getting the body in the bin and time was getting desperately short.

The top of the bin was a foot above her head. She did not know whether it was full or empty. She knew that if she didn't manage it first time her strength would go. She succeeded in getting the arms over the edge but the head kept dropping down. Finally she got head and shoulders over and she was then able to get her full force behind the rest of the body. She heaved with her whole strength. The corpse was slow to go but once the balance of weight changed it began to slip down inside and Annya gave a final shove to the legs. As the body disappeared it made a little sound. There must have been a cushion of refuse already in the bin.

Annya leaned against the bin, shaking, her breath rasping. She managed to pull herself above the rim of the next bin and awkwardly take out some of the rubbish and vegetable remains to throw over the corpse. By the time she finished she was exhausted.

She scuttled to the other side of the wall and was unable to move for a while but panic and time demanded that she did. She pulled herself along to the Volkswagen, sorry now for having cut the leads, which was bound to be linked to the dead man. She made sure that she had left nothing behind and risked shining the torch to check one last time. There was blood where the man had hit his head on the car and she wiped it off with her head scarf and generally rubbed down the parts of the Volkswagen she had touched. As she hurried back she knew that she had blood on her hands and almost certainly on her clothes as well. And she knew that she and Mirek were in terrible danger.

The questioning was not even subtle, as they stood at the bar and Mirek answered the probing from Brus who was quietly getting drunk. Mirek was desperately worried about Annya. Several times Brus asked about Mirek's plans and the answer always came back that they would be returning to Warsaw next day. They had taken a few days off but didn't think much of this part of Poland.

As Brus's questions became more slurred and Mirek's answers more impatient, both men were glancing at the bar clock too often. Obviously Brus was waiting for the return of his colleague and was becoming concerned. Mirek had no way of knowing whether or not Annya was back.

The atmosphere in the bar was becoming increasingly foul and there was a smoke cloud beneath the stained ceiling. The crowd was beginning to thin out and Mirek finally made up his mind. "I must go up. I can't leave my girl to do all the packing." He drained his glass and patted Brus on the arm in farewell.

Mirek went upstairs surprised at how muzzy he felt. He opened the door to find Annya in her underwear, crouched on top of the bed weeping, her discarded clothes on the floor.

"What's the matter? What went wrong?" He staggered over to her and almost fell on the bed.

"Oh, Mirek. Mirek." She clung to him as if she was about to lose him.

He held her, letting her cry, aware of the smell of liquor on his breath. He tried to sober up as he realised that something was terribly wrong; Annya was normally so self-assured. As she began to calm down he quietly asked, "What happened?"

She pushed herself away, her face flushed from weeping.

She could not meet his eye as she said, "I killed him. We're in terrible trouble."

It came out in scattered phrases and at times he had to take her back again over the events. The shock sobered him quickly. When she had finished he dipped his head under a running tap. She was right; they were in deep trouble. "You did fine," he said, drying his hair on a hand towel. "And nobody saw you?" He gazed down at the clothes at the foot of the bed. "We must get rid of those." But he didn't say how.

He picked them up from the floor and they told their own story with dirt and blood stains. "He must have had a weak skull."

"It was the way he fell. Awkwardly. He must have trodden on a bottle. He simply couldn't save himself; his legs shot out. But who will believe it happened that way? Perhaps I should have left the blood stains on the car." With Mirek back, Annya was thinking more easily.

"No. That would have placed him in the parking lot. Unless they find him quickly we should be all right." He was still holding the clothes and he bundled them up. "We'll have to take these with us. There's nowhere to burn them and we can't just dump them."

"We'd better leave tonight."

"That would give the game away. We carry on the same way. Brus, he's the other bloke, knows we're leaving tomorrow anyway. Where are the pliers? I'll clean them." Mirek stood by the bed, screwing up the clothes and thinking as fast as the cloying liquor would let him.

"Brus will send them after us." Annya rose from the bed and when he put his arm round her she was trembling. He said, "We'll be out of the country by tomorrow. Brus didn't suggest we might be crossing the border. I don't think he's expecting it. I'm pretty sure that he followed for some entirely different reason. Maybe they were catching up on our Warsaw capers. Let's try to get some sleep."

It was 1.30 am, when both were dozing, for neither had slept properly, that there was a hammering on the door and Brus was calling out to be let in.

11

Borodin led the way back to the car and together they stripped off the camouflage. Pripy came with them. For Zotov the dog was his warning system; any danger to Zotov, from whatever source, and Pripy would let him know.

The car seemed not to have suffered but as Borodin had pointed out it was going to take some moving. "Right," said Borodin. "Wait here while I go and fetch the tractor. I'll be about half an hour."

He left at a steady walk, used to distances and unhurried, but Zotov was now suspicious of everything Borodin did. There were not many options open to him but he had no intention of staying there like a sitting duck. He headed into the woods for about a hundred yards where it was denser and he could hide comfortably and where there was plenty of cover if he had to move. He squatted against a tree and Pripy lay at his feet lifting his head from time to time. The trees drooped round them silently brooding and watching and it was difficult to shake off the feeling of being observed.

Pripy gave warning before the tractor rumble reached them and Zotov stopped him barking until he was sure. Whatever game Borodin was playing it seemed he intended to deal with the car.

The car came out quite easily once it was expertly chained up and Borodin knew his job. It was pulled clear and placed on the road where Zotov climbed in and tried the engine. It started first time. He switched off and thanked Borodin, not quite knowing what to do next nor what Borodin intended. All the time he was listening for the helicopters.

"Will you be taking the tractor back?" asked Zotov.

"I'll ride it back to the dacha. You take the car and I'll meet you there."

It all sounded reasonable enough but Zotov had been imprisoned for too long to be gullible. He drove back to the *izbi* – he could not think of it as a dacha, and this made him wonder if he'd ever had a real dacha himself somewhere, sometime ago.

Borodin arrived a few minutes after Zotov and they went into the cottage to have what Borodin called coffee. They discussed what Zotov would do next and he told Borodin that he intended to head for the Czechoslovakian border.

"You've come a little too far north for that, haven't you?" Borodin asked.

But Zotov had developed the cunning of the hunted. "Deliberately. I'll go north some more and then cut southwest. It'll keep them guessing."

"You still want to change the car for the van?"

Zotov was no longer sure. The red car was known but so would the van be if Borodin was playing him along. There was something about the whole situation that did not make sense until Pripy started to bark and kept running in and out of the cottage. Zotov chased after him trying to pick up the sound of helicopters. But it wasn't from the air that the sound came, but the ground, and it was carrying on the wind from some distance away. A car engine.

He looked back towards the bog from where the sound was coming. So that was it. They'd probably underslung a car on one of the choppers and dropped it well out of earshot to make a quieter approach by road. He now knew why Borodin had unloaded his gun.

Zotov turned round. Borodin was framed by the door with the shotgun in his hands; it wasn't levelled but he was too far away for Zotov to gamble on disarming him.

Zotov drew his gun very slowly and pulled back the hammer with his thumb. Borodin smiled and did not trouble to raise the shotgun.

Levelling the pistol, Zotov said, "Did you think I didn't know you had emptied the gun? You're a fool. I didn't trust you from the moment I saw you talking to the airmen. I was watching. And listening. I always check the gun; always make sure there's one in the breech with the hammer eased forward for safety's sake. You should have found the spare magazine, Georgi."

Borodin's grip tightened on the shotgun and the butt came off the ground.

"Raise it and I'll kill you." Zotov did not have to pretend desperation.

"There was no spare magazine. You're bluffing."

Zotov took aim. "Then call it. I don't want to kill you but I will if you stand between me and escape. Now put the shotgun on the ground."

Borodin hesitated. He thought Zotov was bluffing but the only way to find out could turn out to be fatal. Of one thing he was absolutely sure; if there were rounds in the pistol then Zotov would fire if he did not lower the shotgun. He had never seen an expression of such intent on any man's face. Zotov was so wound up that the spring was about to snap. Borodin carefully lowered the shotgun to the ground.

"Step towards me and then flatten yourself with arms outstretched."

Borodin did so and lay face down on the ground. While this was going on Pripy, recognising that Borodin was a danger to his master, was growling loudly at the Ukrainian.

"Watch him, Pripy. Don't let him move." Zotov didn't know whether the dog understood or not but neither did Borodin and he was taking no chances as the dog crouched near him. Zotov picked up the shotgun and then went into the open shed to return with some rope with which he tied Borodin securely. As he finished tying the feet he said, "Have you arranged a signal to let them know it's safe?"

It wasn't the pistol that was pressing into the back of his neck but his own shotgun and Borodin knew that he'd been deceived. He turned his head to speak. "I was to fire one barrel. It would have been easy to explain it away to you."

"They won't come until then?"

"They might but they won't know that you've been disarmed until then. They'll wait for a while."

Zotov dragged Borodin into the shed. As he stared down at the Ukrainian he said, "Why? Why help and then betray?"

"They said you are an escaped American spy. They were convincing. A spy is different from someone on the run. I don't like Americans."

"You don't like Americans and you don't like Russians. But you like Borodin and any money offered for my capture."

Borodin shook his head in anger. "I didn't do it for money. I don't need money."

"Where's my ammunition?"

"In the kitchen. In a bag hanging behind the bath."

Before going into the cottage Zotov stood outside. There was no longer the sound of a car. Zotov found the rounds in a small bag nailed to the wall. He put the bath back and returned to Borodin. Standing over him he loaded the pistol.

"You've tricked me well," said Borodin. "Now that you've explained you are not an American spy I can help you again."

"I've explained nothing of the sort. And I would never trust you again, Georgi. You believe too easily." He knelt down beside Borodin and rummaged through his pockets.

Zotov rose with half a dozen cartridges in his hands and dropped them in his pockets. "One barrel you say?" He looked around at the rubbish in the shed and pulled Borodin into the darkest corner behind stacked turfs and then gagged him with some old oily rags. He had no remorse; he was still smouldering at the betrayal. He said, "If you try to warn them in any way I'll come back and kill you. I mean it, Georgi." He covered Borodin up with anything he could find from old bits of carpet to rags and chunks of turf.

He went outside with the shotgun. Suddenly he balled up and fell to the ground holding his stomach in agony. He dropped the gun and rolled about shivering. He called out and Pripy ran round him whimpering.

He lay there groaning and put out a hand to locate the dog. After a while he managed to rise to his knees to find that he was soaked through. "My God." He sat back on his heels wondering how much time had passed. He supposed that the tension had built up in him and the demands on his system were too much to cope with. He would have given anything then for an injection that would settle his nerves.

He climbed unsteadily to his feet, swaying so that he almost fell. His legs would not support him but his mind was screaming out with urgency. He had to act. He dragged himself into the cottage and found Borodin's lethal brew of Vodka. He took a swig and it was like a red-hot poker all the way down to his guts.

The vodka helped. Somewhere out there were men waiting for a signal and if they failed to get one they would come anyway and would be prepared for trouble. He staggered over to retrieve the shotgun, lying where he had fallen. He went back into the shed; Borodin had not moved and, thankfully, probably had no idea of what had happened.

He went back to the corner of the cottage and gazed around at the very restricted view, for Borodin had chosen his spot carefully, and told Pripy to go inside. Zotov closed the door behind him, lifted the gun and fired one barrel. As he walked round the side of the cottage he heard Pripy howling. Once hidden round the corner, Zotov ejected the cartridge and loaded another.

He stood there and waited. Almost immediately a car engine started up. From the position he had chosen he could see both the shed and the approach to the cottage. There was only one route vehicles could take and he would have a clear view of their arrival. And then he began to shake again and he prayed it would stop. The shotgun was wavering and he felt the strong urge to run. He propped himself up against the wall and could hear the engine much nearer now. He fought for self-control and knew that whatever happened he was rooted to this spot. So far he had dealt with every crisis, each time drawing on his reserves, but it now seemed that he could not cope. While he was struggling to pull himself together he had his first glimpse of the car as it rounded the line of spruce.

Mirek signalled Annya to remove her underwear and climb into bed. Brus was still knocking at the door and verging on the hysterical as he called out to be let in. Mirek stripped off his shirt and trousers and rumpled the bed on his side. He grabbed the bundle of Annya's bloodied clothes and glared round hopelessly. Annya held out her hands for him to give them to her and she stuffed them under her now naked body, spreading them out to avoid bumps.

Mirek called out, "Hold on, for goodness' sake. We're in bed. Is there a fire?"

Brus stopped hammering and Mirek tousled his hair. He looked around the room. He had left the pliers on the dressing table and quickly shoved them under his pillow. It was all so basic and so fragile. He opened the door just a little and Brus pushed past him still the worse for drink, eyes red and angry. He stared at Annya who was sitting up in bed looking scared and holding the sheets just low enough to show that she had nothing on.

Sight of her took Brus out of his stride for a second or two, then he recovered and snarled at her, "What have you done with Waleski?"

"Waleski? Who's he?"

Brus had partly sobered since Mirek had left him but he was slow to think and his words came out in a strange order. "You know him. You well know him. And you've seen him disappear."

Mirek intervened. "You're drunk, Brus. You don't know what you're saying. You'd better get out of here." He grabbed Brus by the arm but Brus shook him off.

Brus realised that he was handling things badly and tried to calm down. "My colleague is missing." He turned to Annya again. "And you know where he's gone."

Mirek crossed to the house phone and kept plunging the cradle. He guessed there would be no immediate response at this time of night but it had an effect on Brus.

"What are you doing?"

"I'm phoning the management to kick you out. You're a madman. You come bursting in here when we're both in bed and make crazy statements about a colleague we don't even know. Well, I met him very briefly with you but then he pushed off. Just who the hell are you and what do you want?"

Brus knew that he had made a hash of things. He did not want to admit to being in the UB but had enough sense left to guess that he had already declared himself. He tried to start again. "Put the phone down. Waleski has disappeared. He should have been back a long time ago. And I think the lady knows where he's gone."

Annya and Mirek exchanged glances as if Brus had indeed gone mad. "Is that supposed to mean something to us? And why do you keep talking to Annya? What do you think she's done with him? Beaten him up?"

"Have you been here all the time?" Brus demanded of Annya.

Annya swallowed. "Since I came up from the bar, yes."

Brus glared round the room again so Mirek pulled up the hanging bedclothes. "You think he's under here?"

"Mister Brus," said Annya softly. "What on earth could I possibly have done to your friend? What could any woman do? I've been here since about nine. Why would I be interested anyway?"

Brus was confused. He suspected treachery but the woman had made it all sound so reasonable; indeed what could she have done on her own? Perhaps she had help? He went into the small bathroom and when he returned he opened the old-fashioned wardrobe. By now he realised he had lost any advantage he might have had, and in a rather foolish way was using an authority which he had yet to declare. He had tackled the matter stupidly from the beginning. "So you haven't seen Waleski and you don't know where he is?"

"That's right. But it would help if you told me why you think I should know. I find this most distressing and when we get back to Warsaw tomorrow I'm going to report it. Because, Comrade Brus, I suspect that you are a policeman and that you are barking up the wrong tree. I must assume that wherever Waleski is he's old enough to look after himself. Is he your lover? Is that why you're so upset? I will certainly suggest as much in Warsaw. This whole matter is a disgrace and you offend me."

Brus was about to respond, angry at how he had handled things but even more so at the casual way he was being treated. He began to have doubts. When he stared at Annya he was on the verge of being filled with lust and had to fight his feelings. Could she have handled Waleski on her own?

He moved towards the door and stood holding the handle. His head was beginning to ache and his vision was faulty. He should have waited. He drew himself up in an attempt to gain a little dignity and said as coldly as he could, "This is not the last of it." He opened the door aware that he was still bungling. But then Waleski had usually done the thinking for both of them.

After he had gone Mirek waited a little before opening the door to gaze down the shabby corridor. He closed the door again and turned the key. He crossed to the bed and held the shivering Annya in his arms. They had done well but it wouldn't change things. And when Brus found the cut leads in his car in the morning their position would be infinitely worse. He just prayed that Waleski was not found too soon.

"We must leave very early while Brus still has a thick head. We'll drive towards Warsaw and then cut back on a secondary road." He kissed her on the forehead. "You were marvellous." But she was still trembling.

Mashenka Lubinov was on her way home from the ballet when the Zis drew up beside her. She always walked back to her apartment for she liked the streets of Leningrad and she considered the exercise as complementary to the rigours of ballet mistress. The Zis stopped and someone called out. She glanced back to see that it was the lanky KGB man who had visited her during rehearsals. She turned her head and kept walking; the very nearness of the man offended her.

The car door opened and closed behind her and she heard hastening footsteps. She made no effort to slow or to stop.

"A word, Madam."

"You've already had a word." Mashenka strode on, small and erect and proud. When her arm was grasped she swung round in anger. "How dare you. Take your hand away, you're hurting me."

"You'll be hurt a good deal more if you don't stop and listen."

She struggled in the powerful grip but her spirit was not enough for his rough strength. "There are plenty of people watching your brutality. And many will know me. Let me go."

The lanky man laughed. "They won't complain. Just step into the car for a moment or two."

"No. What do you want?"

"Will you step into the car or shall I call my colleague to force you. If I do you won't see your apartment for some time, I can assure you. Behave; your position does not protect you."

The cold-bloodedness behind the threat finally got through to Mashenka and she suddenly felt insecure. She had heard of these things but had never dreamed that it could happen to her. Her mind was clear, she had done nothing wrong.

She went unwillingly to the car and was almost thrown in. She sat in the back with the tall man who had difficulty in getting his legs in.

"Is it still about Yelena Belenko? I know no more than I've already told you."

"We want to know who she met while she stayed with you."

"She stayed with me most of the time. We had mutual friends in but nobody who monopolised her. It was just a friendly gathering."

"I shall need a list of those people. Every one."

Mashenka was uncharacteristically scared, not for herself but for Yelena. "Didn't she return to her Moscow apartment?"

The question was ignored. "Did she make any special dates while she was here? Did she see anybody without you?"

Fedorovitch Gromov. The little weasel. My God. She had heard Yelena telephone him. She had come in while Yelena was making the call. She had only heard part of what Yelena had said and had thought how strangely friendly she had been. She had thought little of it because she disapproved of Fedor as did most of the ballet set.

"I see you've remembered something."

The flat observation left Mashenka cold. She had forgotten because she had wanted to forget. But could she keep it from this revolting creature by her side?

"You are going to tell us. One way or the other, at some time or other, but tell us you will. Do you tell me now or do we drive on?"

* * *

They met in Szczesliwicki Park about three hours after the LOT flight had landed at Warsaw Airport. On the west side of the Vistula river it was one of the smaller parks with an S-shaped lake running from north to south and had been more convenient to reach from the airport.

As Yelena sat on a park bench she was aware of standing out. Vanity did not aid safety and she belatedly realised that she was over-dressed. Poland was poor and this was particularly evident in the way people dressed; not that the women failed to make the best of themselves. They were a proud race and would always work wonders with what they had.

Maria Janesky approached the bench with delight spreading across her striking features. She was dressed in jeans with an old anorak wrapped round a heavy pullover. Her dark hair flowed out behind her as the east wind tugged at it. She greeted Yelena with unrestrained delight and the two women embraced warmly, hugging each other and even crying a little.

A Pole and a Russian embracing in this way was not often to be seen, but Maria and Yelena had met during Yelena's first trip to Poland and that was now many years ago. And they had regularly corresponded since. Apart from a natural liking for each other they had a culture bond. Maria was a fine contralto and had occasionally sung in Moscow where the two women continued their friendship. And she had managed a singing career without putting on the traditional weight. She swore she did this partly by exercise but mostly by a casual attitude to size. It didn't worry her and she ate what she liked. Her personality bubbled.

"Why here, Yelena? I would have come to the airport to meet you, you know that."

They were walking arm-in-arm through the park with Yelena carrying her grip. Dusk was not too far off and there was the scent of freshly growing shrubs and the sight of bright new leaves on the trees.

"I know you would. But I didn't want us to be seen together at the airport. Maria, I'm in trouble. I must find somewhere to hide and I wondered if you could help me.

Believe me, I am only doing this to you because I don't know which way to turn, or anyone else to turn to."

Maria's arm tightened on Yelena's. "In trouble?" She looked at her Russian friend as they walked. "You've always been a supporter of the establishment. It was one of the few things where we really disagreed. What's happened?"

Yelena shook her head wearily. "It's nothing like that. It's something that happened many years ago. I've done nothing wrong but I know something I shouldn't."

"If it happened so long ago, why the crisis now?"

Yelena gripped Maria's hand. She was tired and not thinking too clearly. "At the time this happened I loved a man. I didn't realise I still loved him so much until he was suddenly in danger after Chernobyl."

"He was there? At the reactor plant?"

"He was in an asylum near Pripyat. He escaped during the evacuation."

Maria stopped walking and turned to face her friend, holding her gently by the arms. "Yelena, you're not making much sense. Why should this affect you?"

"Because I know why he was put away." Yelena forced back tears, mindful of people passing and looking. "Let's sit there for a moment." They crossed to a bench and Yelena continued. "Officially he's dead and has been these many years. Through one piece of careless talk I discovered that he had been put away and I went to see him. It just happened to be at the time when security was closing its net and it was really all a series of mistakes while there was still a flap on.

"Once they realised what had happened I was warned that if I opened my mouth to anyone I would disappear and my lover would be killed at once. What helped me at that time was that his official death had not yet happened and when it was announced I was expected to believe it along with everybody else. I never did and I suppose they realised that."

"What had he done? What placed you in this mess? You look terrifed."

"I am. I can't tell you the story because it would compromise you. I don't want you finishing on the run like me. I've already taken advantage of a friend in Leningrad and I just hope she comes to no harm. I stayed with her for a couple of nights; it is enough to bring her trouble. I am with you now and that, too, is enough to put you in danger. If you knew the full story they would get it out of you and they would have to kill you. I should not have come to you like this but there was nothing else for me to do. Just point me to somewhere safe to stay and then keep away from me. But don't send me anywhere which can be linked to you."

"Come on. Let's keep walking." Maria helped Yelena up and they were arm-in-arm again as they headed slowly for the northern exit, taking the lakeside path. "You'll have to change those clothes."

"I know. It was stupid of me to dress like this. Pride and vanity had to take a fall, I suppose, but sometimes it's been my vanity and, of course, ballet, that has kept me going. It's a poor excuse but I haven't much else."

"Yelena, you were right to come to me. You may not like what I find for you but it will be far safer than any hotel. You haven't stayed anywhere yet?"

"No. I phoned you from the airport."

"Then from now on we keep our eyes wide open. If ever you want to tell me more you contact me, do you hear?"

They didn't trouble to take Fedorovitch Gromov to jail. They did not call on him at his office because it was the wrong image to create in front of his colleagues, and they had, anyway, been warned to keep the whole affair low-key. Someone in Moscow wanted to keep it all quiet. That had been difficult; they were used to heavy-handed methods, finding them more effective, and they had received a reprimand for the way they had handled Mashenka Lubinov in public.

It was different at Gromov's small apartment, though. His wife had left him three years ago for another man and he lived the life of a bachelor. The same men who had spoken to Mashenka came up behind him as he was putting his key in the lock and literally lifted him off the ground to carry him inside.

Gromov shouted in indignation but he was squirming

with fear, wondering which of his shady favours had caught up with him. They wasted no time. They threw him on to a chair and while he was still trying to recover from the shock, one man was closing the door and the lanky man was saying, "What happened between you and Yelena Belenko?"

Gromov quickly accepted that they knew he had met Yelena but they could not know what happened between them or they wouldn't be asking. He had to say something. "She stayed the night here."

"Yelena Belenko? Stayed with you? Did you drug her? Put a sack over your face? You're dreaming, Gromov; working out a fantasy. Yelena Belenko wouldn't get anywhere near sleeping with someone like you."

Gromov was hit in the right place. He swelled with anger, his ego punctured. "It is true. She slept with me here." He suddenly realised that he should have been more cautious.

The lanky man was grinning. "What favour did she need from you, Gromov?"

"None. I've known her a long time." Gromov knew then that he was on the rack. His eyes were darting from man to man.

"The easy way or the hard way, Gromov?"

Gromov tried to get off the chair but was pushed back. "I've done nothing. I made love to her, no more." Even under pressure from these two men he got satisfaction from announcing the conquest. It made him feel good and important and he could see that they believed him now. He was briefly living his moment of triumph when a fist crashed into his face and his spine jarred as he hit the back of the chair with considerable force.

"Just tell us where she went, Gromov, and then you can set about finding another job where you can't corrupt yourself so easily."

12

Zotov could not cope; he was unable to hold the shotgun steady let alone fire it. Pripy's barking reached him from inside the *izbi* as the car drew nearer. The dog was warning him but it seemed, too, that he was trying to give reassurance; he was there and had successfully tackled men like these before.

The dog's presence calmed his nerves as it had done before. Even so he had to back away from the corner of the building out of sight of the approaching car before he could really get a grip on himself. As he stood there he believed he had left it too late. He crept forward again, still unsteady, and peered round the corner. The car came into view a few seconds later.

It pulled up well short of *izbi* and for a while the two men in front did not move. They must have thought it strange that Borodin didn't appear, but the red car indicated that Zotov was still there. And probably they could hear Pripy barking. Their uncertainty had the effect of steadying Zotov. Now that the crisis was actually on him he felt better. But he knew that he was still weak and the gun weighed like a cannon in his hands.

He had hoped the car would stop much nearer to the cottage, and his simple plan now appeared to be shaky. He watched from a low angle hoping that he would not be seen. Nothing had changed and he could only vaguely see the shape of two heads against the light reflecting on the windscreen.

The car engine had been turned off, then it started again. There was space for turning in front of the cottage but only in one sector. He drew back as the car crept forward. The occupants clearly did not trust the situation. Zotov had not appeared, but neither had Borodin. They might have been partially reassured by the fact that Pripy was not loose but it looked to Zotov as though they would turn round and go back for help.

Zotov remained lying flat, hoping that the car would not cross the point where he waited. He heard it pull up and then start the small series of turns that would bring it round to face the way it had come. The rear of the car came past the corner of the *izbi* and continued to come. He saw the face of the nearest man who was craning backwards to view the outbuilding, and then he realised that he had been seen.

The engine changed note and the wheels spun on the spongy soil sending up smoke from burning tyres. When the car tried to straighten Zotov rushed out and fired as it roared past him. He had swung round with the direction of the car and the rear window shattered as it took the full blast. The car skidded as the driver lost control and Zotov emptied his second barrel at the offside rear wheel. The tyre burst and the car veered to crash head-on into a large pile of turfs.

Zotov dropped the shotgun and drew his pistol as he ran towards the car which was now tilted at an angle as it rested halfway up the turfs with steam hissing from beneath the buckled hood. As he reached the car the driver was trying to get out and Zotov kicked the door hard to trap his legs. The man yelled out in pain and Zotov wrenched open the door and pointed his pistol at the driver who was now holding a leg in agony.

The second man was bent forward against the dashboard obviously dazed, his face streaming with blood from cuts caused by the flying glass. "Come out slowly and don't go for your weapons," Zotov ordered. "Both come out this side and put your hands on your heads."

Zotov was wary. They were fit men looking for half a chance but they were in no doubt about his intent. "Walk over to the shed." He kept a safe distance as they went past him. "Stop there, and you," he pointed to the man who was bleeding, "lie flat but keep your hands on your head."

"I need attention. I'm bleeding all over the place."

"If you don't get down, you'll need no attention at all."

The man dropped awkwardly to his knees with his hands

still clasped on top of his head. His cut face looked worse than it was, the cuts superficial. When he was prone, Zotov said to the other man, "Get the rope by the shed door. Don't try anything stupid." When the man returned with the rope Zotov said, "Tie up your friend and do it properly. I'll watch every knot you tie."

When that was done to Zotov's satisfaction he told the airman to get on his knees as his friend had done. When he was just off balance Zotov hit him on the back of the head with the gun and then took his time trussing him. He dragged them one at a time to join Borodin in the shed but he placed them in separate corners to make it more difficult for them to make contact. Then he gagged them so that they could not talk. When he was satisfied, he let Pripy out.

Zotov went back into the *izbi* and took a moderate drink of vodka to steady himself. He wondered briefly for how long he could keep ahead of the pack, then he made up his mind about the cars. The Zis the airmen had arrived in was buckled at the front but he took no chances and ripped all the leads out. He did the same to the tractor and to Borodin's van. He then covered the Zis with turfs from the nearby pile until it looked like another stack. The tractor did not need to be hidden.

He had decided to stay with the red Moskvich. What did it matter which transport he used? They were all known, the Moskvich was reliable and he had developed a liking for it. He loaded the shotgun and went back into the shed to make sure that all three men were secure and then collected a bottle of Borodin's dirty green home-made vodka and checked his own food and water supply. He drove off heading north-west, well aware that he was collecting vastly more trouble the further he went.

Chernov went back late to his apartment. He was in a bad mood and his frustration was growing. He checked the rooms to make sure that Zhadin had not had the place bugged while he was at the Centre, and then he checked the safe. He read through the documents he already knew by heart but he was finding it necessary to re-confirm the importance of what he was trying to do. To have to reassure himself in this way was bad enough but to get nowhere in his searches, and to be unable to use the huge organisation he had controlled for so long, was difficult to bear.

Every time he considered his options he came back to the same obstruction. He needed a blanket search for Zotov and he could not get one without revealing what he knew. Not only his own questionable position prevented him from doing what he knew to be necessary, but the needs of Chernobyl currently outweighed his own.

They had used 1100 coaches for the evacuation and countless helicopters, and the queue of coaches had apparently stretched for twenty kilometres. The whole nation was still punch-drunk and in mourning over the disaster although Chernov found it difficult to feel the same kind of sympathy. The tragedy had been caused by incompetence and that was something he could never tolerate. But what he had on his hands would be a far greater national disaster than a reactor blowing up.

He made himself a sandwich and poured himself a glass of milk. Kanavsky was late; Chernov kept glancing impatiently at his watch. He switched on the television and switched it off quickly as the funereal tones of an announcer reminded him of part of the reason he could not get what he needed. It was ludicrous. Suddenly he remembered that he had not phoned his wife, so he rang her up at Sochi and spoke the same lines he always spoke to her when he was busy and had no intention of being diverted. He might as well have used a tape recorder as she had so often told him.

The bell rang and he let in an apologetic Kanavsky and offered him a drink. Kanavsky sat down. It was obvious that he was very tired and having some difficulty in keeping awake. Chernov needed him and was reluctantly lenient. He put his hand to his lips and pointed to the four walls.

"You are clear, Comrade General. I had the place swept earlier this evening. But why would General Zhadin want to do such a thing to you of all people?"

Seeing Kanavsky's needs, Chernov was generous with the finest Polish vodka. "Drink this, it will wake you up. Something to eat? A sandwich, perhaps?"

"No, thank you. I snatched a bite at my desk. My wife will have somethng hot for me when I get home."

"Then I won't keep you long. The General wants to know what I'm up to. It's a game between us. Perhaps a childish one but it can't last longer than the end of my leave and that's ticking away day by day, so bear with me, Borya. Give me your report."

Kanavsky put his untouched drink down. His words were as weary as his appearance. He too, felt the frustration of failure and the harness with which he was so restricted. He had long since guessed that Zotov commanded an importance far in excess of Chernov's claims, but that sort of thing was not new to him; it was being reduced to so small a cell that affected him most. Both he and Chernov had enjoyed the immense facilities of the biggest and most widespread security system in the world, but now they had been thrown back on to only a few men and some of those Chernov had queried. He could not work this way but he held his tongue and just said:

"We've had no luck. Zotov is still loose and at the moment we don't know where he is. We almost lost another helicopter."

"What?" Chernov could feel his blood pressure rising.

Kanavsky held up a nervous hand. "It's all right. We found it. Two helicopters were sent to search the west side of the Pripyat Marshes. There are several communes out there who cut the turf. And over such a big area there are one or two criminals who live by lifting turfs and selling them. It is too small an operation to worry the local authorities and they are largely left alone. Sometimes they have their uses." Kanavsky reached for his drink.

"A man called Borodin has a small *izbi* out there. The helicopters landed near him and Borodin told the crews that a man on the run was in the woods but warned that he was armed and desperate. Borodin said he could disarm him but it was better done at night and that they should return the next day. They had no reason to disbelieve him and it is quite possible that Zotov armed himself in Pripyat. Borodin suggested that they approach by car, because Zotov would flee at the first sound of a helicopter. The following morning they set off with a Zis slung under the helicopter and they have not been seen since."

"Are you saying that the *izbi* hasn't been searched?" Chernov could not believe the naiveté of it.

"When they didn't report in, another helicopter was sent to find them. The first machine was found about six miles from the *izbi*. It had landed on a secondary road as the ground is not firm. They flew over the *izbi* and could see nothing but the dwelling and a shed and a tractor and big piles of turf. There was no sign of life, and no red car or the Zis. Suspecting some kind of trap they flew back to base to report. They left the other helicopter where it had landed in case the crew returned."

Chernov could not believe it. "They suspected a trap? From one man? What the hell are you saying?"

Kanavsky had been expecting it but his chief was being blinded by his need to find Zotov. "Two men are already dead because of this man. Another two are missing with their car. Did you want another two to disappear, Comrade General?"

"Don't try that with me, Kanavsky. I want Zotov, a man who's been out of touch for decades and who's making rings round our people. So what have you now arranged?"

"The second helicopter went in as low as it could without actually landing. It was odd that there was nothing moving, not even Borodin who lives there. Two choppers are going in at first light tomorrow morning and they will have with them some of our own men from the Kiev Station and they will be armed. On the way they'll drop off a pilot to bring the abandoned helicopter back. But I must stress that there is no sign that Zotov or our people have ever been there."

Chernov drained his drink angrily and banged down the empty glass. "He's been there. He'll be miles away by now. Look, I want you to alert Brest-Litovsk. Sandwich him. He's obviously heading for one of the borders. If you search from both directions you are bound to find him. And that means tomorrow, Kanavsky. He's already covered far too much ground."

"What about General Zhadin?"

"What about him? If you don't tell him, neither will I, Colonel."

Kanavsky rose uncomfortably. "With respect, Comrade General, I still have to work with him after you have left."

"You won't be working anywhere if you don't get Zotov." Chernov could not help himself. When Kanavsky spoke like that it meant that he was beginning to watch his back and it showed that his loyalty was in danger of slipping. And yet Chernov had no alternative to pressurising him. He reached for the bottle. "Borya, sit down and have another drink. I'm on edge and you're tired. It's a crazy situation, isn't it?" He reached for Kanavsky's glass but the Colonel was still standing.

Chernov rose to stand by the fireplace, then he crossed over to clap Kanavsky on the shoulder. He grinned. "We've crushed giants, you and I. We've had the West running round in tight circles. Now we're being baulked by one escapee but you have to ask yourself why. We're doing it on a shoestring, that's why. But I want to show General Zhadin that we're perfectly capable of doing that and it won't do you any harm either. He'll have to notice. Just find Zotov, Borya, and get that extra help from Brest. We'll squeeze the bastard to death."

Kanavsky was not surprised; he had not been expecting anything else when Zotov was found. What worried him more was that an unknown captain in the field office outside Kiev could so quickly be promoted to Major when his own promised promotion had shown no sign of appearing. He was beginning to lose faith in a man he had admired for many years. Long used to covering his feelings he said, "There is one piece of good news. It seems that our fleeing ballerina Yelena Belenko has gone to Poland."

"Poland?" Chernov seemed surpised and was thoughtful for a while. "Have you actioned it?"

"Of course. They are already looking for her there."

After Kanavsky had gone Chernov stopped thinking about Yelena Belenko; she would find it difficult to give up her privileged lifestyle and would soon be found. But Zotov's success at remaining free indicated a lucid mind and, if it became too lucid, the result would be too bizarre and dangerous to contemplate. The problem was long past being simply a matter of Zotov's capture; it was one now of rapid execution.

Maria Janesky kept to the west side of the Vistula. Once leaving the Szczesliwicki Park she took the secondary Wlodarzewska to the main artery of the Krakowska. For a while Yelena, who was sitting beside her in the tiny Renault, thought she was heading back to the airport but Maria turned left on to the Franciszka Hynka to the north of the airport and continued south-east until they reached the Pulawska and then headed south again.

The journey became increasingly depressing for Yelena. They were approaching the industrial area of Ursynow and the buildings were becoming stark and grim and Solidarity signs were painted over the factory walls to remind her of a fight against a system which had hitherto provided a protection that she had largely enjoyed. She saw the signs as a protest against her own country and she wondered if that was why the vivacious Maria had brought her this way. She was shocked when Maria said:

"It's ugly, I know, but it's safer down here. More people are willing to help and if it came to it there would be some solid support." She smiled. "I have many friends who work around here but I have to be careful. Very careful." She glanced at Yelena. "Cheer up. They won't think of looking for you in Ursynow."

Yelena tried to summon a smile. "I'm being ungrateful, aren't I? I'm sorry. But I won't hold out for long like this." She was close to tears and Maria briefly gripped her hand. "Many Poles are used to being hunted and to hiding. It's nothing new. Like them, you will have to get used to the idea. I can only provide a temporary hideout. But you must think of the future. Have you nowhere in mind?"

Yelena waved her hands in despair, indicating the walls and windows as soulless expressions of her own feelings and the grim warning of things to come. There seemed to be a sad expression on everybody's face but perhaps that was a reflection of her own mood. She had never felt so down or so lost. She had not thought beyond Warsaw which had arisen from a youthful dream.

Maria, trying to cope with the narrow streets, was preoccupied for a while. When she glanced again at Yelena and saw her despair she said, "We'll have to get you out of the country then."

"Out of the country? Where?"

"Western Europe. Once over the border into West Germany you can take your choice. Seek political asylum." She smiled briefly. "You wouldn't be the first Kirov ballerina to do that."

Defect! Yelena was terrified. It was the cardinal sin, the final betrayal of her Motherland. She had never been to Western Europe. They were the enemy. And if she tried to get there the KGB would move heaven and earth, and hell as well, to stop her. Nor would she be safe if she did get there. She felt so desperate then that she even considered jumping out of the car, but Maria now brought the car into the kerb and stopped outside what appeared to be a derelict building.

In fact it was an old factory due for demolition and rebuilding. The walls were mainly blank with the occasional window mostly boarded up. The street was short and dingy, and empty except for some youngsters at the far end who all turned when they heard the car; it was not a street for strangers.

"They've seen us," said Yelena.

"No. It's the car they have seen. They are too far away to see us but we are in no danger. Only the police and the security forces are not welcome here. We'll wait until they've gone round the corner."

When the youngsters disappeared Maria told Yelena to stay in the car until she signalled. Maria climbed out, unlocked a door at the top of two concrete steps and went inside. The door reminded Yelena of the depths to which she had sunk. Very little paint was left on it and what remained was a dull, dirty brown. At the bottom, where there had once been a weatherboard, were the jagged holes of wet rot. She tried to anchor her mind elsewhere but all that came to mind was the repulsive groping figure of Gromov.

From the moment she had read of Zotov's escape she had really had no time to think properly or adjust to the penalties of fleeing. She felt she had to get away and that it was all that entered her mind. But from the moment she had let Gromov sleep with her her whole lifestyle had changed. That unsavoury incident had been only the first lesson of survival. And now this dreadful place was another part of her slide down.

Maria appeared, gazed up and down the street and then signalled Yelena to enter. The concrete floor was covered in cement dust and the stairs at the far end were bare. The walls had graffiti scrawled all over them. The plaster had fallen off in great chunks, some of it lying in broken pieces on the stairs. The bare brick beneath looked as if it was crumbling away.

"It's one of the last buildings in a redevelopment scheme," explained Maria as she picked her way up the stairs. "Keep to the sides of the boards, some are nearly rotten."

What was she coming to? Yelena had difficulty in following and did so only because she trusted Maria. But she had never even suspected this side of her. She was both surprised and relieved for, although it was now abundantly clear that Maria was at least connected with the underground movement, she had remained a faithful friend.

They reached the top of the building and the state of it did not improve on the way. Finally, Maria opened another door and ushered Yelana inside. It was an improvement on what she had seen so far. There were two rooms; one had two old armchairs and a couple of ladder backs. There were two single beds stripped down. The mattresses had been soiled and roughly cleaned.

Maria stood in the middle of the room and explained; "These used to be the factory offices. The water hasn't been turned off. Solidarity influence stretches far, but there is only cold." She pointed to the other door. "There's a portable bath in there. A gas stove with a spare cylinder is in the screened-off kitchen section. And the old lavatory still works."

Maria held her arms wide to indicate the room they were now in. She pointed. "Wardrobe. Chest with blankets. No sheets, they need cleaning too often. Pantry with tinned food and milk and utensils. Crude but serviceable. It took a good deal of hard-earned money to set this up." Seeing Yelena's dismay she added pointedly, "A lot of self-sacrifice has gone into this and others in order to help people. Don't be too disappointed."

Yelena sat on the arm of one of the shabby chairs and burst into tears. This was a prison. Maria crossed over and cradled her. "I know, my darling. I know. But it's better than being caught, believe me. You'll get used to it. And it's safe. The moment we think it isn't, we'll get you out."

Yelena didn't want to get used to it. It was a disastrous step to take. Yet behind her despair was the knowledge that if she was caught she would not even have these dubious comforts before being executed. The thought calmed her down. But she realised she would have to have plans beyond this or she would go crazy.

She raised her head and apologised. Then she said, "The man who escaped from the hospital near Pripyat is called Zotov. I don't know whether he's still free, but if he does come to Warsaw, could your friends keep a look-out for him? He'll need more help than I."

Maria knew that this was at the heart of the matter. She crossed to the other chair and faced Yelena. "Why should he come to Warsaw?"

Yelena was wiping her eyes. "I don't know that he will. Perhaps it's all a stupid dream. I don't suppose he'll make it to the border; there is too much against him."

"What does he look like?"

"I don't know, Maria." Yelena hesitated, her lip trembling. "I only know what he looked like twenty odd years ago."

"And he was your lover?"

"In my heart he still is."

"I'll pass the word. Pripyat? The whole town was evacuated. There was a rumour of a helicopter crashing there. Right in the centre of the town. That would have started from Kiev but I can't vouch for it; we get so many rumours. Would that be anything to do with it?"

Yelena looked up, her face animated. She had no idea whether the crash had anything to do with it but, if it had, it meant that that particular crew had not found Zotov if they were searching for him.

Maria's question remained unanswered but she noticed Yelena's reaction. She rose and said, "If they get desperate they may put out a description which we might pick up. Now give me your sizes and I'll get you some clothes to wear. Don't leave this room until I return tomorrow. There are gas lamps in the other room but make sure you put the boardings up at the windows first." She moved to the main door. "Open it only when you hear one hard knock and three quick soft ones." She paused and said as undramatically as she could, "If you feel you're in real danger there's a fire escape outside that window. It's rusty but still sound. Find your way to my place. Okay?"

Yelena gazed round her and nodded. So it had all come to this. She forced herself to smile.

"Thank you, Maria. I know what it might cost you."

They headed south-east through the undulations and occasional woodlands to Lukow. When they approached the small town Mirek was driving and he stopped and told Annya to lie down flat on the rear seat with a blanket over her.

For the whole of the short journey they had been in a state of nerves. They left just after dawn, not waiting for breakfast. They had headed for Warsaw, then circled back and by-passed Siedice. It was a nerve-racking drive but, up to the time they left, Waleski's body had not been found.

The clock could not be put back. Waleski had been killed but the fact that it had been an accident would not stand up in any court, secret or open. They could not possibly have had a worse start to their mission. Mirek drove as if he no longer cared but as they approached Lukow and new dangers he began to function again.

Once Annya was on the back seat he drove steadily into the town looking for a car hire. It was still early and not everything was open but he located a garage with a few battered old bangers on the forecourt. There was such a shortage of cars that either the few on show were useless or the price was too high. He located another, more formal place which was closed, but which advertised car hire although with no visible sign of cars. He then drove back to the fringe of the town and turned into one of the outer and quieter streets and pulled in. He spoke without turning round and told Annya to remain down.

"We must ditch this car. I'll drop you here and take the car about a couple of miles out of town and dump her. I'll then walk back. You meanwhile hire a car. Pascoe at least gave us plenty of funds. I'll walk to the southern limits of town where you can look out for me and pick me up. I'll keep to the main road."

"All right." Annya was staring up above the blanket.

"Fine. You want me to take you back into town or can you manage from here?"

"This is safer for me to get out."

"Take the lighter case." He did turn then. "I love you, Annya. Take care. Don't get yourself mugged."

She laughed as she threw back the blanket. "This is Poland, Mirek, not London. On your way."

He watched her go, admiring her walk, her figure, and knowing what it was costing her in human spirit. She needed to be with him yet she accepted that it was safer to part for the moment. When she had turned a corner without looking back he drove about two miles out of town to a sparse glade standing back from the road.

There was not a great deal of traffic but he waited until the road was empty before he turned off and headed into the thin line of trees. When the car began to buck too much he pulled up and climbed out. The road was still visible and anyone looking his way from one of the passing vehicles must see his car. He looked about him. About fifty yards away was an area of patchy shrubs which might hide the car. He climbed in and drove over the rough ground, at times wondering how the car held up. Finally it dipped into a hidden crater and stopped, nose down. Mirek switched off and climbed out.

When he looked back towards the road it was completely hidden. And he could barely hear the odd swish of tyres. He removed the remaining case and set out towards the town, making his way diagonally through the trees towards the road. The case was weighty and he frequently changed hands but the last thing he wanted was a lift into town and he kept as far back from the road as possible. It was going to be a long two miles and even then he would have to find his way to the other side of Lukow. He closed down his mind and just kept walking, resting only occasionally.

By the time he reached the town it was much more active than earlier and he felt himself to be a focus with the case and perspiring freely. Following the main road he traipsed on to the southern fringes where everything began to quieten again. There was still traffic but now few pedestrians. Pavements petered out further from the town. He dumped the case under a tree which was just budding, wiped his face and waited.

Mirek checked the time. It had taken him almost three hours. He turned his back to the road aware that he must appear like a hitch. Some twenty minutes later he heard a car pull in and he turned to see a mousy-haired woman with a familiar face smiling at him from behind the steering-wheel of a light brown Zis which had seen many better days.

"Climb in, Mirek, you look all in."

"Annya. Thank God." He heaved the case on to the rear seat and climbed in beside her.

"This is my eighth time round," she said. "I was getting worried."

"Where on earth did you get the wig?"

"Never go without one," she replied. "I found a toilet and made the change. Should have done it in the car."

They were moving at a steady 40mph and heading for the Russian border when Mirek voiced what they were both thinking. "We must have left a trail a mile wide but I don't see what else we could do. At least we weren't seen together."

Annya did not reply. Relieved at seeing him again, conversely now that they were together her fears returned. Waleski would be discovered some time. And so would the car, revealing to Brus that they had not returned to Warsaw.

Major Penovitch, feeling the strength of his new rank,

made arrangements that would have pleased Chernov, but not if he had known that Penovitch quoted Chernov's own authority for what he did. Penovitch instructed local KGB headquarters to check trains heading for the border. So trains were delayed at Ovruch on the Pripyat line, and Korosten and Olevsk which connected with the main line from Moscow to the border at Brest-Litovsk. The trains were delayed while they were thoroughly searched for anyone resembling the hospital description of Zotov.

Some arrests were made and a few unfortunates were bundled off the trains to await identification, while Zotov continued his journey by road in the red Moskvich. But the negative result of the train searches ultimately increased the need to concentrate on the roads.

13

Zotov had started off from Borodin's place by rejoining the main road, still largely empty; the traffic on this run was never heavy but with the threat of the Chernobyl radiation cloud still worrying people, it was lighter than usual. Just the same he realised that he had been seen often enough and he finally left the road for any track that suggested it could support the Moskvich.

Using minor roads and tracks was a mixed blessing. He encountered virtually no other vehicle but every track must lead somewhere and he kept his eyes open for settlements. He wanted no more Borodins helping him in order to sell him out. He found a river, a tributary of the Pripyat, and nosed the car carefully into the shrub and tree line along its banks. He quickly hacked down brush to cover the car; to camouflage was now a ritual.

He had stopped early – it was only mid-afternoon – because he wanted time to consider what best to do. The nearer he was to the border the greater the danger. While Pripy trotted round picking up the scent of wildlife, Zotov scanned the area. There was no sign of human life anywhere; the Pripyat marshes were no attraction to casual visitors and only those who worked there would choose to live in the immense, uninspiring country around him.

He sat by the river bank refreshed by the constant sound of running water. It was a good therapy. There would be fish in the river but he wondered if they were contaminated; he would stick to his cans of food. He drank a little of Borodin's vodka. The rough spirit helped to fill the gaps that the drugs had left. The pains in his guts were diminishing but all too slowly and when they chose, they could flare up with no warning and he would roll for a while in agony.

Having escaped from the darkness that had shrouded him for so long Zotov had decided he would rather kill himself than lose his freedom. He knew that the precarious life he was living was hardly a life at all but it was the best he had enjoyed for a quarter of a century. In his late forties there was still time to salvage something if he could get beyond the Soviet borders.

Inevitably, he was trying to recapture his past and as the drugs began to wear off he became more confused. They had blotted out his memory, he now knew that for a certainty, and even that realisation was a giant step forward. He would have to be patient and must not push his mind too far. He could now face up to the belief that he was not a man called Zotov but someone else; someone who, it had been decided, must be buried alive and a new person created. The reasons had to be very powerful.

The things he had learned about himself, like the ability to drive, were too small to help in a real sense. That he could drive pre-supposed that he had had a car or access to one and that could mean a degree of privilege or position. Sometimes he strained so hard to remember that he cried out of frustration. The shutter simply would not open. But in one sense he had breached the blockage with a different sensation of fear. The fear of space, of emptiness, of loneliness, these always returned with darkness and he slept very little at night. Terror was not too strong a word for what he experienced when the light went, and dusk was always the prelude to increasing fear.

Daytime fear was a different matter and was largely reduced to the dreaded sound of helicopters. Scanning the skies had become second nature to him. The only certainty was that those who were searching would come back. He was convinced that when they found him they would kill.

He curled up that night and tried to sleep, Pripy pushing his back into him for warmth. The dog's contact was his lifeline as the shakes started once more and the torment that would not go away until dawn. During the night he awoke screaming with the sensation that he was floating above his own body and that all he could see was eternal blackness.

* * *

In the few days since returning to work, Chernov had lost a little weight. He was eating erratically, reminiscent of his earlier days at the Centre, and he was not eating much. Nor was he sleeping well, and as a result was becoming more and more irritable, which added to his problems, for he needed people like Kanavsky to remain loyal to him.

The report he received from Kanavsky later that morning did nothing to help. He sat behind the desk, looking slightly ridiculous in the small chair, and exploded, "What?"

Kanavsky went over it again, his own temper barely in check. He was now waiting for the day when Chernov's leave expired and he would be free of this man who had been his master for so long. "They found the helicopter crew and the man Borodin tied up in a barn. The Zis had been covered so that it could not be seen from the air. The car had crashed and was unserviceable. Zotov had gone, presumably in the red Moskvich."

Chernov tried to hang on to his feelings. "Anything else you have that might surprise me?"

When Kanavsky hesitated Chernov could see there was worse to come. "They recovered the chopper that burned out at Pripyat. They brought back as much as they could to Kiev. As it was a quick in-and-out job due to the possibility of lingering radiation, they underslung grapples to pick up the wreck. Some was lost on the way back." As he watched Chernov's expression change, Kanavsky added quickly, "But there was enough for the experts to examine. They believe that both men were already dead when the helicopter blew up. They had been shot. There is also a strong possibility that the fire was arson and that the machine did not actually crash."

"You mean Zotov outwitted and killed them and then burned the evidence?"

"We have the evidence."

"After some days. Kanavsky, I simply don't know what to say to you. You've lost your touch. This is unbelievable. All done by a man who has been out of circulation for two and a half decades."

"We don't know that it was done by Zotov."

"It was Zotov at the *izbi*. You said earlier that Borodin had said so, that Zotov made no attempt to hide his name. Stop grasping at straws."

"Do you want the search continued?"

"You're asking me that about a murderer? He can't be too far from the border by now. But which border? Find that car from the air but do no more than that. That's all for now."

When Kanavsky had gone Chernov examined his options. Strangely, they were stronger now than at the outset. The heads of the Czech and Polish security services were old friends of his; he had, after all, virtually assigned them to their posts. And they both had considerably more power than the local influence of poor Kanavsky who was now getting out of his depth.

The important thing was that both heads of the two security services would be feeling their way with Zhadin and if they remembered only part of what Chernov had forced into them over the years, they would not like much of what Zhadin was doing. It was time to call in old and influential comrades. He rang each of them that afternoon on a scrambler. When he had finished he was satisfied that he had battened down the borders of both countries. He was now applying the nutcrackers that should crack Zotov comfortably in the middle. And he was satisfied that he had brought into operation the weight of two highly organised services outside his own country and without Zhadin's knowledge. If he could not use the KGB to full effect he could certainly use its appendages.

Chernov now felt happier than at any time these last few days. Zotov was sandwiched. It would be impossible for him to escape.

As they approached the border with Russia they were in a highly nervous state. On the way Annya had stopped to buy some peroxide to brush pale streaks into Mirek's hair after they had found a quiet spot by the river some few miles from Brest. The danger was, if they changed their appearance too much, they would look nothing like their passport photographs. As the passports and visas themselves were forged and supplied by Pascoe, the risks were doubled.

The traffic gradually increased and slowed as they neared the barriers on the Polish side. Passing through the control this side of the border should be little more than a formality unless Customs and police had been alerted for them. The other side was a different proposition altogether. It was much easier for Russians to visit their satellites than the reverse.

Beyond the Polish and Russian barriers was the old town of Brest-Litovsk, now known simply as Brest. A port dating back to the eleventh century, it straddled the river Bug, and had periodically changed hands as much as Poland had.

Now in the queue waiting for passport control, Mirek and Annya sat nervously in their Zis. They held hands and said nothing, their grip tightening as they gradually approached the head of the queue which was mainly comprised of trucks.

There was never any urgency about these situations. Bureaucracy came in the form of power created by uniforms worn by people who had no power outside them. They took their time while Mirek and Annya's hands grew moist with the waiting.

It was their turn, finally. They handed over the passports through the open car window and waited, not daring to speak. The official glanced quickly at them each in turn, then told them to wait while he returned to the Customs' hut. Those in the mounting queue sat back in resignation.

The Customs officer returned, still holding the passports. Instead of handing them back he said, "Pull into the bay over there and then get out and follow me."

Their hearts were leaden. Another official came from the hut to deal with the rest of the queue as the officer with their passports herded Mirek and Annya toward the hut.

Maria Janesky tried to hide her anxiety as Yelena changed. The discipline of ballet training showed in the still firm and lithe figure of the ballerina as she stripped to put on the faded jeans the opera singer had brought. When Yelena had finished she pivoted to face Maria to ask how she looked, and caught her friend off guard.

"Maria, what's wrong?"

"There's a big flap on. They know you're in Poland."

Yelena held her hands to her mouth. "I used my own name at the airport. I didn't think."

"What else could you have done? They batten everyone down so that they can pull them in on the end of a string whenever they like."

Yelena was still having difficulty accepting this kind of talk but she had only to view her own plight to come closer to understanding the near breakdown of a life-time of indoctrination. What frightened her most at the moment was to see her friend so distraught. For Maria to show her worry meant it was deep. It also meant that if the secret police were looking for her here, Gromov must have talked and a strong sense of shame returned at the thought of what he might have told them.

"How do you know they are searching for me?"

Maria crossed to the window but kept well back. Her arms were folded under her small breasts as she turned to face her friend. "We have some sympathisers in the police. Just a few, but they are helpful in supplying the odd piece of information. At a time like this a tip-off can be invaluable."

Yelena was startled. "They know you have hidden me?"

"Of course not. But they know we might get to know where you are. There's a long chain, Yelena. They don't know I'm involved. At least I hope not. They're unlikely to find you here because I'm the only one who knows where you are. Don't worry. But it does mean that I'll have to keep my visits down and you must not go out in any circumstances. Not until things cool off."

Yelena sank down on to one of the dilapidated chairs. "It will never cool down." Each day brought a new realisation, new fears, and a mounting feeling of hopelessness.

"We have to get you out. But it will take time." Maria gazed round the makeshift apartment. "It could be much worse. You have plenty of food and drink. You could be in the hands of the KGB and if what you know is as serious as you say then they would have tortured and killed you by now. When you are feeling bitter just remember that." Maria spoke harshly because there were times when she believed that Yelena still had not grasped her position.

Yelena crossed the room to embrace her friend. "I know what you are doing for me. I don't mean to seem ungrateful. Couldn't I just go out after dark? Late? To exercise a little?"

"No. Don't take them for fools. The orders to find you would have come from Moscow and when that happens all the stops are pulled out."

Maria crossed to the door. "I parked the car three blocks away. It's safer that way. I don't know when I'll next see you but I will be back. Rely on it."

When Maria had gone Yelena began to worry for her. And if something happened to Maria how would she know? How long could she wait without contact? She would have to get out at night to preserve her own sanity. She would try one small excursion just to see how it went.

They crossed in front of the line of cars and trucks aware of the curiosity they attracted. The official led them to the small Customs and police post.

They followed the officer into the building and across a reception area, past a counter with some desks and chairs behind it, aware of the clack of a typewriter somewhere in the room. Nobody seemed to take any notice of them. The officer took them to a small interrogation room at the far end of the building and a Venetian blind was pulled down to darken the only window. It was gloomy inside, and spartan, just a plain wooden table and several hard chairs.

"Sit down over there." The officer pointed to two chairs on the far side of the table.

Annya was afraid to let go of Mirek's hand; Waleski's body had been found; it could only be that.

The officer stood with his back to the door, a tall, uncompromising figure with a narrow face and thin frame to the point of boniness. He said quite loudly, "When were these passports issued?"

Mirek and Annya exchanged glances. Mirek said, "It tells you inside."

"Don't be funny. You tell me."

"Mine was issued about a year ago."

"The photograph doesn't much look like you."

"Do they ever?"

The officer looked at Annya. "Take your wig off."

Annya, already dazed, was unable to move. It would be useless to deny that she was wearing one.

The officer came round the table and whipped the wig from Annya's head. He returned to the other side of the table but kept away from the door. He opened Annya's passport and studied the photograph and Annya in turn. He then tossed the wig across the table. Apparently satisfied about their identities, he relaxed just a little. "You can put it back on." When Annya had done so, the officer glanced towards the door and hooked a chair forward to sit on its edge.

He waved the two passports at them and then tossed them on the table. "For forgeries they're quite good."

Mirek and Annya sat absolutely still. The officer was playing with them. Mirek said, "You know very well that they're not forgeries. What is the point of all this?"

"The point is that I had to be absolutely certain of who you are. I was warned to keep an eye out for you."

Already stunned Mirek and Annya were now confused and very wary. "Whatever for?"

"Don't you know?"

Mirek thought it best to keep quiet. He knew how Annya was feeling beside him.

The officer suddenly lowered his voice. "We're looking for a man called Zotov. He's on the run from across the border. Last seen driving a red Moskvich. Have you seen such a man?"

Neither knew what to say at first. Both instantly felt it to be a trap. Eventually it was Annya who replied as if to prove to herself that she could face the situation. "What does he look like?"

"Medium height. Greying hair, probably clean-shaven. Drawn features but quite good-looking."

"We haven't seen such a man. We might have seen the odd Moskvich. But I thought you said he was from the other side of the border; we're going the other way." What game was this man playing?

"That's so. But you will be crossing the border. If you see such a man you must notify the authorities at once. He is dangerous."

Mirek felt relieved. It was almost painful as his suspicions took more form. "Are you sure he's coming this way?"

The officer stood up. "No. He could be heading for the Czech border but if he tries to cross the Polish frontier this is the most likely route he'll take. Keep your eyes open and be sure to tell the Soviet authorities if by chance you see him."

"We're taking the Moscow road. Is he likely to be on that?"

The officer shook his head. "He's most likely to be coming from the Pripyat direction. A pity you are not going that way." He moved towards the door. "I would like to search your car now; to make sure you are not smuggling anything. Bring your passports with you."

As Annya rose with the help of Mirek her mind was so filled with the possible discovery of Waleski's body that she had completely missed the sense of what was going on. Mirek was smiling faintly as he helped her towards the door. He put an arm round her and she began to grasp that things had somehow swung their way. Her legs were still unsteady as they walked back towards the car.

14

The trees towered above him like a mass of green soldiers lining his route. Mile after mile they closed him in, making the narrow road a thin ribbon which he followed hypnotically. On impulse he had cut back from the border and had almost gone in the opposite direction. The cunning of survival dictated that he was following too obvious a route so he had detoured. It took him miles from where he wanted to go but it was largely uninhabited and the forests provided the cloak he had lacked before.

Zotov still followed the routine of occasionally stopping to listen for helicopters. It was so silent everywhere, the giant trees supported a winding strip of overcast sky and many a person would have felt too enclosed and even claustrophobic. To Zotov, however, it was bliss, the trees a contact with hard reality to which he could relate. He hoped the forests would go on forever. They cradled his emotions and camouflaged his fears; they were part of mother earth.

He had plenty of petrol, for the small Moskvich was low on fuel consumption. Nor was he short of food or water. He could cope provided he did not lose his sense of direction.

He had no idea what would happen at the border but he did not think it would be so easy a matter as avoiding the border towns. He had no plans for crossing because he did not know the scene. He did not realise that, at some point, he would have to ditch and hide the car. His only certainty was that he must somehow get out of Russia.

Twice during his frequent halts, he heard helicopters and, each time, he edged the car off the road and nosed it as far into the trees as he could. The height of the trees and the narrowness of the road prevented any form of aircraft from coming too low and he made sure he was tucked in. The danger was always when he was actually driving, the car engine shutting out every other noise. He had reached an impasse but was reluctant to admit it. He simply did not know what to do next.

Just before sundown he drove into the fringe of the forest and prepared to bed down for the night. He heard helicopters again, that dreadful thudding he had grown to hate and fear. They were too far away and he could not see them. As the sound faded he accepted that they were on their way back to Kiev before night finally fell. But they would be back.

He found a clearing and spread his bed-roll. A moderate wind whispered through the trees but to him it was a lullaby, a reminder that the forest was his friend which closed in to protect him as darkness fell. He was getting used to stomach cramps and finding it a little easier to combat the sudden pain and the jangling of his nerve ends.

Zotov slept better that night but when dawn broke, a weak sun filtering through the deep foliage in ever-moving shafts, he knew that this was to be the day of decision. The border was within his reach and risks had to be taken. He checked his pistol and the shotgun, making sure that both were loaded and that spare ammunition was in his pockets. After a cold breakfast he eased the car back on to the road, climbed out, searched what he could see of the skies, listened intently for quite a long time, and then drove off with Pripy sitting beside him, his ears pricked, somehow aware of his master's foreboding. Zotov could feel his nerve going and he had to stop for a while. He placed the handgun on the dashboard shelf in front of him and shakily drove off again. He felt he was heading for his own funeral.

Mirek and Annya had no problems on the Russian side of the border except the usual delays and the surly bureaucracy of Soviet officials; but it was increasingly difficult for either of them to hide their anxieties. No longer were they operating in the Polish underground with the strength of the pack around them. They were out on their own, and in Russia, with a dead Polish security agent haunting them all the way.

There were times when they believed they were raving

mad to continue with the mission but the alternative was to turn back which could be even more dangerous. They might just as well go on. Both secretly hoped that they would not find Zotov, for his discovery would only complicate an already volatile situation. Had they known his background they might have felt differently, but all they knew was that he was on the run. So were they.

They had decided not to look for accommodation in Brest; they did not want to be remembered by anyone in the town. So they drove through the ancient port wanting only to get beyond its boundaries and away from the river line. They drove some distance before turning south-east on the Kiev road, not the direction they had informed the Russian immigration officers. They found a lay-by some ten miles out of the town, pulled off the road, and slept on the back seat of the car. They enjoyed the rich, warm comfort of each other's arms. But there was no comfort of the mind. With Polish number plates they would already be noticeable. Fortunately they were on a sparsely used road and heading in a direction most people were trying to avoid.

They awoke long before dawn, stiff and restless. They did some exercises by the roadside to try to instil some life into their bodies. It was cold, damp, still dark, and their motivation was at its lowest. They started off in a sombre silence but their spirits rose as dawn came up and diminished the power of their headlamps. Mirek switched off the lights and turned to view the grey silhouette of Annya by his side. She put out a hand. Touch was the only reassurance left to them.

They coasted slowly between the trees as if they were in a tunnel. "Pascoe has more influence than we realised," he said at last. It seemed as though they had not spoken for days. It was the first reference either had made to the incident on the Polish side of the border, as if they had to be well clear before they could finally accept that it had actually happened.

Annya did not seem to hear him. Nervously she asked, "Mirek, are we going to be all right?"

"After Waleski, who'd have thought we'd have got this far? It's a good omen."

"Maybe they let us. Perhaps they think we might find Zotov for them."

It had crossed his mind, but with the immense coverage the KGB could muster he could not understand why Zotov was still free. There was much about this business that they did not know and he suspected that neither did Pascoe. But Zotov could be anywhere. Even on this main road they had seen little traffic, no doubt because of people's enormous reluctance to pass anywhere near Chernobyl. But the outlying stretches of Soviet roads were never very active anyway. In certain areas it was possible to go for miles without seeing another vehicle.

When Mirek did not reply Annya said, "How far do you intend to go? We must set a limit."

The sun broke through the trees as he was about to speak. The glare cut through the foliage at an angle behind him and reflected blindingly on the central mirror. He adjusted the mirror and replied, "As far as Kovel. It's about ninety or a hundred miles from Brest. From the study we made in Warsaw this road curves out from the border and arches in to Kovel to follow the rail line again. I think Kovel is far enough."

Annya nodded. "Zotov would avoid any towns but this is the only main road. Most people would use the railway from Kiev to Warsaw even though it means changing, so if he's on this road why haven't they caught him?"

The conversation was waking them up, making their minds function again.

"I keep asking myself the same question. It's a strange business. Maybe they think it will be easier at the border."

Annya leaned her head against the seat back. She looked at Mirek thoughtfully. "Have you any idea at all what this is about? Who is Zotov?"

Mirek did not reply; they had been through it so often. They did not have the answers. Zotov might have been captured at the outset for all they knew. It could all be a wasted and dangerous journey.

"Choppers," he said suddenly.

Annya sat up. "Where?"

"Follow the gap above the trees; the road line. The sun

reflected off one of them. I can see two. Some distance away."

Annya shook her head. "I can't see anything."

"They've disappeared below the tree line." Mirek slowed. A convoy of three covered military trucks came towards them, presumably heading for Brest. Mirek gave them plenty of room and the trucks rumbled past. And then a big Zis came up behind them at speed, pulled out and passed them. It was the busiest the road had been. It went quiet again and Mirek searched the ribbon of sky. Suddenly he pulled up, switched off the engine and half climbed out. "I can just about hear them," he said. He started up again.

"Keep your eyes skinned," he bawled out.

"For the choppers?"

"For a red Moskvich possibly hidden in the trees."

Annya glanced at him sharply. "You think the choppers are out looking for him?"

"We are. Why not them? If he's on the road at all he's more likely to be at this end of it than the Kiev area." Mirek's gaze was now totally concentrated on the road, his peripheral vision sharpened to catch an odd splash of colour among the trees.

He was cruising quite slowly now but the helicopters had disappeared and he wondered where they were. When he first saw them he thought that he and Annya might be having a little luck, that the choppers would drive Zotov, if he was around at all, right into their arms. If Zotov was heading towards them on the only main road they would be unlucky to miss him. But the choppers offered both the clue and the help they needed.

Annya, now fully awake, was trying to peer into the woods either side of them. "Don't go any faster than this."

"We're hardly moving." But he knew that she was right. His spirits were falling again, for he reckoned they had reached the point where he had first seen the choppers. He continued on another two miles, despondency mounting after the earlier hopes. He stopped again and just sat there, fingers drumming the wheel. He felt Annya gazing at him.

"You thought it would be so easy, Mirek?"

"No. But I keep reminding myself that this is the only main route. If he's on it we should find him."

"Perhaps the choppers aren't looking for him at all."

"What else would they be doing in this God-forsaken area?"

"We won't find him just sitting here."

But he wouldn't be hurried. They sat there for perhaps ten minutes before he saw the choppers again. And now they were much higher and one was circling while the other hovered. If the crews were watching the road, and it seemed that they were, then their own car would have been seen. The helicopters moved slowly out of his vision as they descended and were lost below the tree line again.

"Let's hope they're doing our work for us. "Mirek drove on at no more than thirty miles an hour. Both he and Annya scanned each side of the road trying to penetrate the tree-line. With Annya trying to cope with studying both sides of the road Mirek coasted along slowly and passed through a very wide stretch, about half a mile long, where the trees receded well back from the road as if some local foresting had been done. It created the widest stretch of sky yet but the helicopters had disappeared.

The trees closed in again and the car was barely crawling along. Mirek increased speed slightly, his nerve ends strumming. The erratic presence of the choppers suggested again that they were searching for something. If a car had pulled off the road there was a limit to how far it could penetrate the forest. He would expect it to be camouflaged but, with the height of the trees, it should be easier to pick out from the road than from the air.

Apart from the engine noise it was quiet and their talk had stopped with the concentration of the search. It was some time later, and the mood had changed again to something approaching despondency, when Annya called breathlessly, "I think I saw something, Mirek. My side."

Mirek braked very slowly. "You don't sound too sure."

"How can I be?" Annya was irritated. "It was a glimpse, no more."

"Maybe we've struck lucky; we could do with some." Mirek pulled the car under an overhang of branches and switched off. "If you're right then I was right about the choppers; they've driven him under cover."

"I'm pretty sure I saw something, but it was so quick."

He smiled. "Stop worrying. Let's walk back. And try to keep under the trees. Don't make a noise."

It was easier said than done. Keeping under the trees meant walking in undergrowth which, inevitably, was noisy. They did their best aided by the loud thudding of helicopters although they were still out of sight. The direction of moving sound is difficult to assess and at times the noise was almost deafening as if the machines were right on top of them.

Mirek suddenly put his hand out to stop Annya who was just behind him. They kept quite still. The helicopter roar was now muted, seemingly by the trees themselves, but there was another sound, much more subdued but distinctive nevertheless. A dog's low growl came from a spot not far ahead and to their left which was the side they were on.

Annya drew her gun. "A wolf?" she whispered.

Mirek wasn't so sure. "Keep that gun handy. Wait there until I call." He crept forward. The sound of the helicopters had stopped altogether which must mean that they had landed and that could only be where the road widened about a mile back. He suddenly felt foolish, thinking that he was reading too much into the situation, and then he saw a red smudge well back from the road.

There was no one in sight and he crept along, trying to avoid the bracken. Then a dog appeared on the fringe of a gap, its head poking through the undergrowth. It was a German Shepherd, its lips drawn back in a warning snarl, its gaze never wandering from Mirek who kept absolutely still. He did not draw his gun, reasoning that the dog would have him if he tried. Without moving he took in as much of the background to the dog as he could. The nape of his neck prickled just before a voice said in Russian, "Move one finger and I'll blow your head off."

Mirek detected the weary desperation in the voice. It

seemed that they had struck lucky but not in a way he liked.

"I mean you no harm."

"You're in no position to harm me. What do you want?"

It seemed crazy. Could he really have located his man like this? It was not the time to think of Walkeski; it had not all been easy. Anyway, he was certain that a gun was pointing at his back and whether or not it was fired would depend on his answer.

"If by chance, your name is Zotov, I've come to help you." Mirek felt his Russian faltering and hoped he was understood.

There was a grating laugh behind him. "To help me? Everybody says that. All they want to do is to kill me."

"I don't. May I turn around."

"No. I've a double-barrel shot-gun aimed at your back. It would make a mess of you. You're not Russian so where are you from?"

"Warsaw. I've come specially to look for you and to get you across the border."

Warsaw! Mention of the place had an odd effect on Zotov and it was as well he was standing behind Mirek for it provoked confusion. Warsaw. Why did that name mean so much?

"Put your hands on your head and turn round very slowly. Sit, Pripy."

Mirek pivoted carefully. The grey-haired man facing him was indeed holding a shot-gun and both hammers were cocked. There was also a pistol in his waist band. The eyes that gazed at him were haunted and the roughly shaved face was pale. He looked ill, but there was character and strength there, and an unshakeable determination. It was easy to see that the man was suffering: the jeans and shirt he wore were stained and torn, but in the way he held himself, Mirek guessed that the man had once been fit and strong.

"You say you've come to help me? Then who am I that you'd want to do that?"

Mirek was puzzled. "I think you're Zotov."

"Don't play with me. That's the name I've been given but who am I? If you're here to help you must know that."

Mirek felt the stirring of alarm. He was ill-prepared for the question. Zotov was Zotov. Now something else was emerging and it began to stink. This man had escaped from a hospital; Mirek began to perceive the kind of hospital it might have been. Zotov did not know who he really was and Mirek was convinced that Pascoe did not know either. Someone must know; someone in London. But right now London seemed a place he would never see again.

"I don't know what you mean." But Mirek was beginning to. "I was told to find a man called Zotov and to get him back to Warsaw and then to London."

"London?" Zotov stared unbelievingly. "England?"

"Yes. I'm English." Mirek watched the trigger finger tremble as Zotov became more confused. He prayed that Annya would have the sense to stay away. If Zotov heard anyone behind him he would fire.

Zotov began to tremble but managed to control himself just in time. "You can get us to Warsaw?"

"We can try. That's what we're here for."

"We?" Zotov backed away a little.

"A figure of speech. I have a car down the road." Mirek was angry at his slip; this man was alert.

Zotov shook his head slowly. "I don't trust you. I don't trust anyone. The last man to help me set a trap."

"I can't force you. It's up to you. If it helps I'm in as much trouble here as you are."

"You are now. I am holding the gun." Indecision was flitting over Zotov's face.

Mirek recognised that there was no way of convincing him. Zotov was being hounded and he would take no risks and he couldn't blame him. "I'm sorry. In your shoes I wouldn't trust anybody either."

Just then there was a loud growl from Pripy who suddenly leapt towards the road. There was a crashing in the undergrowth and Zotov, who had swung towards the direction of the dog, wheeled round again and raised the gun at Mirek who dived sideways as Zotov fired. He heard the roar of the gun and the violent swish of buckshot passing over him and then, as he hit the ground, another gun blasted off and from the corner of his eye he saw a bloodied Pripy limp back to collapse at Zotov's feet.

A great wail of anguish escaped from Zotov as he knelt beside the wounded dog. With tears streaming down his face he lifted his head and screamed at Mirek, "You've trapped me. You're like all the rest, you bastard." He groped for the gun which he had lowered beside Pripy, as two men with sub-machine guns burst into the clearing.

15

"Touch that gun and I'll kill you."

It was doubtful if Zotov heard and if he had it wouldn't have mattered. Pripy whined softly and Zotov put out a hand to comfort him. With loving care he lifted the dog into his arms knowing that there was little time left.

An acute silence enveloped the tragic little tableau for even the two airmen, immensely wary after what had happened to their comrades, felt some of the emotion that engulfed Zotov. The dog meant everything to him, the only creature he trusted, the only friend he had.

There was not a murmur anywhere. The giant trees stood as silent witnesses as the tears flooded unashamedly down Zotov's face. The two airmen were rooted, one with a gun aimed at Zotov and the other covering Mirek who still lay prone, his body angled towards Zotov. Everyone had their gaze on the weeping man and his faithful dog and everyone knew that the situation could not last. Only Zotov was unaware of what was happening outside the grief that consumed him.

The two gunmen glanced uneasily at each other. They should get on with the job, yet something prevented them from moving. Mirek, uncomfortable, yet not daring to move either, belatedly realised what they were all waiting for and why nobody wanted to intrude. And then, as the dog stopped nuzzling his master, it became clear that it had happened.

Pripy was dead; and Zotov's enormous grief touched everyone in the clearing. Oblivious of who was there or of any danger to himself, Zotov cuddled the dog like a baby, his head buried in its fur.

After a while one of the men said, "Put the dog down and stand up. Keep away from the gun." He could not see the pistol in Zotov's waistband as it was hidden by Pripy; even dead, the dog was helping his master.

At first Zotov did not hear but when the instruction was repeated in a shout, he stared up balefully through bloodshot eyes. Still holding Pripy he climbed shakily to his feet and stood swaying from the weight of the dog, the shotgun at his feet.

"Step away from the gun and put the dog down."

Zotov stepped away, unnaturally calm now, his face white. Mirek wanted to warn him but Zotov was on his own. He bent to place Pripy gently in the bracken and as he began to straighten he pulled out the pistol. He did it cleverly and unseen until the last moment when he raised it at the man he believed had killed the dog.

It was a battle Zotov could not win for he was already being covered by a sub-machine gun and it was impossible for him to aim and fire in the time it would take the airman to squeeze the trigger. Mirek could not watch and turned his head away.

There were only two shots and they sounded to Mirek like a hand-gun. He moved his head to see one of the airmen crashing to the ground almost in slow motion, a satisfied smile freezing on his face. Panic surged through Mirek as he realised what might have happened. The remaining gunman was about to fire at everything in sight and his first target was Zotov.

Zotov leaped to one side and fired as he moved but he missed badly as he slipped and fell, losing the gun as he did so. Seeing that Zotov was for the moment out of the action the airman swung round on Mirek who was trying to scramble to his feet. Mirek dropped like a brick knowing that he could not make it in time. With both men on the ground the airman turned back to Zotov and took deliberate aim. Again two shots rang out and the man fell to his knees his gun drooping in front of him. He glared at Zotov only then realising that the shots had not come from him. He keeled over, twitched once and was dead.

Mirek got up and ran towards Zotov who was groping for his pistol. Mirek managed to get a foot over it and struck Zotov on the chin as the Russian tried to rise. He then bent down to collect both the pistol and the shotgun. "Grab those subs," he bawled at Annya as she came slowly into the clearing, her gun still held out.

Zotov shook off the effect of Mirek's blow and crawled on his hands and knees towards Pripy; it was all that mattered to him now that the two airmen were dead. He sat beside the dog and appeared totally lost. The tiny, precarious world he had hacked out for himself had collapsed with the loss of his friend. He no longer had a life-line.

"Do you believe now that we've come to help you?" Mirek looked down at the distressed figure of Zotov who stared back blankly and said nothing. Mirek turned to Annya who had lowered her gun and appeared drained. "Don't let it get to you. You saved our lives. Make no mistake about that. You were bloody marvellous."

"It doesn't help," she replied. "It scares me, Mirek."

"Well, just consider how you would have felt if these bastards had croaked us. Think about it."

At the sound of a woman's voice speaking Polish, Zotov looked up. He met Annya's gaze.

"May I touch the dog?" asked Annya. "He was very brave. I would like to say goodbye to him."

Zotov was on the point of breakdown. Then he nodded with a quiet dignity and stroked Pripy's head.

Annya tucked her gun away. She crossed to where Zotov crouched and knelt beside him. She put her hand out to the dog, avoiding the area of bullet wounds, and laid it on the still warm fur. "You are privileged to have had such a faithful friend." The words sounded stilted to her but it was the right thing to say to Zotov who could do no more than nod almost imperceptibly. "Let me help you bury him."

Zotov looked startled; he did not want to part with the dog. He stared at Annya. She was the first woman he could recall who had not worn a nurse's uniform. And she was very attractive. She had also killed the men who had shot Pripy. He suddenly accepted that the job had to be done.

They had nothing with which to dig except the axe and finally, in spite of Zotov's protests, they had to settle for a large hollow in the bole of a tree and covered the dog with bracken and leaves. They stood in a little group to honour the dog and then turned away.

In a sudden burst of wild fury Zotov started to kick the two corpses as they lay tangled on the ground. Mirek and Annya made no attempt to stop him. When he had exhausted himself Zotov wept again, but quietly now. He started to look around in the bracken and Mirek guessed that he was searching for his weapons. To take his mind off them, Mirek asked, "Can you fly a helicopter?"

The question brought Zotov up sharp. "I don't know. I don't think so. I've been in prison for many years."

"We know. Let's try. We think we know where it landed. But we'll have to get a move on, those men will be expected to radio in a report. Someone will be looking for them."

"Then let's take the car. Help me uncover her."

As they drove back down the road Zotov said bluntly, "I don't trust you any more than the others. But you did save my life and for that I'll give you the benefit of the doubt. But why am I so important? Why is it everybody wants me? What have I done?"

"We don't know." Annya answered after a glance from Mirek. "We haven't been told. We were simply instructed to get you out. And we have placed ourselves in exactly the same position as you. Whatever happens to you if you're caught, will happen to us too."

From time to time Zotov glanced at Annya in the front passenger seat and each time he showed distress; she was sitting in Pripy's seat. It would be a long while before he got used to the dog's absence.

Only one helicopter had landed to one side of the road leaving barely enough room for passing traffic. The tree line receded considerably at this point although the road itself was no wider. The helicopter appeared incongruously large by the roadside but was, in fact, a light six-seater.

Zotov drove the Moskvich under cover of the trees and the three of them hurried back to the helicopter. They all climbed in with Zotov taking the pilot's seat. Mirek sat beside him with Annya behind. Zotov gazed round the cockpit at first with hope and finally with dismay. "It's no use," he said. "It's vaguely familiar but I can't do it."

There was no point in pushing him. Time was passing

and the second helicopter must be somewhere around. "Can you get it off the road? We must get it out of sight."

"I'll try. You two get out, it could all go wrong."

Mirek and Annya exchanged anxious glances.

"If I make a fool of myself I would rather do it alone," Zotov stressed.

They had to take a chance. Where could Zotov go even if he got the machine off the ground. They scrambled out and noticed Zotov's anguish as he studied the controls. They stood well back to avoid the down-draught of the rotor blades if they gyrated. But nothing moved and Mirek and Annya wondered if the aircrew had immobilised the machine in some way; flying helicopters was beyond either of them.

"He's flown one before," stated Mirek as they waited impatiently. "And he knows it. But it was too long ago and maybe it's all changed. Anyway, he's had the stuffing knocked out of him; they've brainwashed him to forget."

Annya gazed anxiously up and down the road. "We can't hang about like this."

As if agreeing Zotov suddenly climbed out. "It's no use. It won't come back if it was ever there at all."

"Does it have brakes?" It was a good question from Annya and Zotov immediately knew what she meant.

"You want me to lose my car as well as my dog?"

"Better than losing our lives. We've got a car. Bigger than yours. And it has Polish registration." Mirek had caught what was in their minds.

Zotov climbed back in and seconds later jumped out and ran to the Moskvich. He drove the car behind the helicopter and nosed under her until he made contact. He was lodged under the rising tail, the hood just touching the rear of the cabin. He put the Moskvich in low gear and slowly accelerated. Nothing happened except the engine strained and the roof of the car began to crumble.

Mirek and Annya ran forward and put their weight against the machine as Zotov accelerated again. They were on the point of giving up when the helicopter gradually moved forward and once it started it gathered a slow momentum. Mirek and Annya shouted encouragement and pushed as hard as they could. When it became clear that the car was coping with the load they grinned and waved, and for the first time since escaping from Pripyat Zotov felt a kind of comradeship, enough to allow him to smile and wave back.

The helicopter would only go so far; once it reached the rough ground it began to resist, but Zotov had pushed it well clear of the road and quite close to the tree line before it angled over and dipped into a shallow gulley on the starboard side to break one of the rotor blades against a tree.

Mirek and Annya ran forward as Zotov climbed out. There was no point in trying to extricate the Moskvich which had buckled under the strain. Zotov hastily pulled out the supplies he had in the rear of the car and bundled them into the brush to be picked up later. As Mirek and Annya helped him the sound they had all been dreading reached them first as a low drone. The second helicopter was approaching.

With Zotov using his axe they rushed to cover both car and helicopter with anything they could find; branches, leaves, peat clods, they all went cascading over the machines as fast as they could be found. Spurred by the increasing noise of the second helicopter they worked furiously to complete the job and when they were satisfied they dived into the trees and hoped they had done the job sufficiently well.

The thudding was almost deafening now and they judged that the machine was following the road and was keeping just above the trees. Leaves and bracken blew into their faces as the helicopter hovered over the wide space. They thought it was going to land in front of them and Mirek handed back Zotov's two guns. The rough camouflage they had erected began to move and looked in danger of blowing off, but it held and the helicopter rose and then went south.

The three waited until the drone had noticeably decreased, then climbed from their cover and hastened down the road. They had roughly covered the bodies of the two dead airmen before leaving but in any event they were in a clearing far too small for a helicopter to land. While they hurried to cover the distance back they could still hear the chopper as it searched.

They reached the clearing, breathless and still anxious. They must get away from the scene as fast as they could. There was no time for remorse, no time for any feelings at all. They dragged the two corpses well into the woods and covered them up again.

The drone was approaching again and they were all tense. If the crew of the second machine was suspicious they would radio for help and they must get away before then. They hurried back to the Zis. Mirek took the wheel with Zotov beside him and Annya in the rear seat. Circumstances had forced them to co-operate but trust was another matter.

As Mirek drove back in the direction of the Polish border he could not be sure that their car had not been seen under the trees. The whole operation had been innovative and there were too many flaws. They had barely covered half a mile when suddenly the second helicopter swooped over their heads, and then it rose just in front of them to avoid the trees. It disappeared round a curve of road and Mirek braked sharply. "Quick, Zotov. Change places with Annya and keep down on the floor."

The change took only seconds and Mirek drove on again. He knew that he wouldn't get far and he was right. As he came round the bend on to the straight stretch the helicopter was lowering itself gently on to almost the identical spot that the first machine had used. It would be a mistake to try to go round it, although there was room; Mirek braked slowly and climbed out as the rotor blades limped to a halt. The pilot climbed out just after and came towards Mirek with a taut face and a gun in his hand.

Yelena Belenko was at screaming point. She had to remind herself again and again of the danger she was in and why she must remain in a makeshift billet. There was space enough, much more than in her apartment back in Moscow, but it was bare and unpainted and desolate. The stark nature of the rooms was enough to depress a person used to the privilege of reasonable freedom; a celebrity. She had nobody to speak to, to complain to. The radio was on but she spoke little Polish and couldn't understand much of what was being said. The music was different but she found it depressing.

She had spent two nights in the safe house and there had been no sign of Maria. The lack of communication was one of her worst problems; not knowing what was happening outside. At night the whole area was deathly quiet except when the wind was up as it had been the first night. The wind found every crevice and crack in the old building and strange, eerie sounds resulted and draughts crept from every corner.

During the day she occupied herself with a broom and brush and dustpan to clean the place through. It was work to which she was not accustomed and she hated it, but it filled in time. She did ballet exercises by the wall furthest from the window but there was no bar. Finally she knew that, whatever the risks, she would have to get out for a spell. She was not conditioned to lead a life of lonely incarceration.

At 11.30 that night she donned a headscarf and a small jacket which Maria had provided, gazed around the apartment and turned off the gas lamps to save fuel. There were two emergency flashlights in the apartment and she carried the smaller, little more than a pencil torch. She took the set of keys which was kept under the mattress, locked the door behind her and crept down the stairs following the narrow beam. She reached the lower hall and kept the torch low so that it would not shine through the door cracks.

She put her ear to the door trying to pick up outside noises but there were none; the only sound was her own movement. She was scared now and almost turned back. She switched off the flashlight as she located the keyhole and the total darkness scared her more; but she had come far enough to be prompted to go on. She turned the heavy lock, waited, and then gradually opened the door. Cold air came in like an icy warning.

She peered in each direction but could see little except a solitary street lamp glowing forlornly at the junction where the youngsters had played when she had first arrived. She closed and locked the door and stood for a while shivering and lonely and afraid. After a while she walked slowly towards the nearest corner, and on reaching it turned round it. The action was like some massive adventure.

At this time of night this old industrial area was deserted and blank factory walls offered no comfort. She did not know where she was going and she knew that it would be stupid to wander too far but the actual freedom of walking outside became exhilarating.

Ahead of her, to the north, was the glow of the city caressing the low clouds with a pastel wash. The symbol of life was too distant, out of reach, and it heightened her solitude. She would never be able to join in under the city lights, never be able to meet people in normal conditions; not while she was here in Poland. She was an outcast, a fugitive and her stolen freedom was an illusion to remind her, much more than the rooms had done, of what was now beyond her grasp.

Yelena clasped her jacket at the collar. She shivered but not from cold. She could see no future. She was stalking the streets in a dilapidated part of a foreign city she did not know, and she felt like a criminal. Yet she had committed no crime except to fall in love and that was so long ago. Something jumped from a wall in front of her and she stopped. It was probably only a cat but it startled her. She swung round to see if anything was at her rear. Suddenly she was highly nervous.

There was a car somewhere and quite close but it was difficult to pinpoint direction. She decided to turn back. She had come from confinement to a prison of another kind; there was no freedom out here. She stopped suddenly, thinking that she had heard someone else's footsteps, and realised she was beginning to panic. By the time she reached the door she was thoroughly frightened.

She opened the door locking up behind her and hastened into the dingy hall. She was relieved and surprised that this shabby and smelly place could give her any comfort at all, but she was glad to be back. She mounted the stairs and used the pencil torch to find her way. Her legs were shaky and, halfway up, she rested. She completed the climb and waited on the upper landing to get her breath back. She was home. Home. She could have sobbed or laughed but she managed to avoid doing either. Her hand was shaking as she fumbled for the key. On the point of inserting it in the lock she suddenly stopped, just avoiding making contact with the door.

Yelena pulled her hand away quickly and almost dropped the key. As she looked down she was sure she could see a light underneath the door. A draught excluder had been tacked on to the door to avoid light escaping but when she looked again she was convinced that it was light she saw. She turned off her flashlight and waited. Just the thinnest strip of light was visible. She knew for certain that she had put the lamps out before leaving. Who was in there?

She stood in the darkness wondering what best to do. There was nowhere to flee to and she couldn't remain indefinitely on the landing. New situations were being flung at her one after another and she felt unable to cope. Life had changed out of all recognition and in so short a time. The pitch black of the landing added to her rising panic and she switched on the flashlight again. After a while, nerves stretched, she decided to go in.

She inserted the key as quietly as she could and turned the well-oiled tumblers; whoever was in there must have locked the door on the inside and that meant they must have keys. Suddenly she began to think more logically, quelling her fears and flinging the door wide open. She closed it behind her quickly and stood with her back to it, relief spreading through her.

Maria Janesky rose slowly from the chair and shouted, "Just where the devil have you been?"

The next moment the two women were embracing, each shedding the different fears which had seized them. At the same time Yelena admitted and at last accepted her prison as a place of safety whatever privations it entailed. She believed too that she had finally discovered her limitations.

Aleksei Chernov was not slow to notice the change of attitude in his old subordinate, Borya Kanavsky. Kanavsky tried to hide it, of course; he still feared Chernov but his respect was waning. Also Chernov's official retirement was coming ever closer and Kanavsky was more often weighing the effect his association with Chernov might have on his new chief, General Zhadin, when Chernov had finally gone.

Another matter was also worrying Kanavsky. So far he had failed to produce Zotov who seemed to be losing his men and machines at a ridiculously fast rate. The losses themselves were deeply worrying but more so was the result his failure might have on his career when Chernov was no longer there.

What at first seemed an almost contemptuously easy job had turned into a nightmare. An escapee from a mental institution was making rings round them even allowing for the ridiculously restricted workforce available to him. Even without the restrictions, and the problems of a radiation area, in truth he should have needed nothing more. And yet, so far as he knew, Zotov was still alive and very much kicking.

Kanavsky was fed up with taking the blame for every failed attempt to capture Zotov. What also niggled him was the secrecy. As the search continued and more men and machines were destroyed it became increasingly obvious that the importance of capturing Zotov was certainly no triviality, yet he knew no more about Zotov now than he had at the beginning.

When Kanavsky was summoned to Zhadin's office he expected trouble. He knew that it would be about Zotov and he felt far less protective of Chernov than at the outset. He knocked anxiously on the door and waited for the call to enter.

It was Chernov's old office, of course, and Kanavsky knew it well. Little had changed for Zhadin's time had been limited since taking up his new post. But Kanavsky had no doubt that the whole décor would be changed the moment Chernov went for good. It was a measure of Chernov's power over so many years that his influence could still be felt around the massive complex, even by his successor.

Kanavsky stood to attention in front of the massive desk behind which sat the new Chairman of the KGB. Zhadin immediately put Kanavsky at ease, motioning him to a chair and pushing across a box of Cuban cigars which the Colonel declined. Kanavsky decided that he did not need fattening up but he was soon to discover that Zhadin's methods, although direct, were not so crude as Chernov's.

"I want an up-to-date report on the Zotov affair."

It was straight to the point and Kanavsky held nothing back. As he spoke he realised that his openness with his new chief was an admission of Chernov's waning influence.

When Kanavsky had finished Zhadin nodded in quite a friendly way. "I'm glad you've decided to give me the complete picture, Colonel. What you have reported is confirmed by what I already know."

Kanavsky controlled his satisfaction; Zhadin must have been in direct touch with Penovitch, the field man in Kiev whom he had promoted to Major. He was relieved that he no longer felt the need to protect Chernov.

"Did Comrade Chernov offer you promotion for your co-operation, Colonel?"

Kanavsky realised he was not yet off the hook. "He promised to recommend me for promotion, sir."

Zhadin waved a hand dismissively. "It wouldn't have helped you; he is in no position to make such recommendations. On the other hand I can give you promotion without reference. Think about it, Colonel. Think about what might happen when the good General has left us. Now tell me what you know about Zotov himself. What's the mystery surrounding him? What has Chernov told you?"

"I know nothing and have been told nothing, Comrade General."

Zhadin stared steadily across the desk, his dark eyes slightly shuttered. For the first time he showed a touch of annoyance. "Nothing, Colonel? You are one of General Chernov's men, have been close to him for many years. Are you saying that you know nothing at all about this man Zotov?"

Kanavsky suddenly felt as if he was tied to the chair. "The General has told me nothing at all. It is part of my frustration that I don't know why I am trying to find the man."

"But you must have suspicions."

Kanavsky shook his head. "I know that Zotov escaped from the institution near Pripyat. That is my sole knowledge." As he noticed Zhadin's features harden he added, "I no longer believe that the man is merely an escapee. If he were, we would not be going to the present extremes of risking our people. I certainly think there is more to Zotov than there appears to be."

Zhadin did not speak for some time and the silence became uneasy between them. Zhadin looked up. "Is the General in his office now?"

"He was about an hour ago. He is there most of the time, sir."

"Tell him I want to see him."

Kanavsky rose, gave a small bow and left feeling Zhadin's gaze on him all the way to the door. The meeting had gone better than he could have expected; no undue pressure had been put on him. He went down to the floor below and approached Chernov's office. He knocked and waited. When there was no reply he knocked again and eventually opened the door.

Chernov was not there. Kanavsky advanced towards the small desk worried without knowing why. There could be many reasons why Chernov should not be at his desk, but Kanavsky suffered a nasty, intuitive feeling. Something was wrong. When he stared at the desk he noticed how tidy it was, as if Chernov had gone home for the day, but his chief usually rang through to let Kanavsky know when he was leaving so that relevant news could then be relayed to his home.

Kanavsky picked up the desk intercom and asked to be put through to Zhadin. He explained that Chernov was no longer in his office.

Zhadin picked up the nuance of doubt that was in Kanavsky's mind. "Even General Chernov must answer the calls of nature, Colonel, so why do you sound so concerned?"

Kanavsky did not know. An hour later, at Zhadin's insistence that he find Chernov, he had his answer. Chernov had gone; he had booked a flight to Warsaw and when Kanavsky checked the departure he discovered that the flight had already left.

Kanavsky personally reported the fact to Zhadin who became thoughtfully quiet. Then he stared at Kanavsky as if accusing him and asked, "Why do you think he has gone to Warsaw, Colonel?"

Why? It was obvious. Chernov was satisfied that Zotov was heading that way. And in Warsaw he could muster all the aid he had been unable to arrange on his home soil. Having set up Polish security Chernov considered it his own. He was going to do what he had wanted to do at the outset: personally take charge of the search, without interference or restriction of any kind from Zhadin whom he detested and distrusted. Chernov had at last got the bit between his teeth and Zotov's days were numbered. "I don't know, Comrade General."

"That's a pity, Colonel. It's also the first time today that you have lied to me. Dismiss."

When a chastened Kanavsky had gone, Zhadin pressed a button on his intercom. "Arrange a meeting for me with Secretary-General Gorbachev as soon as possible. It is a matter of extreme urgency."

16

Mirek climbed out stiffly and walked slowly towards the airman with the gun. "Do you think you need that thing?" He was capable of speaking better Russian but his bad accent and hesitant words made the airman concentrate on understanding him.

"Have you anyone in the car with you?"

Both men had stopped about halfway between the helicopter and the car. "Yes, of course." Mirek turned and pointed. "My girlfriend."

"Anybody else?"

"Just the two of us. Why? Is something wrong?" Mirek was delaying his replies as if having difficulty in understanding the questions. "You want to look?"

"In a moment. First I want to know where you are going? And where you have come from."

Mirek produced his passport. "We're going to Moscow and we've come from Brest." He moved to one side and when the passport was handed back to him the man made a slight turn too, so that he faced Mirek better. It was a move that might make all the difference for at the edge of the forest behind the man's back was the camouflaged helicopter and the Moskvich.

"From Brest? To Moscow on this road? You had better explain."

The second airman was still in the helicopter although Mirek noticed that he was watching them closely. Mirek prayed that he would continue to watch them and not let his gaze wander to the tree line. "We took the wrong turning. We missed the signs and took the Kiev road instead of the one for Moscow."

"It's taken you a long time to find out."

"Our Russian isn't good. As you see, we are Poles. It

wasn't until we saw a sign for Kovel that we had serious doubts. We pulled in to study the map and realised our stupid mistake. We've enough fuel to get us back to Brest. We'll stay the night there."

The airman turned round and repeated to his comrade what Mirek had said. Both men laughed. "My colleague says you need a good navigator."

"Oh, my girlfriend is hopeless," agreed Mirek.

"He also says he saw you on the way down."

"Good for him."

"Which is why we stopped you; your movements didn't make sense. Have you seen a lone man in a red Moskvich on this stretch?"

Mirek appeared to consider it. "No. We've seen an army convoy and a black Zis. Maybe one or two other cars. Nothing red. To be honest we've been too tied up with our own problems."

The airman walked slowly towards the car, his gun now hanging at his side. Mirek shot a signal to Annya but she did not need it. She climbed out showing a degree of leg without overdoing it. The airman was certainly distracted but he walked slowly round the car poking his head in and noticing the stuff piled on the rear seat which had spilled over the floor while Mirek and Annya tried to stay calm.

"You want me to open the trunk of the car?" asked Mirek when he thought the airman was taking too long.

"No. Have you seen another helicopter?"

"Earlier on. I saw two. I suppose one was yours."

"You haven't heard another one since?"

"It's difficult to tell in a car unless one is very close by. Our engine is quite noisy."

The airman shrugged. "I'll make room for you to pass." He walked back to his machine and Mirek and Annya turned towards the car, unable to watch him as he drew level with the area where the other machine and the car were untidily hidden. The rotor blades started to turn and the airman ran forward to avoid the worst of the down-draught.

Mirek and Annya sat in their car deafened by the slowly rising helicopter. They made no move to go forward until the chopper had risen well above them and the barrage of loose leaves began to die down. The rough camouflage they had erected still held good but they could now see a splash of red from the Moskvich. When the noise had subsided and the helicopter had headed south, Mirek eased the car forward.

Annya leaned over the back seat and said, "You can come out now; they've gone."

There was no response so Annya raised her voice. Still there was no reaction from Zotov. Annya leaned over and prodded the pile of clothes heaped on the floor in front of the back seat. There seemed to be nothing underneath them. Growing frantic she knelt on her seat so that she could reach right over and pull the clothes away. "Oh, my God," she burst out. "He's gone."

Mirek braked. "Gone? What the hell do you mean?"

"I mean he's not here, for God's sake. He must have climbed out." Annya slid back on to her seat. "After all that. Damn the man. You'd better not stop, Mirek; that chopper might still be around."

Mirek had already slowed down. "Maybe he's in the trunk." As he pulled up in spite of Annya's warnings, he knew that he was wasting his time. He had to make sure and when he had opened the trunk he gazed round in frustration. Annya had killed two Russians in an attempt to rescue Zotov. It had all been in vain. He climbed in the front and realised how she must be feeling. "Forget him," he said bitterly. "We've got enough problems. We dare not go back for the supplies he off-loaded from the Moskvich but I think we've enough of our own." But he was deeply angry, on behalf of Annya, and because they had actually found Zotov only to lose him. It was a bitter pill to swallow after doing so much and believing that they might have won Zotov's trust.

Victor Belenko stared at the rough walls and began to burble to himself. Apart from the prison guards he had seen nobody for days. He was not in an isolation cell, but he might just as well be. He saw none of the other prisoners and was allowed no exercise. He had been confined to a cell for a reason he did not know, but suspected it to be connected with his wife Yelena. He had no idea what she might have done to get him into this mess but his hatred of her grew by the minute.

The marriage had been in name only for some time now but he could never forgive her for being responsible for reducing him to this. He believed, with some justification, that he had been forgotten and that there was no way that he would ever get out of this filthy cell. Since the earlier interest in him, Chernov seemed to have deserted him completely, for he had not seen the old KGB chief for days. When he demanded to speak to Chernov his pleas were ignored; Chernov was a law unto himself, he did not have to give anyone a reason why the pianist was there.

If anything happened to Chernov, a heart attack, anything at all, Belenko could see himself dying in this cell, an incoherent derelict who had lost his mind. Why was he thinking like this? He gazed to where the dummy keyboard rested against the wall; he hadn't touched it since it had arrived. How could one practise in such squalor? He suddenly started to pray for Chernov's good health. With him there seemed to be little hope, but without him, there was no hope at all.

General Gruszka greeted Chernov like a long lost brother. The two men embraced, repeatedly kissed each other on the cheek, and the affection on both sides appeared to be deep and genuine. Gruszka waved Chernov to a chair. For a while they discussed the horrors of Chernobyl and then Gruszka said, "You should have given me more warning; I'd have put out the red carpet. Retirement sits on you well, Aleksei."

Chernov lowered his bulk to a chair and smiled wryly. "I don't want to attract attention to my visit. And I'm not retired, Lech; not just yet."

Gruszka looked surprised. "But Zhadin is already in office, surely?"

"Oh, yes. But officially, I have still a week or so before my retirement is complete. Rather than waste it on leave, which was boring me to death, I decided, with Zhadin's agreement, to fill in the remaining days doing odd jobs, just to keep my hand in and to fill in the time in a way I best understand. It's not easy to retire after so long in the service. Thirty-five years, Lech. A long time."

"So you've called to say goodbye to old friends? That's nice." Gruszka's bonhomie easily matched Chernov's but behind the smile he was groping for possible reasons why the old KGB chief was here. Chernov was not the type to waste time just visiting old friends.

Chernov gazed round. In spite of his high rank Gruszka's office reflected the serious economic plight of his homeland; it needed redecorating and the furniture was verging on the shabby.

"You want to take in a show while you're here? Maria Janesky is singing at the Opera House."

Chernov inclined his head. "There's one small job you can help me with first." He told Gruszka as much about Zotov as he had told Kanavsky.

"But you asked us to look for this man when you signalled me from Moscow. And I took action on that. The frontier is already under surveillance."

"I knew I could rely on you. It's just possible that he may have slipped through. This is no longer a routine search; this man is dangerous in ways I will explain later. He has to be found."

"So it's not really such a small job?"

Chernov smiled. "No. I shouldn't have tried to fool you of all people. We must find him, Lech. He could be in any hole."

"If we find him what do you want done with him?"

"I'll take him back with me." Chernov shrugged and the chair groaned. He chuckled. "It will be my last job. I'll go out with a whimper, Lech, not the big bang I always dreamed of. But that's life."

Unlike Kanavsky, Gruszka did not believe Chernov from the outset, and ironically that was largely due to Chernov's own teaching. Chernov would never visit Poland on so flimsy an issue. "If he's already in Poland, finding him will be much more difficult."

"But you can do it just the same?" The smile did not hide the sharp edge to Chernov's question.

Gruszka noticed the change and it merely confirmed his first suspicions; there was much more to Zotov than had been explained. "I can give it priority. For an old and valued friend, I could do nothing else." As he gave the assurance he was thinking of the new man, Zhadin; he had no intention of falling foul of him so soon. Meanwhile it would do no harm to placate Chernov. He had to admit though, that Chernov's interest in the escapee, Zotov, intrigued him. He was sure there was an important story here and he wanted to know about it. Chernov had taught him well; none of these doubts, however, showed themselves on his pale, and almost hungry features.

"Good. Can you fix me a hotel? I don't know how long I'll be staying. Until we find Zotov, I suppose. And how is your dear wife?"

Mirek was reluctant to travel on in spite of Annya's insistence on the risk of staying. The helicopter was likely to keep a distant eye on them if for no other reason than there was little other traffic about. By now the radiation cloud was probably well clear of Belorussia but travellers would not be sure of this, so any roads heading towards Kiev, which entailed passing near to the blown reactor, were largely clear.

"Get going, Mirek. Don't make things worse for us." Annya was showing strain.

Reluctantly, Mirek started up again and drove on. He had gone no more than two hundred yards when Annya called out, "There he is. My God, he's waiting for us."

Zotov was tucked into the backcloth of the tree line so that he could disappear instantly if need be. When he saw the car he stepped towards the road and waved.

Mirek pulled over and Zotov climbed into the back. "I hope I didn't frighten you," he said as Mirek drove on. "I knew they would look into the car, and that if I was there they would have found me. I slipped out when you were walking towards the airman. It was only half-a-mile through the woods."

"You might have warned us," Mirek retorted. "We could have missed you."

"It was a question of judgement. It worked, didn't it?"

"All we have to do now is to cross the border with two security services searching for you. You are important, Zotov. If you ever remember why, perhaps you will be good enough to tell us. It would be nice to know why Annya and I are risking our necks for you."

They slept rough away from the road a few miles from Brest. It would be far too risky to book in at a hotel. Crossing the border was going to be a major problem, the more so as the Polish UB were certain to have taken special precautions to make sure that Zotov did not get through.

In the middle of the night Zotov started to whimper and then he screamed. Woken from an uneasy sleep on the rough ground, Mirek and Annya crawled over to him. Clearly suffering a terrible nightmare, they did not know whether to rouse him or not. Finally they decided they must, if only to keep the noise down as his screams penetrated the night.

Annya shook him gently and he began to struggle. Mirek tried to pin down his arms while Annya whispered reassurances in his ear. Suddenly he sat upright and shook as if in a fever. Sweat was pouring off him.

"Zotov; it's all right. You're with friends."

Zotov's eyes opened wide and he stared wildly without seeing them; at that moment he appeared insane. Then his gaze switched to Annya who was still trying to comfort him with soft talk. He closed his eyes and threw his arms round her murmuring, "Yelena, Yelena", over and over again.

Zotov's desperate, clutching arms forced the wind out of Annya but she made no effort to free herself. Gradually he relaxed and after a while was sleeping soundly in her arms, his breathing normal. "Help me lower him," she whispered to Mirek. "Carefully."

When they laid him down again Annya gently dried his face. They stayed until certain that he was all right, and then crept back to their places. "Poor bastard!" Mirek said. "What sort of nightmare could that have been?"

"I don't think it was due solely to drug withdrawal. He was suffering terror. Of what?"

When it was time to rise Zotov was the first up. He looked shaken and tired but active as he prepared food for them from the few supplies Mirek and Annya had brought with them. When they were eating he asked uneasily, "Did I wake you in the night?"

"You had a bit of a nightmare." Mirek grinned. "It didn't seem to last long."

Annya said casually, "Who's Yelena? It's a pretty name."

"Yelena?" Zotov was puzzled. "Yelena. The only women I knew were the nurses and doctors at the hospital. None that I remember were called that."

"Maybe she's from your distant past. You were calling out for her in the night."

Zotov stared at Annya, his eyes haunted. For a moment she was sorry she had mentioned it, but then she saw that he wanted to remember.

"Don't worry," she said. "It means that your subconscious is working. It will come eventually. Don't try too hard."

Zotov stared at her. "But will I want to know? Will I want to know anything about my past? Perhaps it's too ghastly to stand. Perhaps that's why they drugged me and blotted out my memory." Not only did Zotov not know who he was, he was worried that the drugs might have done irreparable damage to his mind.

He had another concern; so far none of them had come up with a formula for escape. The border was well protected for a long way on both sides of the formal control area. Even if they managed to avoid the guards by taking a circuitous route, it would have to be done on foot and transport would be needed on the other side. It was necessary to find a way through border control itself, and to do that it was vital to go into the town, where the real dangers began.

They set off about mid-morning, as too early a start might draw attention, and took the first available turn-off on the fringe of Brest that was routed towards Moscow. Once on that road, they covered a few miles before heading back to the old port, but coming now from the Moscow direction.

Traffic heading for the border was heavy and slowed to

walking pace with frequent halts. Customs were always slow but never as slow as this. Word passed down the line that every vehicle was being examined. Zotov had no papers; to hide on the floor as he had done before would be futile. Mirek drew out of line before it got too dense; nearer to the Customs area trucks and cars were nose to tail.

Even to drink at a café was risky so Mirek stopped near a small bar and took drinks to the car, parked just down the street. As they sat and sipped coffee from paper cups the function of the river port began to unfold as trucks loaded with timber, bales of cotton and engineering parts, rumbled past. The old town seemed cramped and hustling and dusty and noisy. Melancholy cloyed the streets like poisonous fog, the effect of the Chernobyl calamity now part of everyone's dialogue. Life and movement went on but the brooding was almost tangible.

As the day wore on and no solution was reached, despair began to show. The car had become their home and the cramped quarters were depressing them. Finally Annya decided to take Zotov to a small café for a meal and Mirek stayed in the car until they had finished and then went to eat on his own.

It was while Mirek was having his meal that he picked up a Polish newspaper which had been left on one of the chairs. The front page was still full of Chernobyl but he was searching for news of Waleski. He found nothing. Could it mean that the body had not been found? Or were the Polish UB playing a waiting game? He did find something though, and it was shattering. The item was on a centre page. Ian Pascoe was being deported from Poland on charges of spying. It was a severe blow. If they were ever to reach Warsaw, Mirek knew that they would have to lean heavily on Pascoe to help get them out.

It was not just a matter of getting Zotov over the border, although that was tough enough; there was the strong possibility that Annya, and perhaps himself, were wanted for murder. He left what remained of the meal, drained his coffee, and went back to the car. Annya noticed the change in him.

"Something wrong?"

"Pascoe's been kicked out of Poland."

Annya was silent for a while; Pascoe was British and meant more to Mirek than to her. "We have people who can help. They know the lie of the land much better than he does."

"It's not just Poland we're concerned with. We've also got to get through East Germany. Pascoe could have laid a trail of contacts right through."

They were speaking in rapid Polish, and Zotov, on the rear seat, could not understand. "What's going on?" he demanded.

Annya turned. "A contact we have in Warsaw has been deported. Mirek read it in a newspaper in the café. It's a blow but not the end of the world."

Zotov said thoughtfully, "It might be better for everyone if I slipped away and took my chances. You would have no problem then."

They did not disillusion him; it was better he did not know the other problems. Neither replied and Mirek suddenly drove off. He found parking space as near to the Customs' control as he could. "Stay there, I'll see what I can find out."

Neither Mirek or Annya wanted to leave Zotov alone at any time. While he was with one of them there was less chance of his detection but it also meant that they had constant sight of him.

Mirek eased through the long line of vehicles waiting to cross the border. From the Russian side it was usually quicker to enter Poland than the other way round. At the moment it appeared to be impossible although traffic was coming steadily from the Polish side. The queue was much longer now and truck drivers had left their cabs to saunter up and down the line to talk or to find old friends. The smell of diesel and oil was strong in the air.

He walked down the line. Many of the bigger trucks were enclosed and those that had open backs, in the main, had their cargoes covered with tarpaulin sheets roped down. It was the searching of these that was taking the time. Down by the Customs post itself was a huge parking area where drivers who failed to cross that evening could sleep the night in their trucks. The truck crews wore the universal resignedness of drivers the world over; they were used to delays; if it wasn't some sort of search then it was something else. Some played cards in small groups, some dozed, others talked.

There were not an unusual number of border guards and only a sprinkling of police, so it was difficult to understand why there was such a delay. They would be searching for Zotov, of course, but it seemed to Mirek that the build-up of security, and the infuriating delays, were being caused on the Polish, not the Russian side.

As he edged towards the Customs building he heard a commotion. And then, unbelievingly, he saw Russian officials shouting and gesticulating at their Polish counterparts the other side of the border. Whether they were heard or not he could not decide but, in any event, it made no difference to the Poles who were clearly working on instructions from a higher authority. The Russians were furious at the delays.

This puzzled Mirek; Zotov had escaped in Russia and the Russians were looking for him. But it appeared that only a limited number of Russians were involved. It was the Poles who appeared to have been delegated for the job.

He had a few words with a group of Polish truck drivers but learned no more before returning to the car. He gave Annya and Zotov his impressions. "I don't think we'd have much trouble getting through the Russian side; it's the Poles who are causing the trouble."

Zotov had no explanation; he could see the truth of it but that merely added to his frustration.

They camped out of town for two days, coming in each day to review the situation. The queues had grown longer, the parking yard was overflowing, and the complaints were being much more loudly voiced. Some of the murmuring was ugly. Everybody knew that an escapee was being sought; it was common knowledge. The waiting game was becoming nerve-racking. During this time they reconnoitred the banks of the river Bug where ran the border with Poland.

River traffic was no less delayed than that by road. Cargo

vessels were bow to stern and a central lane was difficult to keep open. Mirek, Annya and Zotov, though, decided that the river might be their better chance; if things would only cool down a little. The problems of using the river were considerable, but the opportunities more variable. But there was one problem to which, as yet, they did not know the answer; Zotov did not know whether or not he could swim. As matters stood, they were trapped.

In Warsaw too the pressure was mounting and the tension in General Gruszka's office high. He was being assailed from two sides to both of which he owed loyalty. On the one hand he was trying to help the man who had placed him where he was; on the other, he was being pressured by General Zhadin in Moscow.

The Russian Custom and Immigration officials had bitterly complained of the hold-up at Brest. Some of the trucks going through contained perishable goods and deterioration had already started. At least, that was the assertion. Zhadin had telephoned Gruszka direct; he wanted Zotov found but he wanted the delays to ease up. For his part Zhadin would see to it that help on the Soviet side of the border was strengthened. Meanwhile trucks that were obviously secure, those that were enclosed and had locks on the loading doors, were to be let through unless there was reason for suspicion. That would at least get rid of much of the backlog.

Zhadin also made it clear that he wanted to be notified immediately if Zotov was found and apprehended. Gruszka was under no illusion; Zhadin was his new boss whatever autonomy Chernov had ostensibly been granted.

The moment Chernov arrived Gruszka knew that trouble would follow. He ran his hands over his tired, pinched features and then smoothed down his thinning hair. He looked almost ill; problems were bad enough at home without being pig-in-the-middle between two KGB bosses. He had to decide which side his bread was buttered, and plumped for the future.

Chernov made his daily visit about mid-morning. Gruszka

decided to tell him about the call from Zhadin. The moon-faced Chernov roared with laughter and was almost convincing as he lowered his bulk on to the chair best suited to take his weight. "Joseph Zhadin resents me handling this piddling affair; it goes way back before his time." He raised his hands in surrender. "Do what he wants, Lech. Don't compromise yourself, old friend. Just let me know when you have Zotov. That's all I ask. Then I'll get out of your hair."

Gruszka watched the smiling Chernov uneasily. And then gradually and almost painfully, the seed of an idea pricked his mind and he saw a possible way of getting both Zhadin and Chernov off his back; at least for a while. Enough to give him breathing space.

"I think I'll go down to Brest and supervise things myself," he said.

"I'll come with you," said Chernov, suddenly losing his smile.

"No, Aleksei. Your presence would confuse them. And some would wonder why you were not on the other side of the border. It's best you stay here or go back to Moscow."

A few weeks ago Gruszka would not have dared speak like that to Chernov, whose expression endorsed the thought. But Gruszka had chosen his moment well; he knew Chernov would not argue.

"A fast car will get me there tonight."

Mirek, Annya and Zotov drove out of Brest for the last time. They camped as usual well off the road in some sparse woods which backed on to farmland. They had topped up with petrol and oil and Mirek did a servicing on the car. Nothing had improved at the border so they decided to attempt to cross the next day. Annya would go alone in the car, and Mirek and Zotov would go by river. They had a crude plan which would be slowed down if it turned out Zotov could not swim; but in his courageous way, he agreed to try.

By this time they were so weary from waiting that they sometimes wondered if they were not giving up in a roundabout sort of way. But they all knew they had to try.

Secretly, not one of them held out real hope. Annya was likely to get through but she had no idea what might be waiting for her once she touched Polish soil; the dead Waleski had returned very potently to her mind. However, they each kept their fears to themselves.

17

Mirek, Annya and Zotov returned to Brest the next afternoon. The town was buzzing. Rumours were rife. Some said the escapee had been captured, others that the General Secretary of the Polish Communist Party himself had come to sort out the delays. The talk was mostly contradictory, but there was a general feeling of important developments taking place, and some of the bigger trucks had been allowed through. Mirek noticed a line of army trucks down by the docks, and near the Customs area far more Russian troops were on view.

Mirek drove out of town to the east and noted that road patrols had increased considerably, while jeep loads of troops were now a regular feature. He turned off on to a rough lane which led towards the river, cutting through woods and then on to more open ground. He pulled in and he and Zotov quickly climbed out. They had already arranged to meet Annya at a filling station some three miles the other side of the border. As the two men waved her goodbye and wished her luck, there were tears in her eyes. Then she backed carefully over the rough ground, straightened out and drove off. Mirek turned his head away. As the car disappeared, Zotov observed, "She loves you. You were harsh on her."

"I know," said Mirek. "But it would have been much harsher on her chance of escaping if I had let her stay with us."

But Zotov had surprised himself with his observation. He recognised love, which had stirred something in him; like so often now.

They chose a spot where it was easy to slip down a gorse-covered bank. The spring grass was pushing through and there was plenty of protection provided they were not careless. They were not too concerned about the patrols, for they were clear of the road, but they might easily be seen from the river.

They crawled behind some bushes and tried to get comfortable. Below them was a string of three barges, two carrying timber and another with bales of cotton. At the stern of the last barge a skiff rocked gently on the end of a mooring rope; fore and aft were covered with canvas.

"We'll have to wait till it's dark," Mirek said. "You sure you don't mind going in the water?"

Zotov shook his head and smiled wryly. "Something tells me I can swim. I'm not afraid."

Mirek smiled back. "I know you're not." It was difficult to imagine what Zotov had suffered all those years, and was still suffering as a result. It was incredible that he had come this far with so much against him.

Zotov had his head turned away. At first Mirek thought he hadn't heard him, then suddenly he realised that Zotov was crying. He put a hand out, but stopped before he touched the Russian. This was private grief.

Zotov covered his eyes, then wiped them slowly. "I'm sorry," he said shakily. "You see, I'm not such a strong man as you think."

"I wouldn't have survived what you have. You have nothing to apologise for."

"It's Pripy. The dog. He did so much for me and wanted nothing in return but affection. It was so easy for me to give him that. And those bastards killed him. I miss him, Mirek."

There was nothing to say; no reassurance to offer, and condolence would have been shabbily hollow. Mirek turned to face the river. After a while, without looking back, he said, "As soon as it's dark we'll slip into the water and make for that skiff. If you find yourself sinking just do what I tell you and trust me."

"I'm beginning to trust you; it's not easy for me to trust anyone. Don't worry; we'll reach the skiff."

They had eaten earlier in the day, and had brought no food and water with them in order to travel light. Conversely, they each carried a gun in their waistbands. As they scrambled down the bank it was difficult to avoid obstructions. It was just after nine and darkness had come quite early as the clouds rolled in with a stiff breeze and a threat of rain.

There had been one startling development: river patrols had started just before dusk, heavy launches with mounted machine-guns and searchlights on the bows. Mirek supposed they should have expected this and was grateful that they had at least had some warning.

When they entered the water the coldness made them gasp. Mirek kept close to Zotov who seemed to be oblivious of danger. Zotov wanted to find out about himself and this was one way to do it. He took to the water as if he had been born in it. His crawl was of almost professional standard and Mirek grinned. There was an awkwardness in Zotov's movements and he was using muscles he had not used for years; but he knew how to swim. By the time they reached the skiff, he was panting hard and complaining of aching arms. His elation though, was obvious.

Mirek climbed into the skiff first, not an easy thing to do without making a noise. Once on board he helped Zotov up and they both lay at the bottom of the boat, gasping. After a while they peered over the side, first towards the bank and then up at the towering overhang of the barge's stern.

They ducked down as they heard the put-put of a launch and a searchlight creamed the restive water and travelled the length of the line of barges which had not moved since the two men had arrived on the bank. They crept under the canvas, one at each end of the boat, Mirek insisting on taking first watch while Zotov tried to sleep in wet clothes which became increasingly colder. Mirek prayed that Zotov would suffer no screaming nightmares.

When dawn came at last, the convoy of barges started to move. The chugging of the engines and the wash from the stern screw made the skiff rock furiously. Zotov, surprised, clung to the sides and looked ill, and even Mirek, who had been prepared for it, was queasy. The skiff was hitting each stern wave as if it was solid and the boat was often airborne before crashing down into the next trough. There was nothing they could do but ride it out and Zotov, now grey-faced, was beyond caring.

The convoy stopped again and the skiff gradually steadied while the two men tried to keep under cover of the canvas. Suddenly the barges began to move again; they had waited for only twenty minutes during which time it had become quite light. The convoy made good progress and ahead came the derisory note of a siren as another boat was released. The convoy halted again. The skiff swung out so that, from the stern and just for a second, Mirek had a clear view up river. A police launch had pulled alongside the first of the three barges and policemen were climbing aboard. Mirek ducked down quickly and told Zotov that the convoy was being searched.

Annya slept the night in the car. As she waited in the long queue, she received many visits from other waiting drivers. She did not know whether she was the only unaccompanied woman driver, but the attention she was receiving was both unwelcome and dangerous.

The men were frustrated, of course, and only filling in time, but there were times when she could have screamed at them to leave her alone.

She did not sleep well and toilet facilities had not been designed for this sort of situation. She was also worrying about Mirek and Zotov. She could not get Mirek off her mind. Their affair in Warsaw had been close, but since starting this mad journey to rescue Zotov she had come to view Mirek in a much deeper light. Crisis was forcing her emotions. She only felt safe with Mirek and he now had his own separate problems. Increasingly there were moments when she felt she would not see him again.

At dawn, just as Mirek and Zotov had found, things began to stir. Gradually the waiting vehicles were released and a new feeling of hope crept into the compound. Engines were started up and clouds of diesel fumes spumed into the heavy air. From then on it was a question of awaiting her turn, but only in mid-morning did she actually near the check-point.

As she reached the barrier her heart was thumping. She

was alone in the car yet her sense of guilt was overwhelming. She consoled herself that it was a reflected fear for Mirek. When it was her turn she knew that it was going to take longer than the others. Attractive women drivers were not frequent and the border guards, just as frustrated as the disillusioned drivers, needed light relief. They took longer than usual to search her car and asked unnecessary questions just for the pleasure of speaking to her. But at last she was through.

As she approached the Polish barrier she noticed that the searching of the vehicles ahead was little more than cursory. It was a reversal of the situation when the Russians were cursing the Poles for the hold-up. As a plain-clothes Customs man approached, she had her window down. He held her in polite conversation, and seemed to be about to let her through when she was spotted by the official who had let them through on the way in. He quickly strode over and, apparently of senior rank, dismissed the other man.

"You're back soon. Where's your friend?"

"He's staying on for a while. I'm going back in a week's time to collect him."

His tall frame was stooped in order to face her through the open window. He pushed his cap up a little to show a ridge of blond hair. "That doesn't sound too convincing."

"I'm sorry, but that's the way it is. Is this terrible delay due to this man you told us about?"

"Of course. I see you're not wearing your wig. You look better without it. So where's your friend?"

Annya noticed a difference between this meeting and the first time they met. His pale eyes were almost taunting. Something was wrong. "I told you. May I go through, now?"

"No. Pull over there so the rest can pass."

Her heart sank, and she smelt danger. She pulled out of line but did not get out; she saw the car as her last link with the others, the last hope.

The tall officer came over. He did not hurry and there was a cockiness about him that had not been there before. He bent down and smiled. "Right. Now where are they?"

"They?"

"Your friend and Zotov. Which truck are they hiding in?"

Her hands were damp on the wheel but she was grateful for something to hang on to. "I don't know what you mean. What the hell would I know about this man Zotov? We didn't know of him at all until you mentioned him on the way through. Just what are you trying to do?"

"Why don't you get out. My back is breaking bending down like this." He opened the car door for her.

Annya clung to the steering wheel; if she got out she would never be allowed back in. "No I won't," she snapped. "I don't know what you're talking about."

"Of course you do." Then he smiled more warmly. "I'm sorry. I've scared you. I think you've misunderstood me. I need to know which truck they're in so that I can make sure it is allowed to pass through. If it's searched you'll be in trouble. I'm trying to help you, for God's sake."

Annya didn't believe him. Ever since the fight with Waleski she had lost confidence and now she was afraid of losing her wits. But, about to panic, she suddenly recalled that, when Mirek and Zotov were about to be killed, she reacted without hesitation and saved their lives. It was something else she could hang on to like the steering wheel.

This man was trying to trap her. But what had changed him? She was thinking furiously. To gain time she said, "You're crazy. I've spent hours, days, looking at the back of trucks. Just how do you think anyone could get in without obviously breaking the locks. Are you trying this on everybody?"

"Very good. Well done. But there are a lot of Polish drivers going through. Some of them have close links with Solidarity; some would open the doors for you, especially for someone as attractive. Come on; get it over with and then push off. My colleagues will be thinking I'm spending too much time with you."

"And so you are." Annya wondered whether this man had known more about them on the way down than he let on. Could he know why they had come? Was he the opposite to what they had thought, and had he tried to set them up? Pascoe, after all, had been expelled and something must have been known of his activities. "If I tell you which truck, can I drive away?"

He detected the facetiousness. "Give me the keys. I want to look in the boot."

"The Russians have already looked." But she fearfully placed the keys into his waiting hand.

He went round the back and she watched him in the mirror. He returned holding a can of tomatoes. "You have a lot of cans of food in the back. And your boyfriend's clothes."

"This is ridiculous," Annya exploded. "Of course we have spare food. And my boyfriend has sufficient clothes with him. I told you I was going back. I insist on speaking to your superior."

"And so do I. Get out. Bring your passport with you."

As Annya climbed out, realising that she could no longer resist, she snapped, "You've already examined my passport." But she was sickened by the thought that he might find the gun stuffed under the padding of her seat.

"Perhaps not closely enough. I think you know the way."

A few moments later she was in a small cell at the rear of the Customs building, and was sitting on the edge of a low bed, staring at the stained walls in despair, and wondering where it had all gone wrong.

They rose and fell with the swell, clinging on to the underside of the skiff, hidden by its overhang. They held on precariously but Mirek and Zotov needed only minimum grip to retain a hold. They had let their legs float up under the bottom and were close to floating on their backs.

As the police launch pulled alongside they were almost swept away and had to hang on grimly. They had positioned themselves on the blind side of the skiff, and could cope with the swell created by the launch, but when a man climbed aboard the skiff it started to rock madly. It was touch and go whether they could hold on or not, but they developed a rough knack of clinging to the underside.

Another bad moment came when the man climbed back into the launch and the skiff rolled as if it would capsize. The launch pulled away and set up a further series of waves but eventually the skiff began to settle. Before they could climb back on board, however, they had to be certain that the launch had really gone, and that there were no crew gazing down from the stern of the rear barge as there must have been while the launch was there. They also had to be certain that the immediate river area was clear of other craft.

Once satisfied they helped each other aboard and crawled under the canvas canopies at each end of the skiff. It was a long boat and they watched each other curl up to shiver from cold and wet, knowing that such searches might happen again and again.

The skiff started to move again but this time it was pitching and tossing and the two shivering men managed a grin for each other. Each time the string of barges stopped they would first make sure that the coast was clear and would then slip into the water and take up their positions. Which side of the skiff they clung to was a matter of judgement. As they drew into the port the stern screw was not only throwing up a powerful wash but was also trying to suck them into its blades.

The best places for concealment was on either side of the skiff's bows where the bulge was greatest, and where the wash, difficult though it was, also formed a frothy camouflage. But increasingly it was getting difficult. Zotov had long since dropped the notion that this was some kind of personal challenge; he was beginning to fight for his life and Mirek was not far behind him.

As they reached the real danger area, they saw less and less and dipped into the water more and more. There was a long period when they didn't know where they were, only that stops were more frequent and more painful and that it was increasingly hard to breathe as their heads went under more regularly.

They suffered a period of numbness during which they were in the water all the time, just clinging on, often unaware of what they were doing, so chilled were they. There was no point in climbing back into the skiff as they knew that searches were going on continuously but were beyond caring. They were fast reaching the end of their endurance.

Now they rarely acknowledged each other, as the water boiled behind the barge and pounded into their bodies and faces. It would be easy to let go and just disappear below the water line and leave it at that. Their weariness was almost beyond conscious suffering. They were hanging on blindly, lungs slowly filling with water, but with a thread of survival instinct keeping them there.

As they somehow clung on Mirek tried to pull himself from the brink. They had long since stopped being careful. Their bodies were thrashing out all over the place for anybody to see. They were no longer clinging to the underside of the skiff but simply hanging on for their lives. Something flashed through Mirek's mind, he wasn't even sure what, but he knew that they must let go whatever happened as a consequence.

He bawled out to Zotov who was grey from strain, "Let go."

Zotov made no sign. He looked as if he was about to let go anyway, but Mirek did not want him sliding under to oblivion. "LET GO." Zotov's eyes flickered, water streaming off his face. Mirek signalled and threw up his arms to float away from the skiff. He didn't know whether Zotov followed. The skiff struck him as it passed, grazing his head and almost knocking him out. He spun in the water like a dancer and then lashed out to the surface. The relief of no longer hanging on was enormous but his strength had gone. He trod water and caught sight of Zotov just as the Russian was going down; he struck out as fast as he could.

He lost sight of Zotov and knew that he could not swim any faster, could barely swim at all. And then he literally bumped into the half-submerged Russian and clung on to anything he could find. He hadn't the energy to shout; he simply clung to the sodden bundle in front of him and struck out across the current for the shore. He was heartened after a while when he realised that Zotov was trying to respond. He wasn't sure which side they were heading for; it no longer mattered.

It was not yet noon, but Annya felt as if she had been in the small cell for days instead of under an hour. She had been left alone, which she recognised as an old trick to break her down, to raise fears and generally demoralize her. But it was Mirek and Zotov who really played on her mind.

This was not the first time she had been arrested, but then she had been with many others and release for most of them had been quite speedy. This was more sinister. As she sat on the uncomfortable bed she reflected that the Customs man who had seemed so helpful on the outward journey was playing a double game. Perhaps he had tried the same tactic with others? The border officials had clearly been instructed to look out for Zotov, although then there had been none of the chaos there was now. Something had happened between the time they had crossed into Russia and their return.

The cell was one of a pair and smelled musty, as if it had not been used for years. There was a clear area outside the gridded door and, almost facing her, was another door that led to the more active parts of the building. Shouts and protests from the vehicle queue reached her in muffled form, but mostly, it was quiet. She did not know whether the next cell was occupied; she could hear nothing.

At about one o'clock the outer door opened and three men approached her cell. She was told to stand back against the rear wall and then her cell door was unlocked. Two armed guards entered to make way for another, older man, with a pinched face and an air of authority. He smiled at her but Annya was left with the feeling that he had smiled at many in his time in the same way.

He was an interrogator, she knew at once; but a very superior one. She thought she recognised him, and her spirit suddenly dropped as she realised who he was; General Lech Gruszka, head of the UB. What could he possibly be doing here in person and in her cell?

He was kind in his questioning as if he knew that she should not be in this place and that he understood her fear. He spoke to her about Zotov and she gave him the same answers that she gave the Customs man. Consistency was all-important. He nodded occasionally as she spoke, like a benevolent uncle who sympathised with her problems. At no time was he officious, nor did he press his questions too hard. At times she thought he was about to make her denials for her, he was so reasonable. All this made her more careful in what she said and had the effect of making her much more nervous, and open to error.

While he stood before her with the two guards slightly behind him as if Annya were capable of attacking him, there was a commotion beyond the outer door and a man was shouting protests with obvious fear. Gruszka continued his questions as if he had not heard, but clearly a struggle was taking place.

The Customs man who had arrested Annya came in from the outer office and stood to attention as he asked if he might have a word with the General. Gruszka went to the cell door and listened politely to the eager whispering of the Customs man, then turned to Annya. "Excuse me, my dear. I must leave you for a moment."

The entourage left and Annya was alone again in the tiny locked cell wondering what was happening and why was she so important that the Head of State Security had called at this old border post to question her.

As time passed she became convinced that she would not see Mirek or Zotov again. They would not let her leave here until they were satisfied, and that might never happen. She had expected Gruszka to call back as he had indicated that he would, but it had become ominously quiet beyond the outer door, almost as if everyone had gone home for the day and left things as they were. She worried about Mirek, about Zotov and the mystery he engendered; and she worried about the gun she had pushed into the padding under the car seat.

They hung on to anything they could find, roots, grass, to stay afloat and to recover a little wind. Climbing the bank was not easy and they did it in stages, too weak to help one another. Finally, they were clear of the river and lay face downwards, panting and spitting out water.

A sense of triumph gave them the will to heave themselves on to their knees, soaked, chilled through and shivering. Mirek spluttered, "We've done it." He gazed around slowly. "We must be well up-stream." He rolled over on to his back and stared at the leaden sky. He felt exhausted, and turned his head towards Zotov, who, he realised, must feel infinitely worse than himself. It was incredible how the Russian had managed.

Slow recovery brought with it a sense of panic and, in turn, they climbed shakily to their feet, squelching into the thick grass. The length of river bank was deserted but the river itself was still active with traffic although it had now thinned out considerably and the congestion had disappeared. It left them wondering just how far over the border they had come. They were certainly well clear of the town, there was not a building in sight at this point, nor any sign of life; but they were on the Polish side of the river.

Offering each other a shaky grin they climbed higher up the bank; it was important to get out of sight of the river boats. From time to time, one would slip and the other would help him up. Their sodden footwear was ruined and their saturated clothes clung to them. When they reached the ridge of the bank they crouched low. Agricultural land faced them, shoots struggling up. There was nothing beyond that except a distant line of trees.

They sat with their backs to the bank trying to shake out the damp like dogs. "How far do you think we've come?" asked Mirek.

Zotov was trying to squeeze water from his hair. He looked strained, his face pale, eyes bloodshot.

"I've no idea."

"The service station is about three miles from the border. Could we possibly have come that far? Could we have held on for that distance? There's no sign of Brest so we must be well clear. Are you up to walking?"

Zotov nodded; his arms were on his raised knees and he looked dejected after their ordeal, but there was still fire in him. "If we don't we'll freeze to death, anyway."

They rose awkwardly. Mirek said, "We must find the road." He looked back towards the river, his gaze straying to the opposite bank. "The border follows the river line for some distance. It's just the other side. The road cuts away from it in a V-shape. The service station might be only three miles along the road from Brest but we've some way to go before we hit the road. It's a toss of the coin, Zotov, but we're too near the Russian border for comfort."

As they stumbled along Mirek pulled out the gun that was still in his waistband. Water dripped from the barrel. "These need drying out. The ammo will be all right but we should really strip them down." He talked as if he knew that there would be a stage when they would need them.

Zotov put a hand to his own gun. "Everything needs drying out. We had better pray that Annya gets through; she has your clothing. I hope some of it will fit me."

Mirek did not respond. He was too worried about her. They tramped across the fields hoping that they were heading towards the road. There was no farmhouse in sight nor any building at this point. If and when they found the road they then had to find the service station and that could be in either direction.

They lay flat in long grass on the edge of a small copse, exhausted and dispirited. They had covered far more ground than they expected. When they had encountered trees and wild shrubs it had been a bonus but the going was tough and, never absolutely sure of their direction they kept heading south to where the road must be. The problem was that the road branched south-west from Brest and the river north-east. If they were veering slightly they might never find the road.

It was Zotov who discovered a remarkable sense of direction. It was another gift the Russian was finding within himself; bit by bit he was building up a disjointed picture of his abilities. At times, though, they did not know how they kept going, and here the value of travelling together proved itself. Neither man was willing to admit to the other that he wanted to give up.

When they saw the first suspicion of passing trucks some distance away they almost cried out with relief, for by that time they had been travelling some four hours with only occasional breaks. Their clothes were still damp but their bodies had warmed with the exercise. Now, with something to aim for, they increased their pace.

Their joy plummeted however when, two hours later,

they found the service station with the small café in an annexe at one end. There was no sign of the car, nor of Annya. She would have waited for however long it took them to arrive. As they lay in the long grass they could judge by the frequency of the traffic that the bottleneck at the border checkpoint must have dissipated a long time ago. So what had happened to Annya?

They crept as near to the service station as they dared and got a good view of the activity around it. The smell of coffee wafted their way which reminded them of their thirst and hunger. Because of the border hold-up, trucks were trying to make up for lost time and many drivers who would normally have stopped for a drink or meal, travelled on.

Lights came on at the service station with the heavy dusk. The two men crept even nearer. They crouched in the shadows instead of lying in the damp grass; but there still was no sign of Annya.

"What do we do?" asked Zotov, "with wet clothes and no transport?"

"We can hitch a lift." But Mirek knew that no driver would want to carry them in the state they were in. Explanations would be sought; they had no baggage and, for that matter, no money which had been left with Annya. Mirek had his passport with him because he had not wanted to risk it being found during a routine check on the car, and thus compromise Annya. But the passport was now a soggy mess, nearer to papier-maché than a document. He turned to Zotov.

"If you want to take your chance on your own I've no right to try to stop you. But I must try and find out what's happened to her."

"Even if it means going back?"

"Even that. I can't ditch her."

"I can't go back, Mirek." The haunted look returned to Zotov's eyes. "I can't go back to Russia."

Mirek slapped him lightly on the shoulder. "I know that. I'm not asking you to. But *I* must. I can walk back that far. At least I know that we're only a few miles from Brest."

"You need food. Maybe we can steal something from the café."

"Maybe. But if I were you I wouldn't hang around here while I'm gone. Maybe you could steal a car."

"And go where? I know nobody here. I'll wait, Mirek. But I can't go back."

"Okay. But I'll be some time." Mirek checked the action of his gun. The water seemed to have done it little harm.

Zotov was convinced that Mirek was sacrificing himself needlessly. He was about to lose the first human friend he had made. And, having experienced that friendship, he was going to be lonelier than he had ever been.

The two men shook hands, slapping each other on the back. Mirek detoured the café and was lost to sight for a few minutes. The last Zotov saw of him was his lonely figure heading for the road in the direction of Brest.

18

A light came on in the cell and erased the growing darkness. But since Gruszka left hours ago, all that had happened was that a man had been half-carried to the next cell, protesting loudly that he had done nothing wrong and why was he being arrested? His shouts became muted with the closing of his cell door.

To pass the time, Annya had called out to her new neighbour but he had not responded. Knowing the depressing effect these small cells could have, she assumed that he was doing what she had done, curled up on the bed wondering where it had all gone wrong.

When she checked her watch it had stopped and she cursed herself for forgetting to wind it. There was nothing with which to pass the time except her own thoughts which were becoming progressively more miserable. Her present position seemed so final that she found it impossible to see any sort of future outside these grubby walls.

When it seemed to her that the whole place had died she heard the outer door open and footsteps crossing towards the cells. A key was inserted in the lock and her door swung back. The light was so poor that she could see only that it was a man; it did not appear to be anyone she had so far met.

"You may go."

The words simply did not register and she stood with her back to the wall, waiting.

"For goodness' sake move. Unless you want to stay here."

She couldn't believe it.

"You're free. Get moving."

Instead of glee she felt suspicion, but at last she moved towards the door, her pace quickening with each step. She looked over her shoulder but there was no sign of the man and she began to run until she stood outside on the steps to take in gulps of cold evening air.

The Customs' post was closed for the night but there were very few trucks and cars in the compound behind the barrier. Her own car stood pale and forlorn where she had left it and she hurried towards it, still unable to believe what was happening. When she reached the car she tried to quell the euphoria of release.

The lights in the yard were dull and the visibility bad. The feeling of emptiness was utterly different from the cramped activity when she had first been ordered into the building. She started up and drove towards the barrier convinced it would never lift, that the whole business was some cunning trap. But it did lift and suddenly she was on the open road, on her own, with no congestion of any kind. After a while she checked her mirror but there was no sign she was being followed. The only lights behind her were the frontier lights, and, after a while, even those faded.

The road was lonely, but she resisted the temptation of stopping to check whether the gun was still under the seat. She was so preoccupied that she almost missed the café. The main lights were out, and only one exterior light at the front shone dimly, with the reflection of another from somewhere at the rear. She did a U-turn and crunched over the café's forecourt. She pulled up and doused the car lights.

Annya was not sure whether to wait in the car or get out and try to find Mirek and Zotov. She was so late that they might have given her up. A deeper fear entered her mind; had they made it? She climbed out and looked back down the road. Even though she could see nothing suspicious she could not shake off the idea that she was being followed.

As quietly as she could Annya walked slowly across the wide forecourt towards the closed café. A dog barked, deep and warning, from inside the service station. A huge truck was parked in shadows to one side of the low building, suggesting that the driver was staying the night. She reached the side of the café and went towards its rear. She had an uncanny feeling of being watched.

"Annya."

She spun round. She could see nothing, nor did she recognise the voice. She did not reply but stood still, wishing she had her gun. Someone approached from the shadows of the café wall and she at once realised who it was.

"Thank God, Zotov. I thought you had gone. Where's Mirek?"

But Zotov was suspicious, gun pointing at her, his gaze sweeping behind her. He approached slowly. "You have been a long time. What happened?"

She came towards him realising that he was not entirely satisfied. "They put me in the cells. They thought you were in one of the trucks and wanted me to tell them which. They've only just released me."

He nodded in the darkness. "You'd better get after Mirek. He went back to Brest to find you."

"Oh, my God." She ran towards the car and Zotov followed. When he reached the car he found that he could not climb in. Annya shouted, "What's the matter?"

The same fears filled him. "I can't go back."

"But it's all right for me? A woman?"

He was unable to reply.

She began to understand. "We have the car, Zotov. It makes all the difference. And you owe it to Mirek."

He had known that as soon as Mirek disappeared from sight; his conscience had nagged him. He climbed into the car as if he was going to his own execution. As he joined her, Annya called out, "How long ago did he leave?"

Zotov did not seem sure and she realised how bewildered he was and shivering. She touched his arm to feel the damp clothes. "We must get you changed."

"Find Mirek first. I suppose he left about an hour ago." Zotov sat huddled beside her, but his voice was firmer. After Mirek left he had suffered one of his worst bouts of ague and was violently sick. The friendship he was beginning to build up with Mirek had been ripped away from him almost as savagely as Pripy. Mirek leaving him, threw him back to those first hours of escaping from the hospital bus queue, and for a while he had broken down. Annya, sitting beside him, was the cause of Mirek's departure and, at the moment, he felt resentment towards her.

She sensed some of his feeling. She swung the car round to head back to Brest and, once they were on the road, said, "He'd have done the same for you, Zotov. He's that sort of person."

He gazed at her in the faint, ghostly glow of the dashboard lights. "I know. I'm sorry. It must be difficult for you to understand."

She stared straight ahead as she accelerated and put on her headlights. "It's very easy for me to understand. I don't know how you've coped." She was bursting with questions on how they had managed but this was not the time to voice them. "Now, keep your eyes open for Mirek. Just pray that he hasn't reached the border." Annya was forced to dim her lights as they ran into traffic near the Polish side of the port.

"Why did they release you?"

"For God's sake, Zotov, this is not the time to ask questions. Just keep looking into the shadows off the road." But she too was just as curious about it.

He did not relax his concentration when he asked that question. He would do nothing that might harm Mirek. But her sharp reply jogged him. Without thinking he said, "I once knew a girl like you. She was just as beautiful . . . " and then he stopped, astounded by what he had said.

Annya, sensing the importance of what had happened, kept quiet; she was intent on finding Mirek, but the import of what Zotov said remained. Zotov was remembering somebody from his past; a woman, and the shock of doing so had knocked him back into his cell.

Annya peered to both sides of the road, slowing right down as they reached the outskirts of Brest. Then the blue light of a police car came flashing towards them and Zotov clung to his gun. As it approached the police car dimmed its lights and, in that very moment, on the other side of the road, Annya saw somebody scuttle into the bushes. The police must have seen it too for the car braked hard and began to swing in.

Yelena Belenko lay in an uneasy sleep when the faint tapping on the door woke her up, startled and fearful. She listened carefully but when nothing happened, she began to think she might have dreamed it. She was sleeping badly, dreading every night. She swung her legs out of bed and sat on its edge, head in hands.

The tapping came again, almost too softly to hear. The signal was right and then she heard the key being inserted into the lock. Yelena rushed to the door in her bare feet.

"Who is it?"

"It's me."

Maria came in and locked the door after her. She shone a torch and found one of the gas lamps. When the glow cast some light she said, "After the last time I scared you I didn't want to come in without warning you first. I guessed you might be asleep." Yelena could see traces of stage make-up, so the opera singer must have come straight from a performance.

"It must be bad news for you to call so late."

Maria moved over to the shutters to make sure that they were properly closed and then turned to face her friend. "There is a strong rumour going round that an escapee from a Russian mental hospital has been arrested near Brest. On the Polish side of the border."

"Zotov." Yelena sank slowly on to a chair. Everything changed for her in that moment. Nothing seemed worth doing any more. She felt empty. Possibly for the first time in a life devoted almost entirely to her own needs, she did not care any longer what happened to her.

"Is it true?"

"The late editions have the story and it's been announced on television. I came because I did not want you distressing yourself if you heard it on the radio. Obviously you didn't." Maria crossed over and put an arm round her friend's drooping shoulders. "I'll find out what I can."

"So they've got him at last." Yelena looked up at her friend. "He gave them a run for their money, though, didn't he?"

Maria squeezed Yelena's shoulder. "Don't give up. These reports are sometimes wrong. I'll make you some coffee."

When Maria returned from the kitchen with two mugs she sat on the bed opposite her friend. "We hope to start getting you out within a few days now. It's a question of waiting for the right moment."

Yelena was not interested. She was thinking of a man she had loved deeply and whom she had not seen for over two decades. She doubted she would even recognise him now, but her feeling for him had been rekindled.

"I cannot leave here," she said flatly. "I have to know for sure."

Maria stared over the rim of her coffee mug. Yelena hated this place, yet she was now refusing to leave it because of a man with whom she had lost all touch. Maria wished that she could feel as deeply about a man as that. The values of the comfort-seeking Yelena Belenko were beginning to change; whether for better or worse remained to be seen. Maria hoped that her friend was not in love just with a memory; nor that she was mourning a ghost.

Gruszka was waiting at the border, under instructions from Zhadin which he dare not ignore, whatever his past relationship with Chernov. He was quietly cursing Chernov for putting him in this false position. When Chernov arrived at the Customs post he took him straight to the cell which was next to the one Annya had occupied.

Chernov stood in the doorway, his bulk making it impossible for anyone else to pass him, and stared at the grey-haired man standing by the bed. Could this be Zotov? It was many years since he had seen him. The man was about the height he remembered and the hair was about the same, thicker though than it might have been bearing in mind what Zotov must have suffered over the years.

The eyes that stared back at Chernov were full of fear, but that would be normal for anybody who recognised him and certainly for Zotov himself, if it were he.

"Who are you?" Chernov asked softly.

"Nikolai Botavin. Why have I been arrested?" Botavin's voice shook with the question.

"What do you do, Nikolai Botavin?"

"I am a sales representative for a cotton mill in Brest. I was on my way to Warsaw when I was bundled in here."

Chernov said to Gruszka, who stood behind him, "Has this been checked?"

"Of course. The manager of the cotton mill says that

Nikolai Botavin is on leave. They are not sure where he is. We contacted his home but his wife is not there. We checked with neighbours to find that she has gone away for a few days and we are trying to trace her now. The company in Warsaw say they know nothing of Botavin's visit, but they do know of such a man."

Botavin, who had known nothing of the checks, fell back against the bed, his face pale.

Chernov turned to Gruszka and said, "Can I have a few minutes alone with him?" When he saw Gruszka's doubt he added, "Don't worry, Lech. Just leave me with him."

Five minutes later Chernov left the cell, his expression one of annoyance. "It's a long way to come to find you have the wrong man. He has a mistress in Warsaw. He's deceiving his wife. You could have found that out and saved me the journey."

Gruszka was rattled. "Our enquiries would have thrown that up. It was you, Aleksei, who insisted on coming down. There was always a chance we would get the wrong man; there is no recent photograph of Zotov. Anyway, how can you be sure that he's not lying?"

Chernov sighed; he was trying to hide his anger. "Let him go, Lech, he's not our man." He looked sharply at Gruszka and there was something dangerous about the way he did it. "You wouldn't have pulled someone in just to appease me, would you, Lech? Just to get me off your back?"

It was too near the truth for comfort. "I did not arrest him, Aleksei. The border police found he bore a remarkable resemblance to the description you gave me. And he was travelling under false pretences."

Chernov's eyes were stone hard. He was beginning to wonder just how many old friends he had left. "Zotov will be over the border by now. He'll be through."

"If he is then we'll still find him. The search hasn't relaxed. Botavin will have served his purpose; the news bulletins were designed to cover any mistake. When Zotov hears we have arrested a man it will lower his guard."

"You'd better find him," snapped Chernov, all pretence of friendship gone. "He's shown your security to be useless."

"Yours, too," Gruszka retorted. "He made a fool of you on your own soil. You've been forced to come to us because of your own inadequacies."

Chernov knew then that Gruszka had heard from Zhadin. Gruszka would never dare to talk to him like that, even if he was retired. He became very quiet and calm, and dangerous; the look he gave Gruszka made the Pole uneasy, and he shivered involuntarily. The two men suddenly smiled at each other, the chill in the room increasing.

As the police car veered towards the edge of the road Annya swung to the centre and switched on full beams to blind the driver. The police car skidded as it braked and there was a squeal of tyres. Annya watched her rear mirror as she herself braked and slowed to a stop. Beside her, Zotov was yelling at her for being so stupid. If the police came after them there was nowhere he could hide.

As the car came to a stop she bawled at Zotov to keep down, climbed out quickly, and walked back towards the police car which was performing a U-turn to get after her. She flapped her arms in helpless apology as the police car drew up beside her, the driver furious as he climbed out.

Before he could say anything she said, "I'm so sorry. My hand slipped. I'm not really used to the model. That was really stupid of me."

The policeman, mollified by her admission and her obvious distress, was charmed; but he had to make some show and asked to see her licence which she took from a pocket of her skirt. "Just don't do it again," he growled. "That can be really dangerous. Do you realise you blinded me?"

"That's why I stopped," she nodded miserably. "I really am sorry."

He gave her another warning and, reluctant to let her go, watched her all the way back to her car. He might have followed to prolong the dialogue had his partner not mocked him.

Annya could feel his gaze as she climbed in but she did not look back, believing that it might overdo her act. She continued to drive carefully towards the border with a relieved Zotov by her side. She watched the rear-view mirror and saw the police car turn round again and then pull up. The search was not yet over but whoever had dived into the bushes had been granted a big advantage.

"Did you think it was Mirek?" asked a still shaken Zotov.

"I don't know. If it was I hope he saw me. We can't go on much further or we'll be at the border. We must go back."

"The police might still be there." Sight of them and their proximity to the border had unnerved Zotov.

Annya pulled into a small side street with detached buildings well back from the road. She found she was in a dead-end and turned at the hammer-head to face the way they had been going; but she pulled up well short of the main road. They sat quietly in the car, watching the lit-up dwellings on either side and the few parked vehicles in the street. They were strangers in a strange area.

A door opened across the street and a man stood silhouetted and then could be seen to have a dog on a lead. He turned towards the main road, the dog trotting happily beside him. Zotov thought of Pripy.

"We've got to change this car," said Annya. "The police have now seen it and I've never felt comfortable in it since I was released."

"You mean you were followed?"

"I didn't appear to be. I'm not stupid, Zotov, I did check. And we haven't been followed here. But a description and registration number might have been signalled ahead so that our movements could be monitored."

"Then they must be wondering what has happened to us? They'll come looking. Can we get another car?"

Annya glanced at Zotov who was well down in his seat. "I'm going to steal that van up ahead."

"Do you know how to get in and start it?"

"Oh, yes. I'll drive the van and you follow in this car. I'll use the hazard lights to warn you if we run into the police again. If we're lucky the van won't be missed until morning."

"So you do think the shadow was Mirek?"

"It's the only sign we've seen unless he's already in town. It's our best chance."

Annya climbed out and removed her gun from under the

seat, relieved to find it was still there. Zotov scrambled across to get behind the steering wheel. As she moved up the street he felt anxious for her – her slight figure seemed so exposed and vulnerable. Before she reached the van, the man with the dog reappeared and he wanted to shout a warning. But Annya had suddenly disappeared.

Zotov sank down until he could barely see above the dashboard but he kept his gaze on the man and the dog until they went into the house and the hall light was switched off. He did not see Annya again until he saw the van door open. After a while the van pulled out. There was no sign that anyone had heard so Zotov switched on and drove off to turn left at the junction and follow Annya back to the spot where the figure had disappeared into the bushes. He kept well behind the van, his gaze on its tail lights.

They were travelling slowly, and occasionally a truck or car passed them. There was little traffic going towards Brest. When the van stopped Zotov pulled in and doused the lights, ready to jump out of the car. Then the van moved on again and, after a minute or two, stopped again. The pattern of stop and start continued for some distance but was only performed when no other traffic was in sight. The police car must have gone.

Annya was worried. If Mirek had seen her he would expect her to return; but she could not put the car out in front if the police were somewhere up ahead; it needed to be sheltered from view. But it was the car Mirek would be looking for, which was why she was making periodic stops. She was not sure if they had yet reached the spot where they saw the movement in the bushes, and as she drove on she became increasingly depressed. It seemed a futile gamble.

Behind her, during one of the halts, Zotov was thinking the same. Suddenly the nearside door of the Zis was wrenched open, and a breathless Mirek climbed in and asked, "Is that Annya in front?" Without thinking, Zotov frantically started to flash his headlights.

The car moved up close behind the van and Mirek jumped out to see Annya running back towards him. They embraced fiercely and again Zotov witnessed the love he knew they had for each other. But immediately they broke away and ran back to Zotov.

There was no time for finesse. The river was some distance away, but at least Mirek and Zotov knew the direction to take from the service station. They spent time locating a road that headed north and found that it was not much better than a farm track, but they kept going towards the river with Mirek and Annya in the van and Zotov following in the car.

Near to the river Mirek got out and led the way on foot over rough ground while the two vehicles were driven on sidelights and then with no lights at all. They did not want to be seen from the Russian bank.

It took time to find a spot where the bank was steep enough for the car to run down. They transferred what they needed to the van and the two men at last had a welcome rub down and a change into Mirek's spare clothes.

Holding the door open Mirek drove the car to the top of the bank and remained with it as it gathered momentum down the sharp incline. He jumped out just before the car plunged into the deep waters of the river. He watched the Zis slowly sink, listening to the gurgling as the air was forced out. What little light there was reflected off the oily, concentric circles of water as the car finally disappeared. Satisfied, he went back to the others and they then started back on the difficult way to the Warsaw road.

In spite of their fatigue they decided to drive through the night. It was more than two hundred kilometres from Brest to Warsaw but they took any detour from the main road that offered itself and this slowed them down. It was a tight squeeze for the three of them on the bench seat of the van, but more comfortable than in the back which contained little other than their own supplies and maintenance tools.

They took turns driving and the very act of climbing in and out and changing places helped to keep them going. They kept talking as much as they could, bringing themselves up to date with what had happened. They were all wanted for murder. And with Pascoe deported, there was no outside influence that could help them to get out of

Poland; they were still very much behind the Iron Curtain and well knew the enormous odds that were stacked against them.

As they neared Warsaw the talk began to die; and when they saw the glow of the city in the early morning darkness, it looked like a giant hazy saucer, almost surrealistic in the way it blended with the night. Mirek was driving at the time and he pulled in and switched off the lights. He looked across at the others and knew they were thinking the same. "We can't go in until it's light. We'd be too noticeable on empty streets. But if we go in too late there's a chance that a description of the van will have been circulated. You two have a nap and I'll stay awake until it's time to move."

Annya and Zotov knew better. If they slept, Mirek would sleep too. They were exhausted and needed each other to keep awake.

They managed to keep talking, mainly about trivial things. Both Mirek and Annya knew of safe houses once they were in Warsaw, but that was not the immediate problem, which was how to get over the border to East Germany; and from there to West Germany. It was best not to think of it, for suddenly all their efforts appeared to be in vain. They had come only a very little way although they felt they had been travelling for ever. And yet they had managed so far; to escape from Russia was an almost impossible task; yet they had done it.

Zotov gazed at the lightening sky and the gradually disappearing haze that hung over Warsaw. They must move soon. He said vaguely, "I once made a promise that I'd come here if things were bad. We always talked of escaping to Warsaw. It was a joke between us."

Mirek and Annya were almost afraid to speak. "Who did you make the promise to, Zotov?" asked Annya softly.

Zotov gazed across at them. He was frowning with concentration. "It was a girl. Perhaps the one I mentioned before."

"What was her name?"

Zotov shook his head. "I can't remember. I'm not even sure that I haven't dreamt what I've just said. Maybe it's just wishful thinking."

It was pointless to press him. His memory seemed to be doing better on its own; let it recover in its own time.

"We ought to be leaving," Mirek said not long after. "I think you should wedge yourself in the back, Zotov."

Zotov did not argue. They helped him over the back and Mirek and Annya spread themselves a little. It was time to face whatever was ahead. This was the part that really mattered.

19

General Joseph Zhadin gazed across the immense desk at the grey-faced old man opposite him. "You've been most helpful, Professor Finenko. And I haven't enjoyed putting you through this grilling. But you of all people, know the importance of the matter. Let's have some coffee."

Zhadin rang through and gave the order. He tried to put Finenko at ease but it was difficult. Finenko, and just a few others, had carried the burden for so long and did not expect it to be resurrected, yet, in his heart, he must always have known of the possibility. Finenko was now in his early eighties and the strain on him was almost too much; he had been retired for some fifteen years. Most of his contemporaries were dead.

Zhadin had not wanted to be rough but it had been essential to revive the old man's mind, to stimulate it under pressure, and at all costs, to make him remember. "Relax," Zhadin said again. "I am not your enemy. I hold the greatest respect for you and I guarantee you will come to no harm. On the contrary, I will see that you are well protected, Comrade."

Finenko tried to smile but the thin lips were stiff, and the narrow, lined features failed to hide the disdain he felt. He resented being questioned in this way. His achievements were well recorded and he would go down as a great contributor to Soviet history. In his day he had been idolized and he did not consider Zhadin his intellectual equal.

Zhadin realised this but did not think that Finenko, even now, realised the full political implications of the matter. Or perhaps he was simply beyond caring, the whole issue buried deep in his memory where he considered it should remain. Nothing serious was said until a silver pot of coffee was brought in on a salver, with cups and cream and crystallised sugar. Zhadin poured; both men took their coffee black.

After a while Zhadin said, "I still find it difficult to understand why so few people knew."

Finenko wearily put down his cup. "As I explained, Control was well separated, it was quite easy to convince them. Only those of us at the actual reception at Baikonur knew what had happened. We are talking of half a dozen high officials, responsible people who realised immediately that something had to be done."

"Who contacted Nikita Khrushchev?"

It was the same ground over and over. What was the point? There was nothing more to remember. Finenko closed his eyes, the creased lids flickering as if he was dreaming, and perhaps, after all these years, he was. "Professor Kamensky. We had direct access to Comrade Khrushchev. He told us what to do and had a man flown down straight away."

"That man was General Chernov, who was then a major?"

"As I said before. Nothing has changed, Comrade."

"So Kamensky is dead. That leaves you and Penkov?"

"Obviously it leaves me. I understand that Penkov is very ill. Dementia. A premature senility of the brain; he is a few years younger than I."

"The security clamp-down did not prevent rumours."

"There was no security leak, General. None whatever. We all knew the form. Speculation was just that and no more. There will always be rumours about almost anything. We were sworn to secrecy. The only possible weakness was Drozdof and there was little he could do from Baikonur. He never returned to Moscow; after he was interviewed by Major Chernov he simply disappeared. If any of the remainder of us needed a lesson on the importance of silence, then that was it. And we've been silent ever since, loyal citizens of the Soviet Union."

Zhadin nodded agreement. "If you had not been, none of you would have been there in the first place. I don't doubt your loyalty, Professor. Or that of the others. I don't think

Chernov's heavy hand was necessary, but then, I wasn't there." He eyed Finenko shrewdly, aware that he would soon have to stop his questioning or Finenko might become too confused by repetition. "It's always possible that Comrade Khruschev confided in someone else."

Finenko managed his first genuine smile. "I was not a confidant of the Comrade Secretary-General. If you want my judgement I doubt whether he trusted any of his colleagues. He was a self-cult figure; that was his downfall. He would have enjoyed the power of the knowledge to the last. I am convinced though that, politically, he took the secret to his grave. I've no doubt he trusted Chernov to do the rest; he was Russian to the last."

Zhadin smiled and sipped his coffee. "I've enjoyed our meeting, Professor. I've always admired your work and it has been a great pleasure to see you. I think we've covered everything we can for the present."

"The present? You haven't finished with me?"

"I'm sure I have, Professor. Certainly at such length. If you recall anything else you consider to be of importance you will have immediate access to me. I have nothing but gratitude for your immense co-operation." Zhadin rose and came round the desk to help the frail Finenko to his feet. "Transport has been arranged to take you home."

As they reached the door, Zhadin added with a smile, "I'm sure I don't have to remind you that the act of secrecy you undertook then, still applies now. Nobody must know."

Finenko held on to the door knob. "I'm too old to be foolish, Comrade General. And far too scared. But the secret did escape did it not?"

"I beg your pardon?"

"Well, *you* know, Comrade. I assume that you did not know before. Perhaps Khrushchev did pass it on after all. Someone must have told you. All you've done with me is to confirm it."

Zhadin sat thoughtfully at his desk after Finenko had gone. When he picked up his cup he found that the coffee was cold. He gazed round the huge room, at the portrait of Dzerzhinsky, the Cheka chief, hanging on the wall beside him. He stared at the battery of telephones on the desk, and considered the coverage they had; a direct line to the Kremlin, another with the Politburo and high-ranking members of the Central Committee. There were high-frequency circuits to branch offices throughout the Union and others to the satellite blocks of Eastern Europe. There was direct contact with the GRU and the defence Ministry, and yet another to his six deputies.

Zhadin was reflecting on the power that these instruments yielded during the reign of Aleksei Chernov, an early confidant of Nikita S. Khrushchev, and still loyal to him. But what was the basis of that loyalty? Certainly it was personal and perhaps it resulted in Chernov's rapid rise within the KGB. But Khrushchev's motives had been suspect and outdated, and loyalty should be to the State.

Now the power — which the facilities in this office represented — was his but he was not yet adjusted to it. Yet it was growing to be part of him by the day, and the massive organisation he controlled would perform exceedingly well while he familiarised himself. Most departments functioned efficiently, it would become a question of which way he wanted them to go.

He flicked the intercom switch to his personal secretary and told him to summon Colonel Kanavsky and to hold all calls. While he waited he wondered if he was about to abuse his new power just as he was quite sure Chernov had done over the years. He had made a decision that might have considerable impact, not least in the KGB itself. He was about to sound a terrible warning, but first he had to satisfy himself of its necessity.

Kanavsky was fairly relaxed when he entered. Chernov was in Poland and he felt sure Zotov was no longer his own personal problem; the immediate pressure was off.

"Sit down, Colonel."

At once Kanavsky was warned. He sat and Zhadin seemed to be a mile away across the desk.

"Have you had news from General Chernov?"

"No, Comrade General. Not since he went to Warsaw."

"Any news of Zotov?"

"None." Kanavsky felt a chill creeping over him. "There

was a false alarm at the Polish border near Brest. They had the wrong man."

"Yes, I heard. So you've received no more instructions about the piffling matter of this elusive escapee Zotov?"

"No, sir. I don't see what else I can do."

"You didn't do much anyway. He escaped and is probably over the border now."

"There was the problem of Chernobyl and limited facilities. I didn't think he was that important."

"General Chernov did. Had he come to me in the first place and explained the situation in full, I would have seen to it that he had all the help necessary. Now it might be too late. You are at least partly to blame, Colonel. You operated for Chernov and kept secret from me what it was he wanted. I need to know where your loyalties are."

"With the organisation, Comrade General. With you."

Zhadin smiled thinly. "You certainly had me fooled; I thought you were Chernov's man." He shrugged, his manner relaxing a little. "But I'm going to give you an opportunity to prove your loyalty to me now, Colonel."

Kanavsky dreaded what Zhadin was going to say.

"I intend to take over the search for Zotov myself. But I can't do that while General Chernov is running around in Poland and impeding anything I might try to do. The matter is too important. Now you've served the General for a long time. Do you think he would obey a request from me to return? An order, even? Or is it your judgement that he might pretend to be unavailable while he completes what he set out to do?"

Kanavsky was sweating. It was no time to sit on the fence. "He'll do what he set out to do, Comrade General."

"I think so too. But we can't have two of us doing the same thing and getting in each other's way. Go at once to Warsaw and see that the General enjoys immediate retirement. Only then will I accept your claim of loyalty."

At first Kanavsky did not fully understand the order, or at least he convinced himself that there was more than one interpretation. He felt the blood drain from his face and Zhadin appeared as a blurred figure some distance away.

He pulled himself together and tried to concentrate, aware that Zhadin was waiting for his reaction.

"I'm not sure that I fully understand, Comrade General."

"You understand only too well, Colonel. There is only one way to make General Chernov effectively retire, wouldn't you say?"

Kanavsky stared unbelievingly, his mind numb. "Are you ordering me to kill him?"

"I don't repeat orders, Colonel. You know exactly what you have to do. And it must not be done on Soviet soil. There will be no better opportunity than now."

Kill Chernov! It would be suicide. The shock struck Kanavsky again and again until he could not think straight. He could understand, or at least fully accept, the need to kill someone like Zotov, even without knowing the real reason. But Chernov, the man he had served for so long, that was crazy.

"You find it a problem, Colonel?"

The question was like a cold knife-thrust. He had not seen this side of Zhadin before. "I've never done this sort of thing. Surely it's a matter for Department V." Department V had always dealt with assassinations.

"That would normally be so. But we are talking about the retiring Chairman of the KGB. That requires special attention and I am appointing you a special envoy." Zhadin picked up a steel paper knife and felt its point. "This is your last chance to show that you can be trusted, Colonel. It is not a matter for debate. You can work something out while you're on the plane. I will clear all formalities for you."

Zhadin hesitated and then added, "General Gruszka will be expecting you but you will not report to him officially. He will meet you at the Hotel Bristol where a room will be reserved for you the moment you leave this office. You will be comfortable in the Stare-Miasto among the tourists and with the opera and ballet so near. Take whatever you feel you might need; it will all be cleared."

Kanavsky rose shakily. Maybe he could find excuses for delay.

"Your flight has already been booked, Colonel. You have

two hours to catch your plane. Ring me the moment you have worthwhile news."

Kanavsky walked slowly to the door on legs that did not want to respond. Zhadin had at no time used the word kill, or assassinate, or execute, but that was what he wanted to be done. As Kanavsky opened the door he felt that he was going to his own funeral.

20

They had looped round to join the Lublin Road, a main entry into Warsaw from the south-east. It was quiet in the van, the mood sombre. They picked up traffic as they went. The timing of entry was good for it was the early part of the rush hour with its usual crazy drivers. As they hit the main streets the beetle-like trams were full and pavements were thickening with hurrying pedestrians. Warsaw was meeting a new day with an old routine and it had begun to drizzle. This helped the three in the van for people became less observant.

Mirek was driving but it was Annya who gave the directions. They kept to the east side of the Vistula River and followed the Plowiecka until it hit a junction and became the Grochowska which continued for some distance.

As they neared the centre the roads became busier in all directions, to the factory area of the south and to Zoliborz in the north of the city. At the end of the Grochowska they followed the much shorter stretch of the Jana Zamoyskiego which would lead them into the centre of the city but on the unfashionable side. And when they entered the Targowa they were in the city's east-end.

The criminal element was here, many of them conducting the proliferous, and profitable, black markets on which the country survived. And yet it was directly opposite Old Warsaw, across the river, the beautiful district of Stare-Miasto where the Wielki Theatre sat, with its opera and ballet, near to some of the best hotels. The two districts faced each other but were well separated by the width of the river.

Annya told Mirek where to branch off the Targowa into myriad streets where there was less activity. Many who lived around here were not confined to normal working hours and most of those who were had already gone to work.

"Pull in over there." Annya pointed to a paint-stripped door in a long row of terraced houses in what was a shabby, stunted street. Above them to the rear, rose blocks of residential development, featureless boxes with glass inlets for light.

As Mirek pulled over to the other side of the street, he was well aware that they were being watched although not a curtain twitched. He hoped Annya knew what she was doing.

"Stay there." Carrying a shoulder bag Annya climbed out and knocked on the door. The door opened almost immediately confirming Mirek's belief that they were being observed. A woman, pretty and without make-up, but poorly dressed, asked Annya in at once with barely a glance at the van.

Mirek sat in uneasy silence aware that Zotov, in the back of the van, must be doing the same. Many of the people around here lived from hand to mouth, which was one reason why it was the heartland of villainy. In a country with so many shortages and so little money, crime did pay. Mirek knew that Annya, in her underground capacity, had many contacts, far more than he had, and that they were spread widely over the city.

"She'll be all right. She's a survivor." Zotov had climbed forward to just behind the seat.

"Like you," responded Mirek. He had been letting his mind drift when he should have been alert to what might be happening. But they were all tired out, and his mind had gone into limbo.

Annya re-appeared with the woman who now had a scarf over her head and went up the street without a glance at the van. Annya climbed in beside Mirek. "She's gone off to make arrangements."

Mirek was worried. "Can you trust her?"

"I've used her before. It's a commercial transaction."

Mirek was looking around. "Commercial? We haven't much left of Pascoe's money."

"You can't expect anybody to keep us for free. We let them have the van."

Mirek laughed. "Don't they realise it's hot?"

"Oh, yes. They'll take care of the number plates and the engine and chassis number. Can you think of a better way of disposing of the van? If we had parked it somewhere, it would have either been seen by the police or someone would have stolen it anyway."

"Brilliant." Mirek rubbed his face. He was having difficulty in keeping awake. "It'll be worth a packet on the black market."

A few minutes later the woman rounded the corner and stood there. "Start up," said Annya. "Just follow her."

Mirek drove the van round the corner. They climbed out and a man appeared from a narrow alley, opposite which was a brick wall covered with graffiti; so they were not overlooked. Before they could do a thing the man climbed into the van and drove it away. Mirek and Zotov swung round but it was too late; the van contained their few belongings. Annya seemed unconcerned and followed the woman down the narrow alley.

The alley was cluttered with rubbish. They eased their way round refuse bins which had a visible effect on Annya who vividly recalled the last time she had used a bin. She followed the woman through a tall, wooden gate and along a broken concrete path, with the two men following. The backyard was short and untidy and they were ushered into a scullery which led to a hall, and then taken up narrow stairs covered with a worn and torn carpet which was dangerously loose.

They were left in a room next to an old-fashioned, dripping toilet. There was a double bed, an old wardrobe, one leg of which was balanced by a folded cigarette packet, and a washbasin and jug of water.

When they were left alone, the two men gazed round the room in some despair. Only Annya seemed reasonably satisfied. "They're unlikely to search for us here. She said she'd bring a mattress up. It could be worse, Mirek. We could be in jail."

Mirek put an arm round her shoulders. "It's fine. As long as we can trust the neighbours."

"They're not the type to go to the police. They don't want the law or the UB around here. This is the house we stopped outside, by the way. We simply came in the back way as a little subterfuge. There's a lot to do, Mirek. Have you any idea how we can get out of the country?"

Mirek went to the small window and looked through the net curtains to the short wall at the back of the yard and, a block away, the high-rise residential development. "Oh, yes. But it means taking a hell of a lot of chances." He looked at the other two. "I just hope the locals know nothing about Zotov."

Maria threw the newspaper at Yelena. "Bottom of the second page. Just a short piece." In the end she had to translate it herself. "The man they arrested at the border was not Zotov. Apparently it was a look-alike. They've let him go."

Yelena was overjoyed and for the first time since she had been cooped up showed some of her old animation. Aware that Maria could not have missed her reaction she said, "It's absurd to feel like this after so long."

"I think it's really wonderful." Maria smiled and said cautiously, "It doesn't mean that Zotov has escaped."

"I know." Yelena spread her arms and pirouetted with much of the grace she had once used on stage, "But it does mean that he's still free. He'll escape; I know he will."

"We will have to move in a day or two, Yelena. Don't build up too many hopes about Zotov. Friends are working hard for you. I don't mean to hurt you, but you may never know what has happened to him."

"Yes, I do understand. And I'm so grateful. I will never be able to thank you enough for the risks you have taken." Yelena walked round the room on her toes, still partly anchored in the past. "I never thought I could get used to this. There have been times when I've been a perfect spoiled bitch. I'm sorry." She stopped her movements and faced Maria. "Is it possible to sound out your contacts about Zotov? Has nobody heard anything?"

Maria picked up the bag in which she had brought a few extra supplies. "I do that all the time but I have to be careful how I do it and with whom. There is one possible pointer, although it may have absolutely nothing to do with him."

She glanced at her watch; it was time to go. "There's a security purge on. The word has gone out. Solidarity activists are being harassed all over town. It's the biggest clamp-down for a long time. It could well be that they are looking for someone and it's the political areas where they're searching."

"Does that include this place?"

"Anywhere. This is the safest place of all. Rarely used and only for most important cases, but it does mean that I'll have to be extra careful. Once they're suspicious of me I'm finished. As long as I continue to shine like the red star they think I am, I'll be all right. I'll find out what I can."

Yelena felt the old frustration return. She wanted to help and couldn't. As Maria headed for the door Yelena raised both hands to her lips to blow kisses at her. "Good luck. Be careful, Maria."

"There's a major purge going on." Annya had just come back upstairs from talking to their hosts. "The whole town is in a flap."

"Looking for us?" Zotov had been very quiet since arriving in the room; he saw it as something of a prison.

"It's best to assume so. They must have taken the view that you got through. What we're not certain of is whether they've yet linked us all together."

"Maybe we should move on," Mirek said flatly. Like Zotov, he was beginning to feel imprisoned.

"Where to?" Annya was controlling matters at the moment; she was on her own ground and the men found it difficult to argue with what she did. She turned to Mirek in desperation. "We need new passports." She took a blond wig from her shoulder bag. She opened the wardrobe door and put the wig on with the aid of a speckled mirror screwed to the wood. "The landlord is coming up to take some photographs. We can't get out without documents."

Mirek said heavily, "You're not thinking of going out on your own, are you?"

Before she could reply there was a knock on the door and the man who had taken the van entered with a battered Polaroid. He was short with, hard, non-committal features, and very dark eyes. His once white shirt and jeans smelled of oil. Indifferently, he said, "Let's start."

The day passed more quickly than they expected. As soon as it was dark Annya checked her appearance once more in the wardrobe mirror and said, "I don't know when I'll be back, but I'll be much safer on my own." She held out her hand. "I'm sorry, Mirek, but I'll need what money you have left. Illegal passports are expensive."

He handed over the money, scared for her, but at the same time impatient; he had his own excursions to make but felt that it would not be sensible to leave Zotov on his own. "Make my occupation driver." And then, "Be careful." It seemed such an inadequate thing to say. They didn't embrace, shy in the presence of the Russian. Perhaps it was as well.

Annya blew a kiss. "I'll be as quick as I can."

They met at the church south-west of Wschodnia railway station. Annya had used a pay phone to call her contact and because there was time to fill in she had walked to the station and had then veered well clear when she saw the amount of police activity. Wschodnia was on the Minsk line and any route in from Russia would be well guarded. The way to the church was less hazardous but she had time on her hands so she continued to walk rather than go into the church.

Zigbien was on time and simply walked beside her as Annya was passing the church once again. They both slowed their pace and headed in the rough direction of the Stadium Station. The Targowa, where the three fugitives were hiding, was in a triangle of railway stations, Wilenska to the north-west, Stadium to the south-west and Wschodnia to the east. If all three were under heavy police surveillance, Annya realised it would mean running the gauntlet every time one of them went out.

They walked slowly, arm-in-arm like lovers, and discussed their business, falling silent only when they passed others. They chose their route by instinct, keeping to the quieter streets.

"Is this clamp-down anything to do with you?" Zigbien was a tallish, rather stooped man with a large moustache and small spectacles. His dark hair was usually unruly, but tonight, as a concession to caution, he wore a hat. His overall appearance was donnish, and he certainly had been an academic, but these days he lived by his wits as the only avenue left open to him. He was also an artist of some note and an excellent forger.

"I'm not that important, Ziggie," replied Annya cautiously. She did not want Zigbien to get cold feet. "You know Mirek, of course. Since his embassy contact left he doesn't feel safe. So I'm leaving with him and another friend." She fumbled in her bag. "We need three passports. Mirek wants his occupation to be a driver. There's a note with the new names we want. Our friend is named Wladyslaw Kismurak. He's a salesman. It's all there including photographs."

Zigbien took the packet and rammed it in a pocket. "When?"

"Tomorrow."

"Don't be silly, Annya. You want to be caught with obvious fakes?"

"It's urgent."

"Escape always is. The day after tomorrow is the best I can do, and that will mean working round the clock. And it will cost you."

"But you already have blank passports. You forget that I know who supplied you."

Zigbien instinctively lowered his head as they approached a street light. "There's much more to it than that and you know it. You've had my best offer. Let's not fall out over it. I'll do my best."

They discussed terms for a while and Annya reluctantly passed most of the remaining money over to Zigbien who took it without counting it. He said, "We're getting too near to the station. Let's turn back."

As it was the direction she wanted to go Annya did not argue. They walked in silence for a while and then Zigbien said, "Do you know anything about a Russian called Zotov?"

Before she could stop herself Annya jerked on Zigbien's arm. The question had come as a complete shock and she knew she had given herself away.

* * *

Zigbien was almost as surprised as Annya; he had not expected such a reaction. "I see that you do," he said with satisfaction.

"I tripped," Annya retorted awkwardly, furious with herself. "What was the name again?"

Zigbien laughed. "Do you know, I think that's the first time I've caught you out." And then more seriously, "I don't blame you for being cautious, but the game's up. Is he our Wladyslaw Kismurak?"

"Don't be ridiculous, Ziggie. What the hell would Mirek and I be doing with a Russian? What's it about?"

"All right. I'll play it your way." They turned a corner and were heading back towards the church. "The word has passed down the grapevine; a certain person is trying to get news of this Zotov person. There's been a tiny bit about him in the press."

"Sounds like the UB. I'd lay off it if I were you."

"I don't think so. The source is much respected. Anyway, there's a rumour that you went to Russia. Is there a connection?"

"That rumour was put about by us. We just wanted to disappear for a while, that's all. This Zotov business sounds dodgy, Ziggie. Who's your source?"

It was Zigbien's turn to be secretive: infiltrators were a constant danger to underground organisations. But he knew Annya well, and had respect for her and the work she had done. He, of all people, knew what persecution could do; he had had an academic career ruined by his activities. Yet still he hesitated.

"You can't trust me?" Annya prompted.

Ziggie stopped walking and turned to face her, holding her arms. "You haven't exactly trusted me, have you? But we'll never get anywhere if we keep on hedging. I understand that the person who wants to know is Maria Janesky. She's stuck her neck right out searching for information."

"The opera singer? Good God. She must be working for the State."

"No. Believe me. I can personally vouch for her. She's done some great work for us. But of necessity it has to be limited. Very few of us know about her."

Annya admired the opera star as a singer; but this new role was difficult to accept. "Why on earth would she want to know about this man?"

"I think she can help him."

"We've all heard that before."

"Look, Annya, if you know anything at all about this, would it not be better to meet her?"

"I could be setting myself up."

"Yes, you could. As I've already done many times with her myself without coming to any harm. In fact she helped me when I was really on the floor, just after I was kicked out of the university. We all take risks all the time. If I'm wrong about her I'll attend to her, one way or another."

Annya was thinking furiously. Why would Maria Janesky, one of the privileged, want to know about Zotov unless she had been instructed to tap the underground? It sounded so phony. Yet she respected Ziggie; he had to be more careful than most; already he had served time in prison.

Zigbien did not hurry her. He knew what was passing through her mind and he approved her caution. It would always be like this. He started to walk again and linked her arm through his once more. They were nearing the church.

"Where do you think I should meet her?"

"After tonight's performance at the opera. In her dressing-room."

Closed in. Annya did not like the sound of it.

Zigbien added, "I can arrange to have you covered. If she's against us, nothing will happen in the theatre, it would bring too much notice. But I can see to it that our people watch your back when you leave."

"What time?"

"Ten-thirty. I can get word to her to expect a woman. No names."

Annya glanced up. "Do you think this is safe, Ziggie? I mean, how do I get into the theatre? Even with a wig I don't want to be seen too much."

"You go to the stage door. If she's received my message the doorman will be expecting a lady visitor for her. If he doesn't know about it, go back home. We'll be watching either way."

"Okay, I'll do it. I must be mad." Annya checked the time. "I'll have to cross the river to get to the theatre; I might as well go now and take in a film to pass the time; if you've left me enough money."

"Sorry about that but I have to scratch out a living somehow. Let's go back by the Slasko Dabrowski Bridge."

21

Kanavsky was unpacking in his hotel room when General Gruszka arrived. There was a tap on the door and the General walked in with the familiarity of an old friend; he carried a small paper-covered parcel. Kanavsky recognised him at once and straightened over his case in a stiff, formal greeting. Gruszka had nothing like the authority of Zhadin, but here he was the KGB chief's representative, and particularly so in this instance.

"I hope you had a good flight, Colonel. I just wanted to be sure that you have everything you want."

"All I have is my normal service pistol which seems to me . . ."

"I don't want to know that." Gruszka snapped out the words angrily. "This is merely a courtesy call, as you are General Zhadin's personal envoy. I do not want to know your business, you understand?"

"Yes, sir." Kanavsky reflected that nobody wanted to know. Zhadin had skated round the intent of the visit and Gruszka wanted no knowledge of it. "I'm sorry. I thought you knew why I was here."

"Not the specifics. They are of absolutely no interest to me. I cannot cope with the trivialities of subordinates. I expect, however, that you will want to make contact with your old chief, General Chernov, while you are here, and with that in mind you will find his itinerary, such as we know it, in this parcel." He laid the parcel on the bed as if it was a bomb and then stood well back.

Kanavsky stared down at it; it was big enough to hold a gun. He was still fascinated by it as Gruszka added, "I suppose you know that the General is also staying in this hotel. On the fourth floor. He prefers a back room because it's quieter. Room 405, if you wish to pay your respects."

Gruszka made great play of studying his watch. "He will be my guest at dinner and then at the opera to hear our own great Maria Janesky. If I'd had more notice I might have been able to get you a seat, Colonel. But another time perhaps. I've no doubt he'll be back in his room by eleven. I know he usually has a drink before turning in. It might be a good time to catch him." He smiled, the chill of it making Kanavsky shiver. "Meanwhile, I hope you enjoy our city. Ring my secretary tomorrow and she will find you a guide. Goodnight."

The room was like a tomb to Kanavsky after Gruszka had left. He sat on the edge of the bed and unwrapped the parcel as if it contained delicate china. He did not want to know what was inside. There was a mass of cotton wool and when he had unravelled that, a Colt Government automatic with a silencer already attached. He picked it up to search for the itinerary Gruszka had said was there, but it was not there. That meant only one thing.

Kanavsky examined the gun. It was an ACP, version ·45, and he knew that it had a tremendous recoil, so much so that the manufacturers had had to produce a ·38 for people of smaller physique to handle. But this was knowledge he had picked up in his office and on the firing range. Now he was in the field. The gun also made a good deal of noise and he wondered just how effective the silencer would be, and whether a special adaptation had been made. Perhaps it was intended to be heard.

He knew why the gun was American, and in a way it reassured him. Perhaps he would see his office again. Perhaps. It would depend entirely on how he coped and what orders Gruszka had received from Zhadin. He had no appetite for dinner nor to go to any public place. He lay down on the bed, hands behind his head and wondered how he had got into such a mess. He dozed uneasily, never quite asleep, the intruding nightmares real. All too quickly it was dark. He switched on the television and tried to occupy his mind.

When it was time he rose slowly, his mind clouded, his hands shaking slightly as he checked that there was a round in the breech and that the magazine was full. He then put the gun in his waistband leaving the safety catch on. When he pulled at his jacket it wasn't too bad, the gun quite well hidden. He hoped the silencer wouldn't catch on his waistband as he drew the automatic out.

He screwed up the paper and the cotton wool and threw them in the small metal waste bin by the writing table. Better to get it over. Gruszka had obviously thought so. Why prolong the agony? All he had to do was to kill a man he had once very much respected and feared, who was still, in a way, his boss. The respect had waned but the fear was stronger than ever.

He quickly gazed round the room; he had not yet finished unpacking. It would have to wait. Kanavsky dreamed up every excuse not to go but in the end, inevitably, he found himself walking to the door, locking it behind him when he was in the passage, and then heading for the stairs, rather than the lift, to go up two flights. He was being rushed, he knew it, and he knew he could not turn back.

It was almost as if the hotel had been emptied for him; he met nobody on the way and whole place felt deserted. By the time he reached the fourth floor landing he was panting and he stood there to regain his breath. He pulled in his stomach and felt for the gun again, easing it up and down to make sure that it would come out cleanly when the time came. Taking a deep breath he walked along the empty corridor. He studied the printed signs with the arrows indicating the direction of the room numbers, passed a landing pantry, turned a corner and there it was facing him. Room 405.

Kanavsky looked up and down the corridor. Nothing stirred. He took out the gun, flicked off the safety-catch, and held it behind his back; he would surely hear anyone approaching, and would have time to hide the gun. Meanwhile he did not need to worry about the silencer catching in his waistband. With his spare hand he knocked firmly on the door, barely able to breathe.

Maria Janesky still had on her stage make-up when Annya entered the room. She had dismissed her dresser and given instructions she was not to be disturbed; she was meeting an old friend. The stiff, period dress was on a dummy and the room was filled with the smell of flowers and grease paint. Bouquets were strewn along one wall.

Maria, sitting in front of her mirrors with a white robe draped over her shoulders, could see Annya's reflection and the trace of anxiety in her eyes. She swivelled round on her chair, looking grotesque, close-up, with the deep lines and shadows of the make-up completely distorting her usually warm image.

"Please sit down. Move that stuff there; just drop it on the floor."

Annya was reluctant, but not to sit would be to show her suspicion. She turned the chair so that she could also see the door. She was fascinated by the singer, being unable, close to, to place her in the role that Ziggie had described. She could hear constant movement in the corridor and from time to time someone would tap disconcertingly on the door and call out a farewell as the cast dispersed.

"You don't trust me?" Maria said with a smile. "I don't blame you, especially with this lot plastered on my face. Do you mind if I take it off before we talk?"

Annya nodded. She could not get used to the scene, nor the sounds around her. She watched the make-up melt under the cleansing cream until, with the aid of a towel, a pale, rather vulnerable and very attractive face appeared. This was followed by a light brushing of powder and a touch of lipstick.

"I know you are suspicious. So am I. This dressing-room is usually like a bus station, people coming and going and congratulating everybody else." Maria smiled. "I don't know your name, so you have an advantage over me."

Annya said, "Is it safe to talk here? There seem to be so many people about."

"I agree. We had to meet somewhere and I do get back-stage visitors. Would you come in my car? I'm sure that Ziggie is keeping an eye on you. Please trust me, or we'll get nowhere."

"I can't be long. There are friends who are probably worried sick about me by now."

They walked out together, the doorman calling out a loud good night, and when they reached the street there was a small crowd of autograph hunters waiting for Maria. When they finally reached the small car, Maria drove off and stopped when they turned into a long, nearly empty, cobbled side street.

"I find it difficult to talk and drive. I'm not a good driver and I need to concentrate." Maria watched the mirror and noticed another car pull up some distance behind them and douse its lights. "Ziggie's friends seem to have arrived." She laughed lightly, "Now, where should we start? Zotov. I have a friend called Yelena Belenko in a safe house. She claims to be Zotov's girlfriend from way back; before he was put into a mental institution."

"Yelena Belenko? I seem to remember a ballet dancer . . . " Yelena was the name Zotov had called out during his night of terror.

"The same woman. When he escaped she was lucky enough to read a short report and she fled from Moscow."

"Does she know who he is?"

"Oh, yes. But she does not know why he was put away. By a slip in the administration she visited him soon after he went to hospital but he was so heavily drugged that the visit was abortive. It placed her in considerable danger, though, and she was later threatened, told to forget the whole thing, or else. I think she found out where he was from Zotov's father, when the old boy was still in shock about what had happened. Six weeks later it was officially announced that Zotov died in a car crash. Yelena did not believe it. When she had seen him in hospital he was in no condition to get in a car, far less drive one. But she knew when to keep quiet."

"Was the announcement under the name of Zotov?"

"Yelena won't tell me. She still very much fears for her life with the knowledge she carries. It's not that she doesn't trust me; it's simply that if I come under official scrutiny it wouldn't be long before they got it out of me."

Annya was beginning to warm to the singer. She began to perceive some of the risks she had taken on behalf of a friend in trouble; a Russian friend at that. "What do you suggest?"

"Yelena still thinks she's in love with him. I don't think she ever stopped being in love, and when he escaped it was rekindled with all the old fears. I think they must meet." She turned and gazed at Annya in the poor light. "That's if you know where Zotov is. You haven't said."

Annya was in something of a whirl. She hadn't known what to expect to hear from Maria but certainly nothing like this. "Is your place secure?"

"More secure than most. I've kept it up my sleeve for a very long time. No place is safe but I think this is one of the best. Only a very few know about it."

"Can you drive me part way back to where I have to go? To save time and to stop the others getting desperate. And can you tell me how I can contact you tomorrow morning."

Kanavsky nearly turned back, his nerve almost gone. He could hear the sound of music through the door and wondered if his knock had been heard. He summoned courage and tapped again, more loudly this time. There was no sound of anyone approaching but suddenly the door opened and there stood Chernov, his belly protruding from a loosely drawn, woollen dressing-gown.

"Kanavsky! Of all people. My dear fellow, come in. I'm just having a nightcap; join me."

Chernov turned back into the room and walked towards a dressing-table on which was a bottle, and a half-charged tumbler of vodka. "I'm surprised to see you," he called over his shoulder. "Has General Zhadin sent you to keep me out of trouble? Or have you come to tell me that he wants me back?"

Kanavsky felt more at ease with Chernov speaking; he did not know why, but suddenly it all seemed easier. He followed his old boss into the room, his hands still behind his back.

"We need another glass," said Chernov without looking round. "These damned hotels think we only use glasses for cleaning our teeth. So I bring my own." He opened the central drawer of the dressing-table and fumbled inside.

The bulk of Chernov covered what he was doing but Kanavsky was saved by the dressing-table mirror. He saw the big hand emerge and it was not holding a glass. He almost froze at the crucial moment, but as Chernov spun round in a remarkably quick movement, he brought the heavy gun from behind his back and fired without taking proper aim. He was so hyped up at that moment that he couldn't tell whether the Colt made a lot of noise or not.

Chernov was caught in the shoulder and he fell awkwardly against the dressing-table, sending the bottle flying against the mirror. He straightened and his gun hand was rising as Kanavsky fired again, this time hitting the big man in the stomach. Chernov doubled up, arms across his middle. "You fool, Borya. You've shot yourself as well."

Chernov sank to his knees as Kanavsky watched in horror. Blood was spreading over the dressing-gown and through Chernov's heavy fingers. But even then the old warrior rallied. He turned his wrist and was on the point of firing before Kanavsky broke through his own terror at what he had done, and managed to fire off another shot, the recoil sending him back. A huge hole appeared in Chernov's bald skull and he fell forward in a position of prayer, his head almost touching the carpet.

Kanavsky stood rooted to the spot. When he looked down he was holding the gun in hands that were shaking violently. The last shot had been a fluke, he had never been that accurate. But it was done and the smashed skull confirmed Chernov's death without need to check. It still took time for Kanavsky to pull himself from the fit of terror. What finally made him move was the realisation that the door was still open.

He was wet through as he went through the motions of wiping the gun clean and placing it in front of the body. He had no intention of keeping it and, in a daze, he believed it was intended that he leave it there. He shakily reached the door and closed it behind him, using the handkerchief he had used to wipe the Colt. Routine training was directing what he should do and somehow his weak legs took him down the two flights of stairs to his room.

He went straight to the bathroom and was sick. Later, still shaking, he was unable to grasp that he had killed the great Chernov. He could not accept it, and when eventually he could, he burst into tears. One man had caused all this. Zotov. And if he ever ran across him he would do far worse to him than he had done to Chernov.

"For God's sake, where've you been? We've been worried sick." Mirek had never been so angry with Annya. He had been in a state of utter despair, but the next moment he was hugging her tightly, so relieved that she was back.

Zotov was almost equally relieved. He turned his back as he saw the tears of joy, but within moments was engrossed by what Annya was telling them.

"Yelena." Zotov sat on one of the two rickety chairs. "Yelena." His face was grey with the effort of recollection and yet the others could see that a deep chord had been struck.

"We'll take you to meet her," Annya said. "She's safe and she will be able to help you with some of your past."

Annya and Mirek exchanged glances. Zotov was dazed by what had been said and, after all he had been through, it seemed that he was not now so certain that he wanted to remember. He sat gazing into space, his expression blank.

"You must meet her," insisted Annya. "She still loves you after all this time. She fled Moscow because of you."

Zotov did not respond, going deeper into himself.

"One thing I learned," Annya added desperately. "She came to Warsaw because, when you were lovers, that was the place you both said you'd run to in case of trouble. It was a lovers' joke, but one that meant something to both of you. Perhaps that's why you came here, Zotov. A subconscious pull. Did you ever feel that?"

Zotov nodded slowly. He had felt that, but now he was not so sure that he should have responded to the urge.

Annya gazed at Mirek in despair but he had not had the advantage of speaking to Maria Janesky. She said gently, "You must find out who you are, Zotov. You've come so far. Yelena knows and she won't tell anyone else. She'll help you. And you used to love her ballet dancing."

Zotov's head jerked up. He was worried but the mention of ballet had struck another chord.

Mirek spoke at last. "Don't underrate yourself, Zotov.

We're your friends. We know something of what you've been through and we know you have guts. Don't be afraid of the past. It's what happens from now on that matters. We'll be with you."

Zotov stood up, his thoughts and fears shielded. "All right. I'll go."

"We've got to wait until tomorrow night. I can't contact Maria Janesky until the morning." They all knew that it was going to be a very long wait.

Maria had parked her car two blocks away. She had seen several police patrols on the way and had taken an exceptional number of detours. The city was crawling with police, but the real danger lay with the plain-clothed UB. She had picked up Annya, and then Mirek and Zotov, at different, pre-arranged points. It was very dark for late evening but the streets were far from deserted of traffic. At least that gave some cover.

The factories in the Ursynov had been closed for some time, and here the streets had virtually emptied. When she parked, Maria gave directions and then left with Mirek, on the basis that two separate couples would attract less attention. They reached the disused factory and, once sure that they were not seen, entered. They waited just inside the closed door and, when Annya and Zotov arrived, they all climbed the stairs to the make-shift apartment.

At the top, Maria said, "I'd better go in first and prepare Yelena. I haven't been able to tell her what has happened. It's going to be a shock for her. Wait here. If there's trouble, knock on the door and I'll let you in; there's an escape route from inside."

Maria tapped on the door and then unlocked it closing it quickly behind her so that Yelena would not see anyone outside. The others waited nervously. Yelena was a complication that none of them could have foreseen and they were anxious as to where it might lead. Yet none of them could run away from it.

The door opened and they went in tentatively, Annya, then Zotov, followed by Mirek. During the time Maria had been inside she had helped Yelena to make up, so that she would look her best for a man she had not seen for twenty-five years.

Yelena and Zotov gazed at each other across the large, shabby room, and the changing emotions they displayed touched the others. Neither moved, as they tried to cast back the years to the times they might remember. It was easy for Yelena but Zotov was struggling, yet it was clear that he was filled with a tremendous burst of emotion as his features began to show a joy not previously seen by Mirek and Annya.

"We'll make some coffee," said Maria in a matter-of-fact tone. It was the signal for the others to go into the kitchen-cum-bathroom.

When they had gone, Yelena said, "Oh, my love, don't you recognise me? Have I changed so much?"

Zotov was almost in tears with the frustration of partial memories. "I know you, I'm sure." He raised his hands to his chest. "But it is here that I am certain that I know. My heart is bursting. Were we lovers?"

Yelena came forward; it was too soon to touch him and she stopped just a few feet away. "Of course. We've never stopped being lovers. I recognised you as soon as you came in. You are grey now, a little lined, but still the man I knew. You have not changed that much."

"And you are a lovely vision. But who am I? Why did they do this to me?"

The tears in his eyes were too much for Yelena to bear and she ran forward to embrace him, and he was soon returning her embrace with equal fervour, as they both cried shamelessly.

It was a long time before they separated and when they did they were drained but enjoying a happiness, the strength of which, neither could recall. The years, in the absence of physical contact, had compounded a love that was destined to grow. At that moment it did not matter whether or not Zotov could remember, he knew that it was right to be with Yelena and to hold her in the way that he did. Other emotions were surfacing.

Yelena gently pushed him away. "Don't forget the others. Our time will come."

"Tell me who I am."

"Come, let's sit at the table. We must concentrate for a while."

They sat at opposite sides of the table, for Yelena knew that the yearning must wait until they had sorted things out. "You really don't know who you are? You can't remember anything?"

"Please. Don't taunt me. They made sure that I forgot. They built a barrier in my mind."

"Your father was Sergy Vladimirovich Ilyushin."

He stared, his mind reeling. He knew the name. Everyone in Russia knew the name. But he had never connected it with himself. He did not know that it was considered a triumph at the hospital the day that particular memory was erased. "The famous aircraft designer? My father?" He sat back as if he'd just received a blow. And then something Yelena had said belatedly registered. "You said, was."

"He died in Moscow in February of 1977."

Why didn't he know that, if he remembered the name? Why had that particular piece of news been kept from him? He struggled for recollection and discovered it not too hard. He recalled the elderly man who visited him periodically, once his treatment was well under way. He had never known who it was, he was pumped too full of drugs, but in any event, he realised now that a real name would never have been given. At no time had he recognised the man who had always appeared so distressed. He remembered being told that his father had died but he could not recall the year and it had meant little to him. That had been Sergy Ilyushin?

Zotov struggled to break through the blockage. His veins stood out with effort. Worried, Yelena stretched across the table and they held hands. He shook his head in despair. He knew that it was right to be with Yelena, that they obviously belonged to each other, but in truth, he didn't really recognise her, and she possessed a beauty he surely could not forget. His memory had been clinically blacked out. Yelena felt the strength leave him as he slumped in his chair, the strain too much.

Zotov wearily shook his head. "We'll have to take it in

stages. The doctors, and there were many of them, would be proud of the cabbage they've made of me if they could see me now."

"You are no cabbage, Yuri. It's just a matter of time."

"Yuri?"

She smiled. "I've always called you Yuri, it is my pet name for you. Just as you used to call me Lena."

"Why did they put me away?"

"I don't know. You must have known something they did not want leaked. When you went back to Baikonur . . ."

"Baikonur?" Zotov's face changed and his eyes were a little wild. The name seemed to strike fear. "What happened at Baikonur?"

Yelena saw that he was upset and did not want to continue, but of what help would it be to hide anything. "The Space Programme. I wasn't supposed to know but your father was proud of you and little bits escaped from him. Nothing really secret, nothing that would damage anybody. You were there with Gagarin, and Bondarenko and the others. Gagarin went up and created history. You recall none of this? Nothing at all?"

Zotov stared at her and then his focus suddenly fell short and he was really seeing nothing at all. A look of absolute terror crossed his face, and Yelena rose, frightened, and glancing hastily towards the kitchen door. "Yuri. Yuri, what's the matter? For God's . . ." She stopped as Zotov gave a tremendous yell and collapsed off his chair.

Mirek, Annya and Maria rushed in as Yelena came round the table to crouch by the crumpled figure of Zotov. As he gradually came round they helped him sit up. After a while and looking pale, he said, "I'm sorry. I don't think I've ever fainted before."

They helped him back on to the chair and he tried to smile but behind the effort was a haunted look. "Go on," he said to Yelena as if nothing had happened.

She did not want to but he insisted and when the others started to leave the room again, he said, "Stay, we are all involved. We all need to know what happened."

"But, darling, I don't know what happened. I did not see

you from the day at my babushka's, such a wonderful day, to the day I briefly saw you in hospital. The visit was a mistake and I was quickly ushered out. The next I knew was some weeks later when I read of your death in a car crash in Siberia. I never believed that it was you."

Zotov tried to rally but he was still badly shaken. "What happened to the others? Gagarin, Bondarenko?"

"They're both dead. Valentin Bondarenko was reported to have died before Gagarin's flight. Gargarin died some years later in an air crash." Yelena hesitated, not sure how things had stood between Gagarin and the young Ilyushin. "The official announcement stated that he was on a training flight. The rumours had it that he had been drinking heavily during lunch and crashed his MIG doing stunts. Some thought that being the first man in space had turned his head, others that it had affected him in some way, that he found it difficult to live with."

"And I died some weeks after the flight? It does not seem to be a very lucky time." Zotov's hands were shaking and those looking and listening with such fascination thought he was about to break out into one of his fits of ague. But he controlled himself. Yet, undoubtedly something had changed in him. Apart from Yelena, he seemed totally unaware of the others in the room. Everything he said was addressed to her as if it was of vital importance she should understand him.

Mirek looked in turn at Annya and Maria and was about to signal that they leave the other two together. Yet if they moved at all, it seemed that it would break the thoughts with which Zotov was struggling.

Zotov ran a hand over his face. He had suffered so much for so long, and now he was confronted with another kind of suffering, in many ways worse than before because he did not have the effects of drugs to blanket his feelings and everything in his past. His mind was damaged yet he still struggled to put it right and there was a general feeling amongst the others in the room that, given time, he might eventually succeed.

Slowly he rose and held on to the table edge. He still appeared to be haunted, and then, to everyone's distress, he began silently to weep. He stood there, with the tears running down his cheeks, and Yelena hurried round to hold him and to bury his head in her shoulder, stroking his hair and murmuring soft reassurances to him. Again it was to her that he finally spoke. "Gagarin wasn't the first man in space. I was."

There was only the soft sound of Yelena's comforting murmurs. It was as though, she personally, had not heard Zotov's momentous words, and if she had they did not matter. Only Zotov mattered and he had endured far more than any man should. The other three were stunned into an unnatural silence while they tried to grope with the enormous implications.

None of them accepted that Zotov had actually remembered, but nor did they doubt his words. Zotov knew. And they believed him. It made sense of everything that had happened. It was an awkward time when nobody knew what to say. As the others watched Yelena calming Zotov, there seemed to be a common understanding that Zotov had no actual recollection, but that the fact of what he had said had cut through the mist of his confused and maltreated mind to impart a message like a computer flashing one on to a screen.

Mirek backed slowly away to the kitchen and the others followed as stealthily. It was not a time to intrude; Yelena was coping well; and Zotov was experiencing the only love and care he had received in years.

Back in the kitchen they showed their astonishment. Maria emptied the jug and filled the kettle to make some fresh coffee. Mirek's mind was hammering. No wonder London wanted Zotov back. Ilyushin, the first man in space? It posed the question of whether Gagarin had circled the earth at all. How were they to find out without Zotov's memory returning, yet it was far from doing that?

Mirek turned to Annya. "When is the earliest we can pick up the passports?"

"Ziggie can't get them done until late tomorrow."

"Damn it." He then spoke to Maria. "How did you plan to get Yelena out?"

Maria took the kettle off before it boiled and poured water into the coffee jug. "Two friends were arranging it. They would not say, but I think they were smuggling her out as some form of cargo."

"So she has no passport?"

Maria poured the coffee. She looked surprised. "I've never been in this type of situation before. They didn't mention a passport."

"Do you trust them?"

"Oh, yes."

"Are they experienced or are they just doing their best?"

Maria passed a cup over to Annya. She appeared worried. "I'm showing my shortcomings, aren't I? I just do what I can when I can. This place was set up by my late husband. I'm restricted. Ziggie knows about me because he and my husband were close. He made the contacts for me. Nobody knows who's involved and maybe that's why a passport hasn't been raised. If Yelena goes out as cargo she won't need one, will she?"

Mirek and Annya were shaking their heads. "It's old hat, Maria," Annya said. "Unless they know what they're doing they're chancing their arm and Yelena will be the one to suffer."

Mirek felt his cup, it was too hot and he put it down on the kitchen table. "She'd better come with us."

Maria sat down at the table and the others followed suit. "You have a plan?"

Mirek gazed towards the door and wondered how Zotov and Yelena were getting on. There was no sound at all. "I have an idea. There's no easy way. Particularly now, with such a flap on."

"The flap is worse than you think, Mirek." Annya tossed over a folded newspaper which Maria had brought in for Yelena. "Front page, near the bottom."

He saw Annya's photograph at once and alongside it a small article stating that she was wanted for the murder of Waleski whose body had been found on a refuse tip outside Siedice. Mirek came round the table and cradled her. "I'm sorry," he said. "You must have seen that soon after we arrived and yet you kept it to yourself." He looked across at the puzzled Maria. "A UB man was accidentally killed on the way down to Brest. Annya was blamed for it."

Annya said. "It's not a good picture. And I have my wig; don't worry."

Mirek returned to his coffee. "I don't think things could be any worse. We're in up to our eyeballs. Maria, I think you should go home. Keep well away."

Maria looked tired as she shook her head. "I must see that Yelena is all right. The rest has just happened; it's too bad. What about this plan of yours?"

Kanavsky listened to the sirens and the activity in the hotel. Gruszka had not wasted much time. Within an hour of Chernov's murder the ambulance was taking the body away and within minutes of that a special radio bulletin announced that a Soviet tourist had been found dead in his hotel. The name of the hotel was not given and Kanavsky found it weird that he was sitting in his room only two floors from where he had committed the murder.

The fact that Chernov's name had not been mentioned, or how he had died, or that he was a very high-ranking Soviet official, indicated how Zhadin intended to play the situation. Chernov was simply to disappear.

Kanavsky felt a tremendous relief. He picked up the telephone and asked for a Moscow number, knowing that he should have done it as soon as he returned to his room. It was the number Zhadin had told him to ring but it did not sound like Zhadin's voice on the other end of the line. "This is Colonel Kanavsky," he said in an unsteady voice. "It is done."

"I know," said the voice. "Now you know what to do when Zotov is found. That should be much easier." Kanavsky was cut off.

So Gruszka had already contacted Zhadin. Kanavsky poured a stiff drink, much as Chernov had done. So it was not to end with Chernov. He had become an assassin and was expected to operate again. His problems were only just beginning. Zhadin had him exactly where he wanted him. And it raised the question of whether he too, would disappear. Was Zhadin going to be any better than Chernov had been?

Kanavsky received another blow to his system that night. A staunch patriot from childhood, he had always believed that what he had done in the KGB had been for the good of his country; until now. He had dealt with Department V many times over the years and, via Chernov, had sanctioned assassinations. But he had not personally performed them. For the very first time in years of loyal service he considered the possibility of defection.

He watched his shaking hand raise the glass to his lips, and savoured the harsh spirit going down. The question was, had Zhadin also considered the possibility that he might defect? And just how long had he left?

22

"Each week, two and a half thousand Eastern Block TIR trucks cross the West German border. Three hundred and fifty thousand a year. Under the 1949 Transport International Routier agreement, sealed trucks can cross European borders without Customs inspection. More than forty countries signed the agreement."

Mirek realised that he must sound as if he was lecturing, but the two women were quick to grasp his direction. "The system, originally designed to cut red tape, has been abused by the Eastern Block for years. The juggernauts take routes that are miles off their beat, and pass conveniently near to sensitive military areas in the West. The West know this, of course, and there is talk of a clampdown to make the drivers follow set routes."

Mirek drained his coffee and apologised to Annya and Maria. "Bear with me. Ilia Dschirkvelov, a Russian defector, claims that the drivers of these trucks are officers and tank commanders of the Soviet Army. They gather information on every trip. Some of these trucks carry nothing but sophisticated, electronic surveillance gear, so sensitive that they can pick up pulses from individual typewriter keys."

Mirek saw the growing doubt in the two women. "We must try to get hold of one of these trucks."

"Is this why you're really in Poland?" asked Annya wryly.

"Partly. I certainly discovered that there's no special point where the TIR trucks leave from. There are several places, but most of them leave from Zoliborz, around the general area of Bielanay."

Annya nodded slowly. "I know. You think you can steal one?"

Mirek smiled. "Not at base. There are too many people

around. There's another, old-fashioned way that might work. But it would be desperately risky."

"Staying here is becoming desperately risky," said Maria. "It's a question of time."

"Okay. I'll go back to Targowa and clean up any trace of us there and bring back anything we might need. And then I think, with the exception of Maria, we should all stay here and sweat it out."

"I'll take you," said Maria. "It's getting late for public transport and you'd be too exposed."

Mirek rose. "You've another performance tomorrow night. You'll be exhausted."

Maria shrugged eloquently. "It wouldn't be the first time I've given an indifferent performance."

Annya was worried. "Do you need to go? We have everything here. We can manage."

Mirek went to the door. "I think they should be told that we won't be back. It's not an ethical reason, but if they don't see us again they might begin to worry about their own position, and start asking questions around. Let's keep the lid on it."

When they entered the main room Zotov and Yelena were huddled together on the old settee, talking quietly as they held hands.

Maria raised her brow in query but Yelena shook her head at the unspoken question; Zotov had said no more that was relevant. "We'll be back."

The little Renault purred along with both Maria and Mirek on the look-out for the police. There was still a reasonable amount of traffic as they headed north but it began to fade once they crossed the river and headed for the Targowa. Mirek said, "You're really sticking your neck out too far, Maria. You started out helping an old friend but now you're into something much deeper. If we get away you'll still be left here. They'll begin to work out where the help came from."

"I know the risks. Did you say turn right here?"

Mirek nodded. He did not rate their chances and the scheme he had in mind was crazy which was why he had not given any details. "Now, left here." And then, shouting, "Carry straight on." The words almost stuck in his throat.

Hearing his panic Maria had the sense not to accelerate. As they neared the junction she saw what Mirek had seen. A glow of car lights reflected on the far wall. As they went past the junction, Mirek sank down but turned his head to see what was happening.

The light was not all that good but it was good enough to see the police car parked outside the house where the three had billeted. The blue flasher was off, and there were two police officers outside the opened car door. It was all he had time to see before Maria was turning left again. There were an agonising few minutes when they had to make sure that they were not being followed.

"That was too near," Mirek said. "A few minutes earlier and we'd have been caught."

"The police must have known the house. You think you were betrayed?"

"It wouldn't surprise me, with the number of villains there are around here. We'd better get back."

As they crossed the river Mirek said, "I must steal a car tomorrow."

Maria turned her head. "Won't this one do?"

Mirek, still feeling the shock of seeing the police car, smiled briefly. "You've done more than enough. Anyway, we can't use your car."

"Why not?"

"Because I need a car to steal a police car. If we use yours you'll be arrested after the event."

"I should have met you earlier, Mirek. Annya would have had some competition."

He laughed. "I'm not worth it. Annya and Zotov have done all the hard work. I'm just here for the ride." He turned to watch her. She was attractive in profile, chin held high with a fine neck-line. "Maria, you are pushing your luck too far. Get out as soon as you can. You can come with us if you like."

"Thanks, Mirek. But no. This is my country. I'm not going to be pushed out of it by a bunch of morons."

* * *

After dropping Mirek, Maria at last went home. The others sorted out the sleeping arrangements for what was going to be a long restless night. Too much had happened and the police raid near the Targowa had intimated the possibility of it also happening here. Zotov had gone quiet and was content to have Yelena by his side, a still beautiful woman whom he did not really remember but to whom he accepted that he belonged.

Zotov would have been content to stay in the safe house provided Yelena stayed with him. The comfort was not much but it was better than he had had for a very long time, and his heart was bursting for a glimpse of the past where it concerned the woman who told him they had once been lovers. It was something he wanted to believe and to rekindle, and he would have been happier if Mirek and Annya had left him alone with his old love.

It was as though he had switched off his need to know what had happened to him in his old life so long as he could cling to that section of it; but beneath his present euphoria was the deeper knowledge that they must move out, and he was afraid of losing what he had so unexpectedly found.

They were all up early, waiting for Maria and any news she could bring. They were silent, tetchy and worried about what might happen. The agony of waiting for Ziggie to finish the passports, and the thought of spending yet another night in this place, with the police searching the city for them, played on their nerves. It was made worse when mid-day came and Maria did not turn up, making her overdue by two hours.

"I'd better go to her apartment," Mirek said. "She's in trouble."

Maria always parked in a different position when she visited Yelena. She often left herself with over half a mile to walk. Parking some distance away frequently meant that she left the little Renault outside some busy factory where it could easily be seen. The night visits were different, but equally open to the scrutiny of patrolling police cars. Mirek had been right, of course. There would come a time when the car would strike a chord in someone's memory and an enquiry ensue.

She had taken a risk late last night, and again early this morning, when she visited Ziggie. She knew that the others would be worrying about her but it had all been worth it. She hurried along the grim factory streets, wearing dark glasses and an old floppy hat. Fortunately it was not quite the lunch hour and the streets were not yet buzzing with workers. She turned the corner where the safe house was and immediately came to a halt. With heart in mouth she backed away and rounded the corner again, to lean against the wall and to catch her breath.

At the far corner where she had first seen them were the same group of youngsters she had seen before; but it was the car drawn up beside them, and the two plain-clothes men talking to them that made her heart pound. She edged to the corner and peered round carefully. They were still there and one of the youngsters was talking animatedly and pointing her way. She drew back again.

She could either walk away or stay where she was and try to get some idea of what was happening. She had expected the car to start up, turn, and come back her way. It would be no use running and there were no doorways to dive into; the whole district, apart from factory gates, comprised mainly graffiti-covered, weather-stained brick walls. Even the door to the safe house led directly on to the street.

A car door slammed and an engine started up. Maria summoned her courage and went to the corner, checked both ways, and crossed the street to the other intersection. The car was disappearing round the far corner. Once satisfied that the car was not turning towards her she ventured to the corner and peered down the street. The youngsters had gone.

Maria now realised just how pent up she had been and how inadequately prepared for emergency. She waited a little longer and then crossed towards the blank door. As she approached, it opened slightly, and then more widely, and Mirek stepped out. Maria ran forward. "Go back in. Quickly."

Mirek helped her in, closing the door quickly behind

them. In the gloom of the squalid hallway, he put out a hand to feel her shaking. "I was just going out to find you."

"The UB were at the corner," she gasped. She told him about the youngsters. "Anyway, they've all gone but they might be back."

Mirek followed her up the dark stairs. Maria was rattled. Just before he opened the door for her on the top landing, she pulled on his arm and said, "I don't want to frighten the others. Perhaps we shouldn't tell them."

"They need to be warned, Maria. Are you holding something back."

He could just see her nodding in the bad light. She was still a little breathless as she said, "They've been rounding up all the dissenters. Hordes of them. Ziggie told me when I saw him last night after I left here. It's a wonder he wasn't one of them, but he keeps on the move as much as he can and they obviously haven't caught up with him yet."

Mirek put the key in the lock. "Then you shouldn't have risked seeing him. That was a foolish thing to do."

"If I hadn't I couldn't have hustled him into hurrying your passports. I collected them from him this morning; it's why I'm late."

He gave the signal on the door and turned the key. "I don't know what to say, Maria. Thank you. We'll be eternally grateful. It means we can move today."

Mirek sat in the Renault beside Maria and watched the huge electrically operated door rise. In the gloom of the cavity beyond he could see three juggernauts at loading bays, massive in the comparatively confined enclosure. He looked at his watch. It was difficult to believe it was less than two hours since Maria had arrived at the safe house.

The insistance of the others that she should stop involving herself before it was too late, had fallen flat. Maria wanted to see it through, she was adamant that she at least saw them on their way. The old factory hide-out was now as dangerous as anywhere else.

Descriptions of the three fugitives had been spread everywhere and it was clear that the link between them had been made. The heat was on. At odd times Maria was recognised, but Mirek was ignored; she provided a marvellous cover for him.

They were now in the Zoliborz, north of the city, and so far they had been to three different depots from where the giant trucks left on their long European journeys. They did not stay long at any of them for they were too noticeable in a strictly, commercial warehousing area. Trucks came and went. Most were TIR and they varied from a single driver, presumably on the shorter runs, to a crew of two men.

"I've seen enough," said Mirek. "We'd better get back."

Maria did not reply. She knew what he had in mind. And soon, one way or another, she would see the last of them.

He smiled at her. "We'll miss you too, you know." But as he sat beside her, he tried to keep his mind off the near future. She pulled out of a short queue of parked cars and headed south, making a wide detour to avoid the city centre, but ensuring that they were always part of the general traffic. Only when they approached the district of Ursynow did they begin to feel more isolated, and more vulnerable. Solidarity country was not the best place to be just then.

"Do you have to take Annya with you?" asked Maria, her gaze on the road.

Mirek knew that she meant on the next operation, before they could attempt the final escape. "I know it will be dangerous to be together, but she'll be wearing her wig. I'll need her, Maria. She knows the form. And we're both armed." He stopped talking as they passed yet another patrol car, aware that they were being scrutinised and again thankful for Maria's presence. But the points were building up against her.

"We'd better stop here and walk the rest." Maria pulled in alongside yet another factory wall. Behind it could be heard the faint drone of machinery. They climbed out and she locked the doors. A small truck and a van passed them, the drivers giving them an odd look, as if they could see that neither of them belonged down here.

They slowed their pace as they approached the hideout. They stopped at the corner and Mirek peered round. A patrol car was parked right outside the entrance and a uniformed policeman was scrutinising the door. "There's a car there," said Mirek. "Is it the same one as before?"

Maria peered round and drew back slowly. "No. The other was an unmarked car with plain-clothes men." She was frightened. "He's trying the door."

Mirek was thinking furiously. He put an arm round Maria's shoulder and walked her back up the road away from the corner. "This is going to be the briefest and saddest farewell I've ever made. Go back to your car and don't come back here again." He suddenly embraced her. "Thanks for everything. But it's your time to duck out."

She stood back from him in the sudden certainty that she would not be seeing him again; any of them. It was always going to happen and she had prepared for it. But not like this. There was no time for adjustment. What made it worse was an insight of what he was going to do and she was terrified.

"Oh, God, Mirek." She buried her head in his shoulder.

There was no time to spare her feelings, or to say the many things he wanted to say. There was no time to express the deep gratitude that he felt and of the sorrow the others would feel when they found out that she had gone. He held her head in his hands and kissed her gently on the forehead.

He said in a tone he at once regretted, "For God's sake go, Maria. As fast as you can." Her expression tore at him as she turned away.

23

He checked his gun, took the safety-catch off and returned to the corner.

There were two police officers there now. Mirek glanced towards the car; it was empty. He didn't trust himself to look back to see what had happened to Maria; he rolled round the corner and after the first two paces the policemen swung round to face him.

Mirek smiled widely. "Can't you get in?"

"Who are you?" They were both dark, one of medium height, the other taller with drooping moustaches. They looked tired and bleary-eyed as if they had been on duty too long.

"I'm with the Ministry of Planning. This building is condemned. It's not safe. I have the key if you want to get in. You'll find it empty, though."

The taller man held out his hand. "Let's see your ID first."

"Of course." Mirek put his hand inside his jacket and pulled out his gun. "Don't go for yours or I'll kill you." Over their shoulders, to his dismay, he noticed some youngsters at the far corner, no doubt the same ones Maria had seen. He wondered whether they had seen his gun.

He passed over the key to the shorter man. "Open up. I've nothing to lose if I shoot you."

"Are you Mirek? The whole country is searching for you and the others. You can't get away with it. You'd better hand over the gun."

There was something about Mirek which stopped the policeman from pressing his demand. He turned the key in the lock and pushed open the door.

"Inside, and keep your hands away from your weapons." It was a difficult moment. Mirek wanted them disarmed but the presence of the youngsters restrained him from doing it in the street. Inside it was dark, so he left the door open as he followed them in until he was satisfied that he could see. He closed the door and said, "Drop your belts and don't try a thing." There was barely light enough to see properly.

The taller man tried to undo the strap of his pistol as he unbuckled his belt and Mirek smashed him over the head with his gun without hesitation. He quickly threatened the shorter man. "You want to try the same?"

The police officer gazed down at the crumpled form of his partner and promptly dropped his belt. "You're going to pay for that."

"You won't be alive to see it unless you are very careful. Now drag him upstairs."

As the policeman pulled at his colleague's arms, Mirek scooped up the two belts. He made no attempt to help and closed his ears to the protests about the weight. They rested at each landing and the light was getting worse. Mirek could make out the shapes and was grateful that he had their guns.

The shorter man was exhausted by the time they reached the upper landing and complaining bitterly. But something did not quite ring true. Had the other man recovered? Mirek stepped on his ankle to find out and there was a yell of agony. The short man cursed his colleague for not taking an opportunity in the gloom.

"Stand well back." Mirek tapped the door. He did not want to use the key to create a moment for them to rush him. He knocked again loudly. He bawled out, "It's Mirek. Open up and stand well back."

The door swung open and Mirek ushered the two men in. He felt relieved now that he could see clearly. The others were astounded and worried at the entrance of two police officers even though they were holding their hands in the air. Both Annya and Zotov drew out their guns at sight of them. If the policemen had any hopes before, they disappeared as they saw the desperation of the fugitives, and their cold determination.

Zotov emerged from the emotional shelter of Yelena and came forward ready to kill the two policemen on sight.

Yelena helped to restrain him. "Take off your uniforms," instructed Mirek.

The two men stripped off their outer clothes under the hostile gaze of the others. They were at last thinking about their own safety for they could see that, unless they received help, there would be no escape from here.

"Cut up the blankets and tie these two to the chairs."

Annya and Yelena did the cutting up and Zotov bound them one at a time in a way that ensured they would never be able to untie the knots. He was almost vicious with it, but where his freedom was threatened, he would leave nothing to chance. He gagged them and when satisfied, he dragged each chair backwards into the kitchen from where he removed anything that would cut.

"There's just time to try on the uniforms," said Mirek brusquely. He attempted to hide his tension. "The opportunity just presented itself," he explained to a confused Annya. "I had to take it. We have a car outside."

Yelena took Mirek out of earshot of the policeman.

"What about Maria?"

"She's back home, Yelena." Mirek was stripping to his underwear as he spoke and so was Zotov. The jacket of the smaller man fitted Zotov and so did the trousers of the taller. It left Mirek with nothing that fitted. He dressed again and picked up the spare jacket, the uniform cap and the other gun while Zotov was buckling on a gun belt.

"Let's go," said Mirek. "We don't know how long we've got before they start looking for the car."

It was all a mad rush and, now the time had come to leave, Yelena could not take it in. She did not want to walk out on Maria, whom she could never repay, and she had adopted the safety of the shelter in a way she could not have foreseen. To leave it was to feel unsafe as she had done the night she had gone out on her own. She was now expected to face new dangers at a time when she had found her old love and wanted nothing more than to console and to be with him.

Mirek glanced at Zotov and the two men communicated as they had learned to do during the forging of mutual trust. Suddenly roles were switched and it was Zotov who took Yelena in hand and helped her towards the door. Mirek quickly went into the kitchen to make sure that the two policemen would be no danger for a long time; Zotov had done a thorough job; utensils and knives had been taken and stashed into a blanket, tied with a dozen intensely tight knots and stuffed on a shelf way beyond the reach of the bound men. It was not perfect, but the best that could be done.

All Yelena's old fears returned as they hustled her through the door and locked it behind them. Zotov constantly reassured her as they went down the stairs, feeling their way until they reached the bottom hall. They joined in an uneasy silence as Mirek went to the street door, listened, then opened it a little. He saw the car; the offside door had not been closed properly, which was as he remembered. "As quick as you can," he said and locked the door once they were all out.

The two women climbed in the back. It would have been logical for Zotov to drive as he was the only one in police uniform, but driving over the Pripyat Marshes was one thing, in a city like Warsaw it would be impossible for him to cope. Nor did he speak Polish if the need arose. Mirek took the wheel with Zotov beside him to give some form of credibility. Somebody was passing a message over the radio but it did not seem to involve them and Mirek had made quick note of their call sign, pasted over the facia above the receiver.

The keys were still in the ignition because the two policemen had not let the car out of their sight, until Mirek arrived looking as if he owned the neighbourhood. Ahead of him was the corner where the youngsters had been. He was reluctant to go in that direction, so he pulled out and did a U-turn, and then headed west, keeping to the southern section of the city where there was plenty of anti-government support in the workplaces.

It was now late afternoon and the rush hour was just beginning. In many ways it was an ideal time to travel, since it was more difficult for the police to single out particular cars. As he passed the first corner Mirek glanced up the street and was thankful that Maria had had the sense to leave. It had worried him that she might hang on to see what happened, and he felt strongly for her because she did not know. Perhaps she would never know.

As he eased through the early snarl-ups, Mirek reflected that Zotov was wanted dead. If he was right about his space claim then he was sitting on the biggest fraud in political history. The Soviet Union would lose all credibility, even among its friends. And Mirek was beginning to suspect that there was far more, that Zotov's simple claim was the tip of an iceberg. Suddenly it was easy for him to see why such frantic efforts had been made to stop him. As he glanced at the man beside him, ludicrous in the uniform, he realised that Zotov had no real appreciation of the dynamite he was carrying in his locked memory. No wonder he had been drugged.

Realising that his mind was wandering at a time when he should have every wit about him, Mirek concentrated on his driving. He would have preferred Annya to drive as she knew the back streets of Warsaw so well, but that was impossible. It took some time to reach the city outskirts and when he did it brought little relief. On the peripheral roads were motorised units of the blue-bereted, blue-uniformed, anti-riot militia, as if positioned to scoop up what the city security might have missed. The police car took them beyond the boundaries of the militia and it was doubtful if much attention was paid to them, with so much police activity around. But they would be remembered once the car was known to be missing, and so would the direction they were taking.

During these crucial moments the two women had crouched right down in the back of the car and they only sat up when Mirek told them that it was reasonably safe. With the help of Annya's directions he followed a less crowded route and they kept constant look-out for other police cars.

On the fringe of the built-up area, they were beginning to feel just a little easier when a call came over the speaker with their call-sign. Zotov did not understand, but both Mirek and Annya did. Mirek kept driving. When talking they usually spoke in Russian for the sake of the others, now Annya said in Polish, "That was for us."

Mirek nodded without looking round. "There's nothing we can do. If I answer they'll know straight away that it isn't the regular crew. I don't know their procedure."

They were silent for a while and Zotov and Yelena sensed that something had happened. The call sign was still going out, more insistent, and after a while, impatient.

"They're going to find out," said Annya.

"We just keep going. They were bound to find out sooner or later. They'll probably set up a search in the patrol area. With luck, they won't do it at once. They're not competent. They'll probably assume that the crew are skiving somewhere, having a coffee or something. It will all take time." But how much? Mirek kept the thought to himself. How much time did they need anyway?

"Why are you speaking in Polish," demanded Zotov.

Mirek told him and Yelena gave a little gasp. The thought of capture terrified her. With Zotov it was different, he would rather shoot himself if he felt capture was inevitable, which might mean that he would take Yelena with him. It was a side of him the others had seen, but she had not.

At last they were in open country, the fields stretching out on either side of the road, and the traffic thinned down to a normal commercial level. The car now stood out as the exception but Mirek kept up a good speed, overtaking as police cars do, but keeping in mind the need to preserve fuel. The radio had calmed down but Mirek left it on so that he could at least have some idea of the reaction at police headquarters. He also thought that they might be getting out of radio range.

"How far to Poznan?" he called out to Annya.

"From Warsaw it's about 270 kilometres. And about half as much again to Frankfurt an der Oder. Is that where you're going to cross into East Germany?"

They were speaking in Russian again. The traffic thinned the further they drew away from Warsaw. Farming country stretched for miles either side of the road, over seventy-five per cent of it still privately owned and much more successful than the state farms. Far to the south, on their left, was Silicia and the coalmines, and the foothills to the High Tatras. They were cruising comfortably when police headquarters again started their call sign. It was fainter now but no less worrying. In a fit of nerves Mirek ripped out the receiver.

He stopped himself throwing it out of the window just in time and realised how rattled he had become. He dropped the receiver to the floor. "Sorry, about that. The bloody thing was getting on my nerves." He had spoken in English, which was another giveaway.

Annya leaned forward and put a hand on his shoulder. "I love you, Mirek." She too spoke in English but Yelena understood, almost her sole knowledge of English. "That's how I feel about Yuri," she said in Russian.

They passed the first TIR truck they had seen and it raised Mirek's spirits. Knowing there were so many on the international roads he had almost begun to despair at ever seeing one again. He glanced at the mileage meter; they had already covered over fifty miles but he wanted to get beyond Poznan before making his move. Now he was having doubts about waiting so long. Evening was closing in and dusk was not far off. Darkness would help in one way but would hinder in another.

Reading his mind Annya called out, "I think they would search for the car in the city first. Unless they find the crew they might not connect us with the missing car." She had really spoken to console the others; she doubted that Mirek would push his luck. They were roughly half way to Poznan now, and the country had become more undulating, rising gradually as they progressed.

Mirek delayed putting on the lights for as long as possible, then he said, "Look out for a place where we can get off the road and stretch our legs."

Trucks were spaced to the odd sighting on a road that seemed to go on for ever. Cars were restricted by a general shortage and the prices charged on a prohibitive black market. Farm tractors sometimes appeared but they would branch off to this farm or that, leaving behind a trail of muck.

They found a spot down a lane that appeared to lead nowhere. It was now too dark for farm work and they felt reasonably safe out of sight of the Poznan road and with high hedges either side of them. Mirek had turned the car round in a series of short manoeuvres so that it was facing the way they had come.

They got out but didn't stray far from the car. They had left in such a hurry that they had no food or drink with them, and tension and the long drive had made them thirsty. Mirek opened up the trunk of the car but only the usual police equipment was there: danger triangles to be erected in case of road accidents; an orange flasher to use alongside, and the usual tools and first-aid box. The trunk light was not working so he used the flashlight from the driver's compartment.

Zotov and Yelena had wandered, arm-in-arm, off in front of the car. Annya joined Mirek who seemed troubled.

"What's the problem?"

"It's difficult to see at night. It's too easy for something to go wrong."

"We're armed, Mirek."

"If it's a surveillance truck, they might be too."

"So what are you going to do?"

She sounded calm, yet he knew she was as pent up as he. "You know what we're going to do. We go for it. Let's go tell them."

They positioned the car just below the summit of a long, straight climb. Zotov was standing off the road on the crest of the rise so that he could observe approaching headlights from the Warsaw side. They had already tested that they could hear his shouts. The police car was on the hardcore off the road and the accident equipment was ready to use. The two women stood by to help Mirek as soon as they received Zotov's signal.

It was a gamble. They didn't know whether the juggernauts continued on through the night, the drivers taking turns, or whether they pulled in at known stops or used lay-bys to pass the night. On the big trucks there were bunks at the back of the cab. Different drivers did different things whatever their orders. Once on the road they had their own ways of operating, and their own favourite stopping places.

Several trucks went past without incident. Zotov had

been told that the really big ones had a battery of lights high above the cab, so that there should be plenty of warning. They had to be patient, keep out of sight, and hope that the right truck would come along, and if it did, it would be on its own.

It was almost an hour later when Zotov saw the approach of an array of lights. He had become disillusioned, and detached from the others, and when he saw the lights his voice almost froze. He bawled out and little happened, then he yelled again and it was almost a scream, piercing the night like the cry of a wild animal in pain.

Mirek was momentarily rooted when he heard it, and then he yelled at Annya and Yelena who went into action. They first made sure that there was no other traffic, then placed the triangle almost in the centre of the road, with the amber flasher on. Mirek positioned the police car at the side of the road and just behind the flasher and switched on the rotating blue lamp on the roof of the car. They could all hear the rumble of a massive truck and Zotov became a blurred vision on the crest of the rise as he scudded down towards them, still shouting, as if, having found his voice, he had to keep it active.

The women ran off the road and lay flat waiting for a signal from Mirek. The full beams of the approaching truck shot over the crest, and pierced the dark sky like probing searchlights. The waiting group were pent up, knowing that if it was not a TIR truck, they would have to find an excuse to let it through, and they would then have to start again, with the odds shortening all the time.

The truck, as it crested the rise, looked massive in the night, and the battery of lights appeared to be suspended in the sky. Zotov, the only one in police uniform, felt puny as he stepped forward to swing the flashlight to and fro, the comparatively feeble beam swallowed by the blinding headlamps of the truck. Nothing was happening and he was on the point of throwing himself out of the way when he heard the frantic squeal of air brakes and the lights began to waver as the truck broke into a rear wheel skid.

In the end, Zotov had to jump aside as the truck took time and space to grind to a halt. Someone shouted angrily from the driver's cab as Mirek dived from the other side of the road, gun in hand while all eyes were on Zotov. Once Mirek saw the TIR on the front he did not hesitate. He jumped up on the step to reach the cab and pushed his gun through the open window. He felt blood running down his wrist but he was really only aware of startled, indistinct faces as he shouted, "Switch off and climb out or I'll blow your heads off."

Both men swung to see the gun pointing through the cab window. On the other side Zotov had now mounted the step to raise his own pistol at them. It took a fraction of time for the two-man cab-crew to adjust to a policeman holding a gun on them, and backing up Mirek's threat in Russian.

The startled driver moved his hand towards the ignition and Mirek had sudden insight of what he was about to do. If he jerked the truck which was still in gear, he might dislodge them from their very precarious footholds. In a frenzy, Mirek fired into the roof the cab and yelled at the same time. "Look in front of you, you stupid bastard. If I don't kill you she will." In the blazing headlights, out in front and holding a pistol two-handed, pointing straight at the driver, was Annya. "Switch off now."

The driver switched off. "Right," ordered Mirek, his pistol levelled at the driver's head, "Your mate gets out first."

Zotov opened the cab door as he dropped down to the road. He knew that Mirek was covering his side so he waited for the driver's mate to climb down. He still spoke in Russian but the man clearly understood. "Off the road, and lie flat with your hands on your head." Annya came across to cover Zotov.

Mirek made the driver get down in the same way and when the two men were prone, well away from the road, with Zotov and Annya watching them, and with Yelena awkwardly holding one of the police pistols, he collected the accident gear and rammed it into the trunk of the police car which he then drove well clear of the road. All that stood in the road now was the truck itself.

Mirek was about to climb into the truck cab when he saw

lights approaching from the Poznan direction. He jumped in quickly and dimmed the lights. He bawled at the others, "Keep out of sight. Any nonsense from those two, shoot them."

He jumped out. It was too late to move the truck, but there was plenty of room for passing. He stood on the nearside as the other vehicle approached and he could now see that it was another truck.

The approaching lights dimmed to indicate that they had been seen and the truck slowed down, and then pulled up alongside. The truck was nowhere near the size of the juggernaut and had only one driver who leaned across to call out, "You need help?"

Mirek came round the side. "No. My mate's being sick. I've warned him about the way he eats." He noticed the driver's gaze drift beyond him and he hoped that the others were well out of sight. "He'll be okay."

The driver grinned. "See you." The truck pulled away.

As Mirek hastened back to the others he could see the shape of the police car and wondered if the driver had seen it too. It was a moment of weakness all-round. After the success of the operation, for just a few seconds, concentration slackened on the two TIR crew. They were both still prone, but when one of them noticed that all eyes were on Mirek as he coped with the passing danger, he moved for the gun inside his jacket. He rolled on to his back and aimed at Zotov who was nearest.

Yelena saw what was happening. She glanced back at Zotov, really to show him that she too could cope with these situations. She saw the gun come up, saw the trucker aim at the man she cherished, realised that Zotov could never turn in time, and she screamed and fired in a blind panic until her gun was empty. She was still screaming and still firing the now empty gun as they all descended on her. Zotov wrapped his arms around her to try to calm her down.

The trucker lay on his back with two blood patches just visible in his chest. One had been a lucky shot and must have hit his heart for he was dead, his arms flung wide, the gun still in his hand. His mate lay trembling beside him, hands on head and yelling that he had done nothing wrong. When

Mirek and Annya gazed down at them, they were thinking the same. Yelena had never held a gun before; now she had killed a man in a blind fury to protect her man. It was a miracle she had not hit both crew men or even the man she was protecting.

"Find something to tie him up." Mirek pointed to the remaining trucker. There was no need. Zotov produced police handcuffs and snapped them on the survivor's wrists after pulling the man's hands behind his back.

"What do we do with him?" Annya was standing over the dead body.

"Let's get his clothes off. Zotov, get out of that uniform." Mirek was satisfied that the truckers were military or the driver would not have been carrying a gun; and the truck was clearly a surveillance model.

They stripped the corpse, then dressed it in the uniform Zotov had been wearing. It was a poor fit and the jacket would not do up but it did not matter. Mirek got the truck off the road and doused its lights. Twice they had to take cover as vehicles went by. Eventually, Mirek and Zotov bundled the dead trucker into the passenger seat of the police car and Mirek drove it away saying that he would be away for half an hour.

He drove back towards Warsaw to find the rough lane they had used before. He travelled down it for about a mile. It was utterly quiet, almost desolate, in this stretch of country, but it was impossible to judge how daylight might transform it. There was a risk in leaving the truck and the other three by the main road, but he considered it a bigger risk to leave the police car around.

When he found a crude passing bay he slowed and then drove the car right into the hedge. He opened the fuel cap, unrolled one of the bandages in the medical kit, forced it into the tank, pulling out a long strip like a rough fuse. He gave himself as long a stretch as the length of the bandage would allow. He put a match to the end and ran as fast as he could back towards the road. He covered only a few yards before he was blown off his feet as the petrol tank exploded like a bomb and the car burst into flames.

Bits of metal and stinking rubber were still flying through

the air as he got to his feet. He ran and walked alternately, gasping for breath, but anxious now to get the truck moving and as far away from the scene as possible. At least when the burned-out wreck of the car was found it would take time to determine who had perished with it.

Zotov did some of the driving. It was tough at first but clearly at some time in his forgotten past he had driven heavy vehicles. It took time to sort out the array of gears and get used to the massiveness of the truck, but once it was rolling its heaviness became part of the pattern. Driving at night helped. Mirek and Zotov, each taking turns, were able to get away with mistakes without being seen. They drove at modest speeds until they had the feel of the truck.

Annya, Yelena and the manacled driver were at the back of the cab in the cramped sleeping area. Once in the truck Zotov had tied the driver's feet with strips from the man's own shirt. There was barely room to move at the back, and, periodically, one of the women rode in the cab between the two men. When they saw the distant haze of Poznan they returned to the two-front, three-back arrangement. From time to time the bound driver was warned with a gun at his head. He wasn't gagged but, after what had happened to his colleague, there was no resistance in him.

It was well after midnight when they reached the outskirts of the old city. They followed the ring road to the north of Poznan unaware whether it was normal or not to motor through at this time of night bearing in mind the noise and the vibration which the truck created. They prayed that their transit had raised no interest.

It was a tense time but finally they were out in open country again and it stayed like that to the East German border where they met their biggest obstacle. There was no stopping now and nowhere else to go. And they were tired beyond belief, through lack of sleep and through the tension of the events of the day.

As they neared the border Mirek was driving. He found an unoccupied lay-by some ten miles from it. He pulled in, exhausted and with his mind numbed. With no idea of whether the border was open all night, and if not, what time it opened during the day, it was at least time to wait and get a little rest.

They stretched their legs, one of them always staying with the captured driver who constantly protested that he desperately needed to get out, but his comfort was not worth the risk. Annya and Yelena found some packed food belonging to the truck crew, and they shared out sandwiches and thankfully drank lukewarm coffee from thermos flasks. It was the best moment of the day; the lull before the storm.

The two women slept for a while in the long grass close to the truck but the dew chilled them. Then rain drove them back into the cab. However, by talking, walking, sometimes even slapping one another, Mirek and Zotov managed to keep awake. It became easier as dawn broke and the rain stopped, for they were wet through; but if they had climbed back into the truck they knew they would have fallen asleep.

The road started to become alive again round about seven, but it was still just the odd vehicle. Once there was a pattern to the traffic they joined in and drew out of the lay-by with Mirek driving. Conversation had died and their spirits were low because of exhaustion and because they simply did not know what lay ahead. When they joined the short queue at the border, it was far worse for Mirek and Annya, than at Brest, for this was the one that really mattered. What was more, they were in a stolen TIR truck and had killed one of its crew.

Behind Mirek and Zotov the two women had gagged the trucker, and lay on top of him, cramped but out of sight, with a gun at his head. As they felt the truck move forward they looked at each other across the now stinking body of their prisoner, recognised each other's fear, and silently prayed.

24

No wait had seemed so long. The border was live with troops. Yet the TIR truck itself attracted no particular attention as though it was a protected species. It soon became obvious that the border guards were looking for the stolen police car. Sooner or later it would be found and every waiting second was an agony. Mirek was asked to produce his papers but it was only a formality; these trucks crossed the border throughout the day, every day, and the rear doors were sealed.

The delay was interminable, but it was the smaller vehicles which commanded the attention and trucks were opened, passengers scrutinised. By the time they were let through the Polish border the nerve ends of all of them in the truck were strumming. For those crouched in the rear of the cab it was cramped and difficult to keep still and out of sight. When they finally were through they still had to prepare themselves for the German side of the border. The Germans were always thorough. Mirek and Zotov had their passports ready, but wondered nervously how good Ziggie's forgeries were.

Mirek sat in the cab in a mental hiatus almost unaware of those in the cab with him. It was so quiet he could hear them breathing. He shifted gear, moved up another space and felt sick. Surely they must know by now in Warsaw what had happened. The questions were interminable. Had the police in the factory safe house been found? Had the police car been discovered? Had they identified the dead body in it? It would not need much of a pathologist quickly to see that the man in police uniform, burned or not, had been shot. If Ziggie had been pulled in would they get him to confess to the passport forgeries? And what had happened to brave, loyal, Maria?

Mirek moved forward again, and now there was just one truck in front of him. The frontier officials were being particularly fussy, carefully examining documents, and, quite often, loads when the trucks were ushered into examination bays. He noticed that Zotov was holding his pistol ready. He hoped that the Russian would do nothing foolish, but there was no time to warn him; the truck was being signalled forward.

Mirek's mouth was dry as he made a mess of the gears before sorting them out and edging forward. His cab window was open and he prepared to hand down his passport and the truck manifest from the cab facia compartment which claimed that the cargo was to be delivered to Amsterdam. A grey-uniformed man gazed up at him and, for an awful moment, Mirek thought he was about to salute. Instead, the official offered an embarrassed smile and waved the documents away as Mirek reached down.

The first thing that entered Mirek's head was that the Germans must know that his passport was a forgery and his hand hung limply outside the cab with the documents still clutched in it. The next wave of the hand was more impatient and Mirek realised he was being ushered through. It was impossible to believe. He withdrew his hand, brushed aside Zotov's passport as it was held out for him to take, and tried not to fumble the gears as he eased the truck forward again. He gave the official a wink of appreciation, and the man responded with a knowing smile.

They were through. He drove in a daze, waiting for the mistake to be discovered, for the sound of a police siren. Zotov was staring at him. Behind him the women said nothing, not fully aware of what had happened. It was only when they were clear of the town that Mirek broke from his trance and yelled, "We've done it. Jesus Christ, we're clear."

Yet he only began to accept that they really were clear when Annya spoke. "They think you are a Russian or Polish Officer on surveillance. They must have so many passing through that they have learned not to hold them up."

Mirek began to laugh a little crazily. Zotov gazed at him with some concern and said, "We're still in East Germany."

It was just the cold douche that Mirek needed. He relaxed his grip on the steering wheel, but, yes, they were still in East Germany and had still to get through to Berlin. Unless news came through from Poland to stop this particular truck he could see no problem at the East Berlin frontier. Ironically that was much more likely to happen on the West Berlin side.

His tiredness did not ease with his tension but he could not share driving with Zotov at this stage. He had less than fifty miles to go to Berlin and he decided to stay at the wheel. Less than two hours later he was passed through the East Berlin frontier into the West where he was viewed with the suspicion that all Eastern Block TIR trucks received – but, trust them or not, a treaty dictated that they be let through without the cargo being searched. Unbelievably they had arrived in a pocket of Western democracy and it was almost too much for them to take in.

Suddenly, as they were able to grasp the momentous news but still suspicious of it, they broke into spontaneous cheering, like a bunch of children at the promise of some tremendous delight. For a short while they suffered the insanity of acute euphoria, but it gradually simmered down and Yelena started to weep, and after a while Annya joined her. The two men felt like weeping too, but somehow, they managed to avoid it. It was time to move again.

What followed was like a dream.

Once they had made the right contact and their credentials had been checked with London, the driver was taken off their hands and everything moved very fast. An RAF transport plane was flown out from England with a team of SAS to protect them. While the protection was a relief it was also a worry, for it showed that London considered them still to be in deep danger.

At the Brize Norton RAF base in Oxfordshire they were met by another team of bodyguards and hustled into a mini-bus with an armed escort, and were topped-and-tailed by police cars on the run-down into Hampshire.

They were now in England, yet still under guard. Mirek wondered if they would ever be safe. The estate between

Romsey and the Wallops, was guarded day and night by armed sentries, and had the latest and more effective safety and surveillance apparatus. The parkland rolled back as they approached the magnificent mansion which gave no impression of the battery of arms and sophisticated gadgets that surrounded it. As the mini-bus drew up outside the impressive Georgian porch, the two police cars peeled off and the illusion of peace all around them was complete. Only Zotov saw beyond the tranquillity.

25

"Tell me when you can no longer see my finger."

Zotov waited for the Russian translation from the interpreter who was standing just behind the white-coated doctor. He stared straight ahead as instructed and watched the finger pass across his face until it disappeared on his peripheral vision. He said nothing. The medical apparatus around him was disturbing, and the clinical smell to the place brought back to him terrible memories of the hospitals in which he had been imprisoned. It was just like all the others.

"Well?"

Zotov did not need the interpreter for that. "I object to this treatment. I've had enough. This is what I believed I had escaped from." It all took so long, what with the interpreter grinding out a translation each time. Why could they not find a Russian-speaking doctor? But he had had enough of doctors anyway.

The doctor smiled in understanding. He was middle-aged, plump and gentle in approach but he was really no different from the Russian doctors Zotov had met; they had all tried to reassure him before pumping in the drugs.

"I'm trying to help you. You've been through a lot. I just want to make sure that you are well."

"You want to inject me, fill me with pills as the others did."

"Have we done that to you?"

"It's only a matter of time, once you've decided what I should have. I want to go back to my room."

"You've been in a radioactive zone. We must find out, for your own sake, how this might have affected you. We're trying to help you, Mr Zotov."

"You did that yesterday. You are now leading up to the

condition of my mind. I've been through it all, Doctor, many times before. Please leave me alone."

The doctor straightened and put his podgy hands in the pockets of his surgical coat. He stared at Zotov for some time then nodded. "All right. I do understand what you have been through. Have a rest for a day."

"And tomorrow we start again? Until you have found what makes me tick or have obtained what you want?"

"It's essential to examine you thoroughly, Mr Zotov, and to treat you if necessary. We are not trying to change your personality as happened before."

Zotov rose. He hated the sight of the equipment around him, and shuddered. "But you would like to change me back to what I was? You would like to wring out my lost memory?" He stared back at the doctor, feeling a growing despair. "Perhaps I don't *want* to remember, Doctor. Perhaps, for the good of my health which you are so keen to protect, it is better that I don't. Are you willing to leave it at that?"

The doctor dropped his gaze and shrugged. "We don't want to harm you. Believe me."

Zotov moved towards the door from where a security escort suddenly appeared. "It is strange how doctors all sound the same. Perhaps they are all taught to say the same things. I take it that you are a psychiatrist, doctor?"

"Well, yes, but . . . "

"Then don't take me for a fool. What would radioactivity have to do with you?"

Zotov was standing by the window when Mirek and Annya came into his room. He was gazing across English parkland at its best. The trees were budding with a fresh, pale greenness, against a light blue sky with only the faintest whisps of sun-washed cloud. It was a beautiful day spoiled only by the sombre figure of Zotov himself.

"Are you all right?" Mirek was aware that Zotov had not heard him knock.

Annya called out, "It's us. We can't stay long. Yelena will be arriving soon and you won't want us here then. We just wanted to be sure that you are okay."

Zotov turned slowly, his features grim. "I'm sorry." He came towards them. "You are two good friends, but I don't think you can help me any more."

The room was large with an old-fashioned double-bed with brass fittings. In one corner stood a small table with four chairs round it and there were three easy chairs. It was bright and comfortable and at one end a door led to an en-suite bathroom.

Mirek sprawled into a chair hoping that Zotov might relax but the Russian did not sit down.

"What's the problem?"

Zotov turned back to the window. "It's happening all over again. I escaped to get away from doctors and hospitals and treatment, but now, after all we went through, I find I have English doctors instead of Russian. Nothing has changed."

Mirek gazed round the room. "You mean they treated you as well as this in Russia?"

Zotov turned and sat on the edge of one of the dining chairs. "Of course not. Everyone has been kind. I can order what food I like. I can see my friends and spend time and privacy with Yelena who has been wonderful. But still I am a prisoner."

"Of course you're not." Annya tried to be convincing. "Nobody here sees you as a prisoner."

Zotov smiled bitterly. "Do you know what happens when I open that door? There are two men outside to see that I don't leave. And if I want to walk in the grounds they come with me. At night I am locked in."

"That's for your own protection." Mirek was aware of how hollow that sounded. "Anyway, it won't be for long."

Zotov gazed thoughtfully at Mirek. "I shall be here until your security service gets from me what it wants. It may never get it."

"Then they'll let you go. You'll get money and a new life with Yelena."

"Perhaps. And perhaps, by then, I won't remember any of this either. I might even forget Yelena again." He did not add that, happy as he was to have her back after so long, no matter how hard he struggled he still could not recall knowing her before meeting her in Warsaw.

Mirek glanced up at Annya and they made for the door together. "Cheer up, Zotov. Hang on in there. Ride along with it for a few days. Meanwhile Annya and I will see what we can do with the powers that be."

But Mirek was thinking that it was much worse than was obvious. Zotov was holding back something more than his memory. He hoped Yelena would be able to sway him.

Sir James 'Moggy' Morgan sat in the deep leather armchair facing Mirek across the magnificent Adam fireplace. Both men had drinks by their side and the atmosphere was relaxed. Beyond the tall, paned windows, the lawns rolled away to the beeches and the oaks as Capability Brown had planned it. That Morgan had come in person was confirmation enough that Zotov was of the highest importance. He was not a person Mirek ever expected to meet.

"I hope you find your apartment comfortable," said Morgan, fully relaxed in his chair. He had allocated Annya and Mirek a superb, self-contained suite in the East Wing.

"The apartment is fine, sir. But we are extremely worried about Zotov." Mirek would always think of him as Zotov.

"Why? He's living in style, and Yelena Belenko has daily access to him, and you and Annya can see him whenever he's not under medication. I think you should all keep in touch; it will give him stability."

"He thinks he's exchanged one prison for another."

"That's ridiculous. He gets everything he wants. He has radio, television, excellent food from a wide menu, and his friends are supporting him."

Mirek did not like Morgan's attitude. Zotov had escaped from confinement, and he was again confined whatever the luxury. He had suffered enough. "He certainly doesn't feel free in any way. And he's afraid of being in the hands of doctors again. It's having a bad effect on him. He's very depressed."

Morgan eyed Mirek shrewdly. "I think you deserve to be filled in."

Mirek picked up his whisky. He pushed back his growing doubts so that he could pay full attention.

Morgan lowered his head and seemed to pick up a

middle-distance focus. "Bondarenko was probably the first casualty. He was twenty-four when he died and it took the Russians twenty-five years to grant him an award. He was apparently pulled out of a compressed air capsule when his spacesuit caught fire. Whether he actually reached space is doubtful and will probably remain a mystery."

Morgan spread his hands in a gesture of apology as if it was his fault that his knowledge was incomplete. "On the other hand we believe that Gagarin never went up at all, then, or since. At that time the space team included young Ilyushin who seemed to be a pushy young devil. He wasn't fully trained but he apparently used his father's position to get to the head of the queue against the advice of those who knew better. He went up into space and he returned in a coma. The Soviet hero could not be presented to the world in a gaga state. It was all a ghastly mistake and he should never have been allowed to go. It no doubt explains his present terror of open space, the agoraphobia you reported.

"There's a good deal of supporting evidence too. A Czechoslovak reporter on the Moscow circuit was removed at the time because he cast doubts on Gagarin's claim to fame. He mentioned Ilyushin as the son of the famous aircraft designer and it was the last time he was ever mentioned. A few weeks after the claimed flight the Russian Press published a message of congratulations to Gagarin, signed by all the astronauts in training with him. But there was one important omission. Young Ilyushin hadn't signed, the only one of the team not to. And not long after that he was reported dead in a car accident in Siberia."

Morgan raised his drink and Mirek could see that beneath the apparent calm, the MI6 chief was pleased with himself.

"Another strange quirk was the American reaction to the flight. For years they had scorned the Russian advances in space technology. When Russia claimed to have launched a manned spacecraft on 12 April 1961, NASA reported that they had been unable to track it. If it was up there they could hardly have missed it. Subsequently the White House counteracted the negative claim, and reported that, after all, the US tracking stations had picked it up. If they later returned to their original doubts there was no way they could again contradict themselves without losing all credibility. They had inadvertently gagged themselves."

"You think Gagarin was a substitute?"

"Consider the position of the Russians at the time. They knew that the USA was on the verge of a manned flight and had beaten them to it. But they were in no position to produce their hero because he remained in a state not to be seen outside an institution. At that time they were certainly not a nation to admit to any kind of failure. They had achieved the object but at at what cost? They produced a highly presentable substitute. Gagarin travelled the world and was fêted and idolised wherever he went. He was more than a national hero, he was a world hero.

"Perhaps, as time passed, the world might forgive them for that. Perhaps. Although it confirmed that they could never be trusted and credibility about any of their future claims would be suspect. But what the world would never forgive them was the contemptible way that the man who should have received the accolades Gagarin enjoyed, the man who should have been entered into the history books, was having his brain turned inside out in a Russian mental institution. It was something that had to be kept under wraps for all time. The ramifications of such a ruthless fraud going public opened enormous issues."

Mirek said slowly, "And you hope to get confirmation of all this from Zotov?"

"Only of his crucial part in it. The evidence all points the same way. Even the circumstances of Gagarin's death were distorted. He was full of vodka when he crashed his plane. This much we know. But he was a highly experienced pilot, he knew the risks of too much drink, yet apparently it didn't stop him going up at a time when there was no need to."

Mirek looked beyond the windows to the scene which was so peaceful and at variance to what was being discussed. "If Zotov was such an embarrassment at the time, why wasn't he
killed? Surely it was risky keeping him alive?"

Morgan nodded. "Here we can only speculate. But his father, Sergy Ilyushin, was a powerful figure in Russia in those days. Memory of him, even now, is still strong, and his planes are still flying. I think the son was spared out of deference to the father and the danger he might present. He probably went straight to Khrushchev. There had to be a compromise. The young Ilyushin would live but officially he would die. He would, in any event, have had to have his memory blanked out to avoid recurring traumas of the space flight. That would not make him a zombie, he simply wouldn't be able to recall his past. From that point on they would arrange a personality change. How much of this his father consented to is anyone's guess, but he would have to accept that the credit for the first man in space would not go to his son. It must have been a bitter pill but he knew the alternative and, once committed, was bound to secrecy like the rest."

Mirek stirred uneasily. "Wouldn't it be better for him if he is just left alone? He's quite happy with his old love. He wants nothing more than that. You may never restore his memory and even if you did, it could take as many years as the Russians took in burying it. As you've said, restoring his memory could bring back the old terror. Why can't he be left as he is?"

Morgan put his drink down very carefully. "You're not thinking this through, Mirek. We have the biggest opportunity we've ever had to bring the Russians to the conference table. They are in danger of being exposed to the world not only as blatant cheats but of showing how they slowly kill off their real heroes. The methods they took to cover it up will revolt the civilised world. At the moment they are going through their own traumas but *glasnost* was not intended to cover this sort of situation. They'll keep talking about arms reductions, Mirek, and they'll make more concessions than you would believe over the next few years. But we have to know if we are right."

Mirek drained his drink and was silent for a while aware that he was being studied with some concern. "He has become a good friend. He needs help and love. The last thing he wants is to see another set of shrinks and to be pumped full of drugs again. I doubt if his system can stand the strain. For God's sake, Sir James, the man has already paid the price. Let him be."

"Let him be?" Morgan rose, irritated that someone like Mirek should preach at him. "We're talking of world peace, man. We've been granted something with which to screw the Russians. After some of the treacherous years we've suffered from Russian trained traitors, it's rough justice, wouldn't you say? Do you understand the immensity of that possibility? We can't allow consideration for one man to stand in the way of something as important as this."

Mirek stood up and made no attempt to hide his feelings. As he put down his empty glass and moved to leave the room, he said: "Then we are not much better than the Russians."

Annya put an arm round Yelena's shoulders as the Russian woman sobbed. They had been shopping in Winchester and had gone round the old cathedral but throughout Yelena had been preoccupied and showed little interest in anything. A little distance behind two armed bodyguards followed them, as they were still doing now that they had returned and were walking through the grounds of the house. Admittedly the bodyguards had lengthened the distance behind them, but they were there, and the two women were always conscious of them.

Annya had been expecting an outburst of some sort from Yelena but not the tears. They walked on, Annya cradling the Russian so that the guards would not see her crying. As they reached a huge old oak Annya threw down a raincoat so that they could sit with their backs to the tree while the guards thoughtfully drifted out of sight.

"I'm sorry," said Yelena. "I did not mean to break down like that. You British are better able to hide things like that."

"I'm Polish," Annya reminded her. "You're thinking about Zotov?"

Yelena wiped her eyes. "He's talking of making an escape from here."

"Oh, my God. We're back to square one. You think he's serious?"

"Oh, yes. He's scared, Annya. He's terrified of what they might put him through."

"I'm sure they won't harm him. They won't want to do that. Anyway, where could he go even if he got out?"

"He's not thinking like that. Nothing matters to him so long as he gets away from doctors and needles and drugs."

"Have you tried to talk him out of it?"

"Of course I have. But he's distancing himself from me. He's going into himself and that is where he wants to stay. He feels safe only when he is alone and in control of himself. It's all coming back to him, twenty-five years of being used as a guinea-pig. I can't talk sense to him any more. Annya, I just don't know what to do."

Annya stared round the grounds; the guards were out of sight, but were there somewhere.

"Mirek has already talked to his chief about it. Perhaps if the three of us together insist on seeing him it might help. Come on, let's try."

Zotov sat in the chair facing the windows. The small clinic was on the top floor of the house and the view from where he sat extended well beyond the grounds. In the far distance an old church spire poked through the trees. Yet Zotov saw nothing. He felt numb as if his senses were closing down, the world finishing at the exterior of his body.

"This won't hurt and will relax you."

Zotov registered the doctor approaching with a smile and a syringe. When the translation reached him he wondered how many times he had heard those words before. At the same time it all seemed to be happening miles away and to someone else. "I don't want an injection," he heard himself say. He even struggled as his sleeve was rolled up but someone held him and then another as he struggled harder and in the end he did not feel the needle at all.

Even though he struggled against it he eventually dozed off and years later, as it seemed, the questions began. They were in Russian from the outset but he was beyond wondering how. The voice was talking of the year 1961 and of 12 April at Baikonur, and of the spacecraft Vostock 1. It was mention of the spacecraft that really made him drift and once his mind was on it he could not tear it away, much as he tried and struggled to release his mind from the black terror that was starting all over again.

From the moment he left the gantry and climbed into the

cramped seat to strap himself in he knew he had made a ghastly mistake. The hand-waving and the good wishes were behind him now. Out of sight of his colleagues and the scientists he no longer needed to put on a front. The bravado disappeared with the frightening loneliness. My God, he was scared. And as he waited and waited and those in the control room were making the last-minute checks before the countdown began, the fear mounted, and when the countdown did start he was paralysed.

At first he was unaware of the lift-off for his senses had deserted him but the pressure brought it home and he realised he was hurtling into the sky in a capsule so small he could barely move. He closed his eyes and prayed to any God who might listen. He was so scared out of his wits that he could not look out of the tiny windows as he hurtled upwards faster than any man ever before. He became bathed in his own sweat and after a while realised that the visor of his space helmet was misted with tears.

Why had he not backed down long before? Let someone else go; Gagarin or one of the others? He knew why but remorse had come far too late. He had fought his way to the head of the queue and once there, there was no way he could climb down again and live with himself. The fears had really started once he knew that it was he who would make the first flight. Up to that point it had almost been a game of showing the others how clever he was. If he were to back out, having created so many waves to get there, he would lose face, be derided and laughed at, and his father would never forgive him. Had he been able to run away he might have done but he had been trapped by his own conceit. Now it was too late.

Convinced that he was hurtling to his death he was in a semi-comotose state brought on by acute fear. Something jarred and he realised that the main body of the rocket had fallen away. His last contact with earth had gone and, suddenly, it was dreadfully silent. The radio intruded and he turned it off. It would be impossible for him to talk coherently and he did not want them to know that he could not cope.

He tried to rally but it was a brief, futile attempt before

fear deepened and grew into terror as at last he glimpsed what was outside the capsule. It was so black and so silent and he seemed not to be moving at all. He was suspended in space and he was sick as he believed that this was how he would die; slowly and in space, cut off from the real world, detached from everything he knew, and most of all, alone. Alone and cramped in a black void the immensity of which nobody could comprehend unless they were up there with him.

It was the vastness of space that got to him. It went on for ever into a darkness such as he had never before imagined. He was plunging ever upwards and there was no way that he could get back. The scientists talked rubbish. It was all a big experiment to impress the Americans. It did not matter whether or not he returned to earth; it would still be the first manned space flight. And then he saw earth, a round bluish streaked sphere so far away that he knew he would not set foot on it again. His heart leaped. How could it be? How could he be so far away from it? It looked no bigger than a tennis ball down there. Nobody in the whole world had been this far from it before and he was hurtling round it in a tiny cup.

He tried to tear his gaze away but when he did he was back to watching space. Nothing. Not even atmosphere. He heard himself babble and periodically blacked out. He did not want to die like this; not in a black void. He was terrified and his own weightlessness only emphasised the complete lack of control he had over himself.

He didn't trust anyone down there. They were all fools and he was the biggest fool of them all. He began to believe that the rest of the space crew had let him get to the top so that they would not have to go. He had set his own trap and they had let him walk into it, probably laughing behind his back, knowing that he would not be back and that he would remain a tiny lifeless star racing round earth.

He began to mumble to himself. The atmosphere inside the capsule was foul and he realised it was the stench of his own body. He at last managed to take off his space helmet with hands that shook violently and he sat back gasping for breath. He had to get out. His mind was scrambling, on the verge of complete breakdown. The terror had complete control over him. He really had no idea what he was doing and the myriad controls in front of him had no meaning at all except that he wanted to tear them out. As he lost touch with reality he began to believe that he was receiving a terrible punishment. This was a horrible way to die.

He started to shout, his head rolling from side to side and, sometimes, when he did that, he saw more of space, and for ever it was getting larger and larger and earth was something he no longer understood. He babbled again, then cried, and he felt a tremendous pressure all round his head as if it was being crushed by giant hands. He screamed. He must get out whatever happened. He must smash the window and release himself from this tiny, foul-smelling prison into which he would be crammed for all eternity. They had sent him up deliberately, to die slowly, but, first, to ensure that he became insane.

Cut off from everything he had ever understood, alone for all time, in a dark emptiness that expanded with his bursting mind, he screamed out loud and hurled himself at the window, smashing at it until there was sudden peace as he freed himself to race through space and back to earth. There was no sound, no rushing of air for there was no air. It was uncanny yet peaceful and his body felt so light. A vision of Yelena appeared a long way off and hazy, and he remembered at last.

Annya and Yelena had found Mirek in the billiards room. Seeing Yelena's obvious distress he listened to what she had to say and escorted them out of the house.

"Try not to worry too much," he reassured her. "The medics told me that, on Morgan's orders, Zotov will be left alone for a few days. It will give us more time to work on him. Morgan has gone back to London. Anyway, I'll explain the position to the doctor. He seems a reasonable fellow."

They emerged from the east wing and cut across the massive, circular drive, to head for the west wing where the doctor had his quarters. They trod the heavy gravel, the two women helping each other with Mirek slightly to one side. They were passing the magnificent main entrance with its original porticos when they heard a continuing, terrifying scream coming from the top floor of the west wing. It rose in the air and carried across the grounds in a rising, deranged crescendo which scared the birds into fleeing from the trees in a great exodus and rush of wings. Mirek, Annya and Yelena froze at once, stupefied by the sheer terror in the sound, and the massive despair that was trapped there. The crashing of glass followed as an upper floor window burst out into fragments and a body arched with arms and legs splayed to somersault slowly in front of them before crashing sickeningly to the ground not far away.

They all knew who it was before he hit the ground. Yelena screamed and Annya sank slowly to the ground, hands to face, unable to look at the mangled body. Mirek saw the whole thing as if in slow motion. He had seen the staring, terror-filled eyes, wide open as they now remained.

"He was dead before he hit the ground," he said quietly. It was a strange kind of comfort he was trying to offer. He did not add that Zotov's mind must have been blown, that during the awful moment he had seen the eyes, it seemed that something had terrified the life out of him. Mirek stood there, unable to grasp the tragedy, unable to view the wreck of a friend who had suffered for most of his life. He turned away and was violently sick.

Morgan returned to Hampshire straightaway and the first action he took was to summon Mirek and Annya. They stood before him in the huge drawing-room with its drapes and antique furniture, refusing to sit down in his presence. He made no excuses and came straight to the point.

"Listen, both of you, and listen well. Zotov is dead. He was trapped in the past and would have been an eternal target for the rest of his life. We preferred him to be alive and I think we could have protected him. It was not to be. But remember this; so far as you are concerned he is still alive. Nobody must know he is dead. His ghost can be more effective than his living body. We don't have to worry about it any more. He is still an enormously powerful advantage.

Don't try writing your memoirs. Keep your mouths shut for ever. Is that clear?"

"As clear as our resignations which have already been handed in."

Morgan sighed. "You're impulsive, Mirek, and your loyalties are confused. Apart from anything else, Zotov would probably have died in due course, from overexposure to radiation. In spite of what you think, we were human enough not to tell him that his levels were unacceptably high, which is one reason why we kept him apart and put a time-limit on visits. While he wasn't at Chernobyl itself, he was in the Pripyat area too long. His depressions could even have been a result of that."

Mirek took Annya's hand. He realised that the danger they now faced was potentially worse than any before. "What about Yelena?"

"I'm not as callous as you seem to think, Mirek. She will be well looked after. I've had words with our American friends. It's in their interests too, to protect her. After a little cosmetic surgery she will be given a new identity and she will go to America, and after a year or so, will be able to teach ballet again. Her health will be monitored and she will not want for money. She will have everything she needs."

"Except the man she loved." Annya was quietly scathing.

Morgan shrugged. "That could have happened anyway. I can't tell you any more. You won't see her again. I'm sorry about that, but you of all people will understand the need for security."

"Of course," Mirek nodded sadly. "Please give her our love. Tell her that we'll miss her. And I hope you do a better job with her than you did with her lover."

Mirek and Annya put an arm round each other and walked out into the clean, spring air, towards the distant line of trees. "Well," said Mirek as they got well away from the house. "We'd better start enjoying ourselves while we can. Zotov would have liked us to do that. He may have slipped up on his space mission, but he certainly made up for it later and paid a terrible price."

He stopped and turned Annya round to face him.

"Moggy will have an eye kept on us, but we've coped with worse." He suddenly smiled. "Will you marry me?"

"Would Zotov have recommended that sort of risk?"

"He was going to be best man. We talked about it while you were in jail in Brest," he lied.

"Then I accept, Mirek."

She paused a moment.

"Let's get away from this civilised country. As far away as they'll let us."